PENGUIN BOOKS

Stranger

Karen Perry is the *Sunday Times* bestselling author of *Your Closest Friend*, *Can You Keep a Secret?*, *Girl Unknown*, *Only We Know*, *Come A Little Closer*, and *The Boy That Never Was*, which was selected for the Simon Mayo Radio 2 Book Club. She lives in Dublin with her family.

Stranger

KAREN PERRY

PENGUIN BOOKS

PENGUIN BOOKS

UK | USA | Canada | Ireland | Australia
India | New Zealand | South Africa

Penguin Books is part of the Penguin Random House group of companies
whose addresses can be found at global.penguinrandomhouse.com

Penguin
Random House
UK

First published by Michael Joseph, 2021
This edition published by Penguin Books, 2021
001

Typeset by Jouve (UK), Milton Keynes
Printed and bound in Great Britain by Clays Ltd, Elcograf S.p.A.

The authorized representative in the EEA is Penguin Random House Ireland,
Morrison Chambers, 32 Nassau Street, Dublin D02 YH68

A CIP catalogue record for this book is available from the British Library

ISBN: 978-1-405-94525-7

www.greenpenguin.co.uk

MIX
Paper from
responsible sources
FSC
www.fsc.org   FSC® C018179

Penguin Random House is committed to a
sustainable future for our business, our readers
and our planet. This book is made from Forest
Stewardship Council® certified paper.

Not long after the killings they put me in the back of a car and drive me away.

No sirens, just the rumble of tyres over the asphalt. The car smells of leather and coconut, an air freshener affixed to the plastic grid over the A/C. The officer in the front passenger seat – a woman – looks back at me from time to time, a brief checking glance, but I just sit there, very still, trying to keep myself numb. It's almost midday.

These are the thoughts that occupy my mind: What will happen to the car? I'd left the Cherokee in one of the visitor spaces at the school car park. The whole place now cordoned off, swarming with detectives and uniformed officers, forensics in white zippered suits, the pathologists on their way. I'd dropped my mobile phone when I was running, and now how will I contact Mark? How will I let him know? I lean forward and say:

'Excuse me. My husband—'

'That's all right,' the officer in the passenger seat tells me. 'He'll meet you at the station.'

My stomach turns at the prospect of that encounter so instead I think of the conference call that I will miss now, and briefly wonder what my colleagues will make of my absence – so unlike me to not show up, to not give warning. And then I think of the flight leaving Dublin for Tours at lunchtime, and how Corinne won't be on it now. Her mother will be waiting at the other end in that little airport, scanning the faces of the passengers disembarking, searching among them for her daughter. And I know that my mind is processing these particular thoughts to ward off the horror that waits at the periphery. Conference calls and mobile phones. Flight times and parking spaces. These are what I use to shore up the dam against the dark rumblings of reality that wait to burst in.

At the station, they bring me in through a side door, into the warren of rooms behind the anodyne front desk, the custodians of the law going about their business, the machinery that whirrs and grinds to keep us safe. Numb as I am, I can still detect the current in the air: the crackle of excitement. They won't have seen a case like this in years. If ever. A sort of hush falls as I am brought through; the female officer leading the way nods to some of her colleagues at the desk, and I hear one of them remark to another: 'The mother.'

I hold myself steady, walking carefully like I don't fully trust the ground beneath me. They bring me to a room and ask if I would like tea. I say no but they bring it anyway. And when the officer puts the steaming mug in front of me, I wrap my hands around it and realize that I am freezing. I am shaking.

'Drink it, Mrs Holland,' she tells me. 'It will help, with the shock.'

She asks if there is anything else I need, and I say no. No, I am fine. She looks at me strangely. Her eyes flicker to the blouse I am wearing.

'You'll need to change out of that,' she says, and I look down and see the blood. Smears of it, rust brown, already hardening, embedded into the silk fibres.

'Oh yes,' I say, aware of the rumbling at the edge of my thoughts, getting louder now.

'I'll have them bring you something,' she says. I thank her, and she flashes me another look – it is a cool look of enquiry. There is blood on my blouse, but she is wondering is there any blood running through my veins? I'm the *mother*, for God's sake!

Thoughts buzz in my head like bees.

France, sunlight on the river, the girls in the water, arms about each other, slowly turning.

And then another memory:

We are in the kitchen at Willow Park, Eva and Beth, Mark and me. I am spooning rice and stir-fried chicken on to plates lined up along the island counter. At the table in the alcove, Mark is clearing away his papers while Eva watches him, her hands bristling with cutlery, waiting to set places for dinner. Outside the day is darkening. I'm tired, still carrying some residual stress in my body from the work meetings that afternoon. The mess Mark has made annoys me and I'm taking it out in the kitchen where I tap the serving spoon sharply against the edge of the wok. Part of me is a little apprehensive about the arrival of the French girl the next day, one of twenty taking part in the school exchange programme. It's Friday evening and all I really want is to sink into a hot bath with a glass of wine and listen to the next episode of *Serial*. The overhead kitchen light is casting Beth's auburn hair in a golden glow, her head bent over the letter from school as she reads it aloud.

'*The flight from Tours is due to land at Dublin Airport at 3.30 p.m. on Saturday, 8th April. All host families are requested to meet at the Arrivals Lounge in Terminal 1 at 3.15 p.m. where Ms Doyle will be waiting. Once the students have come through, Ms Doyle will assign each student to their host family.*'

It was just an ordinary evening. There had been hundreds like it, thousands, yet this is the one that plays in my mind, like a scratched record I can't move on from. The last time

3

we were together before she came. The last evening we were 'normal'.

And then I remember Eva, setting the table briskly, efficiently, the cutlery clattering over the polished wooden surface. Like me, she has been listening to Beth's letter.

'*Host family*?' she says sceptically, and then she shudders. 'It's like we're going to the airport to collect a parasite.'

Spring

I

The phone call came shortly before midnight on the eve of Corinne's arrival.

Abi lay slumped against her pillows skimming a novel for her book club, wondering when Mark would get home, when the phone in the hall downstairs began its shrill bleat.

Instantly, her thoughts tilted towards the catastrophic. A mugging on his way home. An accident. She swung her legs out of bed and hurried downstairs, anxiety lending an involuntary sharpness to her tone when she picked up the receiver and said: 'Yes, hello?'

It was met with a corresponding silence.

'Is there someone there?' Abi asked sharply, leaning forward to switch on the table lamp, casting a small pool of light over the polished surface. This time she heard something, a swift intake of breath and then a voice she didn't recognize, saying:

'Mrs Holland, I am so sorry to disturb you at this late hour. My name is Valentina Catto.'

Words spoken softly with a foreign inflection; there was a depth to the woman's voice and a slowness to her delivery that lent her some gravity. Abi's thoughts whirred. Catto – she knew the name.

'You're Corinne's mother,' she said quickly.

'That's correct.'

It was almost one a.m. in France. Beth's exchange partner, Corinne, was due to arrive from Tours at lunchtime the next day.

There had been a picture alongside her details – Abi brought it to mind now: a round, blank face, eyes that were a little wide apart, a suggestion of slightly prominent front teeth in the close-lipped smile. 'She looks like a squirrel,' Eva had commented, which had caused Beth's face to darken. But Abi had been reassured by the photograph. The last thing they needed was some sultry Mediterranean beauty with manners and affectations older than her years.

'I am very sorry,' Valentina Catto said now, 'but I don't think Corinne can come to Ireland.'

'Has something happened?'

'I am unsure if it is wise for her to come.'

Again, that low, soft tone, a certain formality in the enunciation. Abi felt herself simultaneously irritated by the flimsiness of the message while at once being drawn in by the voice.

'I'm sorry to hear that. But surely it's just nerves? Let me reassure you – and Corinne – that she will be very well looked after while she's here. Beth has been so excited about this visit; I know she's been communicating regularly with Corinne. They've been making all sorts of plans.'

It was true that they'd been Snapchatting and Whats-Apping for weeks.

'Corinne told me tonight that you have had a bereavement.'

Abi caught herself then, sudden feeling rising in her chest. Melissa had died a few weeks ago and they were still reeling from the shock. Abi wondered how much Beth had told this girl.

'Yes, that's true. Beth's aunt – my husband's sister – recently passed away,' she said carefully, pressing her thumbnail into the flesh of her index finger to keep herself steady. Her voice remained level. 'But that doesn't have to change things.'

'It would be wrong – Corinne coming to you when you are grieving.'

8

'Really, we are fine. I appreciate your concern, but Beth will be so disappointed if Corinne doesn't come.'

'It is not right,' Valentina went on. 'Someone close to you has died.'

'What can I say to reassure you? Yes, Melissa's death was a shock, but we're coping. And we feel very strongly that it's best for the girls if we carry on as normal.'

Still it was there – the pull of hesitation at the other end of the line. Abi couldn't help but feel that this talk of Melissa's death was just a ruse. That the real reason behind the woman's reluctance lay elsewhere.

'Is there something else, Valentina? Some other reason?'

'I'm not sure how to explain it.'

Valentina's voice had lowered to almost a whisper.

'It's just a feeling that I have. A thought, oh, how do I say it?' She gave a little huff of impatience with herself before alighting on the word. 'Intuition.'

From upstairs, Abi could hear a door opening, footsteps creaking on the landing. She looked up, and saw Beth leaning over the bannister, her face pale in the shadows.

'Something Corinne told me tonight,' Valentina went on, 'it troubled me. She has a good heart, but she is not always reliable in what she says. It made me realize that she's not ready for this.'

Again, there it was – that push of fear in Abi's chest. What had Beth told the girl?

'What's going on?' Beth hissed from the top of the stairs, and Abi shook her head and gestured for her to wait.

On the other end of the line, the voice had broken off. Abi could feel the woman's hesitation, and under the pressure of Beth's gaze, she found herself saying:

'Look, Mrs Catto – Valentina – why don't you sleep on it, both of you. I'm sure once you've had a chance to rest, things will feel different. Corinne will have a wonderful time here – all

9

the exchange kids do. You may rest assured that we will take good care of her,' she added.

'I'm not sure if that's—'

'Please. I promise – everything will work out wonderfully. Why don't you ring me in the morning and we'll see where things stand? Hmm?'

It was a reasonable suggestion, and the other woman softly acquiesced. An instant later, the line went dead.

Abi put the phone down, her mind snagging on those words: *something she told me tonight* . . . But what?

'She's not coming?' Beth asked, interrupting her thoughts.

There was her daughter at the top of the stairs, narrow ankles poking out from the ends of her pyjama legs, hair hanging lank and thin over her shoulders. Abi could hear the note of distress in the question.

'Beth . . .' she said, but the girl had already turned and fled back to her room. After a moment, Abi followed.

Beth's bedroom overlooked the back garden. A second bed had been made up beneath the window for their guest, and as Abi looked around, she noticed other changes to the room. The Jellycat stuffed toys that usually lined the little mantelpiece were gone. So too were the dreamcatchers that had once slowly turned, suspended above the bed. Justin Bieber sulked and preened from the wall above; Billie Eilish on another wall, a tarantula crawling into her open mouth.

'What if she doesn't come?' Beth said. 'What if I'm the only one whose exchange doesn't show up? Everyone already thinks I'm a freak—'

'Shhh, come on now, enough of that. Who cares what people think?' Abi said, adopting the same brisk tone of reassurance that lately she found herself using with all of them – Beth, Mark, Eva.

In the dimly lit room, her daughter's face looked small and

pale, a cross look marring her features. Beth was a worrier. A bed-wetter until the age of seven. An inveterate nail-biter. 'She really feels her feelings,' Mark used to say of her. Of their two daughters, Beth was the one that had always inspired the most anxiety within them.

Abi thought for a moment about reaching out to smooth Beth's hair back from her face, or leaning in to kiss her cheek. But she did neither of these things. Instead, she hung back by the mantelpiece, her thumbnail leaving a crescent-moon indent in the flesh of her finger, as her eyes flickered over Beth's face, trying to fathom the dark run of her thoughts.

'It will all be fine,' Abi reassured her, making her voice bright and as convincing as she could to hide the undercurrent of nerves. Backing out of the doorway, she said: 'Now get some sleep.'

The next morning Valentina Catto sent a text message that read: *All fine.* Somehow, the curtness of the text was more unsettling than the phone call, but Abi said nothing of how she felt to the others, not even to Mark. When he commented: 'A bit weird, isn't it?' his face sceptical and serious, she brushed it aside saying: 'I wouldn't worry about it. Last-minute jitters, that's all!' She was accustomed to answering his concerns with breezy dismissals.

When she suggested that he accompany them to the airport, Mark declined.

'I need to sort out Melissa's stuff,' he explained.

'Liar,' she retorted. 'You just don't want to face the other parents.' Words said half-jokingly, but she watched to see how they landed, observed the nerve being touched.

The uneasiness stayed inside her as she drove to the airport, the windshield wipers of the Grand Cherokee animated as the rain splattered down. Beth was in the passenger seat checking her phone for updates.

'They've landed,' she announced.

Abi glanced across at her daughter. The girl was pale with tiredness, marks of anxiety there in the tight bud of her pursed lips, but it was clear that she had taken some care with her appearance. The old Ramones T-shirt she wore was a favourite, and Abi noticed the touch of lip gloss and the citrussy scent of CK One.

'Listen,' Abi said as she pulled the car into a space. 'Valentina mentioned that you'd told Corinne about Melissa.'

'Yeah. So?'

'I was just surprised.'

'It's not exactly a state secret, is it?'

'Of course not.'

Beth was staring out the window, but Abi could feel attentiveness filtering into her silence.

'I was just wondering what exactly you'd told her, that's all,' Abi went on carefully, as she turned off the engine and looked at her daughter. Beth's jaw tightened, and then she let out a brief frustrated breath.

'Don't worry, Mum. I didn't say anything to cast us in a bad light. God forbid I should shatter the illusion of our perfect family.'

She slammed the door and Abi was left alone for a moment.

Was that what it was? An illusion?

The night's phone conversation revisited her, and she remembered once more the hesitation in the woman's voice, the unspoken sense that this girl had her own problems, her own difficulties.

Abi had been so focused on not disappointing Beth, persuading this woman to send her daughter, that it hadn't occurred to her there might be risks involved. *Intuition*, Valentina had said. Abi had the sudden thought that they'd made a terrible mistake.

But it was only a fleeting feeling. She had long held the view that nerves were merely a loss of confidence. That fear could be quashed with optimism. She stepped out of the car and pressed the lock. The unease lowered its head beneath the surface once more as she walked away from the car, the cabin light fading to black.

2

Contrary to what Abi believed, it was not cowardice that held Mark back from going to the airport, but a hangover.

He waited until the Cherokee had pulled out of the driveway before dropping two Solpadeine tablets in a glass of water and retreating to the quiet of his studio, shutting the door behind him. There, he threw himself on to the sofa and closed his eyes, the luxuriant silence of an empty house on a Saturday afternoon wrapping comfortingly around him as he mulled over the night's events.

It had been a long time since he'd been that drunk. There had just been two of them in O'Donoghue's that Friday night – Mark and his old roommate, Andrew, who was in Dublin to shoot a whiskey commercial. Andrew mainly worked on film productions now but, as he explained to Mark, the ad work was regular, not to mention lucrative. 'The money's too good to turn down, you know what I mean?' he'd said.

Yes, Mark knew. But only anecdotally.

The truth was, whenever he met up with Andrew – which was less and less as the years went by – Mark felt himself exposed to a niggling sense of envy. When they had started out together at university, two enthusiastic film students with differing sensibilities, Andrew's interests had lain in animation – Manga and Japanese anime mainly – while Mark was drawn to Eastern European cinema with its dark themes and slow pacing, its preoccupations with memory. Their friends used to joke that one was a fan of Tarkovsky, the other of Tartakovsky. Regardless of their differences, the friendship had been close, and for a while after university, they had shared a flat, often working on the same productions, both of them as junior designers expected to muck in and complete whatever tasks needed doing from painting the set to fetching sandwiches for the crew when the caterers failed to show up. Exhausting, exhilarating, back-breaking, impecunious – they had been the most exciting years of his life. But then Mark and Abi got together and Andrew had moved to London. Their paths had forked at that point, swerving in different directions.

Now Andrew had his own production design company, his crew working on locations all over the world, involved in film projects that had won BAFTAs and once, an Oscar nomination. Mark was a stay-at-home dad.

'You're the lucky one, really,' Andrew had said. This was after the fourth or maybe fifth pint. 'A wife, two gorgeous kids, a comfortable home. What I wouldn't give.'

The travel was exhausting, he said. You got sick of hotel bars and room service. And some of these directors were total pricks. 'Fucking children throwing tantrums,' he mumbled, swirling the dregs of his glass.

Mark had believed him, but only up to a point. And besides, while Andrew may have to deal with the odd prima donna, Mark was at home with actual children throwing actual tantrums. It was worse now that they were getting older. Two teenage girls with their fluctuating moods, their maelstroms of hormones. Spots and tears and slamming doors. Broken friendships and exam stress. Their endless needs, requests, demands, with no hotel bar to retreat to at the end of the day. And now there was going to be a third girl – this French exchange student of Beth's – adding to the hormonal swamp. He'd said as much last night, griping a little in a self-pitying way, and that's when Andrew had sat up and put his hand on Mark's shoulder, a new seriousness coming into his voice, his demeanour.

'Come and work with me,' he'd said.

'Yeah, right,' Mark had snorted, nodding to the barman. He'd lost track of whose round it was.

'I'm serious, man. Look, there's a shoot coming up in September – a major production. We're talking Canal Plus and FilmFour. Locations in Prague, Italy, London.' Andrew rapped the table with his knuckles, biting his lower lip in a way that was familiar to Mark and signalled his determination. 'I'm sending you the brief. *And* the script. Think about it, yeah?'

At the time, he had allowed himself to get caught up in imagining what it would be like to work on a major project again, an old excitement stirring to life inside him. Now, as Mark lay on the couch, the codeine crawling into his cells, he thought again about the offer, wondered had Andrew really meant it, and even if he was serious, would Mark be able to make things work?

He recalled the agreement made with Abi back in the early days of parenthood. Eva was still in her infancy when Abi's career began to take off, and by the time Beth came along, Mark's career had stalled while Abi's was firmly in the ascendant. It made sense for him to stay at home with the children, and part of him had welcomed it. Once the girls were older and more independent, then he could focus on his work once more. Abi was earning enough to cover their outgoings, and by the time Beth had started school, they were able to sell their starter home and buy the house in Willow Park – their forever home. He was lucky, and the fact was not lost on him. But it was also true that the bargain they'd made had cost him something. He realized now, as his headache waned, that it was not just work he had given up, but the friendships that had gone with it. Yes, he still had friends, but they were closely connected to his family. His social life revolved around the tennis club and, to a lesser extent, the school. He had no close friendships of his own – one by one, he'd let them slip away. When the Campbells had moved in next door earlier that year, he had hoped that some kind of warmth might develop between him and Ross Campbell. They were both stay-at-home dads, both married to high achievers. But Ross was only interested in cars and rugby. And Mark realized now, thinking back on the hours he'd spent in the pub with Andrew the previous night, how much he missed those close friendships that sprang up on set, the easy camaraderie. For a moment, he considered the possibility that he was lonely.

Just as he was having that thought, his phone sounded with an incoming mail, and when he checked the screen he saw that Andrew had indeed sent him the script and the brief, just as he'd promised. *Read these and get in touch*, he'd typed. Adding: *Brain bleeding through my eye sockets. Hung-over to fuck, you bastard.*

It made Mark smile, warm feelings flushing through him. Two minutes later, he was at his desk, downloading the first document, passing his eyes over the opening pages. He was still there a couple of hours later, when he heard the car pull into the driveway, held fast by the images flashing over the canvas of his brain as he read through the script, as though a part of him that had been asleep for a very long time had just awakened, blinking and stretching in the daylight. Reluctantly, he closed down the documents, and went outside to greet them.

3

The pink hair was a shock.

Mark found himself staring as he stood on the doorstep, his hands in his pockets, watching as she climbed out of the car and came towards him. Her hair lifted in the breeze, a tuft of pink spun sugar, and there was a goofiness about her as she struggled with her bag, flip-flops tripping over the gravel, laughing at her own awkwardness. Her hand felt warm and clammy when he took it in his, but her face seemed open and clear.

'You're very welcome to our home,' he said after introducing himself, and she giggled at his formality and hooked the strap of her bag – a bright yellow messenger bag, the type usually seen against cycling couriers' backs – slinging it over one shoulder.

She was small – a good head shorter than him – and when she spoke to return his greeting, he noticed the gaps between her teeth like her gums were too large for her mouth. It made her seem gauche, something endearing in the imperfection.

'Thank you for letting me come. I am happy to be here.'

There was no evidence of the glasses she had worn in her photograph. The lack of glasses coupled with the pink hair gave the disconcerting impression that a mistake had been made – that Abi had picked up the wrong girl at the airport.

'How was your journey?' he asked.

'It was okay. But I don't like flying. It is boring, don't you think?'

He nodded, bemused, then went to the rear of the car to fetch her luggage.

'Where's her suitcase?' he asked, staring at the empty boot.

'She didn't bring one,' Abi replied, the two of them speaking in hushed tones.

'That's all she brought?' he asked, nodding to the messenger bag that rested against her hip.

Abi shrugged. 'I guess she travels light.'

But Mark found himself assessing her more closely – the frayed ends of her jeans, the hoodie that was probably white once but now looked greyish with wear. The way she stared up at the house with obvious wonder and perhaps a little envy too. He knew that feeling, recognized it instantly as one who had himself grown up feeling desperate, longing to escape to something better – something *normal*.

Poor kid, he found himself thinking. Then he shut the boot and went inside.

In the kitchen, she clapped her hands as she looked around and exclaimed:

'Oh wow, I love this! Everything is so modern.'

'I suppose it is,' Mark said, glancing up briefly as he reheated curry in a saucepan. The rice-cooker was already on.

There was something precocious about her, the type of girl who couldn't help but draw attention to herself. The shock of her hair – a clouded tuft of candy-floss pink – she kept fingering it as she giggled, delighted with the novelty of it.

'Everything in your house is so big, so new – everything shiny and bright. It's a mansion.'

'I think that's a bit of an exaggeration.'

He was prickly on the matter of their wealth. When they'd had the kitchen remodelled a year ago, he'd worried about the cost, pointing out to Abi that they could put the girls through college with the money they were proposing to shell out. 'We can always go to Cash and Carry instead,' she'd suggested. He'd kept his reservations to himself after that.

Over dinner, Corinne chattered animatedly about her home in France – a medieval house situated at a bend in the river Vienne. Description flowed from her of sun-soaked walls and diving kingfishers, lazy afternoons canoeing down the slow-moving river.

'It sounds idyllic,' Abi commented.

'You must come!' Corinne said, seizing on the idea. 'All of you! In the summer!'

'Well, maybe,' Abi said, doubtfully.

'No, really! You must!'

Her vehemence was surprising, the force of her goodwill a little disconcerting. Abi flashed a quick glance at Mark, and then he changed the subject, saying: 'Where did you learn your English, Corinne?'

They had all noticed the fluency and ease of her speech, even though her words were heavily accented.

'We spent a couple of years in Canada when I was younger,' Corinne explained. 'I went to pre-school there.'

'How come?' Mark asked.

She shrugged. 'My mother liked to travel around.'

'For work?'

'Oh no! Val never works. It's not her thing.'

He raised an eyebrow but let that pass.

'So why Canada?' Abi asked. 'Do you have family there?'

'No. It's just somewhere that interested Val at the time. Or maybe she'd met someone from there and got an invitation. I really don't know.'

She dropped the bread on to her plate and leaned back to admire the view of the garden. Mark noticed the curve of

20

her long, lean neck. The way she spoke of her mother, calling her by her Christian name, jarred with him. She struck him as a child who spent a lot of time in adult company.

'My sister's there now,' she said, brightening as she turned her attention back to the room. 'She got a place at McGill. She's studying medicine.'

'Sounds like a high achiever,' Mark commented.

'Oh, Anouk's really smart. She got a scholarship to McGill. She's just one of those people – really smart as well as beautiful and talented. Everyone loves Anouk.' She paused, then her eyes fixed on Eva across the table, and she said: 'Actually, you remind me of her.'

'Me?'

Eva, who had barely said a word for the entire meal, looked up, and Mark noticed that as the two girls made eye contact, Corinne's complexion pinked a little.

'Yes,' she said, her voice dropping, shyness coming into her tone as she ventured the opinion: 'The way you look, the way you dress.' Her eyes flickering over the grey silk blouse Eva was wearing, her blond hair brushed straight and swept over one shoulder. 'Like Anouk, you are full of thoughts. Moody.'

Eva's forehead creased into a slight frown. 'I'm not moody.'

'Yes, you are,' Beth countered.

'You're hardly one to talk,' Eva shot back.

'I'm sorry. My English,' Corinne said quickly, becoming a little flustered, 'I do not always know the right word. I meant you are silent – a listener—'

But Eva was already on her feet. 'I'm only silent because it's impossible to get a word in edgeways,' she observed drily, opening the dishwasher and slotting her empty plate inside.

It was true that Corinne's chatter had dominated the conversation.

'Where are you going?' Corinne asked now, as Eva went to leave.

'I'm babysitting next door,' Eva replied, and a swift look of hurt passed over Corinne's face. A minute later, the front door banged shut and the room filled with an awkward silence.

Mark watched as the girl stared down at her plate, the food untouched. He felt a need to apologize for Eva's rudeness but it was Abi who broke the silence.

'Your parents must be very pleased,' she said.

Corinne looked up, uncertain.

'About your sister's scholarship?'

'Oh, yes,' she said, but an air of sulky distraction persisted. He watched her unhappily nudging the rice around her plate.

'Are there any doctors in your family?' Abi pressed gently.

Corinne looked at her with confusion. 'No.'

'I just wondered if Anouk's choice of medicine was because—'

'Valentina was an aid worker, and Guy an engineer. They're retired now.'

This detail interested him. He wondered how old her parents were. The phone call last night from the mother, and now these allusions to a peripatetic lifestyle; he was beginning to guess at an alternative upbringing – anti-vaxxers, home-schooling, living off the grid.

Mark did not think that Corinne was pretty in a conventional sense; her teeth were too prominent, wide gaps between the incisors, and a suggestion of acne in the chaffed redness of skin that lined the grooves on either side of her nose. The wildness of her pink hair was distracting, but really it was her eyes that drew your attention – short-lashed but a deep granular brown. Corinne turned the fork over in her hand and lifted her gaze to meet his, and he noted a splash of orange in the iris, a surprising bloom of colour amidst the brown. Eyes that were playful; they held a spark.

'They are cousins, you know,' she told them now, 'my parents.' The fractional lift of one eyebrow – a challenge there.

Beth's brow furrowed. 'Isn't that like illegal? You know, in case their kids are born with deformities, extra toes and things like that?'

'I don't have extra toes.' She said it mildly, but they all heard the rebuke.

'No, of course not,' Beth conceded, and Mark, trying to smooth things over, said:

'They might be distant cousins, right?'

A delicate pause and then she laughed, her eyes glittering with mischief. 'I was just joking!'

Mark took a sip of water from his glass, watching her.

'Really. I was just fucking with you,' she giggled, and he stifled his discomfort at her casual use of the phrase. He caught the glance that Abi threw at him.

'I'm surprised you're even doing an exchange,' Beth told Corinne. 'It's not like you need it.'

She was giving voice to what they all thought.

'You are sweet to say it,' Corinne exclaimed, reaching across to briefly wrap her arm around Beth's shoulders, drawing her close. Mark saw his daughter's cheeks flush with embarrassment, but Corinne was unperturbed. 'But my English is not perfect. You will see.'

And it was true that she tripped over the occasional phrase, making funny little mistakes. Like when Mark asked about the phone call from Valentina the night before, hinting at some unexpressed reservation, Corinne had shrugged and said: 'It was just cold toes.'

'You mean cold feet,' Mark said, gently correcting her.

Corinne blushed, putting her hand up to cover her mouth as she laughed, eloquent eyes moving quickly around the table.

'You see,' she told them. 'There is still so much that I have to learn.'

She threw a glance at Mark as she spoke, and at the same time, she reached out and touched his wrist, her hand resting there for a second or two. Something conspiratorial in the gesture, the look, like she was trying to draw him in, which confused him as he'd done nothing to earn it.

He was glad when Abi suggested coffee, grateful for the distraction, attention drawn away from how disarmed he felt.

4

Abi had seen the touch and pretended not to notice.

But after dinner, she followed Mark into his studio, closing the door behind her.

For a moment, she looked about at the detritus gathered there – photograph albums, folders full of tax documents, envelopes stuffed with invoices – the room felt oppressive with her sister-in-law's death and the whole mess she had left behind. Sitting in one of the armchairs, Abi felt the shock of it all over again: the little grenade Melissa had lobbed at them from the grave. Her thoughts went to that day in the solicitor's office when the will was read out. At first, she'd thought she'd misheard: that Melissa had left her house to Beth, and Beth alone. Solely and completely. A look of dull confusion had come over Mark's face. He'd had to ask the solicitor to repeat it.

Beth had always been Melissa's favourite niece, but to so blatantly reward her while Eva got nothing? Surely, she must have known the trouble such a bequest would stir up in their family?

Eva's response to the snub had been one of lofty dismissal. 'I never liked that poky little house,' she'd announced airily. 'Beth's welcome to it. The place gives me the creeps.'

But Beth had said little. She'd just sat there absorbing the information, her face giving little away. Later, when it was just the two of them alone, Mark had said to Abi: 'She seemed so composed, didn't she? Almost as if she knew about it already?'

Abi hadn't responded. But she had noticed an unmistakable coolness hanging in the air now whenever both her daughters were in the same room together. She knew Mark sensed it too.

'Have you made any progress?' Abi asked now.

'A little.' Then, sheepishly, he conceded: 'Actually, that's not true. I couldn't face going through all this shit. I was too hung-over.'

'*Quelle surprise*,' she remarked, an eyebrow raised in mock-disapproval. 'So what have you been doing with yourself?'

'Reading a script.'

'Oh?'

'Andrew sent it over. He thought I'd be interested.' Then he added: 'Actually, he asked me if I'd come on board with the production.'

'Really?' The surprised scepticism leaked into her voice before she could stop it.

'That wouldn't be a problem, would it?'

'No.'

'We always said that once the girls were old enough—'

'Of course—'

'And when we had this extension built, and you suggested I use it as my studio, I assumed that meant you'd be happy for me to get serious again about—'

'Mark, it's fine. You don't need to persuade me. I think it's great that you're thinking about work again. Really.'

This was only partly true. Yes, she wanted him to feel happy and fulfilled. But selfishly, she couldn't help thinking of how his revived interest in his career would affect her life. It all seemed so precariously balanced – she was afraid how this might tip things over.

Her glance flickered distractedly over the shelves where some of his old model sets were displayed.

'What do you think of her?' she asked after a moment. 'Corinne.'

'She seems nice enough. Friendly. Confident.'

'Her English is excellent,' she remarked, adding: 'It makes me wonder why she's even here.'

'Does it matter?'

'I don't know. I mean, I thought it was a good idea, this exchange. But now, I just wonder if it's too soon.'

'It's a bit late to have doubts, Abi.'

'True.' When she spoke again, it was in a lowered voice. 'If you'd seen Beth at the airport – my God, the anxiety. So pale and worried.'

'She gets anxious about these things. So what? She seems fine now.'

'No one spoke to her. None of the girls in her class.'

'Not even Lisa?'

Lisa had been Beth's best friend since kindergarten. At least she had been until 'the incident' as they kept referring to it, for want of a better term.

'They didn't even look at each other,' Abi admitted now.

At the airport, Abi had chatted to her friend, Irene Ferguson – Lisa's mother – while they'd waited at Arrivals. All the while they were talking, Abi had kept an eye on the group of girls hovering by the gates. It was such an awkward age, fourteen. Some of these girls still looked like children, and yet others had breasts and hips and attitude to go with it. If what was spoken about today's teenagers was to be believed, then a lot of these girls were already drinking and smoking. Some of them might be sexually active or experimenting with drugs. It was frightening, the stuff parents were warned about these days: cyber bullying and self-harm. Sharing indecent images of themselves with their peers. Paedophiles lurking in chatrooms. Suicide ideation. They were just kids. Why were they in such a hurry to grow up?

Lisa had stood alongside Sasha Harte and Nicole Nash,

showing them something on her mobile phone. Abi observed the tight little triumvirate they had formed. Sasha with her arched brows, sweeping her hair over one shoulder and making some comment out of the side of her mouth. Nicole, small-eyed, sneaky, her hand moving to cover a mouth full of braces as she giggled at Sasha's aside. And Lisa – mild-mannered, waifish, thin brown hair and sad eyes – Abi had known this child since she was four years old. All those years Beth and Lisa had spent going in and out of each other's houses, it seemed to Abi as if Lisa was almost as familiar to her as her own children. It pained her to see Beth – pale, copper-haired, freckled – standing alone, not talking to anyone, a distance between her and the others. Abi had felt a push of silent alarm.

'Have you talked to Irene about it?' Mark asked now, drawing her attention back to him.

'I've tried to, but she keeps being evasive. Whenever I bring it up with her, trying to find out if she knows what actually happened between them, she just says something non-committal about how flakey teenage girls can be and how they'll work it out between themselves eventually.'

'Maybe she's right. Maybe they will patch it up themselves, in time.'

'I sense that Irene feels embarrassed by it all. That she doesn't want Lisa hanging out with Beth after what happened at the school. Has Craig ever mentioned anything to you?'

'No.'

Mark sometimes had a pint with Craig at the tennis club, and occasionally they paired up for doubles. But Abi knew Mark didn't trust Craig, that he regarded him as shady. Rumours swirled about Craig's business dealings, his links to Nicky Kehoe, a major gangland criminal. And while Abi was prepared to turn a blind eye, a lasting distrust lingered between the two men.

'She must have some friends, surely?' he asked, a nudge of irritation mixed with worry sounding in his voice.

'I can't remember the last time she's had a friend home. There've been no invitations to parties or sleepovers. The other girls go to discos – I read about it on the mums' WhatsApp group – but Beth doesn't go. I look at Eva, all the friends she has – she's hardly ever home—'

'That's hardly fair, Abi,' he said, exasperation leaking into his tone. 'You can't expect Beth to behave like Eva – they're completely different people.'

'I know that.'

'You're always holding Beth to Eva's standard and I just don't think that's right.'

'No, I don't,' she said, affronted, and he seemed to pull back then, softening his tone.

'Things will change,' he said. 'Kids do this – girls especially. One minute you're out of favour, next minute you're back in.'

'It's been a year, Mark.'

'Yeah . . . well.'

'Sometimes I think we did the wrong thing, leaving her in that school.'

'It was your idea that she stay there, remember? You were the one who went and sweet-talked Helen Bracken into keeping her.'

She shot him a look. The accusation was there in his tone.

Most of the time Abi could convince herself that what had happened – what Beth had done – was just a blip. It was only when she was confronted with Beth among her peers – or rather not among them, but standing off to one side, head bowed, scanning her phone, while the other girls made jokes among themselves, giggling and fingering each other's hair and jewellery in the easy tactile way of teenagers – it was only then that Abi heard the alarm ringing inside her head.

She thought about admitting this now to Mark, but at that moment there came a burst of laughter from upstairs and both of them looked up instinctively.

'If this girl can be a friend to Beth,' Mark said after the laughter died away, 'then I don't care how good or bad her English is, or what her reasons are for coming. Perhaps it will be the best thing that ever happened to Beth.'

'Yes, perhaps,' Abi replied. But her voice sounded weak and unconvincing, even to herself.

5

Beth couldn't take her eyes off the girl. The candyfloss hair, the ease with which she moved beneath Beth's avid gaze. It was like an exotic bird had suddenly landed inside the bedroom, making everything around her look drab and grey.

They were at an age where assessing each other's appearance was instinctive – irrepressible – but Corinne conveyed little interest in studying Beth, and if she was bothered by Beth's attention, she didn't show it. She touched the keyboard of the laptop, and Beth's eyes travelled to her fingertips – nails that were bitten down, the stubs painted a deep purple.

'This is yours?' Corinne asked, surprised.

It was a silver iMac, gleaming with newness.

'My mum got it for me. She gets like a special discount through her office.'

Beth tried to sound nonchalant. She didn't want to get into a conversation about the row that had erupted the day she came home from school and found her old computer was gone. Tearful protests over the loss of documents, photographs that she'd saved, privacy breached. Abi, tight-faced, had looked at her and said in a low voice: 'It's for the best, Beth. You know that as well as I do.' And as she'd moved to leave the room, Abi had paused at the door, taken by a sudden ferocity, and hissed at Beth: 'My God, you should be *thanking* me!'

Disturbed by the memory, she looked down quickly, but Corinne didn't seem to notice. Impetuously, she kicked off her flip-flops and hopped up on to the bed. Leaning into the poster of Justin Bieber, she kissed his pouting lips, turning to look back at Beth, her face shining with mischief, before jumping down off the bed again.

Beth liked the way Corinne laughed. And she liked the way Corinne moved around the room, so sure of herself, a liveliness within her mannerisms, the busy way her attention flitted from one thing to another. It made her think of Lisa – not because Corinne and Lisa were alike, but because they were so different. Lisa was always quiet, thinking her big, deep thoughts. 'She's like a nun-in-training or something,' Eva had once remarked. 'A fucking postulant.' But Beth had loved that about Lisa: the quality of her stillness, her grace. It made Beth feel calm. Lately, whenever Beth thought about Lisa, it was the loss of her gentle serenity that hurt the most. She missed her friend.

Corinne was different. To be near her was to feel excitement, the lick of an electric current, the fizz and jolt of her personality lending a charge to the air.

She was at the wardrobe now, briskly looking through the clothes that hung there. Most of the clothes were Eva's cast-offs that Beth couldn't bring herself to wear, the rest a boring selection of jeans and tracksuits, everything shapeless and muted, like she was trying to make herself disappear. Corinne plucked a dress from a hanger and held it up for inspection. It was a green satin slip that Beth hadn't the courage to wear.

'Anouk has a dress just like this,' she said.

Beth didn't answer because at that moment, Corinne pulled the T-shirt she'd been wearing over her head, and yanked down her jeans, and Beth found herself staring at the thin body exposed to her, alert to the blue underwear, silky bra-straps cutting through tanned skin. There was a shrugging carelessness to Corinne, like she was unaware of her exposure as she reached for the dress. It made Beth twitchy with envy and longing.

The satin rippled as the slip fell over Corinne's body.

'What do you think?' she asked.

'Beautiful,' Beth breathed.

Corinne was hunting around now for her smartphone.

'Here,' she said, handing it over. 'Take a picture of me.'

Corinne pressed herself against the wall, drawing one leg up so the sole of her foot rested against the skirting board, her chin tilted up, her face unsmiling. Impressed by the readiness of her pose – the *professionalism* – Beth took the photograph. But when Corinne examined it, she frowned, displeased.

'I look fat. Take it again.'

She altered her pose, changed the angle of her face. Still it wasn't right. After five attempts, she was satisfied.

'I will Instagram it,' she announced, her thumbs flickering rapidly over the screen.

'You can keep the dress if you like,' Beth offered shyly. 'I'm never going to wear it.'

'Why not?'

'It's just a bit . . . I dunno, revealing or something. I'd feel too exposed.' She ducked her head, aware she was blushing again.

'It would look cute on you. The green colour with your hair.'

But Beth hated her copper-coloured hair. Just as she hated her pale freckled skin and her teeth that still felt furry and strange since the braces had been removed barely a month before. She hated her stupid body with its flesh bulging in all the wrong places, her ugly feet, her sloping shoulders and flat chest.

'Anouk used to tell me what to wear,' Corinne said then. 'For a whole year, it was a game we played. Every day, she

33

would pick my clothes for me. And it didn't matter what she chose, how silly or unsuitable for the weather – I had to wear what she picked.'

Beth frowned. 'Didn't that annoy you? Giving up control like that?'

'No! It was liberating!' Corinne laughed. Her whole face lit up when she laughed. 'To not have to choose – to not have to worry what people would think.'

Beth thought of Sasha and Nicole and some of the other girls at school. The way they scrutinized what everyone wore, allocating points based on your appearance. That stupid *Outfit Of The Day* group they'd started on WhatsApp and now everyone in the class was on it. Everyone except for Beth.

'Hey, we should play that game!' Corinne announced, suddenly seizing on the idea. 'Why not? Every day, while I am here, I shall choose your outfit and you can choose mine!'

'I don't know,' Beth said, uncertain.

But Corinne was already flicking hangers across the rail, scanning the clothes in the wardrobe before seizing on a bib-shirt Abi had bought for Beth last Christmas, hard fold-marks from the packaging still visible through the cotton.

'Here. Put this on,' Corinne instructed, waiting with the hanger dangling from a crooked index finger.

Beth felt seized with indecision. She baulked at the idea of shedding her clothes under Corinne's watchful eye. But it had been so long since Beth had brought a friend up here to her room – over a year. Whenever her parents asked if she wanted to bring Lisa back to the house for pizza or a movie, she made excuses. But now, under Corinne's steady gaze, she felt the hard carapace of her defences begin to melt.

Head down, she took off her T-shirt, clutching it in a ball against her chest while Corinne took the shirt from the hanger and placed it over Beth's head. She pushed her arms into the sleeves and reached to loosen her hair from beneath the collar, and as she did, she felt a hand go to her neck, the lightning touch of a finger trailing over her skin. She jumped aside as if she'd been burned.

'What?' Corinne asked.

Beth stood there with her hand clamped hard across the back of her neck. 'Don't touch that.'

'What is it?'

'Nothing.'

'Let me see it.'

Corinne was coming towards her now and Beth backed away.

'Please don't.'

Corinne moved quickly, one hand reaching for Beth's arm and pulling her around, the other hand plucking at the neck of Beth's shirt.

'Hey!' Beth shouted, alarmed by the sudden move and taken aback by the girl's strength, the shock of this physical contact. Corinne's grip was strong, and Beth felt herself pinned against the desk, unable to shake free.

'It's just a scar,' Corinne announced, sounding disappointed. She released her grip and Beth turned around quickly to face her, heart beating fast, sweat on her back. She felt the French girl's proximity; the curl of her smile seemed teasing.

'I don't like people touching it,' Beth said quickly. She couldn't say why she felt so alarmed, tears threatening to spring in her eyes.

'How did you get it?'

'An operation when I was twelve. I had scoliosis.'

'What?'

'My spine grew curved.' She gestured with her hands to demonstrate. 'They had to put metal pins in my back to straighten the curve and to make sure it grew properly.'

'That is awful,' Corinne said, and Beth felt shy beneath her gaze which had grown serious and intent.

She shrugged. 'It was okay.'

'No,' the girl said, her voice insistent. 'It must have been terrible.'

The statement, solemn and clear, sat in the air between them. The way Corinne held the silence and the change that came into her eyes – empathy, sadness – it was as if she glimpsed something of what Beth had endured. Not just the physical pain but the anguish of all the things you could not see, a history of names that had been affixed to her: hunchback, gimp, spastic. Names that adhered long after the unruly line of her spine had been disciplined.

'Do you want to see something?' Corinne asked, leaning forward slightly, her voice dropping.

Beth's heart gave a small kick, and she watched as the other girl half-twisted, pulling up the hem of the green slipdress to reveal her hip. Beth leaned forward.

It was a tattoo of a tiny flower. Delicate white petals surrounding a yellow centre, the outline of the flower inked in a thin black line. It was no bigger than a real daisy, and there was something tender about the sight of it nestling there on the band of skin above the blue cotton of her underwear – Beth felt an urge to touch it but didn't dare.

'What type of flower is it?' she asked.

'In French, we say *laurier-rose*. But in English, it is oleander?' Her accent tripped upwards, questioning her own pronunciation. Then she added, almost bashfully: 'I looked it up so I could tell you.'

'It's beautiful.' Beth's eyes were still fixed on the furl of petals. Her unease had dissipated.

'But poisonous,' Corinne added. 'You must take care how you handle it.'

She said this lightly, almost carelessly, and Beth, who was still leaning forward to examine the delicate flower, felt the touch of Corinne's fingers once more against her neck. A feathery caress.

'I have an idea,' Corinne said.

Beth allowed herself to be steered into the desk chair, and when Corinne tugged down at the back of her collar to reveal the scar, she didn't flinch or protest. Instead, she remained still and perfectly calm as Corinne picked up a pen from the desk and began to draw. The coolness of the pen's nib gliding over her skin. All the nerve endings tingling, a sensation that stilled her heart and yet sent ripples of feeling all through her.

When it was done, Corinne took a photograph, then held the phone so Beth could see the image on the screen. The tenderness of lines drawn along the curve of the spine – the curlicued leaves, the delicate petals. The ugly gash rendered gentle – artful.

'You see?' Corinne said. 'This is beautiful too.' Her voice close to Beth's ear, her breath hot on Beth's neck.

In the shadowy corners of her mind, Beth heard those words echoing in a different voice, a different room. The silky voice dredged up from her memory, words spoken to make her still and attentive, like a snap in the grass that alerts the deer to danger.

'What is it? What's wrong?' Corinne asked.

'Nothing,' Beth replied.

But Beth knew that Corinne had seen it – the shiver that went through her, even though the room was warm.

6

Eva waited until the Campbells had left and little Jo was settled in his room. Then she found her phone and opened up WhatsApp. 'Coast is clear,' she typed.

Ten minutes later, she heard the sound of brakes screeching outside and when she went to the door, Callum was locking his bike to the railings.

'Hey,' he said, scooting in through the open door quickly before they were seen.

He didn't kiss her, even though they had kissed a week before outside the tennis club, both of them a little high after their wins.

'I brought wine,' he said, following her into the kitchen, where he slid a bottle of red from his backpack and presented it to her. 'I stole it from my old man's collection. Hopefully it's not super-valuable,' he added, glancing at the label with a nervous laugh. 'My dad will fucking crucify me if it is.'

Eva knew Callum's father from all the years he'd been coming to pick up Lisa from her house. Craig and Irene Ferguson were a fixture at the tennis club, both shouty and flamboyant – both voluble when drunk. 'Dirty money,' her father had commented after returning from a particularly splashy event at the Fergusons' Victoria Road house, but it didn't stop him from drinking their wine or eating their food, she thought glibly. She wondered briefly what her father would think if he knew Callum Ferguson was here, right next door, about to be seduced by his own daughter. Because while neither of them had spoken of it when they'd made the arrangement for this evening, Eva knew that her baby-sitting gig was an opportunity for them to have sex.

Half the girls in Eva's year had already been relieved of their virginities, if not more. At least two of her peers had taken the abortion pill. But sex was something that troubled Eva. Some part of her clammed up with fright whenever things got heated. Steve Klein, a guy from the swim team she'd kissed a few times, had snapped at her one night after she'd shoved him back violently, panicked when he'd steered her hand to the button-fly of his jeans: 'You're fucking frigid, do you know that, Eva? You strut around like you're God's gift, but you're a fucking icicle.'

Secretly, she worried that there was something wrong with her. A genetic flaw, perhaps. Her aunt Melissa had been forty-four years old when she died, and she'd never even had a boyfriend. Eva was horrified at the thought of being so abnormal. Sex was a burden she was determined to shrug off before university began, and she had made the decision that Callum would be the one.

There was something clean-looking about him – hygienic – his fingernails always spotless, his hair neatly cut. Everything he wore looked box-fresh like it was brand new. She watched him now as he moved about the kitchen, swirling the wine in his glass, her eye following the taut pull of muscle beneath his pink sports-shirt, that particular hue emphasizing his toast-coloured skin. He'd turned his attention to the framed photographs of the Campbells that lined one whole wall of the kitchen. Black and white studio portraits of the family, dressed in jeans and white T-shirts, barefoot and smiling, a collage of stylishly happy family life.

He was peering closely now at a portrait shot of Jo, the Campbells' three-year-old son. They had adopted him from an orphanage in Vietnam – or maybe it was Thailand, Eva couldn't remember. His hair was cut into a pudding bowl shape that made his flat little face appear rounder, more cherubic. Jo had Down's Syndrome and Eva couldn't imagine any child being more adorable.

'They sure do think a lot of themselves, these people,' Callum remarked, bringing his glass to his lips.

Eva said nothing, but a shimmer of disappointment passed through her. She'd wanted more from him than this. Eva loved Jo, his unabashed joy whenever he saw her, his sticky impulsive hugs. Ross was okay in a balding rugby-dad sort of way, but Becca was nice. Smart, glamorous, always immaculately dressed – one time, when Eva was babysitting, she'd spent a full hour going through Becca's wardrobe, trying on her clothes, her shoes, imagining what it was like to be Becca.

And what was wrong with the photographs anyway? Eva nursed fantasies of her own wall of pictures, posing barefoot with a handsome husband and their gorgeous children. Recently, she had allowed Callum's image to slot into her fantasy – how well they would look together, how cute their kids would be! When she'd told her best friend, Alicia, about her crush, Alicia's reaction had been instant and emphatic: 'Oh my God, how perfect you guys would be together! You're like made for each other!'

Eva focused on that thought now as she approached Callum, touched his shoulder and said 'Hey,' and then he kissed her.

She tasted the warmth of the wine on his mouth, his lips soft against hers, the pleasing strength of his hand pressing into her lower back. They paused briefly so he could take the glass from her hand, and then he was back with her, his face on hers, his fingers plucking the blouse loose from the waistband of her jeans, exploring beneath it. She liked the sensation, the loose swimmy feeling in her tummy as instinct began to take over.

The guest bedroom was upstairs at the back of the house and it was to this room that they retired, shedding their clothes quickly and coming together under the feather duvet. It was not quite dark outside, the evening light falling through a gap in the curtains, magpies clacking in the trees beyond. Eva could hardly believe this was finally about to happen, her heart beating fast, feeling the weight of his body on hers, his face rearranged into an expression of fierce concentration. She steeled herself, willing her body to relax, to thaw, and it was at that precise moment when the door behind them opened.

Light from the hall shone off Ross Campbell's bald head. He didn't say anything, just stood there for a few seconds, long enough to survey what was happening, the brief scuffle under the duvet as the two lovers hastily came apart.

'I thought you said they'd be gone for hours?' Callum hissed, after Ross had closed the door and thumped back down the stairs.

He was already pulling on his boxers, his jeans. The room was suddenly filled with his panic, Eva's heart giving out its own unsteady beat.

'I thought they were. Something must have happened.' She was leaning over the mattress, hunting for her underwear while trying to conceal her nakedness. Embarrassment was crashing over her. Ross Campbell, whom she hardly knew, barely ever thought of – and he'd caught her like this!

'Do you think he's down there waiting?' she asked as Callum hopped on one foot, trying to get the other into his sneaker.

'The fuck should I know?' His tone was terse, and there

was something accusatory in the way he wouldn't meet her eye. It wasn't as if she'd planned for it to happen, Ross barging in like that. 'Do you think he'll tell your folks?'

'I don't know.'

'Fuck! If my dad finds out about this, he'll have my balls!'

She felt her lip trembling, and he must have seen it, because he paused, seeming to soften. 'Listen, I'll call you, okay?'

'You're going?'

'I'm sorry, Eva. I like you, but this just isn't what I had in mind for this evening, you know? I'll be in touch.'

He kissed her swiftly and then he was gone, his feet rumbling down the stairs, the slam of the front door, the shush of his bicycle wheels as he pushed away down the drive.

Ross was waiting for her in the kitchen. He looked up as she came in, and Eva noticed the half-empty bottle of wine on the counter by his elbow. The sight of it made her wince.

'I'm sorry,' she said softly. 'I'm so embarrassed – please don't tell anyone about this.'

She realized how self-centred she sounded, more concerned with her reputation than the act of trespass she'd just committed.

'He just came over to hang out with me. I didn't mean for things to get so out of hand.'

Still he made no reply and that was somehow worse than him losing his temper and making accusations.

'Please don't think that I'm a slut,' she said, and his brow furrowed into a quizzical expression, and then he smiled.

'Christ, is that what you think?'

'No—'

'I'm not some sanctimonious old codger. I can still remember what it was to be a teenager, grasping opportunities when you could.'

He shook his head, still grinning, but there was a faraway look about him, as if he was reminiscing on exploits in his own past.

'You're not mad at me?' she ventured.

'I'm not thrilled, but I'm not mad either.'

He scratched the dome of his head and laughed once more. 'Seeing that young fella running out the door, his jeans practically around his knees, it reminded me of myself, getting chased out of a girl's bedroom, half-dressed, leaving my shoes behind in a panic! I can't have been much older than you are now.'

She wondered if the girl whose bedroom he'd been caught in was Becca, and then she thought of Ross as he might have been back then and found herself looking at him more closely.

Her father always referred to him as 'the petrol-head next door' and Eva had been mildly irritated on occasion by the loud growling of engines while she was trying to study. Now she took in his height, the blue cotton of his shirt stretched over wide rugby shoulders. Under the spotlights of the ceiling, she could see the contours of his skull, his hair shaved to the scalp – a concession to advancing baldness. She guessed he was about forty. She was normally dismissive of any man over the age of thirty, but there was something very calm about him – a solidity that was reassuring, attractive even. The thought startled her.

'I'm guessing your parents don't have a clue about any of this,' he made a vague gesture towards the wine, the bedroom upstairs, and she shook her head.

'Please don't tell them.'

He snorted. 'Is that really what you think I'd do? Come on!'

'What about Becca? Will you tell her?'

He considered that for a moment, holding her in his gaze.

'I'm not sure, to be honest. It's not that I keep secrets from my wife, but just, when it comes to Jo, she gets . . . Well, she can be overprotective.'

He lapsed into a distracted silence, and then roused himself. 'Speaking of which, I'd better go. She'll be wondering where I am.'

He held aloft the mobile phone he'd forgotten – the reason for his return – and then winked at her.

'Be good now. And don't drink any more of that wine, yeah?'

She laughed and agreed but still some awkwardness lingered.

As soon as she heard the car pull away once more, she snatched up her phone and called Alicia. 'You are not going to believe what just happened,' she began.

Alicia hooted with laughter when she heard, and then consoled Eva that the whole thing would blow over.

'Give that guy a wide berth for a while,' she advised. 'Maybe even ditch the babysitting job.'

Eva knew it was good advice. But later she wondered if avoiding Ross would only serve to magnify the incident. Already she felt the push of new and strange feelings inside her, like the hollowing out of a dark, quiet space around the memory. Feelings she couldn't admit to or yet fully understand.

7

Things might have been different – the incident forgotten – had Abi not invited the Campbells for Sunday lunch.

She had made the arrangement with Becca a few days before.

At nine o'clock on Sunday morning Abi began preparing the food. By eleven thirty the lamb was in the oven and she went upstairs to dress.

Passing Beth's room, Abi heard a raised voice saying:

'You have to! We agreed, right?'

She paused in the hallway, put her ear close to the door and listened.

'I just think I look stupid, that's all,' Beth said. Words spoken softly, but Abi heard the bullish undercurrent.

'You don't look stupid! You look cool. You just need to be a bit more brave, yes?'

There was a gaiety to Corinne's tone, but an insistence too.

'I'm not like you,' Abi heard Beth say. 'I can't carry it off like you can.'

'Remember the rules. You cannot question – you must just obey, right?'

Abi opened the door.

'Everything okay?' she asked, looking from one girl to the other.

Beth, she saw, was wearing a purple vest with a black gypsy skirt. The outfit, Abi observed with a pang of tender feeling, made Beth look lumpen and ungainly. It emphasized her curved shoulders, and the shapelessness of her waist and hips. Next to her, Corinne looked fresh and casual in a clean white T-shirt, dark skinny jeans. A swift expression of shame crossed Beth's face as she met Abi's gaze, disappearing just as quickly as she looked away shyly.

'Everything all right in here?' Abi asked again and Corinne perked up, rousing herself from whatever stand-off they'd been having.

'Sure! We were just talking.'

She flashed her bright, sunny smile, but Abi was not convinced. Turning her attention to Beth, she began tentatively: 'You look nice. Are you two going out somewhere?'

'No, why?'

Abi's eyes flickered over Beth's clothes. 'I just thought—'

'Can't I just dress for myself? Why do you assume it's for someone else?'

Beth's cheeks flared with colour, and Abi felt her daughter's discomfort.

'There's been some chatter on the parents WhatsApp group about an outing to the Epic Museum this afternoon. It looks like most of the girls in your class are going, and I was just wondering if you two might be interested.'

'You want us out of the way so we don't interrupt your little lunch party, is it?'

'Not at all! But I wouldn't have thought you'd be interested in a boring lunch with your parents and the next-door neighbours.'

'Well, if the alternative is hanging out with all those bitches from school—'

'Watch your language, young lady.'

Calmly, Beth brought her eyes up to meet Abi's, coolly finishing her sentence: '—then I'd rather swallow razor blades. If that's what you're serving.'

Abi flinched. It was the mention of razor blades that did

it. Instantly, her mind bolted to that phone call from the school a year ago, Helen Bracken's voice at the end of the line, formal and calm but with a sharp note of tension at the back of it, telling Abi that she needed to come to the school at once, that something serious had happened.

A whole year had passed, and she was still unnerved by the memory.

'Come on, love,' Abi pressed gently. 'If you don't make an effort, how on earth do you expect to have any friends?'

'She has a friend,' Corinne said, taking a step towards Beth and linking her arm.

Abi read the challenge in the gesture, but it was pointless pursuing the matter in front of the French girl, and besides, the Campbells would be there in an hour or so. There wasn't time for confrontation.

'Very well,' Abi said, backing out of the room, 'I'll set places for you both at the table.'

She did her best to be magnanimous, ignoring the look of triumph that had come over Corinne's face.

The Campbells arrived shortly after one. Little Jo brought his own transport – a wooden balance bike with racing stripes in red dashed along the sides – 'his go-faster stripes,' Becca explained apologetically as the boy charged through the hall on his little bike, the rubber wheel colliding with the Hollands' kitchen door.

'Whoa!' Mark laughed, reaching down to right the boy, setting him back on the saddle and tussling his glossy black hair. 'Easy, cowboy!'

'Sorry about the bike. He insists on bringing it everywhere,' Ross explained, pride in his voice, as he added: 'He's mad for bikes and cars. Anything with wheels.'

'I wonder where he gets that from?' Mark joked, referring

to the row of cars that lined the Campbells' driveway. Apart from Becca's Golf, there was a 1973 Fiat 127, a Karmann Ghia minus its wheels, an ancient, mud-splattered Land Rover, a Mercedes and a small red Toyota bearing signage for a school of motoring. When the Campbells had moved in, they'd had the whole front garden bricked over to accommodate Ross Campbell's car collection. At the time, it had filled Mark with dismay, but on this particular Sunday he didn't mind so much.

'Guilty as charged,' Ross laughed, holding his hands aloft in surrender.

They went into the kitchen where Mark reached up into one of the presses for a tin box filled with animal cookies. In the past, he'd kept it stocked with treats for the girls, but they were beyond such juvenilia now. These days, he mainly kept it stocked for Jo.

'What would you like, buddy?' he asked the child. 'Lion? Elephant?'

The boy chose a chocolate-covered seal, gripping it in his chubby little hand and rewarding Mark with a gummy smile, his eyes – crinkling with delight – disappearing behind their epicanthic folds.

'Oh, he just gets cuter every time I see him,' Abi declared.

In the months since the Campbells had moved in next door, never once had Mark or Abi heard the child have a temper tantrum. No screams of annoyance, no demanding shouts. 'He's even cute when he's crying,' Beth had commented once, observing Jo's plaintive whimpers, big tears rolling over his rounded cheeks.

'Full of energy too,' Mark added as Jo began wheeling around the kitchen table.

'Tell me about it!' Ross joked.

'It's exhausting,' Becca admitted. 'But I just keep thinking back to how he was the first time we saw him in the orphanage – so quiet and still, almost like he was afraid to make a sound.'

'The poor little lamb,' Abi remarked.

'It just makes me grateful every time I see him whizzing about the place.'

Mark poured glasses of white wine for the ladies, uncapping beers for the men, and when Ross expressed an interest in seeing the studio, Mark was happy to oblige.

It wasn't a large room, but it was well appointed with a little wood-burning stove in one corner, skylights in the pitched roof and French doors opening on to the patio. He'd lit a fire in the stove earlier in anticipation of this moment, and now he sat in one of the armchairs, sipping his beer, while Ross Campbell peered at some of the models that were displayed along the shelving unit – miniature stage sets made from balsa wood, Ross's thick fingers occasionally picking up some delicate piece.

'Did you make these yourself?' he asked, making an appreciative noise when Mark admitted he had.

Mark felt that perhaps he'd been too hasty in writing off a possibility of friendship with Ross. So what if the man liked tinkering with engines? It didn't necessarily follow that he had no soul.

'I can't imagine it,' Ross said, 'spending your time making these things. It's like Lilliput, yeah?'

Mark gave a brief explanation of his working method and Ross listened politely, the bottle of Heineken held casually by his hip, but it was obvious he was baffled by it all. And when he said: 'Would you not be tempted to clear out all this stuff and put in a pool table? Get yourself a flat-screen TV and a decent sound system, a little fridge in the corner?' Mark tried to hide his disappointment.

'Yeah, it's tempting. But how would I get any work done with all that distraction?'

'Looks like you're already distracted.' Ross nodded towards the table where several translucent bags full of matchsticks lay next to a half-hearted attempt at construction.

Approaching the table for a closer look, Ross wrinkled his nose and said: 'What is all this? Are you building something? Or is it like a really complicated Jenga?'

'It's an old hobby of mine. Something my sister and I used to do as kids,' Mark explained, fondness creeping into his voice. 'We'd build miniature models of well-known buildings, recreate them from matchsticks. We used to spend hours working on them.'

'Did you not just watch television like the rest of us?'

'We didn't have a television.'

'What?' Ross laughed, straightening. 'Jesus, talk about a deprived childhood!'

Mark caught the derision in his voice, the quick flicker of his eyes, and he recognized it at once: the same assessment every boy in his class, every kid on his street, had ever made about him. That he was a weirdo, a freak. From a family of freaks. His ancient, bookish parents, his frumpy, introverted sister – it was all there in that look. Sometimes, as a child, he'd looked up from his book, or his model-making, his attention drawn by a sharp snapping sound breaking the silence, and his mother would dash outside just as the kids disappeared on their bikes, the egg yolks and albumen dripping down the stippled masonry, sliding over the windowpanes.

Somehow, when Ross Campbell looked at him, Mark felt the man glimpsed all those dark days of his childhood, got the measure of what had formed him, the way a bully always spied a weakness.

'We don't have a television either.'

Both men turned towards the voice.

Corinne was standing in the doorway, her hands in her pockets, one shoulder leaning against the door frame. She was smiling, but Mark could see the challenge there in her open face as she held Ross's gaze.

'And who are you?' Ross asked, bemused.

'This is Corinne – Beth's friend. She's visiting from France for a couple of weeks.'

'Is that so?' Ross smirked. 'Like the hair,' he added, shooting an amused glance at Mark who didn't reciprocate, resenting the attempt at forced collusion. Despite all his good intentions at focusing on the positives, he felt in that moment a trickle of dislike for the man.

'What sort of tower will it be?' Corinne asked, stepping into the room, moving confidently past until she was at the little table, picking up a matchstick and testing the sharpness of it against her palm. 'The Eiffel Tower, perhaps?'

She said this playfully, smiling at him, and Mark found himself warming to her.

'Perhaps. Or maybe the bell towers of Notre Dame.'

'Just the bell towers? Why not the whole cathedral?'

He laughed. 'That might be overly ambitious.'

'But why? Maybe I could help you!'

'If you like.'

'I would like that.' She put down the match and stretched expansively, sighing with pleasure. 'I just love this room, so full of nostalgia!' she declared. 'It reminds me of home. Even the smell – so familiar.'

Mark could feel Ross's interest cocked by this girl. She was so guileless and free in her expression. There was something embarrassing about her openness and yet he found it refreshing too. Both his daughters had become so closed to him during their adolescence – remote in their differing ways. But now, while he watched Corinne picking through the things he had amassed here, taking delight in them, he found himself struck by the light and colour she brought into the space. He hardly noticed it when Beth poked her head around the door.

'Didn't you hear Mum calling?' she asked, her voice tetchy and suspicious. 'Lunch is ready.'

There were six of them at the table. Jo, having eaten earlier, sat in a corner watching cartoons on his mother's iPad.

'No Eva?' Becca observed, and Abi explained that she was upstairs studying. The Leaving Cert exams were only a few weeks away.

'She's a good girl,' Becca replied. 'You've got no worries there. Always has her head in the books whenever she babysits for us. Isn't that right, Ross?'

'I'll tell you what, I want this guy's life,' Ross said, changing the subject and nodding in Mark's direction. 'He gets to sit at home all day in his room, playing with his little models while this lady here —' he nodded to Abi '— goes out and earns the dough!'

He laughed to show there was no malice intended, and Becca giggled and poked her husband in the stomach, saying: 'Like you can talk. Playing all day with your cars. What do you think, Abi? How did we wind up in this position?'

Abi, putting down her glass of wine, said: 'Honestly, I'm the lucky one. It's such a relief to be able to go to work knowing that your children are being cared for by the person who's invested in their needs, who best understands them. And Mark's always been more attuned to them than I have.'

Mark said nothing. He'd heard Abi do this before: exclaim over his parenting skills while simultaneously disparaging her own. Mostly, he didn't mind when she did this, understanding that she was not just trying to make him feel better, but assuaging her own residual guilt for the lack of time and attention she had been able to bestow on the girls over the years. Her job demanded so much. Perhaps it was the recent discussion with Andrew, reviving old passions, but he felt a prickle of resentment now.

'You're so lucky,' Becca remarked. 'You seem to have the whole thing sorted out between you. It's like you've managed to achieve the perfect work/life balance.'

Beth snorted, saying 'Yeah, right,' while reaching across the table for the potato salad.

Abi flashed her a warning look, and then Mark sat forward, saying: 'Actually, that balance is about to shift a little. A friend of mine in the business has asked me to come on board with the production design of a movie he's working on. Filming begins in September.'

'No shit,' Ross said, impressed. 'Where?'

'Prague. London.'

'Cool.'

'Well, we still have to agree the arrangements,' Abi said, laughing nervously as she handed around the basket of bread. 'Nothing's set in stone.'

A flicker of doubt went through him and he tried to catch her eye.

'You should do it,' Corinne said, and his gaze moved to her, surprised by the intervention. 'I love your models. You are really talented.'

'Thank you,' he said, and Beth snorted again.

'Mum doesn't think so. She thinks his stuff is boring.'

Mark frowned, wounded by her comment. Abi was already protesting vehemently against the charge, but Beth stood firm. 'Didn't you hate his stuff when you first met?'

'I think that's an exaggeration,' Mark said coldly.

'We met in college,' Abi explained to Becca and Ross. 'We were both involved in a DramSoc production of *Our Town*. I was acting, and Mark designed the set. It wasn't exactly love at first sight, was it?' she asked him teasingly.

The truth was, when he first knew Abi, he'd found her overly opinionated, critical and fussy. She had worn her blond hair tied back in a ponytail that had a jaunty bounce to it – even that was annoying. But it was her reaction to the reveal of his set that cemented his negative feelings towards her.

'It seems a little bland,' she'd said, the corners of her mouth tugging downwards as she cast her underwhelmed gaze over the artwork he'd spent weeks working on.

Bland.

He could barely stand the sight of her after that.

'Some years later, we met again,' Abi explained now, 'at a Radiohead gig. You liked me better then, didn't you?' she challenged flirtatiously.

Mark remembered how he'd found himself next to her in the pub after the gig, and she'd said: 'Well? Do you approve?'

'What?' he'd asked, confused by the quizzically amused expression on her face.

'You've been watching me all evening. Have I changed in the intervening years? Become more bearable?'

She was smiling up at him playfully, waiting for him to speak, and he'd felt a queer lurching inside, a sudden flash of intuition.

Oh no, he'd thought, contemplating his future, his fate. *Not her.*

'Yes, I liked you better then,' he admitted, feeling like he was surrendering something with those words. From across the table, Corinne was still looking at him with her clear-eyed gaze.

At that moment, Eva came into the kitchen and both Ross and Becca looked up.

'There she is!' Becca declared. 'How's the study going?'

Mark, distracted by his thoughts, didn't listen to the answer Eva gave. Instead, he found himself caught in that moment before lunch when Corinne had come into the studio, her lightness and ease, the bright flare of colour she brought into that drab room. A butterfly in a cave, he wondered, or a canary in a coalmine? His attention only returned to the kitchen, and the conversation, when he heard Becca say:

'You should get Ross to teach you!' and he saw Eva's cheeks flush with colour.

'What's this?' he asked, and Eva rolled her eyes.

'Driving lessons, Dad.'

'I can teach you.'

'Yeah, right! I've been asking you for like two years and you just keep telling me how your parents wouldn't let you drive their car, and how you had to wait until you were in your twenties and able to afford your own—'

'All right, all right,' he said, uncomfortable at having his own words repeated back to him in front of Ross.

'Mark's terrified she'll scratch the car,' Abi offered.

'No, I'm not—'

'Honestly. You've no idea. If he had his way, we'd all have to walk up one side of the stairs and down the other so the carpet would thin evenly. And we'd never have taken the shrink-wrap off the furniture.'

Ross roared with laughter. Mark glared at his wife, who ignored him.

'So what do you think, Ross?' Abi asked. 'Reckon you'd be able to teach this young lady to drive?'

Ross nodded, glancing up at Eva again, a little shyly, Mark thought.

'Why not? I'm game if you are,' he said.

It was a straightforward arrangement. But Mark saw the lift in Eva's brow, caught the quick movement of humour in her eyes. Something was unexpressed between them, and Mark felt the weight of it. He didn't like to think about what it meant.

8

There was a Benjamin Franklin quote that Eva's aunt Melissa used to trot out whenever she came to stay: 'Guests, like fish, begin to smell after three days.' Every year, she would arrive on Christmas Eve, sleeping on the fold-out bed in Abi's home office until the morning of St Stephen's Day, even though her own home – a mid-terraced two-up-two-down – was less than four miles away. Eva's parents would always press her to stay longer, and that's when she'd make the remark about the fish.

Eva thought there was truth to the phrase. Even someone as peaceable and familiar as Melissa became an irksome presence after a while. The same, she found, was true of the French girl. After the first couple of days Corinne began getting on Eva's nerves. She was pass-remarkable which had been kind of amusing at first, but now seemed just plain rude. Her laugh was irritating – a sudden high-pitched honking that could be heard all over the house. Also she had zero respect for people's personal space. Eva avoided engaging her in any kind of conversation, made uncomfortable by the way Corinne leaned towards her when she spoke, so close that you could feel the heat of her breath. And twice now, Eva had walked into her own bedroom and found Corinne there, fingering an object on her desk or just gazing dreamily out the window. She had cornered Beth about it.

'Keep that fucking freak out of my room, okay?'

'She's not a freak,' Beth had said, rising to the defensive.

Freak was too strong a word but there was something

about Corinne that wasn't right, like she'd been dropped on the head as a kid. It wasn't a cultural difference; it was more that her neurons fired and sparked in a different way to other people's. Despite her facility with the English language, she had a habit of staring that Eva found unnerving.

At school, Eva steered clear of both Beth and Corinne, which wasn't hard. As a senior, all her classes were taught in a different part of the school to the junior years. It was only during assembly on Thursday mornings when the whole school gathered in the hall that they were forced to mingle.

Assembly, that Thursday morning, began as usual with a droned recitation of the school prayer.

'Come, Holy Spirit, open our hearts,
Bestow on us the gift of faith . . .'

The voices of five hundred girls rose in unison.

The chairs for assembly were arranged in giant rings around a central space where the principal, Mrs Bracken, stood at the microphone. A small woman with an owlish look, she wore a black academic gown over her clothes, her sharp gaze passing over the uniformed rows of girls in front of her.

'Grant us strength when we are weak,
Courage when we are afraid . . .'

The words came out of Eva's mouth automatically. She slumped in her chair and stared down at her shoes. Patent leather brogues, a little scuffed at the toe.

'Wear different shoes next time, okay?' Ross had told her.

This was at the end of their lesson the previous evening, when she'd turned the car into the narrow driveway, and he'd reached for the wheel to correct her steering. She'd glanced down at his hand, noticed the tiny blond hairs pushing through at the backs of his fingers. He had big, powerful hands. She had watched from her bedroom window as those hands tinkered with engine parts under the bonnet of a car. His instruction was calm and measured. He teased her about the boots she was wearing, the heel inappropriate for driving. 'No one can see your feet when you're in the car, you know,' he'd said, and she'd heard the grin in his voice. *You can see them*, she'd thought, and felt the heat at her neck.

Now, as Mrs Bracken's voice crackled through the speakers, Eva found her mind replaying the lesson once more, every word of their conversation unspooling in her head in all its delicious detail as she slipped down in her chair, her eyelids lowering.

He told her it was admirable that she wanted to get her driver's licence before she started college. 'Everyone should, in my book,' he'd said. 'It should be part of a person's education. Far more practical use to you than the Pythagorean theorem or reproduction in plants.'

'And this way I can drive myself to college,' she'd said, 'instead of relying on my parents for a lift.'

'Jesus, what's wrong with the bus?' he'd laughed, and she'd liked the way he kept looking at her, waiting for her reaction.

'I'll take the bus sometimes. But when I'm in training, I have to be at the pool for like six a.m. That's too early for the bus—'

'Wait, so you're an athlete?'

She'd guessed he'd be impressed by that, and it was gratifying to feel his attention as she'd detailed how she'd been swimming competitively since she was ten years old, how she was hopeful of making the university swim team.

'So how often do you train?' he'd asked, and she'd listed the early morning starts, getting an hour in before school, as well as two evenings a week and racing at weekends.

'That's some commitment,' Ross had said. 'I remember what it was like when I was your age.'

'You were an athlete?'

'Rugby,' he answered. 'I played for Terenure. Tried out for Leinster once.'

'Really?'

'Yeah. Back in the day.'

'What position did you play?'

'Hooker.'

'I'll bet you were good.' She glanced across at him, a coy smile playing on her face. 'I'll bet all the girls were mad about you.' She couldn't believe how daring she was, and a little thrill had shot through her as he'd grinned bashfully and pointed to the steering wheel, saying: 'Here. Eyes on the road, young lady.'

They'd talked about school, about the subjects she was taking, about her impatience to be finished with that part of her life so she could start university, adulthood, independence. He'd sighed wistfully and said:

'God, I envy you. All that you've ahead of you.'

'The parties, the booze, the drugs, the endless shagging,' she'd teased him.

My God! Had she really said that? The man was forty years old! In her world, that was ancient.

'I'd say you're already covered on at least three of those,' he'd remarked, deadpan, and just for an instant, they were back in that bedroom, her naked body beneath the covers, the air between them holding the silence, but something was communicated all the same.

Lately, in idle moments, whenever Callum messaged her and she allowed her mind to drift to the little patch of dark chest hair she'd discovered nestling over his sternum, the smoothness of his back beneath her fingertips, Eva often found her thoughts interrupted by the moment Ross opened the door, reliving the awkwardness of their conversation afterwards. It was as if the incident had awakened within her a new awareness of Ross Campbell. She watched him from her window cradling his little boy against his hip, pointing out in a soft, affectionate tone the different cars, patiently repeating the words. She observed the tender way he leaned down to touch the boy's neck, to kiss the glossy black hair. Ross was not some adolescent boy like Callum, prey to his own desires and clumsy about expressing them. He was past all that. He was a grown-up.

'Thanks,' Eva had said, after handing over the money to him. 'You're a really good teacher.'

'Ah, there's not much to it,' he'd replied.

She liked that about Ross – his self-deprecation.

'See you Saturday,' she'd told him, then stood and watched while he reversed.

She hadn't seen the figure in the window upstairs, the outline of frosted hair, the ardent gaze. And when Eva turned back to the house, she was unaware that she was being watched, the secret smile on her lips noted, the light in her eyes astutely read as desire. She ran up the stairs and into her bedroom.

'You like him, don't you?' Corinne said, almost as soon as she'd walked in the door.

'What are you doing in here?' she'd demanded, snapping on the light, unable to conceal her annoyance.

'I can see it in your face. I recognize the look.'

Eva had stepped past and thrown her wallet on to her desk.

'Kindly get the fuck out of my room.'

'Anouk fell in love with a man in our village. He also had a wife and child. It was a scandal.'

'That's fascinating, but I'm not like Anouk,' Eva had retorted.

Corinne had stood in the doorway for just a moment, the

smile on her face enigmatic, infuriating, her eyes lit up with the strange workings of her own convictions.

'Yes, you are,' she'd said, before stepping softly away.

It was stupid to feel unnerved. At the time, Eva had convinced herself that she was more enraged by the girl's trespasses than unsettled by her calm intensity. But even now, in the school hall surrounded by hundreds of girls, she experienced it again: that same shiver of unease.

Eva looked up, her thoughts interrupted by the loud scrape of a chair, a voice she recognized travelling across all the heads of those gathered there, saying:

'Sorry, but can I leave now?'

Mrs Bracken blinked in surprise. No one ever interrupted her address at assembly. Eva strained to see above the girls in front of her, and then she saw the candyfloss hair, the familiar smirk.

'No, you may not,' Bracken snapped, rustling her notes before resuming her speech.

'Who the fuck is that?' Alicia whispered to her.

Eva didn't answer. She kept her gaze fixed on Corinne, who continued to stand there, zipping and unzipping her hoodie, a challenge in her expression.

'Take your seat, young lady.'

'But this is boring.'

Laughter rippled through the crowd.

'Sit down. *Now!*' Bracken barked, irritation spilling over into anger, and Eva noticed the smirk hardening on Corinne's face, before she sat down and Eva couldn't see her any more.

Bracken's speech continued but the mood in the room had changed. Next to her, Alicia's foot was tap-tapping against the leg of her chair but Eva sat perfectly still. A familiar feeling of disquiet roused itself in her chest. She strained to see her younger sister but Beth was hidden from view.

A year ago, Eva's younger sister had almost gotten herself expelled. Soft, dreamy little Beth, who never raised her head above the parapet. Eva could still remember the day she arrived home from the pool and found her mother sitting at the kitchen table, red-eyed, a tissue balled up in her hand.

'Have you noticed anything in school?' Abi had beseeched Eva. 'Anything at all? Has anyone said anything to you about Beth? About anything she might have been involved in?'

'Why? What's she done?' It had been the obvious question, but her mother had ignored it, ploughing on with her interrogation.

'Has she said anything to you about what's been going on in her class?'

'No.'

'Does she talk to you at all about Lisa? About Sasha and the others? Have you seen them together in school?'

'I'm not her keeper, Mum—'

'Would you just answer the fucking question!'

She had never seen her mother like that. Her voice screechy with shredded nerves, cheeks wet with tears. It had frightened Eva to see her so untethered. And that was before Eva knew what Beth had done.

They didn't discuss it. That was the way things were in her family. Her father was emotionally repressed and her mother was relentless in her optimism – doggedly putting a brave face on things – so between them they conspired to curtail any analysis or even discussion about the points of pain in their lives.

Still, Eva remembered sitting at the top of the stairs, listening to the whispered conversation between her parents about Beth, about what had caused the rupture.

'Perhaps it's a genetic thing,' her father had suggested. 'I mean, when you consider Melissa – how she is sometimes . . .'

He had sounded morose, bewildered. Or maybe he was just wrung-out.

Aunt Melissa had suffered from her nerves. Eva had known this all her life. Most of the time she was fine, but then the phone would ring and her father would speak in hushed, calming tones before taking his car keys and disappearing for a few hours – sometimes for a whole night. Her mother would offer them a tight smile and, by way of explanation, would say: 'Auntie Melissa's in a bit of a tizz again, that's all.'

A bit of a tizz. A little frazzled. On edge. Her nerves are at her again.

All these different terms her parents had for what was a clinical mental problem.

It had never occurred to Eva that it might be an inherited condition, one that could be lurking within her own DNA. Or Beth's.

After the incident, Eva had wanted Beth to change school. But in the end, her parents decided that there had been enough upheaval in their lives. Beth's act was marked down as a one-off. She had been 'acting-out' as teenagers sometimes do.

But Eva knew that it was not all right. One by one, she'd watched as Beth's friends had peeled away from her – even Lisa. Beth roamed the school corridors alone. At lunchtime, she sat in the library, reading. She didn't volunteer for the school play, or for the Young Scientists Exhibition, or for Junior UN. At home, she seemed swathed in a dreamy silence, but at school it took on a different shape. Beth was unpredictable, nervy, and now, as the scraping of another chair announced a further interruption, Eva felt a familiar dread as Alicia elbowed her sharply and said:

'That's your sister.'

Beth stood, stalk-like above the sea of turned faces, her voice rising in an arc, 'Missss!'

A ripple went out through the crowd, chairs around her pushing back, girls hastily getting to their feet and leaping away in horror, the acrid smell of vomit percolating through the air.

Assembly proceedings were brought to a halt. A path was cleared, and Eva watched as her sister walked Corinne out through the hall, the French girl pale-faced and drawn, Beth's arm wrapped protectively around her.

The girls filed out, returning to their classrooms. The care-taker was summoned to clean up the mess.

Later, Eva heard it said that the French girl had stuck her fingers down her own throat.

But Eva had not seen this for herself. She dismissed it as an unsubstantiated rumour. There were lots of them going around.

9

'Trouble?' Corinne asked.

Mark put the phone down and looked up. She was standing on the stairs, barefoot, wearing that perpetual hoodie of hers. It was just the two of them in the house.

'Not really,' he replied. 'That was Helen Bracken. She was calling to check you're feeling okay.'

They had decided it was best for Corinne to stay at home that day, to make sure she was fully recovered. Beneath the flare of pink hair, her face was wan, her complexion waxy, but still there was the characteristic spark in her eye.

'That was very kind of her,' she remarked pointedly which made him wonder how much of his phone conversation she had overheard.

On the surface, the call had been to enquire after Corinne's health, but it had quickly segued into a discussion about Beth. Her behaviour at school, while nothing like the alarming display of last year, was still a cause for concern, Helen had said. Her grades were poor, she displayed little interest in her schoolwork, and her participation in class was limited.

'Her lack of social interactions,' she had told him, 'is worrying.'

'Right,' he'd said.

Perhaps he'd sounded defensive, for she quickly added:

'I say this only because we don't want her slipping back into depression.'

Inwardly, he baulked at the word. Depression was for adults, a psychological response to serious loss – bereavements, financial disasters, betrayals, broken hearts. It was not for fourteen-year-old girls who were loved, cherished, provided for, safe.

'Has Beth been a naughty girl?' Corinne asked now, smiling mischievously as she came down the stairs towards him.

He considered his reply, before answering carefully: 'Her grades have slipped a little. She needs to put in a bit more effort.'

'Would you like me to talk to her?'

'Do you think she'd listen to you?'

She leaned against the newel post and shrugged. 'I think so.'

He was reminded of something Abi had said earlier in the week – an observation she'd made about the control Corinne exerted over Beth. It was after the lunch with the Campbells and he'd been up to his elbows in soapy water and dirty dishes when she'd raised her suspicion that Corinne was instructing Beth in what to wear.

'I overheard them,' she'd answered when he asked how she knew this.

'You were eavesdropping on their conversation?'

'Don't put it like that. I just happened to be passing and I paused to listen. Beth didn't sound happy.'

He had scrubbed at the pan in the sink, while Abi went on: 'Didn't you see what she was wearing today? My God, she was like some kind of child prostitute.'

'That's harsh.'

'Didn't you notice how awkward and uncomfortable she looked?'

'She's a teenager. That's how they look, most of the time. Either that or like they've just committed murder.'

Abi shot him a look.

'I just don't like the idea of this girl controlling her,' she said. 'Beth's so impressionable—'

'Oh, just give it a rest,' he'd snapped.

It irritated him, the way she was always harping on about Beth – how vulnerable she was, how impressionable. Just leave the child alone, he wanted to say to her. And now he had Helen Bracken on the phone stirring up his anxiety. Sometimes, when he dropped the girls to school, the feeling crept over him of other parents casting their gaze in his direction, judging him. He almost imagined their thought patterns: 'Oh, so *that's* the father . . .' Paranoia, that's all it was.

In the quiet of the hallway, he thought about Abi's assertion. Tentatively, he remarked: 'You have a lot of influence over Beth, I've noticed.'

'You think?' she asked, raising her eyebrow. She couldn't seem to help her flirtatiousness.

'What's your secret?'

She laughed and sang in her soft, husky voice:

'Let's play "Master and Servant".'

He smiled with surprise.

'You like Depeche Mode?'

'I like Nouvelle Vague. They cover it.'

'Have you heard the original?'

'No.'

His smile broadened. 'Come with me,' he instructed.

She followed him into the studio and perched on the arm of a chair while he fiddled with his iPod until he found the track. When the opening lyrics sounded in their falsetto pitch, Corinne laughed, moving her head in time to the beat as the synthesizer kicked in.

'I like it,' she told him.

'Yeah?'

Both of them were raising their voices to be heard above the music blasting through the speakers.

It surprised him, the rush he felt – youthful nostalgia, an old euphoria – as the sounds filled the room. But after a moment, he began to feel embarrassed, and so he turned down the volume and watched as she walked around the room.

'These are so good,' she remarked, pausing in front of the design models he'd displayed along a shelf. 'They were for your job?'

'Some of them, yes.'

'You must miss it,' she said, and he was surprised by her perception.

'I do,' he admitted. 'I'm looking forward to getting back into it.'

Since the night out with Andrew, the idea had grown larger in his brain, taking up more and more of his thoughts, his imagination. He'd read through the script twice now, and, excited by the images that sparked to life, he'd taken to sketching out a few ideas on paper, firing off some observations in an email to Andrew.

'It must be lonely for you,' she remarked, 'here, on your own in this house, this room, every day with no one to talk to.'

'I manage,' he said, trying to laugh it off, but in truth he felt moved by her assertion. How strange it was that she should see this in him, that she should be aware of this hole inside him while his own wife and daughters seemed blind to it.

'I get lonely sometimes,' she told him now.

'You do?'

'Since Anouk left. I miss her.' She said the words plainly, a little half-shrug that implied resignation. 'Beth is lucky – she has Eva.'

'Yes,' he agreed, although he doubted either of his daughters drew much comfort from each other. Especially not lately; there had been a distinct coolness between the girls ever since Melissa's will had been read.

69

'What about you?' she asked him now. 'You must miss your sister.'

'Yes, I do.'

'Beth told me what happened. It must have been awful for you.' Her face had grown serious, her eyes narrowing into a frown of concern, and he felt a familiar lurch inside himself – a feeling akin to nausea. It came upon him anytime Melissa's suicide was touched upon.

'Yes, it was awful,' he replied, his voice stiff. 'Particularly awful for Abi. She was the one who found the body.'

'But you were her brother. It's different,' she insisted. 'You must feel so sad.'

He looked down, the nausea lapping at his insides.

'It's guilt more than sadness, to be honest.' How strange it was to hear himself saying these words. 'When she died I felt like I'd let her down. I'd failed her.'

'Beth said she had been ill.'

He closed his eyes briefly, pressing a thumb against the lid.

'Multiple sclerosis. It was hard on her. I just hadn't realized how much she was struggling.'

'Poor Mark. Minding everybody.'

He opened his eyes and met her gaze. Touched by her compassion, the tenderness with which she'd expressed it, but confused by it too.

'You don't need to pity me, Corinne.'

'I don't pity you. I admire you. Actually, I am a little envious,' she told him, turning away as if embarrassed by her admission, fixing her attention now on the model he had started to construct – the cathedral of Notre Dame. Her suggestion.

He watched as she picked up a match, considering where to position it.

'Envious?' he pressed when the silence persisted.

'Beth and Eva are lucky you are here so much. And they are lucky with the life you have made for them. This house, the school they go to, the neighbourhood – everything is so normal. I wish my life was normal like theirs.'

'What do you mean?'

She put down the matchstick and rubbed at her forehead – a pinched look had come over her face.

'Where I live, everyone thinks we are strange, you know? My family – the way we live. Everyone thinks we are odd.'

He remembered again how she'd said they didn't have a TV, as well as his own early suppositions about her parents as hippies of some kind, a view that was only reinforced as Corinne revealed more of their strong views on sustainability and the pernicious nature of capitalism. This seemed to translate into shopping in vintage clothing stores and eschewing anything manufactured in the last twenty years. Mark remembered the flash of pity he'd felt for her on the day she'd arrived with her paltry belongings, her tatty flip-flops, and he felt a surprising lurch of recognition.

'It's not easy, is it,' he said, 'growing up in that type of environment?'

'No,' she admitted, her usual high spirits dampened. Then her eyes flickered up and met his, and she said: 'It was like that for you too, wasn't it?'

He nodded. 'My parents were old when they married,' he explained. His mother had been in her mid-forties when he was born – his father in his fifties. 'The house I grew up in was very hushed. Making noise or raising our voices was frowned upon. We were encouraged to read or draw or make jigsaws. Other children were never invited into our house. I guess it must have been hard for my parents in some ways, but ... well, it felt stifling and sort of loveless. And I did feel that we stuck out as oddballs. I took a lot of stick in school over it.'

71

'You felt ashamed of them,' Corinne stated, and her voice was soft, not judgemental. She seemed older to him in their conversation, more mature and considered in her spoken words, with a poise he hadn't noticed before.

'Yes, I suppose I did. Ashamed of them – ashamed of the house we lived in, the meanness and poverty of it.'

It was why his own home was so important to him – a sort of fortress against the old wounds of his childhood. On occasion, when he became agitated over a crack in the wall or fretted unduly over the risk of flood from the rising water-levels of a nearby river, Abi would lose patience with him, saying: 'It's only a house, Mark! It's just bricks and mortar!' Equally, she was scornful whenever he expressed concern about what the neighbours might think. But Abi didn't have his insecurities. She had no understanding of what it was like to grow up as he had done. But now, Corinne sitting across from him with her understanding air, her gentle gaze, it occurred to him that of all the people in his household, she was the one person who did understand. She shared the same sensitivity, the same need to shrug off the shaming cloak of one's childhood.

As if reading his thoughts, she said: 'I think you and I are alike, Mark.'

It was disconcerting, hearing her use his Christian name. And the seriousness of her expression communicated a need that confounded him, made him want to turn away.

'Do you want a coffee?' he asked, getting to his feet.

'No, thanks.'

Alone in the kitchen, he stood for a moment, leaning on the counter, replaying what had just occurred between them. It was all perfectly innocent, and yet he had suddenly become aware that it was just the two of them alone in the room. He had felt the heaviness of her steady gaze.

When he brought his coffee back into the studio, he found her peering into a cardboard box full of old T-shirts.

'Are these yours?' she asked.

He nodded. 'I used to buy them at gigs,' he explained. 'Tour T-shirts, you know. I sort of collected them for a while.'

'Do you ever wear them?'

He shook his head. 'Nah. I was half thinking about framing some of them and hanging them up in here.'

He didn't like to admit it, but Ross's contempt for the studio's furnishings had gotten to him, the sneering way the other man had joked about installing a pool table and a beer fridge. Privately, he had worried that Ross thought him unmanly. Effete.

'I like this one,' she remarked, taking a black T-shirt from the box and turning it towards him so that he could see the red warning-sign logo and instantly recognized it.

'That's my Radiohead T-shirt,' he explained. 'It's from their OK Computer tour. I was at their gig in Dublin, 1997. You weren't even born.'

She held it against her like something precious, one hand smoothing the fabric down over her belly and hip.

'I like it,' she said, flashing him a smile, a hint of mischief in it. Her earlier seriousness had dissipated, and he welcomed the return of her naturally sunny disposition.

It occurred to him that the last half-hour spent with her had been more meaningful than any exchange of views he'd had with his own daughters – or his wife – in quite some time. That she should recognize things about him that they had failed to see – it moved him. He realized that he enjoyed her company.

'Why don't you keep it,' he said now, nodding towards the T-shirt.

Her whole face lit up with unabashed pleasure.

'Really? You're sure?'

'Absolutely.'

It occurred to him that she must have realized that this was the T-shirt from the Radiohead concert where his relationship with Abi had been kindled. He felt a slight creep of guilt. But it was just an old T-shirt, he told himself. A fragment of nostalgia forgotten in a box.

10

Colour streamed through the lens as Beth pointed the phone while Corinne posed: the pastel shades of the ice-creams she held in each hand, her frosted pink hair lifted gently by the wind, behind her a swathe of blue sky.

Boats moored near the yacht club clinked in a gentle sway, and the water lay green and still, the horseshoe arms of the twin piers hugging it close to the land.

Beth took the photo, but when Corinne examined it, her mouth twisted into a moue of dissatisfaction.

'No. You are in it,' she remarked tersely. And it was true that if you looked closely enough, there she was – a tiny Beth reflected in the dark lenses of Corinne's heart-shaped shades.

'Sorry,' she mumbled.

But Corinne just twitched her head to shake out her hair, held the ice-creams a little higher and said: 'Take it again.'

Beth was getting better at taking the shots, more mindful now of keeping her own shadow out of the frame. The ice-creams were melting but Beth knew not to mention it.

Corinne licked the little tributary of strawberry ice-cream that was running down her arm, and handed the other cone to Beth. It was pistachio – a flavour she didn't like, but so what?

She was getting used to Corinne making choices for her.

'You need to try new things,' Corinne was always telling her. 'Be brave, not boring.'

It had started as a game, but now it was something that she just accepted: that Corinne laid out her clothes for her every morning, that she instructed her on what to order in restaurants and cafés, that she told her what messages to post on Facebook and Instagram. Bit by bit her reluctance had fallen away to the point that she now welcomed the instruction. Besides, Corinne only wanted what was best for her.

'You have ice-cream on your face,' Corinne said, reaching forward and sliding her finger upwards over Beth's chin.

'I'm such a slob,' Beth admitted, embarrassed by her own happiness, basking in the radiant glow of Corinne's attention.

There was an easy familiarity between them now, like friends who'd known each other all their lives. When they sat on the sofa in the evenings, watching *Stranger Things*, their legs slung over each other's on the ottoman, Corinne idly curled strands of Beth's hair around her finger. Only that morning, she had popped a zit on Beth's face with a needle Beth kept for that purpose on the mantelpiece in her bedroom, Corinne's gaze cool and detached like a surgeon, but she was careful with the needle, afterwards dabbing the weeping pinhole tenderly with a cotton pad. Beth thrilled to her touch.

They followed the crowd moving towards the People's Park, pausing so Corinne could tip her ice-cream cone into a bin.

'Didn't you like it?' Beth asked. They had queued outside Scrum-Diddly's for fifteen minutes at Corinne's insistence.

'It was too sweet. It made me feel sick.'

She often did this, Beth noticed. Made a big fuss about ordering food and then, when it came, she lost interest.

'I need to pee,' Corinne announced, so they headed into the park where a small queue had formed outside the toilets.

'I'll wait outside,' Beth told her, as the door closed behind Corinne.

A warm wind was blowing. Beth licked at her cone and looked about. Everywhere there were people stretched out on picnic blankets strewn across the grass, kids swarming around the fountain, the spray careening madly in the breeze.

Distantly, she became aware of someone calling her name. She looked around, a hand shielding her eyes from the sun, and there was Nicole Nash, smiling and waving and coming towards her. Confusion washed over Beth at this display of friendliness, uneasiness rising like a tide as Nicole approached, saying:

'Hey, Beth! We thought it was you! What're you doing here?'

'Nothing.'

'A few of us are hanging out by the bandstand,' Nicole said, jerking her head in that direction. 'Come on over and join us!'

Beth's eyes flicked to the centre of the park where teenage boys in low-slung jeans were skateboarding along a run they'd set up, doing jumps off a sheet of plywood propped on stacked bricks. Music was thrumming from a speaker, hip-hop with a heavy beat, and leaning over the railings of the nearby bandstand were the girls, about seven or eight of them – Beth's classmates and their French exchange students – flicking ash from their cigarettes or swiping through their iPhones. There among them was Sasha, leaning over the railing to share a joke with one of the boys, Lisa beside her smiling shyly. Catching sight of Beth, Sasha straightened up and raised her hand, waggling her fingers in a little wave, but Lisa kept her hands on the rail, her face a blank oval.

'So, are you coming?' Nicole asked, cheerful but impatient.

'I can't. I'm waiting for Corinne.'

'Who?'

'You know – my exchange—'

'Oh yeah. Pink,' Nicole sniggered. 'Come on. We'll wave to her when she comes out of the loo. It's not like she'll be hard to spot.'

Reluctantly, Beth allowed herself to be led away, stuffing the rest of the cone into her mouth as she walked.

'Sasha was the one who saw you,' Nicole explained. 'It was her idea that we bring you over.'

'It was?'

'She feels really bad, you know,' Nicole went on. 'About what happened at her party. I mean, it's been like over a year now and still there's all this animosity between us. And over what? Just a stupid misunderstanding, right?'

'Sasha said that?'

'Of course. We all agree that this has gone on too long.' This close to her, Beth could see the braces clenching Nicole's teeth, the tight line of dry skin that had formed on her lower lip.

'Here she is!' Nicole called as they reached the steps, and she ran on ahead.

Afterwards, Beth would think back over the signs that she'd missed – the note of giddy excitement in Nicole's voice that made no sense, the glance exchanged with Sasha as they approached, the way Lisa stood off to one side, refusing to meet her gaze. But at the time, any little warning voice sounding in her head was drowned out by the screaming want inside her, the need to be forgiven, accepted, enfolded into their group. Her longing must have been so obvious to them, so easy to manipulate, and all the time she'd thought she kept it so well hidden.

'Good to see you, Beth,' Sasha said. Then, over her shoulder to the boys, she said: 'Guys, this is Beth.'

'What's up,' Beth said, her eyes sweeping the ground, and Sasha laughed, not unkindly.

'Hey, cute outfit,' she pronounced, her gaze settling on the green slip-dress that Corinne had selected for her to wear that day. She'd paired it with her red Converse and a denim jacket. It had felt all right – better than some of the clothes Corinne had persuaded her into – but now she felt exposed under Sasha's assessing gaze. Her legs were too white, her hips and waist too lumpy.

'Do you smoke, Beth?' Sasha asked, her head to one side. This close, Beth could see the dusting of purple mascara on Sasha's lashes, making her eyes look more richly brown.

'Here. Have one of mine,' Sasha said, flipping open her carton and taking a cigarette for herself before holding the pack out to Beth.

'No, that's okay—'

'Oh, come on! Let's have a smoke together, huh? Seal our friendship with nicotine.' She took a step towards her and Beth felt the force of her enthusiasm. It seemed rude to decline.

Almost as soon as she put out her hand to take it, she felt the air tightening with expectancy, announcing the trap. Touching the cigarette, she knew something was wrong – it *felt* wrong. She drew it from the carton and saw the tight cotton pellet in her fingers trailing the tell-tale blue cotton string. Instantly, laughter erupted around her, and Beth stared at the tampon in her hand, the bandstand tilting beneath her, the sickening drop happening in her stomach.

Nicole was guffawing like a crazy person. Sasha leaned into Beth's face, saying: 'Now stuff that into your fanny, you filthy little gimp,' delivering the words so sweetly, sugar laced with poison.

One of the skateboarders said: 'I don't get it,' and Sasha turned to explain it to him.

But Beth's eyes were on Lisa. Lisa who stood with her head lowered, refusing to meet her gaze.

'That's fucking gross,' the boy remarked, and the girls collapsed into gales of laughter.

Head down, cheeks burning, Beth moved quickly through the crowd. It was easier to just keep walking, to concentrate on the motion of her feet, counting out her steps, counting out the number of cracks in the paving, counting, counting, counting. The same way she counted when barrelling down the school corridors, briskness masking her loneliness. Distantly, she heard Corinne calling her, but she was propelled by something bigger now, the swell of her humiliation carrying her across the street and on to rocks, moving closer to the sea until she found a flat slab to sit on, something to anchor her shaking limbs.

'Hey! Why did you run from me like that?' Corinne demanded once she had caught up with Beth. 'Did you not hear me calling?'

'I heard you,' Beth said quietly, her eyes fixed on the mass of water in the bay.

'So why did you not stop?' Her voice was crisp with annoyance but Beth, for once, didn't care.

She kept thinking about Lisa back there with the others. She hadn't joined in the mocking laughter, but still. Her presence among them made her complicit. Lisa had been her best friend and might be still if it hadn't been for Sasha.

Perhaps Corinne saw it in her – the surge of sadness – for the sharp rise of her anger seemed to dissipate, and she came and sat by Beth, close enough for their arms to touch.

'What is it?' she asked softly. 'What happened with you and those girls?'

Beth looked down, picked at a scab on her knee. 'You saw what happened,' she said mulishly.

'No. Not that. Why do they hate you?'

The reluctance was there like a wall between them, but then Corinne reached for Beth's hand, held it gently in hers. Beth felt the soft sweep of Corinne's thumb over the flesh of her palm. A thrill of nerves went through her.

'It was Sasha,' she began quietly. 'Sasha and her stupid party.'

How easy it was to summon the memory – girls giggling in their pyjamas, the smell of popcorn lingering in the air. Sasha's fourteenth birthday. Over a year ago now but each detail remained vivid. All the girls from their class invited for a sleepover in Sasha's house – a massive mock-Tudor mansion with a home cinema, tennis courts in the garden, a hot tub on the deck.

They'd watched Zac Efron movies back-to-back while eating hot dogs and pizza and shovelling popcorn into their mouths. Beth remembered feeling light and floaty, the Baileys she'd stolen from her parents' drinks cabinet coating her tongue. She'd grown bored and then sleepy. It was almost three a.m. when she drifted from the home cinema, leaving the others playing Truth or Dare. She stumbled into the sitting room and fell face-first on to the sofa.

'As soon as I woke up, I knew something was wrong,' she told Corinne.

It wasn't the strangeness of her surroundings in the thin light of early morning, or the tackiness in her mouth, the unfamiliar blur in her head.

'I was lying on the couch and there was this pull deep in my insides, this unfamiliar ache.' Her voice trembled a little, thinking back on it. Nerves twisting in her stomach. 'Without thinking, I just rolled over and sat up and that was when I felt this dampness and I looked down and saw what had happened.'

A smear of brownish blood screamed from the soft white

fabric of the upholstery, the same blood plastering her pyjamas to her skin. Her instinct was to hide it, but when she attempted to flip the cushion, she found it was sewn to the frame. A small whimper escaped her lips – panic rising inside. She needed to clean herself up and change, and she needed to escape from that house. But the stain on the couch—

'*Oh. Sweet. Jesus.*'

Nicole Nash – her small eyes screwed up into a perfect sneer. Sasha behind her, saying:

'Nic? What's hap—' Words cut from her mouth as she caught sight of Beth. 'That's fucking disgusting!' she shrieked. 'My mum's gonna kill me!'

Beth fled the room, Sasha's voice ringing in her ears – 'Use a fucking tampon, gimp!'

She had grabbed her bag and locked herself in the bathroom, the tears coming uncontrollably as she dressed. By the time she emerged, the others had all assembled in the sitting room – she could see them gathered there, surveying the damage, hands clapped over their mouths in horror or disgust. Lisa was among them. She looked up and caught Beth's gaze, returning it with a fierce little look of her own. But she made no attempt to approach with any words of comfort or solidarity. She had picked a side and in that moment the world around Beth went cold.

'Hey, don't do that to yourself.'

Corinne's voice shook her back to the present. She looked and saw the French girl's expression and then followed her gaze to her own arm which she had been absently pinching. A neat little row of pink welts lined the skin of her inner arm. She hadn't even noticed she'd being doing it.

'Sorry,' she muttered and moved to pull down her sleeve, but Corinne grabbed her arm and drew it towards her for inspection.

'Some of these are deep. Look – you are bleeding.'

Beth pulled her arm away and folded her legs up so her knees were under her chin, resting her cheek against them.

'My period ruined my life,' she said softly. 'How pathetic is that?'

She sniffed and felt the breeze lifting her hair, waiting for Corinne to say something, shamed by what the French girl knew about her now.

But Corinne didn't speak. There was the sudden catch of a lighter, the smell of tinder, and when she turned her head to one side, she saw Corinne's eyes narrowed against the film of smoke exiting her mouth, the joint in her hand held out for Beth to take.

'Go on,' she urged. 'It will be good for you.'

'No, I—'

'Go on,' she repeated, calm but insistent.

'Where did you get this?' Beth asked, glancing around before bringing it to her mouth, the dank taste of it, the dry crackle of paper as she inhaled.

'Skateboarders.'

For a few minutes they just sat there, staring at the sea, passing the joint back and forth between them, ignoring the long looks from middle-aged women speed-walking in their joggers, the loud tutting of an old man ambling past with his dog.

After fleeing Sasha's house, Beth had run to her aunt's house, letting herself in the front door. She had sought comfort, the warmth and familiarity of an embrace. *It's a thing of beauty, Beth. It marks you out as special.* The smell of Melissa's breath, still sour with sleep.

A calmness came over her, the weed working through her. All the little knots and pressure valves inside her seemed to release. She was filled with serenity, like an empty church hall with all the radiators on, rain rattling distantly on the roof.

'It's stupid to hurt yourself,' Corinne said now, straightening one leg out to gently kick Beth's shin. Something teasing in the gesture, in the playful smile on her face.

'I suppose,' Beth said.

'You should hurt those bitches. Not yourself.'

The anger was always inside her – the low hum of it there in her thoughts, her feelings, weaving through her dreams as she slept. But here with Corinne, she felt not free of it but a little unburdened. She felt like she could cope.

Corinne ruffled her pink hair, leaned back on the rock and Beth watched her, awed, sensing something pulsing between them, a charged mist. Corinne was brave in ways she could never be, but when she said this out loud, Corinne just laughed.

'Courage is a choice,' she declared happily.

And Beth thought: *I can learn from this girl.* Eyes hungrily eating her up.

Mark found the letter on Good Friday.

He was in his studio, Tom Waits growling on the stereo, an open bottle of beer beside him – his Catholicism had lapsed long ago. A box containing the emptied contents of Melissa's desk was open in front of him. For weeks, he'd been putting off going through it, but now, on this evening, he'd felt relaxed – buoyant even. There'd been another email from Andrew full of enthusiasm about Mark's ideas. Again, he'd pressed Mark to commit to the project, outlining dates and deliverables, locations and timescales. It was in this bright mood of optimism that he'd decided to tackle Melissa's effects. He'd been sifting through a pile of her paperwork when he discovered the note.

'Jesus,' he said, holding it out in front of him, his hand trembling a little as he realized what it was.

Corinne looked up, one hand holding a matchstick suspended over the foundations of Notre Dame. 'What is it? What's wrong?'

She was working on the model while waiting for Beth. Distantly, the hum of the shower could be heard. Moments earlier, Eva had popped her head around the door, informing him that she was going out.

'Where to?' he'd asked.

'Just out. Alicia's waiting,' she'd said, evasive and impatient.

'Can I come with you?' Corinne had asked, and Mark had noticed the frown coming over Eva's face.

'No,' she'd snapped. 'Find someone else to stalk for the night.'

'Hey, easy,' he'd warned.

But Corinne wasn't offended. Tentatively, she'd offered a compliment, as if attempting to smooth over the spike in the atmosphere between them. 'You're beautiful,' she'd said. Eva had slammed the door on her way out.

Now Corinne got to her feet and came towards him, but he held the letter back from her, reluctant to share it yet.

How easily he might have missed it. How innocuous it looked! At first glance, it was just a series of instructions: how to set the heating, how to turn on and off the house alarm. Account numbers listed along with PIN codes, passwords for online banking. Instructions for the payment of utility bills. It was only when he flipped it over that he realized what it was he held in his hand.

The writing, which had been neat and orderly, now turned into a looser scrawl.

I hope this all makes sense. And I'm sorry about everything. Mx

Aware of Corinne standing next to him, waiting for some explanation of his behaviour, he said:

'A note from my sister. I had hoped there'd be some indication as to why . . . I thought she might at least—' He broke off, overcome, and Corinne reached out and touched his shoulder, squeezing it gently.

'I'm fine,' he told her quickly, exhaling sharply.

She withdrew her hand and sat down on the floor next to him.

Carefully, she suggested: 'Perhaps she didn't want you to know why.'

'Perhaps.'

He thought about his sister – still a mystery to him, especially after her death. What came to mind now was her love of nature, how she had turned the scrubby patch at the back of the little house in Beaufield Court into a miraculous haven of leafy green calm, a sharp contrast to the drab, poky rooms of the interior which remained filled with the brown furniture from their parents' time. She'd had friends but no one special. His whole life, he never once recalled mention of a boyfriend. It had crossed his mind that his sister might be gay. One year, issuing the annual Christmas invitation, he had said to her: 'You know if there's anyone you would like to bring with you – if there's a man in your life, or a woman-friend – we'd be only too happy . . .' His voice had trailed off when he'd seen the brief flash of horror in her eyes. 'Just me,' she'd snapped, and he'd felt cut by the unfamiliar sharpness in her tone. *Woman-friend.* He cringed at the memory of it.

'When was the last time you saw her?' Corinne asked, and he replied that it was a few nights before her death.

'We had just moved back into the house after all this had been completed.' He waved his arm to indicate the studio, the kitchen, the utility room. 'We'd invited her for dinner to show off the new building work.'

'How did she seem?'

He hesitated, part of him reluctant to discuss it with her – she was just a girl, a teenager. And yet . . . there was something about Corinne that invited openness, the sharing of confidences. Her gentle questioning, her genuine interest – it had felt like a long time since anyone had probed his feelings so delicately and persistently.

'She was out of sorts,' he told her now. 'Nothing major, but she was quiet.'

He remembered how excited he had been that night, pointing out details like the Crittall windows, the reclaimed blue limestone floor. Melissa had made appreciative noises, but a lack of enthusiasm was coming off her in waves. Eventually, he'd said: 'What? What is it? Why are you acting like this?' Sharpness in his tone because he'd read her reaction as evidence of envy or disapproval, neither of which he was prepared to tolerate. But instead of being offended or aggrieved by his attack, Melissa had said:

'Could you ask your builder to take a look at my house? I'm worried that soon I won't be able to get up the stairs any more.'

'I'd felt immediately ashamed,' he told Corinne now as he gave his account of that evening. 'There I was, all excited about my new improved home, and there was Melissa, bursting my bubble with her loneliness, her future that seemed blighted by paralysis and decay.' The injustice had been stark.

'We talked about modifications to the house to accommodate her disability – a stair-lift, ramps and widening of doorways for wheelchair access, that sort of thing. I tried to get her to consider moving to more suitable accommodation, but she wouldn't countenance leaving her garden.'

The following morning, he'd made arrangements for his builder to quote for the work that Melissa's house required, but a few days later, Abi had called over to Beaufield Court and found Melissa in her room. Empty pill bottles on the bedside locker, the body cold.

'What I felt – if I'm really honest,' Mark told Corinne, 'was not sorrow or shock. I felt trapped. I was in my forties and still dealing with my oddball family. It was like no matter what I did, no matter how far I moved on, moved up, moved away, I would always be that kid in the weird family in that fucking house . . .' His voice petered out.

She was fixing him with an expression of complete absorption, totally focused on what he was saying. Her hoodie was pulled down over grey leggings and he saw that she was barefoot, a tiny silver ring clasped around the second toe of her left foot. So much about Corinne seemed awkward-fitting, out-of-shape, but he observed now how neat her feet were – pretty, in fact, if feet could be called such a thing.

'Why am I even telling you all this?' he said quickly, lowering his head.

'You miss her,' she stated plainly, and he felt – for the first time since Melissa had died – the hammer-blow of loss.

A hard lump filled his throat, and he blinked away the tears. He felt her hand rest on the back of his neck, and almost without thinking, he reached out and touched her bare foot, felt the warm softness of her skin beneath his touch.

His hand rested there for just a moment. And then, with a sudden flash of recognition at how inappropriate this was, he pulled it away and got to his feet. Flustered with embarrassment, he listened for the hum of the shower and heard only silence from upstairs, followed by the loud closing of the front door, footsteps in the hall.

'You should go,' he said to Corinne, aware of her sitting there staring up at him, and he unable to meet her gaze.

'Please,' he said, and the door opened just as she stood, so that when Abi came into the room, she saw Mark standing there staring at the floor, scratching the back of his neck, and Corinne alongside him, her face flushed with confusion, a stunned look about her.

He knew how it appeared to her – how guilty they both seemed.

'I'll see if Beth is ready now,' Corinne said softly. Closing the door behind her, she left the two of them alone.

Abi had gone into work that day. Most of her co-workers had left for the long weekend with only the dedicated few remaining, and in the quiet calm of the almost empty office she was able to get some real work done. She had been writing up a report for the management meeting on Wednesday, when her boss approached.

'There's something I want to run past you,' Richard had said, glancing around to make sure they were alone. 'Head Office have been making noises about us taking over the Asia-Pacific branches. Bringing them in under our remit. This is all on the q.t., you understand, not something we want to spread throughout the company until we're ready to announce.'

'Of course. You know you can rely on my discretion, Richard.'

'If this goes ahead then things are going to get a lot more hectic round here. I've been swamped since the merger and I'll need someone I can trust to handle things on the APAC side. To cut to the chase, we'll need someone to manage the new links and your name came up.'

'Me?' A flush of pleasurable nerves went through her.

'Yours among others. Obviously, there'll be an interview process, but you'd be in with a good chance. I'm not going to lie to you – it'll be a ton of work. A fair bit of long-distance travel too. But you'd be well rewarded. A decent bump in salary plus share options. You'd be a non-equity partner, Abi. Are you interested?'

Her pulse quickened with excitement.

'Definitely.'

'Good.' He dropped the file he was holding on her desk. It landed with a small thud. 'Cast your eyes over this before next week. We'll talk again then.'

All the way home in the car, she had felt the glow from Richard's recognition. With her ringed finger she had tapped out a rhythm on the steering wheel, excitement making her impatient, eager to get home and tell Mark. Now the file was sitting on the hall table beneath her handbag, but within two seconds of finding him there in the studio with Corinne, guilty looks on both of their faces, she knew she would not tell him.

'What's going on?' she asked once Corinne had left the room.

Her voice was low and controlled, but she felt tightness in her facial muscles.

'It's not what you think,' he said, his eyes red-rimmed, his face pinched with tiredness. 'I was just a bit thrown, that's all. She caught me at a bad moment.'

'What happened?'

It was only now that she noticed the page in his hand.

'Here,' he offered it to her. 'Read it.'

Melissa's familiar handwriting caused a slight jump of alarm in her throat.

'Where did you find this?'

'In one of the boxes I took from her house. Somehow, I missed it when I was clearing things out. Look,' and he held up the envelope it had come in for her to read. *For Mark, in case*, it said in Melissa's familiar writing.

'Was there anything else?' she asked.

'Nope. That's it. Some suicide note, don't you think?'

'She was never one for words,' Abi said, her thoughts racing.

'I shouldn't have gotten upset in front of Corinne,' Mark admitted. 'It was just that when I found the envelope it was almost a relief. The prospect of finally understanding why. But then I opened it and read that. I just couldn't believe it. The disappointment and sheer frustration.'

It was there in him again, the swell of anger in his voice, his face crumpling with disgust.

'We'll probably never know why,' she began. 'I'm not sure

Melissa found it easy to communicate what she was feeling, deep down.'

'I was her brother. Her only family member. Am I that hard to confide in?'

'No, of course not.'

'She should have told me she was struggling. I would have helped her.'

'You did help her, remember? All those times she fell apart, you were the one who picked her up, set her back on her feet again.'

Abi felt a small pulse of anger, thinking of all those nights when the phone would ring, Melissa sobbing down the line, *I can't cope, I can't cope.* She thought of family occasions where they'd have to ignore Melissa's dour expression, the fug of depression she carried with her like a staleness in the air. All the time and energy they had devoted over the years to propping up his sister's fragile ego, seeking new and diverse ways to rouse her from inertia, distract her from the shadows that crept across her mind. Never once had Abi seen Mark lose his patience over it. Each time the call came in the night, he dutifully got into his car and drove over. She knew now what he was thinking: years of patience and care, his quiet devotion, and after all that, she had left him this paltry note? No wonder he was shaken and angry. No wonder he was bewildered.

Tiredness crept up through her legs and she sat down in an armchair. It was one of the ones from Melissa's house, small-framed in a Laura Ashley fabric. Privately, Abi had always found her sister-in-law's furniture to be mean and fussy. The little house in Beaufield Court had seemed cluttered with furniture, dust-covered knick-knacks and framed photographs; the walls and floors swarmed with frenetic prints. She wondered how Melissa had been able to breathe in the stifling atmosphere of that house.

'We need a holiday,' she told him without much conviction. But it was true that she'd been thinking about it recently. One evening, Valentina had rung while Corinne and Beth were out, and Abi ended up chatting to the other woman for almost an hour. And what a conversation it had been – so cordial and relaxed – a far cry from the stilted awkwardness of that first phone call barely a week beforehand.

'You must come to us in the summer,' Valentina said towards the end of their exchanges. 'It is beautiful here – you will love it.'

Mark drained the last of his beer and then held up the empty bottle. 'Yes, we need a holiday. But right now I need another beer. Do you want one?'

'Sure.'

While he was in the kitchen, she leaned forward and looked at the spill of matches on the tray, her eyes tracing over the contours of the structure that had grown since the last time she was in this room.

Mark returned and handed her a beer, and she said:

'What's it going to be when it's finished?'

'Notre Dame cathedral.'

'Was that Corinne's idea?'

'Not really.'

'But she has been helping you with it, right?'

'A little.'

With the tip of her index finger she circled the rim of her glass.

'She seems to like spending time in here,' she commented softly.

'What are you saying, Abi?'

'Do you think maybe she has a little crush?'

He coloured and laughed. 'Don't be ridiculous.'

'Why not? She's a teenage girl. They have been known to get crushes on older men.'

'Come on! She's bored, that's all.'

'That's what worries me. You shouldn't encourage it, Mark.'

'For God's sake, Abi,' he said, grinning, as if what she was suggesting was ludicrous. But beneath it she could sense something else – embarrassment perhaps. Or guilt?

'You would tell me, wouldn't you? If there was something there – something I should worry about.'

'Of course I'd tell you. But I really don't think you need to worry. And besides, she's leaving soon.'

He must have seen the doubt that lingered on her face, because he softened now and reached for her. She felt his arms go around her, leaned into his chest. 'There's only you,' he whispered, and she tightened her grasp, needing the warmth of that connection between them, wanting to stay there, to hold on to that feeling of safety.

There was a knock on the door, and they pulled apart quickly.

'We're going out,' Beth informed them, Corinne standing in the hall behind her.

While Mark ran through the usual drill with Beth of being careful and staying safe, Abi's eyes passed over Corinne. The girl was zipping up her hoodie covering the black T-shirt she was wearing. But Abi had caught sight of it already. It was the black Radiohead T-shirt from the concert where she had hooked up with Mark all those years ago. It troubled her, that he had given it to her, but she didn't question him about it. Like so many other things they didn't talk about, she was afraid of what the answers might reveal.

12

'Are you nervous?' Alicia asked.

They were walking to the party on Victoria Road. Word had gone round that Craig and Irene Ferguson were flying to Malta for a long weekend, and soon afterwards Callum had WhatsApped the invitation.

'A little,' Eva admitted.

'Do you think it will happen tonight?' Alicia probed, 'it' meaning sex with Callum.

'I don't know. Maybe.'

But Eva wasn't sure that nerves accurately described how she was feeling. 'Unsettled' was closer to the truth. An image crept into her head: the look on Corinne's face that evening. The breathy quality to her voice: 'You're beautiful,' she'd said. Eva supposed she ought to be flattered but there was something about Corinne's expression that bothered her. The unabashed adoration. Something slightly batty about it, as if she was mesmerized like one of those religious fanatics, eyes lit up with ecstasy.

'Relax, Eves,' Alicia said, squeezing her arm comfortingly. 'He's majorly into you – I know that for a fact.'

'How do you know?'

'I've got eyes, haven't I? Trust me. You guys are perfect together. You make sense.'

The Fergusons' house was already heaving, Jay-Z pounding through the speakers, and as they navigated a path through to the kitchen, Eva felt a hand grabbing her wrist and turned to see Callum grinning widely. Before she could say anything, he had his arms around her, and his mouth landed wetly on hers, a spark of excitement flaring within her. Leaning into him, she wrapped her arms around his narrow waist, the heat from his body coming through her dress as others whooped around them, someone shouting 'Get a room!'

He pulled back from her, saying: 'You came.'

'Of course I came!' she laughed, a warm relief flooding her entire body at his obvious happiness, all her insecurities instantly fading away.

The temperature in the house soared, and Eva could see the sheen of sweat across the back of Callum's neck as he led the way through the crowd. She liked the proprietorial manner of his hand holding hers, the way the sea of people parted as he led her into the living room where they danced and kissed and gyrated against each other, both of them taking swigs from a bottle of Coke laced with rum. Across the room, Alicia mouthed 'Told ya!' moving in her own synched rhythm with her boyfriend, Josh.

After a while, Callum pulled Eva close and said into her ear: 'Come with me.'

He brought her through the kitchen where two girls from her class were belly-dancing in bra-tops and mini-skirts while a couple of guys snorted lines off the veined marble surface of the island unit. Callum led Eva outside to the back garden where the party had spilled on to the darkened lawn.

'I'm so glad you're here,' he told her. 'I felt like a dick after what happened the last time. That guy scared the shit out of me. I shouldn't have legged it though.' He looked genuinely concerned, and she slipped her arm around his waist and snuggled in close to him.

'That's okay. I could handle it.'

'But God, what a perve.'

She stiffened. 'What do you mean?'

'I mean him, standing there like that, eyeballing you for like ages!'

'Was it ages?'

'Jesus, Eva, his tongue was practically hanging out.'

She'd had two driving lessons with Ross since that night and while she harboured a casual interest in him, it had never occurred to her that it was reciprocated. Could it be true that Ross had lingered? That he had stayed a fraction longer than necessary not out of shock but out of arousal?

'Not that I blame him,' Callum went on, pulling her close. 'You're super fit. I just wish I'd got to spend a bit more time checking you out myself.'

'Well, that could be arranged,' she said, smiling into his mouth as they kissed.

'There's something I want to show you,' he said, drawing her further from the house.

Eva giggled and stumbled over the damp grass. 'Where are we going?' she asked, but he just shot her a devilish grin.

They had reached the end of the garden black with shadows thrown from the trees that lined the property. Behind them, the house was lit up against the night, shrieks of laughter and music pouring out of the open windows and doors. Callum took a key from his pocket and unlocked a gate that she had not noticed. It was a wrought-iron affair, all scrolls and spikes, and he led her through it now towards what she saw was a small house with a shiplap exterior, vines trailing around the windows.

'What is this place?' she asked, and he turned to her and pushed her back gently against the wall. He kissed her softly at first, then moved her lips apart and she felt something papery pressing against her tongue. Her instinct was to pull away, but he held her firmly, his fingers massaging into the small of her back, until the tab dissolved between them. For a moment, they just stood there together, his forehead lightly touching hers in the quiet shadows, the moon high above them.

'What was that?' she asked.

'I want us to party – just you and me.'

'I do too, but—'

'It was just half a tab,' he assured her. 'Don't worry.'

Then, he added softly: 'I really like you, Eva,' and there was a seriousness about the way he said it that melted her distrust. When he unlocked the door and led her inside, she felt the fear within her dissipate, a lightness coming into her. He switched on a lamp and she looked around at wood panelling, shelves bowing under the weight of books, a battered leather sofa and an old partners' desk.

'It's my dad's,' Callum explained. 'He works from home a lot. This is kind of his office.'

'I like it,' she said, trailing a finger over the bookshelves, conscious of him watching her as she moved slowly through the room. 'So, is it true?'

'Is what true?'

'That your dad represents Nicky Kehoe?'

Callum leaned back against the desk and smiled slowly. 'You heard that rumour?'

'Well? Is it?' she asked teasingly. 'Does your dad launder money for a criminal gang?'

'He doesn't launder money. But yes, he does give Nicky financial advice.'

She widened her eyes, feigning shock. She was enjoying herself – Callum's attention, the masculine feel to the room, the looseness of her limbs, her body light as a feather. Why had she been so nervous?

'He's actually pretty sound, you know. Not like how they portray him in the media – some sort of gangland thug.'

'You've met him?'

'Once or twice, he's called into the house.'

'Aren't you scared? You know, getting caught in the crossfire of some gangland feud?'

He snorted. 'No! Dad's got nothing to do with any of that. It's just business, that's all.'

'Are you allowed in here?'

'Nope.'

'Naughty boy,' she said, laughing at the mashed sound of the words coming out of her mouth. 'God, I'm so wasted,' she giggled.

It was easier this time, in a way. Shedding their clothes as they'd done before and coming together under a blanket on the couch – all of these actions had already been played out between them. There was a moment of resistance, but she fought against it in her mind, silencing the nagging doubt. She had come to this party in the full knowledge that sex was on the cards, and so what if he was operating at a pace that was faster than her desire? She never told him to stop, even though it felt like she was trying to get him to slow down but he wouldn't listen.

Afterwards, when it was over, she curled up into a corner of the couch, her cheek pressed against the leather, and she closed her eyes and thought about an old chair in her grandparents' house that had smelled like this, horsehair tufting loose from a split in the seam.

'Hey, Eva?'

Distantly, she heard him, like he was calling to her from another room. Pressure on her back, his hand shaking her.

'Hey, come on. Wake up.'

How long had she been asleep? Her breasts were sore, the room colder now, drawing goosebumps over her flesh. The dryness in her mouth felt huge; it was difficult to swallow.

Her skin peeled away from the leather as she tried to lift her head.

'Check this out,' she heard him say, but the lightbulb hanging from the ceiling was too bright and she had to look away, a dizziness announcing itself.

'Come on, Eva, look,' he said, his voice louder now, impatient with her, and she tried to sit up, rubbing her eyes, flakes of crust caught in mascara. She blinked her eyes open and saw the gun.

'Where'd you get that?' she asked, instinctively drawing back into the couch.

'It's my dad's.' He was holding the gun out for her to see. 'He keeps it for protection. You know – just in case.'

'I thought you said he wasn't involved in anything dangerous. That it was just business.' He wasn't pointing the gun at her, but still she felt the threat of it.

'It is . . . Hey, what's wrong? Are you mad at me?'

'No.' She was dressing quickly, her heart strobing in her chest.

'Then why are you being like this? Hey, where are you going?'

She was at the door, pausing to put her shoes on.

'Alicia's probably looking for me.'

'Come on, don't go. Look, I'm sorry, okay? I was just fucking around. You know it's not loaded, right? I didn't mean to frighten you—'

She shut the door and hurried out through the wrought-iron gate, stumbling back up through the garden, tripping over shrubs, the heel of her shoe sinking into the soil. Glancing back, she kept expecting to see him running after her, waiting to hear him shouting her name. But she didn't stop.

The spirit of elation in the house had hardened into a more deadened beat, the air now tinged with the acidic smell of vomit. She didn't even look for Alicia, fleeing to the safety of the street.

Once outside, the nausea in her stomach eased, but there was a wobbly sensation in her limbs as she found the number. After making the call, she waited by the side of the road, her muscles turning to jelly. The clouds in her head wouldn't clear, and she had the strangest sensation that her lips were blubbery, her face flaccid like she'd just had a stroke. Her heart was beating too fast and by the time she saw the car swing around the corner, her dress was drenched in sweat.

She'd expected the little red Toyota, but he'd come in the Merc.

'What happened? Are you okay?' he asked, once she was sitting in the passenger seat.

Instantly, she burst into tears.

She tried to speak but the words were mush in her mouth, and she felt his alarm while trying to regain control of her emotions.

'Just tell me this much,' Ross said. 'Are you hurt?'

She shook her head, no.

'I was at a party,' she croaked.

'Right. And you've been drinking, obviously.'

She snuffled in response.

'Anything else? Did you take anything?'

She nodded quickly, unable to meet his eye.

'Okay. What was it?'

'I don't know.'

'What do you mean, you don't know?'

And then she'd explained about Callum passing the tab into her mouth while they were kissing.

'He said it was just half a tab,' she said.

'Yeah, but of what? Ecstasy? Acid?'

She sniffled and wiped at her cheek with the back of her

hand. He leaned forward and popped open the glove compartment, taking a packet of tissues out.

'Here,' he said, handing her one and watching while she wiped beneath her eyes and then blew her nose.

'I'm sorry,' she said, embarrassed at him seeing her like this. 'I'm a complete mess.'

'Let's just worry about what went on back there.'

'Okay.'

'Did something happen between you and this boy?'

She looked down at her knees, pulled the hem of her skirt down to cover her thighs.

'Eva, did this guy try to have sex with you?'

She bit the inside of her cheek, tasted the metallic taint of blood.

'I can't talk about it,' she said at last.

She knew that the word 'rape' was bouncing around in his head and she wanted to dispel it but didn't quite know how to explain what she felt – her reluctance, her fear.

'Listen, I'm probably not the person you should be talking to about this stuff. But you've called me here to get you and now I feel responsible, so you've got to tell me if I should be bringing you to a police station or a hospital. Do you understand what I'm saying?'

There was a sharpness in his voice that set her off crying again, and she felt his hand on her shoulder then, his voice softening: 'Hey, hey. I didn't mean for that to come out so harshly. I'm just worried.'

'I know. And you're so nice to come and get me. I feel so stupid now.'

He gave her a moment, his hand still on her shoulder, softly coaxing her, and she took a deep breath and said:

'Callum and I . . . I thought it was what I wanted, but now . . . I don't know.'

Embarrassment flooded through her. There was no way she could tell him about the gun.

'Oh, Eva.' He shook his head and when she snuck a glance at him, she could see the anxiety had fallen away from his face, replaced by an expression that seemed closer to pity.

'This guy, Callum – this is the guy you were with in my house? Your boyfriend?'

'He's not my boyfriend. We're in the same tennis club.'

'And you like him?'

She didn't answer, just stared hard at her knees, waves of uncertainty washing over her.

'Look, I don't know what happened back there,' Ross said. 'And I've got to tell you that when I hear this guy slipped you a tab first, that sets alarm bells ringing in my head. But Eva, you're just a kid. And relationships can be confusing. Sex can be confusing. Especially at your age when you're still figuring these things out.'

'I just thought it would be different.'

'Yeah, well. Listen, I'm not sure if anyone's first time is ever really what they expect it to be. In fact, I'm pretty sure that ninety per cent of the time it's a disappointment. But it gets better. Trust me.'

She gave him a watery smile. 'Promise?'

'I promise.' He grinned at her, relief visible on his face. 'Listen, I know you've had a crappy night and you're probably thinking there's no way you're going to do that again, but in a few months' time you'll be finished with school and embarking on the next stage of your life, and once you're in university, then it will be all parties and boys, boys, boys. You're going to have the time of your life, and you'll look back on this night and laugh about how worried you were.'

It felt good to hear him say this even if her limbs still felt shuddery and strange.

'Take my advice: be safe but have fun. Enjoy this time, because believe me it passes too soon. And then you get older and it gets even more complicated.'

The way his voice trailed off and the grim expression that had taken over his face made her wonder about Becca, about their marriage.

'Right, I'm going to drop you home now,' he said. 'Do you feel up to that?'

She nodded and he started the engine and eased the Merc out on to the road.

'You should talk to your mum about this,' he suggested.

'Are you crazy? There's no way.'

'Well, how about your dad then?'

'My dad would have an aneurysm if he knew what just happened.'

Silence fell between them as the car moved in and out of pools of light thrown by the streetlamps. Her uneasiness fell away as she became distracted by the distorted light, the way it flashed across the bonnet of the car. Her legs stretched out into the footwell, warm air blowing around her knees and calves, quietening the shivering in her limbs. The car smelt of something minty, the dashboard was empty, the cabin scrupulously clean. She allowed herself to sneak the occasional glance at Ross, taking in the heft of his shoulders bunched in his sports jacket, the gleam of his head. There was something honest about his baldness, like he had nothing to hide. She imagined what it would feel like to place her hands on it, a charged sensation running through her at the thought.

'What did you tell Becca when I rang?' she asked as the car slowed and came to a halt at the side of the street.

'I told her it was one of the lads from the Rugby Club needing a lift.'

He had turned off the engine and was looking at her now.

He lied to his wife for me, she thought.

There was something dangerous in the air between them as they approached goodbye.

'I'm sorry for calling you. But I didn't know who else to ask.'

'That's okay.'

'I knew you'd come for me.'

'You did?'

She nodded, holding his gaze. His breathing was audible, the streetlamp catching the little spikes of stubble along his jaw, casting them silver. The T-shirt he wore beneath his jacket was wrinkled and creased, and she wondered if he'd been wearing it in bed when his phone had rung. She imagined she could catch the warm funk of sleep from it still. The length of time they were looking at each other, unspeaking, seemed to stretch to a point where what happened next felt inevitable. She leaned towards him, her lips finding his, the dry smoothness of his mouth sending shooting sparks of desire pinging around her body. And then he pulled back and said: 'Whoa there,' and her eyes snapped open. She saw his expression clarifying into one of alarm. With a plunge of horror, she realized he was leaning away from her, shaking his head in the negative, saying:

'Listen, Eva, I'm flattered but you've got the wrong idea . . .'

She clapped her hands over her face, not wanting to see the look he was giving her, needing to block it all out.

'I'm sorry if I gave you the wrong impression,' he went on desperately.

'No, it's my fault.' Her voice came weakly through the nest of her hands. 'I'm so embarrassed.'

'Don't be. Hey, if I was ten years younger . . .' He let the sentence trail off.

'God, I'm an idiot.' The tears started flowing.

He didn't say anything, just let out a loud exhalation, as if he'd been holding his breath the entire time.

'Your wife is so pretty,' she said then, and he remarked:

'Yeah. But it's not everything.'

She thought he sounded a little bitter, hidden layers of meaning caught within those few words.

'Please don't tell her about this,' she said, taking her hands away from her face, and he lowered his chin and gave her a serious look.

'I'm not going to keep secrets from my wife, Eva.'

She wanted to say that he'd already lied to his wife about the phone call.

'I'll wait here until you're safely inside.'

Her legs felt wobbly, the whole strangeness of the night washing through her, but for just those moments, she was able to put all of that to one side, remembering the dryness of his lips against hers and holding fast to the knowledge that his eyes were fixed on her as she walked all the way to her house.

13

There was another party happening that night: Sasha Harte was hosting a goodbye bash for the French students. Beth — and by extension, Corinne — had not been invited.

They sat at the counter in Eddie Rocket's, Corinne lazily flicking through the little jukebox on the countertop. Beth nibbled her veggie falafel. She didn't like beetroot. Even slathered in Eddie's Secret Sauce, it still tasted like dirt. But she had grown used to submitting to Corinne's choices, deferring to her friend on decisions about clothes and food as well as other things. Beth wondered now, as the earthy taste filled her mouth, how she would manage on her own without Corinne's guidance.

It was their last night together and already Beth felt the loss. A glimpse of impending grief had settled on her mind's eye, and perhaps it had on Corinne's as well, for she was quiet that evening, unusually pensive as she picked at her fries, her face resting on her hand.

'You're sure you don't mind about the party?' Beth said.

Corinne arched an eyebrow. 'You have asked me this maybe twenty times already.'

'I know. Sorry. I just hope you're not feeling like you're missing out.'

'What are you going to do about her?' Corinne asked, lifting her face from her hand.

'Who?'

'Sasha. She treats you like shit. You can't let her keep doing that.'

'I know.' She pushed a nacho into her mouth unhappily. 'But what can I do?'

Corinne shrugged. 'You could kill her.'

She picked up the little knife by her plate, made a quick stabbing gesture. Instantly, Beth thought of her mother preparing roast lamb for Sunday lunch. She had a fleeting image of Sasha trussed like a joint of meat, her fake-tanned skin bristling with rosemary needles.

'You know I'm kidding, right?' Corinne laughed.

'Sure.'

'But there are things you can do. Things to make her feel uncomfortable, to feel scared,' Corinne said casually.

But Beth dreaded the idea of confrontation, especially with Sasha, who commanded such power – her ready confidence, the crowd of fawning sycophants that trailed around in her wake.

'There was a teacher in school who was mean to me,' Corinne went on. 'Teasing me about my hair, shit like that. So I started a rumour that he liked some of the girls in our class but in a sexy way, you know?'

'What happened?'

'He left.'

'He was fired?'

'No, but it didn't matter. Once people start to think something about you, it's hard to make them change their minds.'

'But didn't they know it was you?'

Corinne rolled her eyes and giggled. 'I was careful.'

'It sounds complicated.'

'Not really. With the internet and a smartphone, you can do anything.' She nudged Beth with her elbow, adding kindly: 'Don't worry. I will show you.'

But when? Beth wondered.

The two weeks had flown by, and already Beth had learned so much. She had come to know her friend's sounds and her smells – the intimacies of early morning breath, the fug of night sweat lingering in the little room – just as familiar to her now as Corinne's tics and habits. Every morning, the surprise of her frosted hair, like icing on a child's birthday cake. It felt like Beth was shoring up all these little details so that when Corinne was gone, there would be something left to sustain her through the weeks and months of their separation.

'We should go somewhere,' Corinne said, pushing aside her fries and tapping a rapid rhythm on the countertop, already looking towards the door.

It startled Beth sometimes, the speed at which Corinne's mood changed. One minute she was morose and withdrawn, the next she was commanding, fizzing with energy.

'Where?'

Corinne flashed her a conspiratorial smile. 'I have an idea.'

The house was in darkness.

Beth felt her stomach dropping with sudden nerves while she fumbled with the keys. She pushed the door open and reached for the lights. Flicking the switch a couple of times, the hall remained in darkness.

'They must have turned off the electricity,' she whispered, a sinking feeling of disappointment inside.

But Corinne was not put off. She took out her mobile phone and used the torch function to light their way. There was an odd echoey stillness to the place. Most of the furniture in the rooms remained: the couch, the nesting set of coffee tables, the old writing desk. But the clutter that filled the shelves and cabinets had been cleared. The air carried a familiar smell, but the thin light cast by their phones through the gloom lent a strangeness to the house that inspired both unease and a peculiar excitement within them both.

In the kitchen, Beth watched as Corinne flipped open the cupboard doors, hunting for food, but there was nothing there. The fridge had been unplugged and cleaned, but it still gave off a rank odour like sour milk.

'Let's go upstairs,' Corinne suggested, and they felt their way through the shadows, the torchlight swinging wildly in front of them.

Darkness made the house feel smaller, and as they reached the top of the stairs and stepped into Melissa's bedroom, Beth felt the chill in the air of the unheated house. The curtains were drawn back and behind the bare window was the skeletal outline of branches of the mock orange tree growing in the garden.

'Is this where she died?' Corinne asked, and when Beth nodded, the French girl giggled and gave a shudder.

'Spooky!' she said, her teeth gleaming through the darkness. 'Abi found her?'

'Yes. She had died in the night. Mum found her the next morning.' She listened to the weird echo of her voice in the silent room and it felt disembodied, like the words were spoken by someone else.

The bed was made up with the coverlet and scatter cushions Beth remembered from her aunt's time. The same pressed flowers hung in frames above the bed, and when Corinne opened the wardrobe, some of Melissa's clothes were still hanging there. Beth felt the cold hollow of her stomach and wished they hadn't come.

'Do you think Eva minds?' Corinne asked.

'Minds what?'

'That this house is all yours?'

'I don't think so. We talked about it after we found out – after the will was read. I told her that it was hers too – that I'd share it with her.'

'And?'

'She said she didn't want it.'

There had been a coolness about Eva that day, Beth remembered. A sense that she was holding herself stiffly, back ramrod straight, attempting to show she was immune to the hurt of her aunt's expressed favouritism. 'I couldn't give a fuck,' she'd said breezily when Beth had clumsily addressed the issue. 'I don't want anything belonging to that fruitcake.' Her voice was tight, and Beth had perceived this as an attempt to disguise the hurt. But Eva's coldness had persisted since that day.

'She must be pissed about it, though. Right?'

'We don't talk about it,' she said quickly, a stiffness in her voice.

It was just one of those things in their family – an understanding that the relationship between Beth and her aunt was close, special. Her parents often said it: how Beth was the daughter Melissa never had. It was different with Eva, who was more intolerant, more judgemental. She'd thought their aunt was a drip and a leech. 'Pathetic' was what she deemed her. 'A sad sack.'

Outside, in the garden, the ghostly trumpet-heads of bindweed crawled over the dark shapes of the bushes and trees, colonizing the flower beds her aunt had tended so carefully. She was confused by the sadness coming over her in great waves. Grief, she supposed. She put her hands out to the glass.

'Put this on,' Corinne said, and when Beth turned around, she saw the dressing-gown held out to her. Silk shining under moonlight, the outline of a heron along the front panel, instantly recognizable.

'No,' Beth said.

'Come on. You're shivering.'

Corinne took a step towards her, and Beth tried to back away but the window was right there behind her.

'I . . . I don't want to.' Her voice faltered, and the intimacy of the night became charged, an edge to things now in the quiet of the deserted house.

'Remember the rules,' Corinne said. Her voice was soft but there was insistence there. 'You must wear what I tell you to wear.'

It was a thing of beauty, so different from the clothes Melissa had usually worn which were shapeless and utilitarian – mannish even. But the dressing-gown was her secret luxury, *my little indulgence*, Melissa used to say, a gift from a friend Beth had never met or known, brought back from overseas. How strong the memory was: the flash of silk over cotton pyjamas, the draped sleeves, the sleekness of the long-billed heron, his elongated neck. And when Beth slipped her arms into the sleeves and Corinne fixed it over her shoulders, she caught a sudden whiff of Pears soap, an undertone of something musky – the little rollies Melissa used to smoke. That smell, so familiar to her, it was as if her aunt had slipped into the room, was standing right behind her in the shadows. Turning to the window, she caught sight of her own reflection, and in that moment, she recognized the likeness: the dressing-gown, her own pale face in the glass – it was uncanny.

She sat on the edge of the bed, her breath coming quickly.

'Hey, what is it? What's wrong?' Corinne asked, and Beth shook her head.

'Nothing, I'm fine.'

But Corinne's gaze was worried, and so Beth said it again: 'Really, I'm fine.' But her skin was clammy, a shakiness in her limbs like a sudden drop of sugar in her bloodstream. She closed her eyes, wished herself back in the brightly lit warmth of Eddie Rocket's. In the lidded darkness, she felt Corinne take her hand, turning it over to reveal the soft inside of the wrist.

Beth felt the gentle drag of fingertips over her skin and began to feel calm. Corinne watched her carefully like a tentative nurse, and it was the tenderness of her gaze as much as her touch that quelled Beth's anxiety.

'I will miss you,' Corinne said.

'Me too.'

'We are best friends now, yes?'

'Yes. Oh, yes.' Her heart filling up.

'We should do something – something to seal our friendship.'

'Like what?'

'I don't know . . .'

Beth suggested cutting their palms and holding them together so their blood mingled, but Corinne was squeamish and recoiled at the idea. She had a better idea, something more intimate that required trust.

'Tell me a secret,' she said, her voice whispery. 'The biggest secret you have. The one thing that you lie awake at night, thinking about. The thing you are afraid to tell anyone.'

The room around them felt cold. It was getting late and they'd have to cycle back in the dark with no lights.

'I don't know,' Beth said. 'I can't think of anything.'

Looking down, she felt the silk beneath her hand, the feathery lightness of it.

'I will go first,' Corinne offered.

She was sitting cross-legged on the floor and Beth saw the curl of Corinne's eyelashes as she looked up at her on the bed.

'Last summer,' she began, 'Anouk went on holidays with some friends. She told my parents they were going to Italy, but really she went to Croatia to visit our grandparents. We had never met them, you see. Guy's parents had died before I was born and Valentina had lost touch with hers. They had made it clear that the past was not somewhere that should interest us, but Anouk didn't care. They didn't find out until she came back.'

'And what happened?'

'As soon as she returned, I could see how changed she was – so serious, she hardly spoke to me any more, just walked around in a daze. She kept going into rooms with my parents and closing the door, all of them talking in hushed voices. I couldn't hear what they were saying.'

There was a grave look on Corinne's face and Beth realized that her friend was afraid.

'You can't ever tell anyone this,' Corinne said now, her voice dropping so low it was almost a whisper. 'Do you understand, Beth? Not anyone. Not ever.'

'I won't, I promise,' Beth said solemnly.

Reassured by this, Corinne continued: 'You know those stories your parents tell about how they met? How they fell in love and got married and all of that shit?'

'Yes?'

'My parents used to tell us how they met in a camp for refugees. In Angola during the civil war. Valentina and Guy were both volunteers, you know? Dreamers. Thinking they could change the world. It sounds romantic, no?'

Beth nodded, wary of the barely-holding-it-together air of Corinne's account, something slightly manic in her delivery.

'But it was all a lie.'

'What?'

'My parents may have met in Angola, but they were already related.'

Confusion swept over Beth. 'What do you mean, related?'

Corinne's eyes flickered, then she said: 'Brother and sister.'

Beth experienced an instant drop in her stomach and at the same time a clamouring in her head. Corinne saw the way the information hit her, and nodded in recognition.

'I know. It's horrible, right?'

'I don't understand. How could they—?'

'Their parents knew each other. They were friends. Part of a group of Croatians living in Paris after the war. They used to go to each other's apartments, hang out in the same places, you know? My father was a small boy when Valentina's parents moved away. They left Paris and moved to Nice. Valentina was born there. So, when Guy and Valentina finally met in that refugee camp in Angola, they didn't know. Not at first. They had no idea that Guy's father and Valentina's mother . . .'

Her words drifted into silence, but the picture was already formed in Beth's imagination.

'When did they discover it?'

'When they returned to France, they told their parents they were married. Valentina's mother went very white, Anouk says. She nearly fainted. This secret she had held on to for so many years. She had to tell them.'

'And they ignored her? Did they not believe it was true? Maybe it isn't true,' Beth suggested, but felt the flimsiness of her optimism. The weight of certainty hung heavily in the air between them. The truth giving off its own peculiar pulse.

'It was too late. Valentina was already pregnant with Anouk.' Her voice flat, a faint hint of despair.

'When did you find this out?' Beth asked in a small voice.

'The day before Anouk left for Canada, she told me everything – how she had found our grandparents in Croatia, how they had explained it to her. Everything made sense somehow. All those years of moving from place to place like we were running from something. The strange way my parents looked at each other sometimes.'

Beth felt the mattress hard beneath the seat of her bones. Corinne's revelation appalled her. She had no idea of what to do with this information, what words of consolation she might offer. It went too deep. A betrayal so profound it infected the blood.

A shiver went through her, of excitement, of fear. She felt Corinne's eyes on her, felt the dry heat of her skin, their bloods jumping and communicating through their held hands, an air of watchfulness in the quiet house around them.

'Now it's your turn,' Corinne said solemnly. It was not a request, and Beth felt the immutability of the pact they'd entered into, the sanctity of truth required after Corinne's own brave admission.

Beth's heart began thrumming away, nerves prickling over her skin as Corinne fixed her with a direct gaze, eyes wide and compelling. Beth had no choice, and part of her had been yearning to tell.

'Tell me a secret,' Corinne whispered. 'The one thing you could never tell anyone.'

Summer

The girls are dead.

The knowledge of this sits inside me, pulsing with its very own heartbeat – a living, breathing thing.

'I think I'm in shock,' I tell the detective.

She is a young woman with a pale face and amber eyes. Cassins is her name.

'I haven't cried yet. I don't know why. It's not that I don't—'

I stop because the tide of emotion is swelling in me now and I'm not ready for it to unleash itself. So I stare hard at the floor, a black flecked linoleum, striation marks evident from the sweep of a mop. The room smells strongly of disinfectant, like it's recently been cleaned down. Which makes me wonder what this room has held: people crying, people puking, people pissing themselves. You don't know how your body will react when subject to this kind of pressure. I myself have become frozen. As if I'm observing myself from a distance. Sitting still like a china doll on this hard plastic chair. One of my daughters, when she was little, used to think dolls came alive as soon as humans left the room. Beth. Always the more imaginative, the more fearful of the two.

'I would like to see Eva,' I tell Detective Cassins shakily. 'My daughter. I should be with her. She shouldn't be alone.'

She nods, keeping her eyes on me. 'Of course. We will arrange it. But for now, I need to ask you some questions, Abi.'

She asks me what time we arrived at the school. What was the plan? Did Beth know we were coming? Did Corinne? I tell her about the phone call from Mark, about what he'd discovered in the house, and how I had flung open the car door and begun to run. When she leads me through to the moment of impact, the moment I witnessed their fall, I have to hold on to the edge of my seat with both hands, as if the force of memory might carry me away.

After a while, the door opens and a uniformed officer enters with a bag. Cassins nods to her, then says to me:

'Perhaps you'd like to change out of that blouse, Abi.'

I look down, shocked all over again by the blood. I had forgotten it was there.

Inside the bag there is a navy cotton blouse, with a bright red strip of ribbon banding the inside of the collar. I'm momentarily thrown because the blouse is mine. It was on my bed this morning, folded with the other clean laundry. Only now do I realize that the police are in my house. Of course they are. Crawling all over our home, combing for evidence, peering into every nook and cranny of our lives. I imagine my neighbours gathering outside on the street, gazing in amazement at the police cordon that has been set up, at the parade of uniformed officers going in and out of my house, carrying away computers and laptops, stowing them in their white vans to be driven away, their contents trawled through for anything incriminating, any clue at all that could point to a motive, a reason behind this terrible act. My neighbours will be shaking their heads in bewildered dismay. Willow Park used to be such a quiet, respectable road. And now the police are there again – the second time in twenty-four hours.

Wait until the press gets wind of this, I think. Although I imagine they already have. Tabloid hacks swarming to the school, questioning the other parents, the other pupils – the witnesses, the survivors. And when word leaks out as to the *identities*, then they'll come for us – our neighbours, our family members, my work colleagues, our friends – they'll descend like vultures, come to strip the carcass of our lives to the bone.

'Lindsey here will show you to the Ladies,' Cassins says, interrupting my thoughts.

Her amber eyes follow me as I leave the room.

Alone in the toilets, I break down. My ruined blouse in my hands, I stand there in the cubicle in my bra and skirt and bawl. The sound frightens me. I will myself to stop.

'Pull yourself together,' I snap, as if it's one of the girls I'm scolding, Beth nursing bruised feelings, Eva losing it over a poor performance at the pool.

I blow my nose, then flush the tissue away and pull on the clean shirt they have given me. At the sink, I avoid contact with my own reflection, washing my hands quickly, wiping them on my skirt rather than the sour-looking towel on a rail. I've put my blood-stained blouse in the same carrier bag that had held my laundered shirt, but now I realize that I don't want the thing. How could I ever wear it again? There's a flip-top bin in the corner of the room; I open it and shove my blouse deep inside, then step away briskly, holding my breath against the smell.

In the corridor, the officer waits for me. It's busy out here, the hum of voices increases as we move away from the Ladies, and I see people milling about the desk – some in uniform, some civilians. There's a bench against the wall lined with people, all of them waiting, and as we reach the interview room, a woman turns her head and looks over at me, and I realize that I know her. It is Siobhan Harte – Sasha's mother. What on earth is she doing here? But then I think, oh. Yes, of course. And I suddenly feel afraid. Are there other parents here from the school? The way she is looking at me, the hard varnish of her stare.

'All set?' the officer asks, opening the door for me.

I take one last look at Siobhan. She sits up straighter on the bench, lengthening her neck and fixing me with a look that contains neither pity nor hatred. Rather it is a look of vindication. And it all comes tumbling back – our conversation, her assertion, the descriptor she'd used, pinning my daughter with a word.

'There,' it seems to say, her cool, arch gaze. 'Didn't I warn you? Didn't I tell you so?'

14

'Slow down,' Abi told Mark.

Her eyes flicked towards the speedometer of the unfamiliar dashboard. They had picked up the rental car at the airport. The traffic leaving Bordeaux had been murder and now Mark was looking to make up for lost time, fields of sunflowers and crops whizzing past, heat shimmering above the tarmac.

'I'm not speeding,' he said.

'You don't know the roads.'

He let out a short bark of a laugh. 'It's a motorway, Abi, not some winding country lane.'

'What if you miss the turn-off?'

'We've got the Satnav,' he said tersely.

In the backseat, Eva let out a loud sigh of irritation, catching Abi's attention. Wan and tired after her exams, she'd hardly spoken to either of her parents throughout the journey from the airport. Abi watched now as her daughter put her earbuds in, zoning out of the situation in the car.

Mark glanced at her. 'Are you all right?'

'I'm fine,' Abi answered, her voice strained with insistence.

'You seem tense. Is there something wrong?'

'Just tired,' she said in a way that communicated her desire to let the matter drop.

Tension crawled beneath the surface of her skin. Impatience to get to their destination married with an anxiety she'd been carrying since the incident in Tesco's the day before.

She had been hurrying around the aisles, looking for a few holiday essentials, when she'd turned a corner and found herself face-to-face with Siobhan Harte. For a few minutes, they'd chatted about school, the holidays, the French exchange programme, Abi explaining how Beth had remained in France even though her classmates had returned.

'My husband and I, along with our older daughter, are going out tomorrow to join Beth. A week's holiday,' she'd said.

'Oh, lovely!' Siobhan responded, but Abi picked up on a certain reticence.

She didn't question it, and was about to say her goodbye when Siobhan exhaled loudly and said:

'Look, Abi. I wasn't going to say anything, but something's been going on between the girls. Something upsetting.'

'Oh?' The basket on Abi's arm felt heavy all of a sudden, her muscles automatically tensing.

'It's this WhatsApp thing they do – Outfit Of The Day.'

'Right. Beth's mentioned it.'

'I'm sure she has,' Siobhan said quickly, and Abi's antennae twitched.

'Lately, whenever Sasha posts a photograph of herself, she is immediately bombarded with questions posted online, asking: Where did she buy the outfit? How much did it cost? What size is it? Did it come in any other colours? These are just some of the questions – there are normally many more. It's the same with every single outfit she posts – instantly the questions start, ten, twenty messages in a row. I know it sounds silly, but it really bothers Sasha.'

'I imagine it would be a little annoying,' Abi replied carefully.

'Oh, more than annoying,' Siobhan countered swiftly. 'It's

intimidating. Some of the questions are just downright mean, suggesting that Sash looks fat or unhealthy.'

Her smile was gone now. A strident tone had entered her voice as she clutched the handle of her trolley, a challenge there in her eyes.

'Hang on a second,' Abi said, trying to adopt a reasonable tone. 'Are you saying that Beth has been intimidating your daughter?'

'Yes.'

'You're sure about that?'

'She's been posting the messages under a false name but everybody knows that it's her.'

'Oh, come on—'

'And when Sash confronted her about it, she didn't deny it. It's online bullying.' Siobhan's face had gone quite red.

'I really think you've misunderstood. Even if it is Beth, it sounds to me like she was just trying to join in, granted in a clumsy way. But instead of being nice about it, Sasha has shunned her.'

'Now, just a minute—'

'In the same way Sasha and her little gang shun Beth at school. Constantly.' Abi's voice had risen, and she saw the flash of indignation in the other woman's eye.

'I don't want to have an argument about it,' Siobhan said, mustering up some dignity. 'But if it continues, I'm going to bring it up with the school.' She fixed her handbag on her shoulder and pushed her trolley forward towards the end of the aisle, but before she rounded the corner, she looked back at Abi and said, her voice wobbling a little:

'I know you think this is nothing. And as her mother, it's only natural you'd think the best of her. But we all know about your daughter. We all heard about what she did to herself. She's disturbed. If you were in my position, you'd be worried too.'

The word stayed with Abi even after Siobhan Harte had scuttled away. *Disturbed.* It reverberated now in the filtered air of the rental car as Mark pressed down on the accelerator, and Abi sat there quietly fuming. She had held back from telling him about the incident. Instinctively she had known that bringing it up would only have caused an argument between them, with Mark accusing her of being overly concerned about Beth's social behaviour, expecting her to conform with the little vixens in that school, and Abi would be forced to bite down on her words, and suppress what it was she was really concerned about.

Over the past two weeks, Abi had spoken to her younger daughter on the phone a number of times as well as a daily text message. Beth had seemed her usual self – brief, yes, and unforthcoming with information, but she had sounded content. No alarm bells had gone off in Abi's head. She realized now that a complacency had drifted in.

Up ahead on the motorway, a plume of smoke rose in the distance, blue sirens whirling past. It was the second accident they'd come across, and the traffic slowed, clogging as it met the blocked artery. But at the next exit, they veered off and soon found themselves on narrow roads that skirted wide expanses of agricultural land, trees and hedgerows cropping up then disappearing again, the car passing through shade to sunshine. Metallic grain silos were dotted about the sloping countryside. Muscular brown cows grazed in the dusty heat. The further they got from the motorway, the more the character of the place announced itself, becoming concentrated in the villages with low terracotta roofs, church spires, twisting vines and potted geraniums dotted around empty civic squares.

'We should stop to pick up groceries,' Mark said, but Abi was impatient to get there, visited by a sense of excitement that intensified with the heat of the day, the realization that they were finally away from it all. A holiday they badly needed.

'Valentina said there's a supermarket in the village.'

'Let's hope there's a bar,' Mark replied. 'I'm gasping for a cold beer.'

He was hunched forward over the wheel, eyes fixed on the road, and Abi felt a sudden tenderness towards him. All the grief he had been carrying silently inside him was visible to her in his pallor, the sinewy strain of muscles in his neck. He needed a holiday as much as she did. She put out a hand and touched his forearm.

'Me too, love,' she said.

They reached the house just before five. The road brought them down into a valley where a wide river cut through, green water moving slowly beneath a stone bridge with several arches, houses nestled along the banks. The village, they understood, was very old, some of the buildings medieval, and as they followed Valentina's instructions and turned on to the little road that travelled alongside the wall of the river-bank, they marvelled at the higgledy-piggledy nature of the houses somewhat precariously balancing against each other in alternating heights and states of disrepair.

'It looks Photoshopped,' Mark commented, the car slowing as they sought out the house.

'It's beautiful,' Abi said, and it was.

Trees grew at a bend in the river, branches sweeping down to touch the water. A stone cross stood as a monument on one side, faced on the opposite bank by a small chapel, itself flanked by stately looking houses. Norman turrets, slate roofs, many-paned windows glinting in the sun between half-closed shutters. Something safe and wholesome and other-worldly about it all, like nothing bad could ever happen here. The knots of tension in Abi's muscles began to ease.

The house was at the end of the lane. It rose imperiously above the bank, caught in the full orange glow of the early-evening sun. The heat hit them as they opened the car doors and climbed out. Abi felt the hot air wrapping around her bare legs and she rubbed the back of her neck and looked up at the old stonework of the house swarming with the still-green leaves of Virginia creeper. Shutters in peeling blue paint were opened to show tall casement windows, and high up in the eaves, she could hear a bird singing.

Mark was opening the boot, already looking to unpack the car, but she motioned for him to wait.

And there was Valentina at the top of the run of steps. She stood for a moment with one hand raised in welcome, the other lifting the hem of her voluminous dress to reveal dainty brown ankles over silver sandals. The dress was sky-blue, a string of large yellow beads hanging over it. With her hennaed hair piled high on top of her head, she seemed drenched in colour. There was something stately and regal in her manner, her poise, as she descended the steps slowly, her dark eyes crinkled by her broad smile and fixed on Abi as the two women approached each other. Val was small, diminutive against the backdrop of the large house. She reached up for Abi, kissing one cheek then the other, the brush of her skin soft and warm and faintly scented.

When she drew away, Val clasped both of Abi's hands in hers, exclaiming: 'You are here at last! It makes my heart glad to see you!'

It was the first time they'd met, although through their

phone conversations Abi felt a bond had already formed between them, Valentina exacting a promise from Abi that she and all their family would come and spend a week at their house in the Vienne. There was a separate apartment – an annex, Valentina had said – where they would be comfortable, with their own space and privacy. She had been insistent, and Abi – charmed by Valentina's warmth, the easy eccentricity of her expressions – was persuaded.

And so now they were here, and Abi watched as the small woman approached Mark and then Eva, both of them laughing and blushing as they were embraced in turn.

'Where's Beth?' Mark asked, and Val clucked, her expression mischievous and twinkly in a way that reminded Abi of Corinne.

'They will be back soon. They have a surprise for you,' she said, wagging her finger at each of them. 'Those girls. Wait. You will see.'

Something about Val's private amusement, the way she turned away from them at that moment, brought on a small internal lurch in Abi. But when Mark caught her eye and she saw the question in it, she smiled to deflect any note of worry, then followed Valentina into the house.

It was cooler inside, the heat kept at bay by the tiled floors, the thick walls. There was a dark moodiness to the place with its blackened beams, bookcases rising up to the high ceilings. All living was done in one large room with windows giving on to a view of the river, a twisting cherrywood staircase rising up through the house. Valentina guided them through, creating a little flurry around her as she threw out various asides about the house and the village – how La Grange, as the house was called, had once been a tithe barn for the local clerics; how the water level of the river was perilously low, there having been no rain for months. Abi observed how theatrical Valentina was, creating a little swirl of chaos around her as she absently picked up various objects to show them, one hand waving a lit cigarette about in airy circles, the other hand fingering the yellow beads swinging from her neck or teasing a stray tendril of hair back into its nest on the top of her head. The similarities were there between mother and daughter – both small and birdlike, quick glittering eyes, the flurry of energy that surrounded them. There was a sort of chaos to the house also, towers of books and magazines in sliding piles on the coffee table, a haphazard arrangement of spider plants covering the window ledges, vast amounts of unmatched platters and bowls piled on top of each other along the open shelves of the kitchen. The mantelpiece was adorned with various photographs in patterned frames, and Mark stood there now with hands in his pockets peering from one to the other. Eva hovered by the door, scratching her arm and casting a wary eye up at the slanting ceiling.

'Is this Anouk?' Mark asked. He was looking at a black and white picture of a young woman, draped across a couch like an odalisque, remote and serious, heavy-lidded eyes staring back at the camera out of an oval face. Mata Hari, Abi thought.

Valentina said: 'Oh, yes,' and smiled myopically at him.

'She's very pretty,' he offered.

'Anouk is a beauty,' Val declared, before adding: 'It is very hard for Corinne.'

Mark's expression grew quizzical. 'But Corinne has her own charm, surely.'

'Oh, yes. Yes, she has,' Val answered but her vagueness made her sound insincere. 'And of course, Corinne has character.'

'That's certainly true,' Mark laughed.

'Yes? You have noticed?' Playfully, she prodded his arm, and Abi saw Mark's cheeks redden.

'So? Do you see a likeness?' she asked, glancing once more at the photograph of Anouk.

Mark examined the image, frowning a little. 'Well. I suppose you can tell they are sisters,' he began uncertainly, but Valentina laughed.

'No, not with Corinne. With this girl,' wafting the hand holding her cigarette towards Eva.

'Me?' The word came out of Eva's mouth punched with doubtful surprise.

'Yes, you, my dear,' Valentina said. 'When Corinne told me, I didn't believe her. But now that you are here . . . yes, I can see similarities between you and Anouk. Your hair, your physique. Your *hauteur.*'

Eva's frown deepened but this just made Valentina more amused, her tinkly laugh rising. Reaching out, she briefly stroked Eva's face, before adopting a brisk tone:

'Now, come! I must show you to your accommodation.'

She led them back outside and across the terrace to another door they had not noticed. As she walked, Valentina told them: 'You know, they are so happy together, the two girls. So close.'

'Really?'

'I have never known Corinne to connect with anyone like this. Apart from Anouk, of course.'

'She must miss her sister greatly,' Abi ventured. 'But how wonderful for Anouk. A scholarship to McGill!'

Valentina looked back and smiled, but there was something myopic about it, and then she opened a door that led into a small, narrow room with a large, cluttered desk and filing cabinets. A bed was made up in the corner.

'Your room, *chérie*,' she said to Eva, indicating with a waft of her hand, then leading them to a small staircase concealed behind a curtain.

'They have been inseparable these last two weeks,' she went on, picking up the earlier thread of conversation as she led them up the steep run of steps. 'So good at sharing, at helping each other. Such devotion. And so independent now. I have hardly seen them.'

'Oh?'

'You know what teenagers are like. They don't want parents hanging around. And it is good for them, is it not, to exercise their own free will?'

'Within reason,' Abi said. It worried her a little, how much Valentina may have left the girls to their own devices. The word 'devotion' stuck in her head, pairing with its sister 'disturbed'. She knew her own daughter well enough. Beth was soft but prone to fierce emotions. Abi couldn't help but wonder what dark feelings might have been summoned to life from her innocence.

'Here we are!' Valentina announced, twirling with a flourish, her blue dress briefly inflating like a jellyfish at the centre of the room.

It was a loft space, anchored by a bed covered with a plush red blanket. High above, the Velux windows were thrown open to the evening light, but the room still felt airless and heavy with heat. Some of the chaos of the main house had crept its way up here into the loft, old suitcases piled in one corner, towers of paperbacks leaning against the walls. The place felt crowded with heavy furniture.

'It's lovely,' Abi said, turning to Mark. 'Don't you think?'

'Charming,' Mark replied, straining for sincerity.

It was just the kind of place that he hated, cluttered and airless – a reminder of the cramped mustiness of his childhood. A heavy odour hung in the air – a mélange of old cooking smells and bodies, underlaid with damp. Abi heard a cough, a loud guttural hacking from beyond the wall.

'That's Guy,' Valentina explained without any hint of embarrassment or apology. 'He must be waking.'

Abi's heart sank. The walls were paper-thin.

'And the bathroom is just over here,' Valentina said.

She was launching into an explanation of the vagaries of the plumbing when a door opened downstairs and they heard Eva's voice, raised in surprise.

'Oh. My. God,' she said.

And then the shrieking delight of Corinne's laughter coming up from below, at once distinctive and strange.

Mark reached the steps first, Abi following. Over his shoulder, she saw Corinne standing there alongside a boy in an oversized sports jersey. The pink dye in Corinne's hair had started growing out. A strip of dark roots an inch wide ran the length of her parting. Her limbs were thin and deeply tanned beneath denim shorts and a lemon-yellow T-shirt, her hands cupped over her mouth so that her face showed only her eyes, lively with humour, exchanging glances with the boy. Abi looked beyond them for Beth, but the terrace was empty, shadows creeping over the cracked pavings.

'You look like Justin Bieber,' Eva said with disgust, and the boy answered in a voice that was soft and light and instantly recognizable:

'No, I don't.'

Abi's eyes snapped back to him.

'Beth?' The name escaped her lips like a gasp.

Mark had already taken a step towards his daughter, reaching out a hand to touch the newly cropped hair. 'Jesus,' he said, sounding amused.

But Abi didn't find it funny. Instead, she experienced a painful rush of love for her child mixed with anguish. All that Beth had suffered in the past – her raw vulnerability to every slight, every harsh remark – how could Abi possibly protect her when she invited this derision?

'What have you done to yourself?' she asked with dismay.

Beth's hair had a hacked look to it, like the job had been done with nail scissors. It was shorn close to the scalp at the back and sides, the hair on top left a little longer – a small mercy – the ends bleached a horrible yellowish-white colour that made Abi think of rancid butter. The skin of Beth's face looked pinkish and mottled against the lurid blond and there was a crusty-looking spot nestling in the crease to one side of her nose. The brutality of the haircut made her look vulnerable and exposed, like a mollusc ripped from its shell.

'Do you like it? We did it ourselves.' Beth's smile was both nervous and gauche – a blithe embarrassment to it that made Abi melt a little.

'I don't know what to say. Is this a permanent dye?' She brought a hand up to touch the hair, which felt coarse and dry.

'Don't worry, it will grow out.'

'Oh, Beth.'

Disappointment leaked into her tone and instantly, the hope in Beth's face closed down. She looked sideways at Corinne – a quicksilver glance but Abi caught it, taking in how their eyes locked, the slight nod of reassurance that Corinne gave, the way it steadied Beth.

'Is that a nose-piercing?' Eva asked, her own nose wrinkling with distaste.

Abi hadn't noticed it, but now she saw Beth's hand instinctively going to her face, the pad of her index finger pressing to what Abi had thought was a spot, but as she peered closely, she saw that it was in fact a tiny stone embedded in the flesh around Beth's nostril. A crusty layer had formed around the circumference and the skin looked scratchy and raw.

Corinne's laughter rose, too loud for the room. Abi felt it scraping inside her skull, heightening her sense of alarm. She looked around for Mark, but he had already turned away from her, unperturbed, stepping out into the sunlight to fetch their luggage from the car.

15

It was hard pretending everything was normal. Especially now after the arrival of her family.

Beth stared up into the eaves and said:

'Do you think they noticed?'

'Noticed what?' Corinne asked.

'About your parents?'

All the heat from the day seemed to have gathered into the dark attic space. They lay in their underwear with the coverlets kicked off, Corinne fanning herself with a book while she considered her answer. Beth could hear the dull flap of pages from across the room.

'What would they notice? They act normal, don't they?'

'I guess.'

Whenever Corinne's parents spoke to each other in rapid French, Beth found it hard not to stare, after what Corinne had told her. She watched them from the corner of her eye as they prepared the dinner alongside each other in the little kitchen; Valentina – small and animated, tossing ingredients together with a flourish; Guy, a large, humourless man, seemed hulking beside her. Beth was intimidated by Guy – his long silences, the directness of his watery gaze. She could find no trace of filial resemblance between the two adults. Still, it was impossible to observe even the smallest interaction between Guy and Val without a small tremor of revulsion. Sometimes, she would stare at them wide-eyed and then Corinne would kick her sharply under the table and flash a warning glance.

It seemed like years had passed – not months – since that night in Dublin when Corinne had revealed her family secret. Ever since, the secret had consumed Beth. She had googled around, looking for information that might help to tease out the strands of this problem. She became familiar with the terms: *consanguinity, endogamy, autosomal recessive disorder*, getting lost down rabbit holes bristling with facts about social order and genetics that she didn't understand and that hurt her brain when she tried to.

A secret that burdensome was hard to keep. Sometimes, when Beth had been in her father's den in the evenings, the two of them working in silence on their matchstick construction, and her father would momentarily glance up at her from the blueprints and ask was she okay, that shading of concern in his voice made her long to tell him, lay the facts in front of him and have him make sense of them for her.

'I thought my mother might notice something,' Beth said now.

'Your mother?' Corinne snorted with derision. 'If anyone would notice it's your father. Mark sees much more than *her*.'

Corinne thought Abi was flakey and false. There was a vein of acid running through her impersonation of Abi – the way she swept into a room, both bossy and inattentive. It made Beth feel guilty when she laughed. But for all Corinne's assertions, Beth knew her mother was astute, her father perceptive. And she had wondered on the eve of their arrival whether they would meet with Corinne's parents and instantly guess that something wasn't right about them.

The answer, it turned out, was no – they didn't see it. All they were concerned about was Beth's hair.

It had been Corinne's idea. Sort of. On one of the days, hot, listless, bored, she'd fingered the brightly coloured ends of her own hair and mused about cutting it.

'Don't,' Beth gently urged. 'It's nice the way it is.' Love leaking into her tone.

'It's boring. I'm sick of pink.'

Beth had seen photographs of Corinne with her natural hair colour – a glossy, unexceptional brown. She couldn't imagine her friend without the cloud of bubble-gum hair, the flighty eccentricity of it like a special mark, an anointed sign.

'Maybe I should cut it all off,' Corinne suggested.

'No way!'

'Why not?'

'Your parents would kill you for a start.'

'But that is the point, right?'

She'd seen the confusion in Beth's face, and it made Corinne laugh.

'I did it once before, you know. When I was ten. Cut my hair off to this short. Ksk-ksk,' she made snipping gestures close to her ears, her eyes taking on the familiar gleam of mischief. 'You should have seen Valentina's face!'

Beth tried to imagine it but couldn't.

'After that, they kept staring at me – Val and Guy. Could not take their eyes off me!' She sounded delighted with herself, and then she caught Beth's gaze and her expression grew serious, a touch of defiance in her arched brow. 'For once, they were looking at me. Not at Anouk.'

Pictures of Anouk were all over the house. A sulky beauty, she stared out from frames in the sitting room and kitchen, in the bedrooms and hall. Some were studio shots, others less artfully taken but just as persuasive. Corinne was hanging there too on the walls with their flaking paint, but it did not require an actual accounting of all the images dotted around the house to know there were far more of Anouk than of her younger sister. Beth had wondered was it only that way since the girl had gone? But now she began to suspect that it had always been so, and her heart felt pained at the thought of Corinne constantly eclipsed by this sister, a feeling Beth could relate to.

'You should do it,' Corinne said then, her eyes flickering quickly over Beth's head and shoulders. A challenge there.

Instinctively, Beth's hand went up to touch her hair. Long, nondescript, fuzzy in the humid heat, it was hardly the lodestone of her appeal. But still, the thought of cutting it all off caused her insides to seize with fright. Corinne was already upon her, enthusiastically fingering strands and tucking them up and under.

'Like this,' she said, 'and this,' turning Beth so she was confronted by her own startled reflection in the glazing of a cabinet.

'I don't know . . .'

'It would be chic! It would be cool. You could finally see your face. All the time, you are hidden under all of this. It would free you.'

Corinne's voice was charged with excitement. All traces of boredom had fled from her tone, her manner.

'And you have this freckle here,' she went on, touching the place just underneath Beth's jaw and sending a thrill of nerves shooting down her neck, 'so cute, but never seen. Think how sweet you would look!'

Beth was scared, but equally she burned with pleasure under the heat of Corinne's attention, her vivid ministrations, and was desperate to prolong it.

'What about my scar?' she asked, fingers reaching to trace the familiar ridge of it running down the back of her neck.

'But that would be the whole point! Why hide it? It's beautiful! To show it is to be brave. Don't you see? You have to do it!'

Seized with conviction, Corinne declared: 'I could do it for you. I've cut hair before.'

She was shuffling through the contents of the utensils drawer in the kitchen before Beth could even voice an objection. It was only when she turned and came at Beth, the scissors gleaming in her hand, that Beth drew back from her and said:

'No. Please. I don't want to.'

A short pause and then all the animation that had taken hold of Corinne drained away.

'Fine,' she said, putting down the scissors and throwing herself on to the couch, lapsing into sullen silence.

'It's just that I—'

'No. I understand.' She turned her face away.

Whenever this happened – her sharp withdrawal – it made Beth think of a light suddenly switched off. A room bathed in warm sunshine sharply plunged into darkness. These moments left her feeling bereft and a little panicked, scrambling for ways to reverse her friend's mood. When she had Corinne's attention, she felt warm and whole and understood. But with the attention snatched away, she became once again the old Beth she despised – stupid, worthless, hardly there at all. She didn't deserve Corinne's friendship, that's what she thought. Corinne was only trying to help her by compelling her to be fearless and daring, as Corinne herself was. What was she so afraid of?

She'd picked up the scissors, and standing in front of Corinne, had snatched a handful of her dull, frizzy hair and sheared it straight off.

'There,' she said flatly. 'It's only hair after all.'

It had been worth it. For the delight in Corinne's reaction alone. It had been worth it.

She had given herself over to Corinne's fussing, nervily

surrendering control. Corinne had snipped and washed and dyed, butterfly fingers flitting over Beth's hair, and when she was finished, Beth was unrecognizable to herself. She looked at the pale triangle of her face, alarming in its new naked-ness, the greased blond locks like a corona of lemon peels above her forehead, and felt an inner trembling. But what-ever doubts she held were waved aside by Corinne's bright assertions, her coos of rapture. Somehow, her good opinion carried more weight than the heft of Beth's own insecurities – it was more prized because it had to be earned. It was not until Beth saw Eva's appalled expression, and the alarm in her mother's face, that the full volume of her insecurity came screeching to life within her head. For one horrible moment, she was sure Abi was going to cry.

All throughout the evening, while the seven of them ate on the terrace, she kept catching her mother sneaking little glances at her, glances suffused with dismay. Through the stilted polite-ness of the meal, Beth could tell her mother was impatient to get her on her own and she knew what that would mean. When it was airily remarked upon that Beth would continue to share Corinne's room for the duration of the holiday, she'd seen her mother's mouth tighten, her lips thinning with fury.

'Maybe we should tell them,' Beth suggested now, and this caused Corinne to sit up suddenly.

'Are you crazy?'

'Why not? We have to tell someone. It's not right that this should go on – your parents, living together like this when they're . . . you know. I mean, isn't it illegal?'

Corinne's secret felt too large and explosive to be con-tained by just the two of them.

'If you tell your parents,' Corinne said, 'then we will never see each other again. Do you understand that?'

'But—'

'Do you think they would allow us to be friends if they knew what a freak I am?'

'But it's not your fault! They'd understand that. And you're not a freak.'

'You made a promise,' Corinne hissed through the darkness. 'How would you feel if I told Val and Guy yours?'

The words reached Beth and a coolness swept over her limbs. They didn't talk about it much but now she felt her own secret in the room with them, throbbing in the darkness, so much worse than what Corinne had admitted to.

'It is better this way. Trust me,' Corinne whispered, her voice softer, sinuous. 'You do trust me, don't you, Beth?'

'Of course I do. More than anyone.'

Corinne flopped back on to the bed, satisfied. She dropped the book on the floor and a few minutes later, Beth heard the steady sounds of her breathing through untroubled sleep.

Abi did get to speak to her, eventually. The next day, as Beth idled on the terrace, waiting for Corinne to finish in the shower, her mother gently took her by the arm and walked her down to the river.

'I just wish you'd thought this through,' she said, casting her eyes over Beth's ruined hair.

Beth knew Abi was trying to keep her frustration muted, but disappointment was coming off her mother in clouds. She felt herself tense against it.

'I did think it through. I want to look like this.'

'How could you have wanted this? You had such lovely hair, Beth.'

'No, I didn't. You never said that before.'

'Of course, I—'

'You were always at me about it, telling me to get it out of my eyes, to tie it back and do something with it, remember?'

'Well, you've certainly done that now,' Abi remarked, tartness entering her tone. 'I suppose this was Corinne's idea?'

'No!'

'You mustn't let her talk you into doing things you're uncomfortable with. This business of her telling you what to wear. I've seen her do it. You have to stand up for yourself. Be your own person.'

'I am—'

'It's time to grow up a little. Stop being so naive.'

'For fuck's sake, Mum . . .'

'Watch your language, young lady.'

Beth stared at the river, silently fuming. For a moment, both mother and daughter were silent.

Frogs lived at the water's edge. Corinne had pointed them out to her, their tiny slick forms splayed on the rock or crouching among the weeds. Beth had felt so happy then, before her family arrived, so relaxed and at peace. Now her insides were churning, rage pummelling the undersurface of her skull. What did Abi want from her? On the one hand she was telling Beth to grow up, but with the next breath she was berating her like a child. Corinne was right – her mother was clueless as to how to speak to her, emotionally retarded.

'Look, I didn't mean to upset you,' Abi said, adopting a gentler tone. 'I only want what's best for you.'

Still Beth said nothing.

'So, what have you girls been doing during your stay? How have you spent your time?'

Beth shrugged, then mumbled something about hanging out together, swimming, her answers vague and noncommittal.

'Did you see much of the other girls from your school while they were here?'

'A bit. Not that much. We tended just to do our own thing.'

'I bumped into Sasha Harte's mother in the supermarket. Sounds like Sasha had a good time.'

'Great,' she said, her voice impassive.

She could feel her mother's hot gaze and knew Abi was straining towards further questioning, worry knitting through her faltering silence. Beth kept her eyes on the clump of weeds by the bank, where the willow tree dipped into the water. Rats lived there, Corinne had said.

'I just want you to be happy,' Abi said, 'to be kind to others as well as to yourself. It's important.'

The words jarred, stirring up questions in Beth's head, but she said nothing, allowing a silence to open up between them. Eventually, Abi turned, casting a glance back at the house.

'Your dad should be ready now. Why don't you get your things and come with us, hmm? We thought we'd go towards Angles and rent some canoes. Eva's keen. How about it?'

'Can Corinne come too?'

Beth kept her gaze on the riverbank, but she didn't need to look at Abi to know her jaw was tightening.

'Can't we have a day to ourselves? Just the four of us?'

'We can do that anytime we're back in Dublin,' Beth said, quiet, determined. She felt her mother waver, hovering on the brink of argument.

'Very well,' Abi relented. 'But I would like to spend some of the holiday just the four of us. It would be nice to have my family to myself for a change.'

Something slipped from the riverbank. A small splash, and then the sleek back of the rat breaching the surface.

Despite Abi's wishes, it proved difficult to prise the families apart. Valentina was an attentive host, insisting on cooking for them every evening, elaborate meals served on the terrace,

Guy generous with the wine. Beth watched her parents going through the motions of polite cheerfulness, exclaiming over everything, but she knew that beneath the surface they were pissed off. Mark was unhappy with their accommodation, and Abi resented the forced togetherness. And during the day, wherever they went, Corinne was always there.

'Do you think your parents still have sex?' Beth asked.

They were at the viewing spot by the ruined fortress high above Angles, just the two of them. Down below, Abi and Mark were on the terrace of the English tea shop, the brims of their sunhats casting their faces in shade. Eva had disappeared, scorning the company of the younger girls, and now Corinne was moody and distracted. Beth hated it when she got like this – resented her friend's persistent hankering after Eva's company. She longed for the days when it had just been the two of them, before her family had arrived and spoiled things.

'I don't know. Probably,' Corinne said. She shrugged as if it were no big deal. '*C'est normal, non?*'

It baffled Beth, the way Corinne could be blasé about something so huge.

'Your parents still do it,' Corinne remarked.

Beth didn't like to think about it, but she answered: 'Yes. I suppose so.'

'I heard them.'

'You did? When?'

The walls in La Grange were thin. She'd heard her father complain to her mother about waking in the night whenever Guy took a piss. 'I wish he'd lay off the sodding wine for once, give us all a night's sleep,' Mark had grumbled.

But no, Corinne corrected her, it was back in Dublin when the incident had taken place. Beth had a sudden picture of Corinne pressing her ear against the door of her parents' bedroom, eavesdropping on their intimacy. She wasn't sure how she felt about the idea.

'When do you suppose people stop having sex?' she asked.

Corinne shrugged and rooted about in her bag for her mobile phone which was ringing.

They often talked about sex, Corinne sharing her experiences. She was comfortable in her body, a casual sloppiness about her that Beth envied but couldn't imagine possessing. Corinne flirted with strangers when they were in the Proxi in the village, making eyes at guys queuing for lottery tickets and cigarettes, smiling coyly and twisting a strand of pink hair around her finger. When they sat together just the two of them in the village square, Corinne liked to point out different men and quiz Beth over whether or not she would sleep with them. It was just a game to pass the time, idle speculation. It didn't mean anything. Although Corinne had claimed to have slept with guys who were older than her. A lot older. Like Bruno.

She knew Corinne was talking to Bruno on the phone now. She could tell from the way her friend changed her voice, her tone, like she was sidling up to him, coquettish and suggestive. Her laugh was different, throatier, less natural. Even her mouth became pouty, her lips full. Beth had met him once on one of their walks. A tall, thin man who might once have been considered handsome but there was a wasted look about him now. He'd been wearing a singlet with jeans and while his arms were muscular in a wiry way, she could make out the mound of a pot belly above his waistband; he spoke with a drawl and his complexion was grey.

She heard her name being mentioned, Corinne asserting something, and she knew the arrangement was being made and felt a corresponding flip of nerves in her tummy. The view from where they were sitting seemed suddenly vertiginous, unreliable. She put out a hand on either side to steady herself against the rock.

'He said yes,' Corinne said with excitement. 'It is all arranged. Tomorrow evening. He'll be ready.'

Beth didn't say anything. Her silence made Corinne look up.

'Beth? Are you okay?'

'Yeah.'

'Hey. What's wrong?'

Beth thought of what her mother had told her, about not getting forced into anything she was uncomfortable doing. She thought of Bruno's nicotine-stained fingers. Fear sat like a stone in her belly. But then Corinne reached out and touched the back of her neck, her busy fingers moving over the scar.

'Relax. It's going to be beautiful. You'll see,' Corinne said. The soft reassurance of her voice and the light flutter of her touch working their dark magic. She only wanted to help. Beth desperately wanted to change, and Corinne understood this. A reinvention. It involved stripping away layer upon layer, making herself new. It frightened her but that was the whole point. Fear would awaken courage, and as Corinne always told her, courage was a choice.

'You will thank me for this later,' Corinne promised, a smile in her voice as Beth's nerves quietly vanished.

16

The heat was unbearable. There was a thermometer attached to the wall of the terrace in the lee of La Grange and Mark stared at it in disbelief. The mercury was nudging forty degrees and it was only mid-morning.

'*Le canicule*!' Corinne called out cheerfully.

She was sitting at the little wrought-iron table in the shade of the house, a woven bag collapsed by her feet. One foot was tucked up on the seat so she could rub oil into the skin of her calf which was deeply tanned. In her presence he felt pale and watery and acutely Irish.

'What's that?'

'Heatwave,' she translated, offering up her gap-toothed grin. She seemed perfectly unperturbed by the fug of hot air thickening around them.

'Putting on your sunscreen,' he remarked, and she laughed.

'Eczema,' she explained, capping the bottle with brisk efficiency and then getting to her feet.

She stretched out her leg, toes pointing like a dancer, and said: 'You see? It is very ugly, no?'

There was a small patch of scaly skin near her ankle, inflamed from scratching. The oil on her leg glistened in the sun. In her denim cut-offs and white T-shirt, she looked fresh and at ease while he was sweating. He had always thought her gawky, but now he saw that her legs were thin but shapely, her eyes lively, and he was struck momentarily by her coltish beauty.

'Does it itch?' he asked.

'A little. At night, mostly. Sometimes I wake up and it is bleeding.'

'Right.'

'It's best in the water. When I'm swimming, I don't feel anything. And my diving is spectacular!'

She giggled at her own boastfulness, pointing and flexing her foot, then twirling on the spot with arms outstretched. When she came back to face him, she dropped a small curtsy that was so obviously cute and flirtatious, he was momentarily disarmed.

'Take my photograph?' she asked suddenly, producing her smartphone from the back pocket of her shorts and handing it to him.

She issued him with some brief instructions and then stood with her arms stretched towards the sun, eyes closed, face lifted to receive the warm rays, smiling serenely. He took the picture and said: 'There.'

She came to stand beside him, cupping her hand around the phone to view the image. Satisfied, she told him she'd Instagram it, and then put her hand out and touched his forearm. Briefly, their eyes met, and he felt hot with confusion.

'I am roasting!' she declared loudly. Putting a hand to the back of her neck, she lifted her hair. 'I can't wait to get into the river!'

Inside the house, the others were getting their swim bags ready. There was a bathing spot further upstream that Val had promised to take them to.

'What about you? Will you swim?' she asked, smiling up at him. 'Will I show you my dives?'

But now, as Abi emerged from the house with her sunglasses pushed up into her hair, a tote bag slung over her shoulder, Mark felt embarrassed, like she'd caught him out.

'Actually, if it's all the same with you ladies, I think I'll give the river a miss today.'

'You never said,' Abi remarked, a look of mild irritation crossing her face. He tried to ignore it.

'Yeah. I thought I'd drive over to Châtellerault. There's that vintage car museum I was telling you about. I want to check it out. You don't mind, do you?'

'It's miles away. Are you sure you want to be sitting in the car in this heat?'

'We have air con. Besides, I like the idea of being in a museum – a cool, vaulted indoor space – rather than outside getting toasted. You know how easily I burn.'

After a second's hesitation, she said, 'Well, it's your decision.'

It was the heat, he reminded himself, as he caught the dismissive note in her voice. The heat was making them both irritable. That, and the forced proximity to these people. They were perfectly nice but Valentina's hippy-schtick was beginning to grate, and he found Guy a bit of a chore. Whenever he was alone with Abi she worried aloud about Beth. It seemed to Mark that as a couple they had little to talk about these days except their daughters – first Eva's exams, and now Beth's wayward direction. It was tedious. A few hours apart would be good for all of them, he told himself, the thought creeping into his head that more and more lately he wished to be alone rather than in his wife's company.

'Do you want a lift to the bathing spot?'

'No, that's all right. We'll walk. Don't trouble yourself.'

She said it brightly, but he caught the sting in it and Corinne did too. She was still stretching out her leg, but it was less playful now, more watchful.

'Can I come with you?'

He hadn't seen Eva coming out of the house, but now he

turned and saw her standing there with her hand raised to shield her eyes from the sun. She was squinting at him and there was something tentative and shy about her request.

'But I thought you were coming with us to the river?' Corinne said. She had straightened up and was watching Eva now with a look of naked disappointment.

But Eva just breezed past without looking, saying: 'Come on, Dad. Let's go.'

They drove in silence. Outside, the air shimmered with heat as the rental car clung to the corners of the roads wending through the French countryside. Mark's eyes passed over hay bales dotted across yellow fields, squat farmhouses that teemed with bougainvillea and climbing roses, their shingled roofs nestled between hedgerows. It was impossibly beautiful – a bucolic scene so steeped in colour, like something Roderic O'Conor might have painted. Mark spoke this thought aloud and Eva said: 'Yeah, I guess,' while leaning back in her seat with a sigh.

Ever since her exams had ended Eva had looked strained and thin. He worried about her pushing herself too hard.

'Thanks for coming with me. It's nice to have the company,' he told her.

'No worries.'

'I didn't know you were that interested in cars.'

'I'm not. Anything to escape Beth and her sidekick.'

Mark laughed. 'Are they getting on your nerves?'

'Please. They're insufferable. All that whispering to each other, the constant in-jokes. That inane giggling.'

She had a point, although for Mark it was something of a relief to see Beth happy, that she had found someone her own age to connect with after all the difficulties she'd had at school.

'The hair and the nose piercings?' Eva went on, scorn in her voice. 'What's that all about? Can't they be friends and still maintain their own identities? Why does Beth submit to her like that? It's so spineless and infantile, not to mention weird. I mean, doesn't it smack of infatuation to you?'

'Beth can be a little intense, I know—'

'Intense? Jesus, Dad, she nearly suffocated Lisa. The poor girl could hardly breathe with Beth attached to her like a limpet. Before their big bust-up, of course.'

He glanced across at her. 'Is that why they fell out? Because Beth was too attached?'

Briefly, Mark's mind flitted to an occasion when he had opened Beth's bedroom door to tell her that dinner was ready, and found Lisa with her back to the wardrobe, a look of mild alarm on her face, Beth fingering the ends of her friend's hair, touching them with what Mark could only think of as reverence.

'Fuck knows. I'm just saying that Beth has form,' Eva said. 'First Lisa, now Corinne.'

'Come on, love. I think you're getting carried away. They're just experimenting, that's all. Having a bit of fun.'

'Beth would do anything Corinne suggested. She's more like Corinne's puppy dog than her friend.'

He glanced across at her. He had the feeling that there was more to it than she was letting on.

'You don't like Corinne, do you?'

'She freaks me out. Always staring at me, constantly comparing me to her sister.'

'I think she means it as a compliment, love.'

'Please. She's a fake. And a liar.'

'That's a bit strong.'

'Is it? All the crap she comes out with – it's so boastful. And it can't possibly all be true.'

'Like what?'

'Like she can drive a car.'

'Okay. Fair enough.'

'Like her sister's at McGill.'

'Isn't she?'

'Come on, Dad. You saw the way Valentina looked when Mum mentioned about Anouk's scholarship. Like Mum had three heads. Corinne made it up the same way she makes everything up.'

Mark was silent, absorbing this new perspective. He thought about Corinne, wondering whether Eva's assessment of her was altogether fair. He brought to mind the upward tilt of Corinne's nose, the determined set of her chin. Something plucky about her that he liked. So what if she made up a few stories? It showed she had imagination and a type of bravery that he couldn't help but admire. And something else occurred to him: that Eva had no understanding of what it meant to grow up ashamed of where she'd come from. She knew nothing of the desperation involved in escaping the net of an impoverished childhood – he and Abi had made sure of that. Their eldest child was now a confident young woman, and while he took pride in that, he felt slightly alienated from her too. Her self-assurance was so different from his latent insecurities. Beth had always been the one mirroring his personality. And it struck him that Corinne, in her own way, was like him too. There was something in her that he recognized: a discomfort within her own family that she couldn't mask. He knew something of what that felt like.

'Beth's happy,' Mark said, trying to placate Eva. 'I say let's just indulge her, if only for the next few days. At the end of the holiday, we'll go home and then Beth and Corinne won't be hanging around together any more. My guess is that after a few months they'll have dropped all contact beyond being friends on Facebook.'

'Fine. It's your funeral.'

She was already slipping her iPhone buds into her ears, locking him out of her thoughts once more.

The museum was a giant industrial-looking complex on the banks of the river. According to the information booklet it had served as a munitions factory from the time of the Franco-Prussian War until it was abandoned in the 1960s. Now it was home to a museum charting the evolution of transport, but to Eva it still felt abandoned, a sepulchral silence filling the air, broken only by the sound of her flip-flops gently slapping on the concrete floor.

She was glad of the silence, glad of the opportunity to drift past the exhibits alone, her dad trailing some distance behind her. Eva had not wanted to come to France on this holiday. A group of her friends were going to Greece for a week, but when she had raised the suggestion her mother had pleaded with her. 'This might be the last opportunity we have to go away as a family,' she had said. Eva had to concede there was some truth to that. With her exams completed, she was excited about starting university, impatient for that part of her life to begin. She just needed to get through the summer first.

Earlier that morning, she'd FaceTimed Alicia who had looked blurry with sleep, her voice ragged from the night before. They talked a bit about the party, who'd been there, and Alicia had casually mentioned that she'd seen Callum.

'That creep,' Eva had said, and Alicia had made a face.

'Come on. He's not that bad.'

'How can you say that?' she'd asked, indignant. 'After what I told you?'

'Maybe you misread the situation, Eves. It sounds like he

was just messing. You know what guys are like. He probably thought you'd be impressed or something.'

'Oh yeah, cos that's really impressive. Waving a gun at me after he'd drugged me and fucked me.'

'It was half a tab. And we both know you wanted to fuck him too, so you can hardly plead lack of consent.' Alicia's voice softened then. 'Listen, he feels pretty bad about the whole thing. You know he really likes you.'

'You talked to him about it?' A coolness crept into her voice. She was watching Alicia's face carefully, the slide of her eyes as she looked away and then back again.

'Yeah, a little. I mean, it was a party – I talked to lots of people.'

'Where was Josh?'

Instantly, Alicia rolled her eyes. 'Don't mention his name to me. We are so done. Do you know, he applied to colleges in the UK and never fucking told me? And when I said I didn't think I could do a long-distance relationship, he just laughed and said, "Suits me," and walked off! Prick.'

Their conversation moved on to other gossip from the party and Eva let the moment pass. But it stayed: this new suspicion twitching around inside her.

Some of the cars in the museum were like tractors. Others were sleek and enormous, polished to a gleaming perfection. There were little information plaques about each vehicle, but after reading the first few, Eva gave up and allowed her mind to drift. Her thoughts turned to Ross and the row of cars that lined the front drive of the Campbells' house. Of all the people she knew, he would get the biggest kick out of this museum. Her father was admiring the vintage cars with a restrained speculative air, but she knew that if Ross was here, he would loudly exclaim over each new vehicle, peppering her with facts like a nerdy but excited kid unable to contain his passion.

She paused in front of a 1913 Peugeot Type BB – a fire-engine red convertible with black leather interiors, spokes on the wheels. She snapped a picture of it with her iPhone, and then opened up messages, wracking her brain for something smart and cool to type. Attaching the picture of the Peugeot, she typed: *Thinking of this for my first car. Does it get your approval??* then sent it quickly before she changed her mind.

Instantly, her cheeks flushed with colour at the thought of Ross's phone lighting up with her message. It was a bold move on her part – unmistakably flirtatious. Risky too given how he had pushed her away. Weeks had passed since they had spoken. Her last lesson with him, he had seemed detached, and she'd wondered if he was distracted by the memory of her lunging at him in his car after he'd rescued her from the party. She couldn't blame him for feeling uneasy. At the end of the lesson, when she was handing over the money, he'd said: 'Well, I think that's it, Eva. There's not much more I can teach you,' and she'd felt something plummeting within her – a horrible disappointment laced with panic. 'Your best bet now is to get yourself insured on either your mum's car or your dad's and then get out there and practise,' he'd told her. She'd stammered something about not feeling ready yet, but he'd waved her words away. 'You'll be grand,' he'd said before getting out of the car.

She couldn't blame him. Not after what had happened between them. Eva still found herself arrested by the vision of it returning to her again and again: that moment in his car when she had leaned in and kissed him. The awful confusion that followed as he pulled away from her, aghast. How deluded she must have seemed to him! How brazen! Even now, her embarrassment rose quickly to the surface bringing a rush of dampness under her arms, her heartbeat quickening.

Deep in her bag, she heard her phone ping and she hurriedly fumbled for it.

Sweet! I approve. Where r u?

A wave of feeling came over her: relief, excitement, a quickening of nerves.

Car museum in France. It would blow your mind.

She pressed send, biting down on the smile that kept surfacing while she waited. And sure enough, a new message pinged back:

Oh yeah? What else have they got?

She sent him a photograph of a 1947 Georges Irat MDU with a black body and soft white top. *Exquisite* was his verdict. To the picture of the grey 1950 René Gillet motorbike, he responded: *Cool.* She sent him images of a 1961 Dodge Lancer alongside an antique Total petrol pump; of the first electric car as well as early Vespas. His responses were immediate and positive. She felt the rhythm of their communication flowing backwards and forwards, wondered where he was right now, what he was thinking.

She had reached the final part of the car exhibits, and now she paused, an idea coming to her.

'Hey, Dad,' she said, waiting as he approached. 'Will you take a picture of me?'

'Sure.'

He reached out and took her phone and she pulled her hair from the elastic that was holding it back, then arranged herself so that she was leaning back against the 1962 Sunbeam.

'I don't think you're allowed to touch the cars,' her father said.

'Just take it quickly.'

He took a few different shots and when he handed the phone back, she flicked through them and selected the best.

'Who are you texting?' Mark asked.

'Alicia,' she lied.

The last part of the museum was dedicated to its history as an armaments factory. Glass cases held samples of swords and knives, rifles and pistols. Briefly, she thought of Callum standing over her, the gun in his hand. She remembered her heart pumping madly, the light gleaming on the barrel, and wondered at herself now for having felt so afraid.

Her phone sounded with an incoming text.

Beautiful, it read.

A split-second later, a second text: *The car's not bad either ;)*

She blushed to the roots of her hair.

Thoughts and feelings tangled inside her. What did it mean, this message? It was openly flirtatious – she wasn't imagining that. She remembered again the brief press of her lips against his, and how he'd pulled away, laughing but embarrassed. His response at the time had made her feel foolish – too young, too easily humiliated. But now this text changed things. Had he had time to reconsider? Was it possible he'd been thinking about her too? That he had missed her?

Eva knew that they were on the cusp of something. How she responded would determine everything. The image of Callum lingered until she dismissed it.

Callum Ferguson was just a child – a boy playing with his father's gun.

The feeling crept over her that she'd started something she shouldn't have, something illicit. Ross was a married man. There were rules about that kind of thing. But Eva was tired of being good and responsible. She was done with childish things. Drifting past the exhibits, she smiled to herself, a kind of recklessness taking hold of her. In the quiet of the museum, she thrilled to the danger.

17

Four of them went down to the river.

Val had promised that it was not far to the bathing spot, but with the heat and Valentina's leisurely pace, by the time they saw the break in the trees and the flash of sunlight on the green waters that flowed slowly beneath, the sweat had broken through the cotton of Abi's sundress, drenching her back and sticking to her underarms. The car park was jammed and as they approached, she could hear the screams and splashes of kids playing in the water, hip-hop music filtered through speakers high up in the trees. A crescent-shaped beach was carved into a bend in the river; the sand was littered with towels upon which teenagers sprawled listening to music, mothers flipping through magazines or paperbacks. When Valentina had suggested coming here, Abi had pictured somewhere peaceful and pastoral, a glade where they could cool down and relax, so she was relieved when Valentina picked her way past these bathers and led them up into the grass. She walked with purpose, until they reached a spot beneath the trees a hundred metres or so beyond the beach. The music and the screaming were still audible, but there was more privacy here.

'The water level is higher at this part of the river,' Valentina explained. 'So the girls can swim. And maybe us too?'

'Yes, I'd like that.'

The women put down their things, Valentina spread the rug over the grass near the bank and then pushed off her sandals and sat down, unpacking their picnic of bread and cheese and fruit. Closer to the water's edge, the girls were stepping out of their shorts.

Beth's swimming suit was cerise pink and she wore a loose white T-shirt over it. Abi's eyes automatically went to the scar at the base of Beth's neck. It curved like a sickle blade over her spine. Even now, two years after the operation, it still sent a mild shudder through her whenever she caught sight of it.

'Quit staring at me, Mum,' Beth said quietly, her tone terse, and Abi found herself embarrassed to be caught in that way.

'Why don't you take your T-shirt off?' she suggested. 'Let the sun get at your skin.'

'I'm fine,' Beth snapped and then seated herself on the bank, dipping her feet into the water.

'You're not going to wear that T-shirt while you're swimming, surely?'

'So?'

'For goodness' sake, love!' she laughed, slightly exasperated. 'That's just silly.'

'What's it to you if I do?'

'You've a lovely figure. I don't see why you're trying to cover it up – especially in the water—'

'God, just leave me alone, would you?'

Beth lowered her head, furious and embarrassed, and Corinne, sitting alongside her on the bank, dipped her feet in the shallows and grinned up at Abi. She was wearing a black bikini, spaghetti straps tied in two fussy little bows over the nubbed bones of her shoulders. She was skinny and tanned, shoulder blades sharp like webbed wings, droplets shimmering on her feet and calves as she lifted them in and out of the water.

'Just go, Mum,' Beth snarled.

'It's not easy, is it?' Val said, when Abi came to join her on the rug. She felt the woman's sympathetic smile.

'It's because of her scar,' Abi explained, feeling the need to account for her daughter's behaviour. 'That's why she wears the T-shirt. She's very self-conscious.'

'That is understandable.'

'I keep telling her that she shouldn't be embarrassed about it, but still.'

'She had scoliosis, Corinne says.'

'Yes. She was always a little hunched forward. I was forever telling the poor child to stand up straight, to put her shoulders back. But by the time she turned ten, we realized it was serious. That she would need an operation before she was thirteen.'

'It must have been frightening for her – poor child.'

'Yes, it was.' Then, Abi added: 'I wasn't there for it – the operation. I had wanted to be, but . . . Well, things went wrong.'

The week before the operation, Abi had flown to San Francisco for a series of work engagements. Tired and stressed, she'd started coughing in one of her meetings and couldn't stop. Her colleagues, alarmed, had sought medical attention for her. An X-ray at the hospital revealed she had pneumonia, and while it could be treated with antibiotics from the comfort of her hotel, it meant that she could not fly. And so, Abi was stranded in California for six extra days and Beth had her operation without her mother present.

'It felt like another instance of letting her down,' Abi admitted now.

'But that was outside of your control,' Valentina reasoned. 'You were sick. It was not your fault.'

'Yes.'

But it was also true that Beth had drawn closer to Mark afterwards. They were alike – thoughtful, quiet, introverted – attributes that in Mark she found sphynx-like and attractive.

But in Beth, these same qualities were often infuriating. She felt like her child was deliberately blocking Abi access to her life, like sheltering her schoolwork with the curve of her arm.

The operation had also brought Beth closer to Melissa, who'd spent long hours in the hospital with her. And even after Beth's recovery, she continued to rely upon her aunt, spending long afternoons in the little house at Beaufield Court, just the two of them. Abi supposed she should feel grateful that Beth had a responsible adult to confide in, but she felt her child pulling away from her, and was helpless to do anything about it.

All of these thoughts, she found herself admitting to now, speaking in a low voice to Valentina, both of them breaking off small pieces of baguette and nibbling.

'Can I tell you what the worst thing was? It was the way Beth never expressed her annoyance.' She shook her head. 'I knew she felt I'd let her down, but she just bottled it all up, refusing to confide in me. I know it's wrong to compare them, but if it had been Eva, she'd have made accusations, thrown a tantrum and we might have had a terrible row but then the air would be clear. Beth keeps everything locked up so deep inside it's like the atmosphere will always be clogged with these unspoken things.'

'It's hard being the mother of two daughters,' Val offered after a moment. 'Getting the balance right between them, trying to be fair and equal. And it just gets harder as they get older and start judging you.'

'Yes, exactly. I mean, we may love our children equally but that doesn't mean we understand them equally, does it?'

Valentina reached out and touched Abi lightly on the arm. 'You feel closer to Eva,' she stated simply.

'It feels wrong to admit that,' Abi said softly, idly picking at the grass by her feet. She was assailed by a sense of guilt even saying these words, and yet there was something about Valentina that invited these kinds of admissions.

'But why? It's only natural. After Anouk was born, I felt like my whole heart was possessed with love for her – that there was no space there to love another child. But then Corinne came along and it felt like I grew a whole new heart – a second heart full of love for her. But I have learned that you can have two hearts beating in your breast, but only one brain in your head. Sometimes, it's impossible to understand both.'

Abi smiled at the metaphor. It seemed a little touchy-feely. She imagined Mark turning away with disgust were he here. But Mark was not here, and Abi was still a little angry at him for that.

'Does Guy feel this way too?' she asked, and Val's face crumpled into an expression of derision.

'Oh no! No, it is completely different for men. Fatherhood does not come with the same baggage; I don't care what anyone says. They have no understanding of the worry – of the huge burden of guilt we carry around with us.'

Abi watched her daughter getting to her feet and wading unsteadily into the water. Ahead of her, Corinne was advancing into the depths, sweeping water over each of her shoulders before dropping down to immerse her whole body, grace in that one fluid movement, while Beth stood there and watched, shivering.

'Just because she keeps her thoughts and feelings hidden from you doesn't mean she doesn't love you, or that she doesn't feel loved,' Val said gently.

Abi felt a lump creep into her throat, her emotions rising suddenly to the surface.

She watched her daughter, pale and shivery, and knew she

was trying to pluck up the courage to surrender her flesh to the cold. And then Corinne rose up from the water, droplets pouring and sliding over her skin, and reaching out her hands, she took both of Beth's in hers. They stood like that for a moment, Corinne's mouth moving, uttering words that Abi could not hear, her gaze steady and intent. And then she stepped backwards and drew Beth into the water, a gasp rising up into the trees followed by a joyous shout. There was something so tender in that gesture, the lump burst in Abi's throat and she found tears were flowing hotly down her face.

'I'm sorry,' she said, leaning down so that she could sweep her wet cheeks with the hem of her dress.

She felt Valentina's hand coming to rest on her back and realized with embarrassment that her dress was drenched with sweat.

'You are under so much pressure,' Val said soothingly. 'Your work – the stress of your career – and then trying to be a mother to both of your children at this most difficult of ages. You push yourself too hard.'

'Do I? Sometimes I feel I'm not doing enough.'

'What more can you do? You are only human,' Valentina countered vehemently.

Abi managed a watery smile. 'I don't know what's come over me. This past year has been tough. Things with Mark . . . well, they're not always easy, especially after his sister died. And then Eva had her exams. And Beth . . . She was so lonely.' Clouds moved across her thoughts. Tentatively, she added: 'Troubled.'

Beside her, she felt Valentina waiting. It was curious, the desire that rose within her now to unburden herself of this information. She had never really discussed what Beth had done with anyone apart from Mark and the therapist they'd sent Beth to see. But something was pushing her to talk, and it didn't feel strange at all when she turned to Valentina and said:

'There was an incident last year at the school.'

The words came hesitantly at first, but Valentina's watchful silence drew her on.

'One afternoon last autumn, I got a call from the school principal. There'd been an argument between some of the girls. Beth was upset. She's not a very verbal child – she never has been. When people tease her she gets flustered. She's helpless to defend herself.'

Abi heard the words coming from her mouth and knew how pathetic they sounded – how delusional. But she still clung to the belief that what had happened was not really Beth's fault.

'We never did find out what was said that upset her. But it must have been bad because she just lost it. All hell had broken loose by the time the teacher got involved. Beth had a craft knife in her hand, and she was threatening one of the other girls with it. She was very upset. The teacher tried to calm her down and that's when she . . .' Abi paused – it was still shocking to her. 'She turned the knife on herself.'

Beside her she could hear Valentina's intake of breath but didn't dare look at her. Beyond, in the water, the girls were swimming in the sunshine, the wet cotton of Beth's T-shirt plastered to her body. That day in October seemed so distant. Surely there could be no harm in talking about it now?

'It wasn't a deep cut, thank God. She needed a couple of stitches, but that was all.'

'It must have been frightening for the other girls,' Valentina remarked, not unkindly, and it was true. Whenever Abi imagined the scene, she pictured the blood spreading through the fabric of Beth's shirt, her eyes wild, that knife in her hand. Helen Bracken told them afterwards that some of the girls had been hysterical.

'She was suspended from school for a week,' Abi said. 'We never did find out what led her to do such a thing. She was teased by some of the girls about her back, the way she was hunched. Even after the operation, she still got a lot of flak. Girls can be cruel. And in hindsight, things weren't great at home. I was away a lot with work, Mark was unhappy.'

Valentina listened but didn't interrupt, letting Abi's words run on.

'After the incident, I cut back on my travel. We found a counsellor for Beth and that seemed to help. The only thing we couldn't decide on was what to do about school.'

Mark thought they should move her – find someplace else to start over. But Abi disagreed. She told herself that it was a small blip and that things would return to normal. Besides, it was better for Beth to be in the same school as her older sister – to have Eva there to protect her. And deep down Abi felt that by moving her they were somehow admitting to Beth's culpability.

'I felt it was better for her to stay, thinking that it would pass.'

'And did it?'

'Yes and no. Things settled down. There were no more incidents. But all her friends fell away, even her best friend, Lisa, and they had been so close. Beth became isolated. We tried to help, encouraging her to invite some of the girls over, offering to take her to discos or concerts, wherever her peers might be hanging out.'

'It didn't work?'

Abi shook her head. 'She's been so lonely. Mark and I were beginning to think she'd never find a friend.'

She smiled now, a warm rush of feelings going through

her – gratitude, mainly. Any misgivings she had about Corinne seemed to quiet themselves. Abi looked towards the river and she saw the two girls bobbing about together. They were deep in the water, only their heads and shoulders visible. Beth had her arms slung around Corinne's neck, both of them slowly spinning. There was something beautiful about the image – a serenity to their poise, their held gaze, the gleam of sunlight on the water around them, their faces in shadow.

As Abi watched, the thought came to her: *they are in love.*

It came to her naturally and without shock or warning. It felt like something blindingly obvious and yet she hadn't seen it until now. She continued staring at them locked in their private clinch, impossible to look away. A cold feeling swept over her shoulders, the back of her neck, even though the sun was blistering down.

At that moment, her phone began to ring and she realized that she had been holding her breath as if waiting for something terrible to happen – an accident, a fall, swift and alarming.

Turning away, she rooted in her bag, expecting to see Mark's number or Eva's, but instead it was Richard, her boss.

'Congratulations,' he said as soon as she answered.

'Oh my God, really?' she laughed.

'Really. You deserve it. The best candidate for the job, hands down. No question.'

'Oh wow, that's wonderful! Thank you, Richard!'

Excitement coursed through her, delight making her forget the heat, her anxiety over Beth, all the troubles clamouring inside her quelled by this news. They talked for a few moments about the next steps – contract negotiations as well as advertising to fill the post she'd be vacating – and all the while her brain was whirring with thoughts of what this meant.

After the call, she clutched the phone to her chest, her

heart beating madly with excitement. When she looked up now the girls were standing hip-deep in the water. Abi watched as Beth lifted her arms and allowed Corinne to peel the wet T-shirt off her torso, lowering her head as the soaked cotton came away revealing her pink swimsuit, childish in comparison with Corinne's bikini. At first, Beth's arms went instinctively to cover her chest, but then the other girl said something Abi could not hear but knew the words spoken were quiet instructions, and Beth's hands fell away to her sides; she stood simply in the water, looking to Corinne, like a sinner offering herself for a benediction. Corinne had twisted the T-shirt into a rope, wringing the water out. She held it over her head and swung it towards the bank where it landed with a wet slap and then she eased herself back into the river, but her eyes were on Abi now, her face serious and calm, and Abi felt sudden anger bristling in her throat, a directionless alarm. She had seen the look of triumph in Corinne's eye — recognized it clearly. The girl had succeeded where Abi had failed. *I have the power now*, the look seemed to say.

From her place on the rug, Valentina was still and oblivious. She looked up at Abi, offering a benevolent smile. 'We must celebrate,' she said.

18

'*What?*'

Mark paused in the buttoning of his shirt and looked at Abi who was dressing on the other side of the bed. Evening light fell through the Velux windows above them. The room was very hot.

'You heard me,' she said, calmly dabbing perfume on to her wrists.

'Do I think anything's going on between them?'

'Yes.'

'As in . . . ?'

'As in a relationship of some sort. A sexual relationship.'

He could hardly believe what he was hearing.

'No, of course not!'

The words came out terse and more aggressive than he had intended. He caught the way Abi glanced at him and tried to pull back a little.

'They're just good friends, relaxed in each other's company. I wouldn't read anything more into it than that and nor should you.'

'I'm not saying she's gay—'

'Aren't you? Because that's what it sounds like.'

'She's a teenager, Mark. They like to experiment. And it's different for kids these days than it was when you and I were their age. They're more open about these sorts of things, more likely to question and explore their sexuality.'

It amazed him, the light conversational tone she was adopting.

'What makes you think they're having some kind of . . . romance?' He struggled with the word.

'Just something I saw today,' she answered in that same blithe tone. 'They were in the water together with their arms around each other. There was something so intense about it . . .' Her words drifted into the air between them, and then she stepped into her shoes and said: 'Well, you used the word "romance" – that's how it struck me. Romantic. Dreamy.'

He shook his head, having difficulty absorbing this.

'Did you say anything to Beth about it?' he asked.

'No.'

'Good. Let's not have her write out her gay confession just yet.'

'Why are you being so prickly about this?'

'I just think you're barking up the wrong tree. Give the kid a break.'

'All right. Fine.'

Her blitheness was starting to irritate him, and he was already cross with her. The news of her promotion, sprung on him barely an hour ago, was still percolating through his brain, stirring up all kinds of unwelcome emotions. It hadn't helped that he'd found out third hand. He and Eva had just returned from Châtellerault; he'd parked the car alongside the boathouse and was walking back towards La Grange when Corinne appeared beside him, half-hopping as she attempted to fit her foot into an espadrille while trying to catch up with him, giggling at her own clumsiness.

'Did you hear the news?' she asked, reaching out to grab hold of his arm, steadying herself against him as she successfully fitted the shoe over her heel.

'What news?'

'About Abi. She got that big job. We were having our picnic when she got the call.'

Confusion had swept over him and she'd seen it in his face.

'You didn't know?' she asked, the amusement draining from her features. Instead her eyes grew serious, searching his face for evidence she might have upset him.

'No, it's fine,' he stumbled.

She bit down on her lip. 'I'm sorry. I should not have said.'

He'd shrugged it off, but when he'd confronted Abi and she'd confirmed it, she'd been more upset about Corinne spilling the beans than sheepish over her own deception, keeping the promotion from him.

'What the hell does it matter who told me?' he'd hissed.

But she'd been quietly furious. 'I wanted to tell you myself.'

And now they had to go through the charade of this celebratory dinner with Val and Guy when all he really wanted to do was sit alone by the river with a book and a beer. His thoughts and emotions were all tangled up. He really didn't need this added complication – Abi's spurious and baseless imaginings about Beth and Corinne.

'We should keep an eye on her anyway,' Abi went on. 'There's no point putting her on the spot – you know how she is. If I'd said anything about it, she'd just have gotten all defensive and prickly and buried the truth of her feelings even deeper.'

'So why are you telling me?' he asked, although he knew the reason. Often, he felt he was used as a conduit between his wife and Beth, some attendant third party to their mother–daughter communication difficulties.

'In case you'd noticed something too.'

'Right.'

'Well? Have you?' She was standing now, fully dressed, a clutch bag in one hand. She'd made some effort, he could see, and it shocked him to discover that he felt not the slightest stirring of attraction for her in that moment.

'No, I haven't.'

He went back to buttoning his shirt, but he could feel her still watching him. Her blitheness had evaporated and when she spoke there was tension in her tone; something of his irritation had transferred to her.

'You are all right about this, aren't you?'

'About what?'

'My promotion.'

'Sure. It's great news.' But he kept his voice deliberately flat, and sensing her waiting, he added: 'I just wish you'd asked me first before accepting it, that's all.'

Even as he spoke, he knew the incendiary effect it would have.

'*Asked you?*' The words came from her mouth dripping with disgust. 'It's the twenty-first century, Mark. I don't need to ask your permission to accept the promotion that I have worked my ass off to get – that I deserve.'

'I'm not saying you needed my permission. And I'm not suggesting you don't deserve it—'

'Then what?'

He shook his head, angry at himself for getting drawn into this dispute when he would have preferred more time to think things through. But they were already in the middle of it. There was nothing to be gained from backing down.

'Well, have you thought about how it's going to affect me?' he put to her.

'Of course I have.'

'Really?'

'Yes!' She had one hand on her hip and her face bore a look of genuine confusion. 'Why are you acting like this? Why can't you be happy for me? Why can't you be proud of me?'

'I am proud of you. I just wish you'd discussed it with me

first instead of hiding it from me until you were sure it was in the bag and then presenting it as a fait accompli.'

'I wanted to surprise you,' she told him, unconvincingly. 'I thought you'd be pleased.'

She dropped her bag on the bed and sat down, shaking her head, nonplussed and annoyed.

'This promotion,' he continued, 'it's going to mean longer hours and more travel, right?'

'Probably,' she answered without looking at him.

'And who's going to be there for the girls while you're flying all over the world?'

'Oh, come on. It's not like they're toddlers any more, is it? Eva's about to head off to college, for Christ's sake.'

'What about Beth?'

'She's fifteen, Mark!'

'I know her bloody age,' he said, his voice low and level. 'If you're that concerned, we can get a child-minder or something.'

'Don't be ridiculous. I'm not talking about someone to pick her up from school. I'm talking about someone who'll be home in the evenings to make sure she eats a dinner and studies and gets to bed on time. I'm talking about parenting, Abi, not child-minding!'

'This is absurd. And sexist.'

'Don't even think about playing the gender card.'

'Why not? You know as well as I do that if the situation were reversed – if it was you with the chance to take your career up a gear – that you would expect me to fall over myself with gratitude and support.'

'Abi, you clearly didn't give my career a second thought.'

He watched her absorb the venom in his tone, then he continued:

'What about the project I'm working on with Andrew?'

'What about it?' she asked, and he thought she seemed more reticent now, something sneaky in the way she turned away at that moment and started looking through her bag, checking the contents.

'Filming starts in September. I'll be gone for the duration.'

'And how long will that be?'

'Six weeks. A couple of months maybe.'

'Is that set in stone?' she asked.

'Pretty much.'

'I don't remember us agreeing to that.' She looked up at him now, and he saw her jaw set, readying herself to dig her heels in.

'I told you about the project months ago,' he insisted. 'I've been working on plans, drawings – I've even shown them to you. How can you be so obtuse about this?'

'I'm not being obtuse, I'm being realistic.'

'Realistic?'

'Well, have you signed a contract yet? Has Andrew actually paid you for any of this work?'

'No, not yet.'

His voice lost some of its stridency, and she raised her hands in a gesture that implied she'd proven her point. It infuriated him. 'What?' he demanded.

'This always happens,' she cried, exasperated. 'Andrew comes home, you meet for pints, and then for weeks afterwards you tinker with ideas for whatever grand project he's boasted to you about, fooling yourself that it's actually going to come to something, and always – *always* – it fizzles out. Something happens: the funding is pulled, or there's a schedule clash, or Andrew falls out with the director . . . I've lost track of all the times he's let you down. How can you still fall for it?'

The blood flowed hotly up into his head, and he moved quickly to the door. Her accusations of gullibility galled him, and yet part of him wondered secretly if she was right. Had he been fooling himself, thinking there was a firm commitment when Andrew might only have been half-serious, an offer made out of drunkenness and pity?

'Don't get me wrong,' Abi said now, keeping him in the room, 'I'm happy to see you reviving your interest in work. And with this promotion, well, the difference it will make to our finances is substantial. Don't you see? You'll be able to pick and choose which projects you take on now. Ones that are closer to home, perhaps – that fit around our lifestyle.'

'That fit around *your* lifestyle, you mean.' The words came out sounding acidic, but he couldn't help it. 'Why must everything always revolve around you?'

'That's unfair.'

'Is it? You call the shots. And I think you like that.'

'This is ridiculous.'

'We had an agreement—'

'Oh yes. Our agreement. You know, most people would look at our situation and think you got a pretty sweet deal, Mark. I work long and hard to pay for our house, our holidays, our cars, school fees, the tennis club—'

'And we all have to bend over backwards in gratitude—'

'Gratitude?' She spat the word at him. 'I don't get gratitude! I get sullenness and resentment from the girls, and from you, I get bloody martyrdom!'

'What?'

'St Mark the martyred husband. Minding the kids, doing the shopping, cleaning the house – and never letting me forget the fact of it. Jesus Christ, expecting me to get down on bended knee and give thanks—'

'Oh, that's bullshit!'

They were both shouting now, and he could feel the vein pulsing in his temple.

'Admit it, Abi – our arrangement suited you.'

'Yes, it did. And I have no problem admitting that. I mean, let's be pragmatic here.'

'How?'

'Well, the fact is that your work is unreliable. It comes in spurts. It's just the nature of the business that you're in. Like it or not, my career is steady and well paid.'

'Better paid, you mean,' he said acidly.

Her jaw tensed; her eyes grew cold.

'Yes, I earn more than you do. And I don't see why I should have to apologize for that.'

'It would be a damn sight easier to swallow if you could be a bit less smug.' The words were out of his mouth before he could stop them. 'And can we please put to bed this notion of a so-called "agreement"? When the hell was it decided that my career should take a backseat to yours? Because I don't ever remember us sitting down having *that* conversation. You just ploughed ahead with your career and assumed I'd row in behind you. But that's you all over, Abi. Unilateral decision-making to suit your own needs, expecting the rest of us to just sail along behind you.'

'That line sounds rehearsed,' she remarked, and he felt his cheeks redden. It was unnerving the way she could do this: hold up a mirror to expose his petty failings.

'I'm not going to pretend this isn't something I've thought a lot about,' he began, but before he could go on, Abi let out a shriek of impatience and fury.

'God! That is just so like you! Thinking about it but not *talking* about it! You sit in your little man-cave, conducting these arguments in your head while you allow years to pass before actually opening your mouth to tell me what you're feeling! Don't you see how unhealthy that is?'

'What difference would it even make? Are you honestly

trying to tell me you'd alter your behaviour if I was more open about my unhappiness?'

Her eyes flared. 'You know, I'm really sick of this notion of yours that somehow I am to blame for your unhappiness. As if your miserable childhood is my fault. Because that's what it all stems from, Mark – your insecurity, your obsession with our house, with keeping up with the neighbours—'

'I am not obsessed with the house!'

'Oh, please! If it wasn't for the house, I think you'd have left me already—'

'If it weren't for the girls, I'd have left you!' he snapped, the words flying out of his mouth before he thought to check them.

She stared at him, her breath caught, and he felt his own heart kick out in sudden fear.

'What are you saying?' she asked, half-laughing but it was a nervous laugh.

Had he meant to say that? Even now, he couldn't be sure.

An image came to him then – the two of them, standing together on a precipice, peering over the edge, wondering which one of them was going to jump first. Vast tufts of cloud obscuring the drop, but the temptation was there. Go on. *Go on.*

Words came into his head. A notion of how to wound her. The threat pulsing in his temples.

'I'm not going to leave you,' he said quietly.

Shakily, she answered: 'Well, thank God for that—'

'—until Beth's finished school,' he added quickly.

He met her eyes, saw the shock registering, and something shot through him that might have been fear, but also might have been a thrill of excitement. Because that's what you got when you leapt off the precipice: a rush of adrenaline to shave the ragged edges off the terror.

'Don't be ridiculous,' she told him, that half-laugh coming again, a horrible nervous hiccup.

From outside on the terrace, he heard Valentina's sing-song voice calling up to them.

He glanced at his watch. 'It's getting late,' he said. 'We'd better go.'

'You can't just leave things like this!'

He shot her a look loaded with unspoken grievance.

'I'm not the one who made this arrangement,' he reminded her. 'I don't even want to go out with these bloody people. Not that you'd even considered that.'

He left the room before she could have a chance to reply.

You've gone very quite. No more pics?

Eva was lying on her bed contemplating this message when her dad put his head around the door.

'We're heading out now, love,' he told her. 'You're in charge, okay?'

'Sure.'

Through the open door, she caught a glimpse of her mother passing behind him, heard the thunder of her footsteps on the stairs. She'd heard the rumble of their argument through the wall, the words inaudible but the tone unmistakable. Her parents hardly ever fought – her father was too repressed and her mother too slippery to pin down. Instinctively, Eva rolled her eyes. She wasn't in the mood for any of that crap. Her father was still hovering in the doorway, trapped by his indecision.

'What?' she snapped.

'Keep an eye on those two downstairs, will you?'

'I'm not their babysitter.'

'I know. Just . . . if you notice anything . . .'

His voice drifted. The look he was giving her was hapless and pathetic.

'Fine,' she said. Satisfied, he backed out of the room. A minute later she heard the front door slam.

Returning her attention to the text, she considered how to respond. Ross had misspelled 'quiet' which was funny and sort of endearing, although she'd have scoffed had it been anyone else.

No more cars, she typed, then sent.

A few seconds later, his response came back: *Doesn't have to be of cars*.

She sat up a little on the bed.

Where are you? Still in the pub? she asked.

Back home now, came the answer.

She wondered if Becca was there. A guilty flush passed through her as she pictured them in their kitchen, Becca tossing a salad, little Jo making a jigsaw on the floor, Ross beside him pretending to play while secretly texting Eva.

But then her phone pinged again.

All alone here. Looking for distraction ;)

Her heart beat faster. She leaned forward and bit her lip.

She knew what he was asking. She wasn't a fool. But her feelings towards Ross were complicated – a mixture of tenderness and forbidden longing and trembling excitement. She wanted him to woo her – to make her feel special. And yet this was special, wasn't it? There he was, alone in his house on a Saturday afternoon thinking of her. Not his beautiful wife, but her, Eva. It was clear from his texts that he didn't think of her as some stupid kid he gave driving lessons to who occasionally babysat his son. What had passed between them that afternoon was charged with a sexual current. He had opened a door and now she stood on the threshold, waiting to be ushered in.

Eva got off the bed, slipped down on to the floor, her back against the wall. Light was angling in through the open window, casting shadows over the bare boards, the rough plaster. Beneath her T-shirt, she unclipped her bra and slipped it off. The T-shirt was thin cotton with a wide neck that fell over her shoulder to expose it. A simple adjustment as she leaned forward, the camera-phone angled above her, revealed the delicate curve of her breast, the barest shadow of a nipple. Keeping her head turned to the side, her eyes averted, she allowed herself the slightest smile, then clicked.

She did this a few times, playing around with the filters. Finally, having made her choice, she held her breath and pressed send.

As soon as she did it, she was seized by a feeling of intense regret. Scrabbling for her bra, she clipped it back on, re-arranging herself. The room was still hot, but she felt cold now, a dozen questions filling her head: What if that wasn't what he'd been asking for? Had she taken things too far? What if Becca saw it by accident? All of these questions crawled around inside her brain – she felt itchy with them.

When the door to her bedroom opened and she saw Corinne leaning a shoulder against the frame, she almost welcomed the intrusion, anything to escape her own thoughts.

'Hey. What're you doing?' Corinne gave her a lazy smile.

'Nothing.' Eva tried to keep her voice nonchalant, but she could hear the jump of nerves in it.

'We're going out,' Corinne said. 'Will you come? There's something I want to show you.'

Eva didn't really want to spend any time in their company, but the thought of being alone, waiting for Ross's response, filled her with despair.

'Come on,' Corinne said in her wheedling tone. 'I need you to do something for me.'

19

There were only two places in the village to buy alcohol: the *tabac*, and the Proxi – a small supermarket situated up a side street behind the *boulangerie*. Beth and Corinne waited outside by the shelter where discarded cartons and crates were stored, while Eva went into the Proxi with the money. Wasps buzzed around them, attracted by fruit rotting in the bottom of a crate. Beth swatted them away, then kicked at a stone on the pavement.

'What's wrong?' Corinne asked. She had her eyes closed, her head leaning back against the shop window.

'Nothing.'

Corinne smiled lazily, then opened her eyes. 'Tell me.'

'Why'd you have to ask her along?' Beth grumbled.

'I already told you. We need her to buy the alcohol.'

'I know, but—'

'What?'

The truth was Beth didn't much want the booze. She'd have been as happy just smoking a few cigarettes between the two of them, maybe taking a couple of bottles of her dad's beer. She resented Eva's part in all this – had been surprised, in fact, when her older sister had agreed to the plan considering how her response to anything from Beth or Corinne was usually one of disdain.

'You're nervous?' Corinne asked.

Beth shrugged. 'A little, I guess.'

'Don't be.' Her smile broadened and she pushed herself away from the wall, her right hand reaching out to touch

Beth's shoulder, fingertips brushing against the skin of her neck. 'It will hurt a little, but it will be beautiful – I promise.'

Hope kindled in Beth's heart. Then Eva emerged into the evening sunlight, a paper bag holding her purchase, saying:

'So. Where to now?'

It was too far to walk, but Corinne seemed confident of a lift. They trudged along the side of the road with their hands out and soon enough a van pulled over and the three of them piled in, Beth squeezed against the window feeling the heat from Eva's thigh alongside her own. Corinne rattled away in rapid French to the driver, a middle-aged man in overalls, oil stains covering his hands and forearms. The van reeked of cigarettes and sweat.

'How're we going to get back?' Eva murmured as the van picked up speed, but Beth ignored her and stared outside.

The countryside was a blur, her mind's eye turned instead on that moment earlier in the day when they'd gone down into the water together.

'Why do you wear this?' Corinne had asked, tugging at the wet cotton of Beth's T-shirt clinging in folds against her skin.

'So my shoulders don't get sunburnt,' she'd answered, but Corinne had known it was because of the scar.

Even before the operation, Beth had hated the idea of people looking at her, the horrible curve in her back, the solid mass of flesh around her stomach like the trunk of some thickened tree. Her curves were in the wrong places – her body an amorphous shape that she despised. In a way, she was grateful for the scar – it gave her the perfect excuse to hide herself away while others around her chose to bare all in bikinis, labouring to perfect their flawless tans.

'Liar,' Corinne had said, her eyes flaring with humour.

She'd been inches away from Beth, her arms gently moving through the water. The river washed around them, brackish and cool. Beth, crouched in the shallows, could feel the silt of the riverbed beneath her toes.

'Come,' Corinne had said, beckoning her out into deeper waters.

Corinne's arms shone with sunlight catching the droplets on her skin. Her breath held the faint whiff of something sweet. Beneath the damp folds of Beth's T-shirt, she had felt Corinne's finger gently tracing the silvery white line of her scar. Distantly, she was aware of her mother on the bank, watching, always watching. But the nerve endings in her body rose to the touch. She raised her arms and allowed Corinne to peel the T-shirt off, and in that moment, it felt like shedding skin.

'*You don't know, oh-oh, you don't know you're beautiful,*' Corinne sang, her rasping voice yielding to a pure, sweet tone.

Beth had wanted to stay in that moment – the gentle movement of water, Corinne's fingertips, their legs tangling below the surface. She felt the full force of Corinne's attention, and didn't want the moment to ever end.

The van braked suddenly. Corinne said:

'This is it.'

They climbed down from the van and watched it speed away.

'Where are we?' Eva asked, frowning as she looked around at the scrubby fields, hazy in the evening sunlight.

'Come on, it's this way.'

Corinne led them towards a low house with a bowed roof that sat alone among a thicket of nettles and briars. Tiles were missing in patches from the roof. It appeared derelict until a blond-coated dog limped out into the yard, her handsome features drooping and sad. Corinne bent to rub her muzzle and the dog suffered her attentions for a moment then turned and moved away, revealing a dark streak of shit running down her flank, ribs flashing beneath loose skin with every painful hop.

'Gross,' Eva remarked, disgusted.

'She's got cancer,' Corinne declared, shrugging with indifference, before disappearing through the open doorway.

Beth and Eva hung back. Nerves announced themselves in Beth's stomach now they were actually here. The prospect of what she was about to do gave her pause. It was too real, too immediate. From inside the house came the high-pitched yelping of a small dog.

'What are we doing here?' Eva asked her, and Beth felt the ripple of her sister's unease inspiring her own jittery reflex.

But then Corinne was leaning out the door, smiling her encouragement. 'Come on! He's waiting.'

Brave was not something you were – it was something you decided. That was what Corinne had told her, again and again. Courage was a choice. Beth tried to hold on to that thought as she moved past Eva and stepped into the gloom.

The reek was the first thing she noticed. The house smelt of wet dog. Then, as her eyes became accustomed to the dimness, she saw that they were in a living room, sparsely furnished. The mantelpiece bore a garland of dulled tinsel. Snuffling and squealing on a bunched-up blanket on the floor was a litter of pups. Beth counted seven in all.

Corinne bent down and scooped one of them up, exclaiming over it with delight.

'Oh, they are so cute! I want one!' she announced, hungrily nuzzling the little puppy as it scrambled in her embrace.

Beth could have ignored the squalor if Eva hadn't been there. If it had just been her and Corinne, she might have been able to shrug off the conditions of the place. But instead she saw the horror in her sister's unguarded expression and saw the room through Eva's unblinkered gaze: the stack of dirty plates on the countertop, the array of squashed cans and empty beer bottles that littered the surfaces of the room. A tatty sofa bore the sprawling weight of a huge black dog with weeping eyes, ropes of saliva swinging from his jaws; another dog – clearly the mother of the pups – prowled around the kitchen, slack teats swinging, claws clacking on the filthy lino. There was a thick, dense, stupefied air to the place – even the dogs seemed sedated – and when a toilet flushed in a distant room, the sound startled her. Seconds later, Bruno appeared, hitching his jeans up over narrow hips and buttoning his fly.

Instinctively, Beth took a step back while Bruno exchanged kisses with Corinne. He put the cigarette he'd been smoking back between his lips and then took the puppy from her arms, pinching hold of the skin at the back of its neck and holding it aloft. He spoke but Beth couldn't understand what he was saying – words tripping and slurring into one another. She understood it was to do with the dog's masculinity, something coarse and rude from the growled tone of his delivery, the way Corinne squealed with horrified laughter, clutching at his arm as she leaned forward.

Given what he was about to do to her, Beth looked at Bruno more closely, taking in the T-shirt clinging tightly to his narrow frame, a chain looping from the back pocket of his jeans to the belt hoop at the front. When he laughed, he looked like a goofy farm-boy, but then he'd stop abruptly, as if remembering the persona he was adopting, sweeping the long fringe out of his narrowed eyes, the cigarette held to his mouth between middle finger and thumb.

Eva was making her own silent assessment. The spatters of tomato sauce speckling his T-shirt, the reptilian eyes darting from one girl to the other in a speculative way that made her feel nervous. He kept snorting loudly, rubbing the underside of his long, thin nose with the heel of his hand. It was disgusting. She glanced at her sister whose face was blank.

'Do you have any idea what's going on here?' she whispered.

Beth wouldn't look at her. 'You'll see,' she said.

One of the puppies was pissing on the floor, and Bruno swore, bending to snatch the puppy by the scruff of its neck. Holding it aloft, he showed it to Eva, saying in heavily accented English:

'You like my little doggies? Eh?' Then sniggered at the disdainful look she shot back, Corinne joining in the laughter.

'You would like to 'old 'im?' he persisted, advancing towards Eva, the pup yowling.

'No, thank you.' The primness of her response seemed hilarious to him.

'Take 'im, 'e likes you,' he persisted, so close to her now she could smell his fetid breath, the stink of his armpits. He pushed the puppy against her folded arms and Eva exploded.

'I don't want your fucking dog!'

Bruno held her furious gaze for a moment, then dropped the puppy on the ground. It scuttled under the sofa and hid there.

'It's okay,' Corinne reassured Eva. 'He's just joking.' But the mood in the room had changed.

'*Laquelle?*' Bruno asked sharply and Corinne nodded at Beth.

Eva watched uneasily as this guy with the haunted face, the druggy drawl, conducted a hushed conversation with Corinne. She didn't understand much beyond the sense that some kind of negotiation was underway. Beyond them, Beth stood in silence, grave and wraithlike in the gloom as Bruno turned his gaze back on her. He flicked a finger impatiently.

'*Enlève ton T-shirt*,' he said.

Beth's eyes snapped to Corinne who simply nodded at her to obey. Alarm jumped in Eva's throat as she watched her sister shyly shedding her top.

'Hey!' she said, catching Beth by the arm. 'What are you doing?'

But Beth just wrenched away from Eva's grip and moved closer to Bruno, offering herself up for inspection. Thin and shivering, knobs of bone protruded from her spine as her shoulders slumped forward. She looked so pale and vulnerable, standing there in her grey bra, the rounded cups barely filled by the meagre mounds of her small breasts. Bruno ran a fingertip over the ledge of Beth's collarbone and Eva saw her flinch.

'Would someone please tell me what the fuck is going on?' Eva asked, her voice shrill with fear.

Corinne had put the puppy down and she stepped towards Beth, urgency coming into her voice as she said: 'Remember. Brave is what you choose. Brave is what you can be.'

But Beth didn't look brave. Terror flashed in her eyes.

'I don't know,' she said, her voice barely audible.

Bruno had moved away from her now, stepping into the next room. Briefly, Eva's eyes followed him. Through the open door she saw an unmade bed, a sour look to the tumble of sheets. Her eyes snapped back to Beth.

'Put your top on,' she commanded. 'We're leaving.'

Beth's eyes met hers and for a fleeting moment, she saw the gratitude in them – she wanted to be saved. And perhaps Corinne saw it too for she grabbed hold of Beth's arm, and with her other hand she pinched the skin, gave it a hard, sharp-nailed twist. Beth cried out, shocked to tears by the sudden savagery.

'That is all you will feel,' Corinne hissed with angry urgency as she brought her face close to Beth's. 'Nothing worse than that. The pain will be worth it, I promise you. You trust me, right?'

Beth nodded, cowed with shock but her eyes still tearful.

Bruno was back in the room with them, a leather pouch in his hand. He went now to a low table with a lamp on it and crouched there to flick the switch. The sudden light in the room was jarring, casting a cold, harsh spotlight on the scuffed wood of the bench. Eva felt within her a tremendous urge to leave, and yet she was compelled to look as he unzipped the pouch, unfolding it to reveal a set of needles.

'It's all right,' Corinne was whispering to Beth, leading her forward.

'*Est-elle sûre?*' Bruno asked, fixing Beth with a frank stare while snapping on latex gloves.

Dumbly, she nodded, then knelt down.

'Jesus Christ, Beth! Are you out of your fucking mind?' Eva was beside herself, nerves, fear, jumping in her throat.

But Beth didn't answer. Something had come over her – a sort of serenity, like she was closing herself off from Eva, from the grotty surroundings of the place, from everything except this man and her own decision.

'It won't hurt,' Corinne told her, gently rubbing her arm.

'No, Beth, I can't let you do this,' Eva insisted, grabbing sharp hold of her arm, but this time it was Bruno who pushed her away.

A hard shove; Eva stumbled backwards, feeling the queasy softness underfoot, the shrill scream of the puppy. '*Eh! Attention!*' Bruno shouted.

Her heart kicked out in fright, but still she tried with Beth.

'Don't be so fucking stupid. Mum and Dad will kill you.'

'I don't care.' Beth's voice sounded dreamy and faraway.

Eva wanted to slap her. To shake some sense into her.

'It's fine! It's okay!' Corinne laughed but it was a nervous trill.

'You're seriously going to do this?' Eva persisted with her sister. 'Here? In this hovel? You could get hepatitis. You could get HIV.'

But Beth ignored her. She turned away and offered up her flesh.

'I'm calling Mum,' Eva said, hurrying away from them.

She stumbled out into a small clearing that might have once been a garden. A clump of nettles brushed against her bare calf – a sudden rash of stinging lashed her skin. She fumbled in her bag and found her phone. Thumbing the screen, she saw a message there – she hadn't heard the ping of receiving it – but she could see that it was from Ross.

A snap of dry grass underfoot, and she turned and saw Corinne coming towards her.

'Don't call your mother,' she said quickly, her voice coming out in a breathy rush. 'It will be okay – you'll see. She needs this.'

Eva ignored her, inputting her pin.

'I needed it too,' Corinne went on. 'I wasn't always brave, you see. But Anouk brought me here. She knew that I needed to do this. And Bruno is careful. He knows what he's doing.' She pulled up the hem of her vest to show her own tattoo. An inked flower, Eva glanced at it, unimpressed. She didn't like tattoos or body piercings, thought them cheap. But Corinne didn't notice the look of disgust. 'Anouk knew that it would be good for me—'

'Well, I'm not like your fucking sister,' Eva said, cutting her off. 'I actually care about my sister's health.'

The expression on Corinne's face faltered, the light in her eyes dimming. 'Don't say that—'

'All this talk about Anouk – the way you go on and on

about her. It's so fucking boring.' Eva turned away from her. 'And as for your deranged notion that I am somehow like her. Please! You might mean it as a compliment, but she sounds like a complete asshole. Self-centred, erratic, a fucking nutcase—'

Eva felt the bite of nails in her shoulder, the stinging scrape of them. Corinne snatched the phone from her grasp. It happened so fast, Eva hardly had time to react. And there was Corinne, backing away from her, one hand held out, warning Eva to keep her distance, but Corinne's eyes were on the screen, widening as she scrolled through the message.

'What are you doing?' Eva asked, her voice high-pitched with alarm.

Eva lunged, but Corinne was quicker.

She turned and flung the phone high into the air. The cry caught in Eva's throat as she watched the arc of it sailing into the distance, landing somewhere among the long grass in the next field.

A surge of fury and despair rose up through her.

'You bitch!' she cried, swinging around to face Corinne. 'What the fuck did you do that for?'

Corinne's eyes were hard grey pebbles. Cool and impassive, she returned Eva's stare.

'They're still going to find out,' Eva said, her voice thick with anger and panic. 'And when they do, they'll kill Beth, and then they'll make sure you never see each other again. This stupid idea will end your pathetic crush on each other, but both of you are too dumb to have thought that through.'

'They won't find out unless you tell them.'

'I will tell them.'

Corinne's eyes flickered over her face. 'No, you won't,' she said. 'Or I will tell them about you and that man. The married neighbour. Sending him pictures of yourself. Think how shocked they will be.' Her voice was soft, playful, but her expression was hard.

Fury turned quickly to shame.

'You wouldn't dare.'

'Wouldn't I?'

Corinne drew herself up and smiled sweetly at Eva.

'Watch out for snakes,' she said softly, already turning away.

20

The restaurant was called l'Orangerie and it was situated
in the heart of a village some forty kilometres away. Guy
drove, Mark in the passenger seat alongside him, a moody
masculine silence between them. In the backseat, Valentina
chattered away, making pleasant little asides that breezed past
Abi. It was as if she was observing the scene from afar. Four
strangers in a car travelling sinuous roads over unfamiliar
terrain.

Don't be ridiculous, she'd told him, that horrible nervous
laugh escaping from her throat. As if what he'd said couldn't
possibly be real or serious. Some awful joke of his.

But now, with the evening sunlight in her eyes, the devas-
tating blow of his words revisited her. Abi's head swam,
nausea rising in her stomach. She had no idea how she would
get through the meal.

At the restaurant, they were shown to a table in the corner
of a large courtyard. Leafy potted plants gave the space a
jungle feel, the heat of the day cooling between the brick
walls and the tiled floors, a glass ceiling overhead – hard surfaces that trapped the din of conversation and intensified it
into a storm of words.

When Guy suggested champagne, she was thrown, and
when he raised his glass and announced: 'To your great success,' she'd had to blink away her confusion, the memory of
her promotion obscured now by the sense of crisis inside her.

The champagne slid coolly down her throat.

'This dinner is on us,' Abi said, her voice sounding shaky

to her, so she leaned forward, making an effort now to regain control of her emotions. 'You have been so kind in organizing everything for us. This is our way of saying thank you.'

Guy, who was sitting next to her, said: 'As you wish,' then shook his napkin free of its fastidious bunching and spread it across his lap.

Valentina explained: 'We discovered this place not long after we first moved to this part of France. Oh, but it has been so long since we last came here.'

'There was no point,' Guy declared, his eyes fixed on the menu. 'Why bring an anorexic to a restaurant?'

A shadow crossed Valentina's face. 'Please, Guy,' she said, her voice tight and cool in a way that Abi had not heard before.

'It's not as if it's a surprise to them,' Guy went on. 'You knew this, right?'

His eyes flicked to Abi.

'Corinne is skinny, certainly. But I didn't think she was anorexic.'

'She is skin and bone. No meat at all.'

'All the young girls are thin nowadays. Am I right?' she asked the table.

Her tone was light and amused. She allowed herself a glance across the table at Mark, hoping to draw him into the conversation. But his eyes were fixed on the placemat in front of him, his face inscrutable, and she felt a further push of resentment at his lack of engagement, leaving it to her to carry the conversation.

'She doesn't eat – she picks,' Guy pressed on. 'A small pick at this, a tiny pinch of that.' Little mincing gestures accompanied his description.

'But she seems interested in food,' Abi persisted. 'When she was with us, there were several occasions where she cooked for us. She went out of her way to prepare us a meal. We were really impressed, weren't we, Mark?'

'Oh yes. I'm sure it was quite the performance,' Guy said drily. 'But it's just a ruse. A smoke-screen to disguise her illness.'

'That's terrible,' Abi remarked. 'It's an illness that's just so hard to understand, isn't it? How to treat it, what caused it in the first place—'

Mark said: 'It is always the fault of the mother.'

There was a single moment of shocked silence while his words reverberated around the table. Valentina's eyes filled with swift hurt. Guy sat forward in his chair.

'He's joking,' Abi said quickly, seeking out Mark's eyes with her own searching glance, but he picked up his fork, turned it over in his hand as if examining the tines. She wanted to kick him under the table.

Left to explain, Abi went on: 'It's a family joke. You see, when Beth was a baby, I went to Vienna on a business trip, and at a dinner on the last night, I ended up sitting next to the husband of one of my Austrian colleagues. He was a child psychiatrist. His patients, he explained, were aged between zero and eighteen. "Zero?" I asked. "Why would a baby need a psychiatrist?" And he gave me a list of problems: crying excessively or not crying at all, refusing to sleep, refusing to feed. But after running through this list, he looked at me with a dry expression, and his words I will never forget. He said: "Of course, it is always the fault of the mother."'

Guy laughed, a deep chuckle, and Val cried out: 'But that is ridiculous! And such a typically male response – blaming the woman. You didn't believe him, I hope?'

'No, of course not!'

But Abi remembered how, when eventually she'd arrived home to Ireland, the baby had caught a bad cold and developed a furious rash all over her body. Mark had thought it was a reaction to the formula milk, but Abi couldn't help feeling it was more than that. The baby refused her breast – she wouldn't even take a bottle from Abi, only Mark, wailing whenever her mother came near.

She's mad at you, Eva had stated – three years old, sitting at the kitchen table, her hair in bunches, scribbling with her new crayons.

Sometimes Abi felt like Beth was still mad at her. That she'd been mad at her mother ever since.

'I made the mistake of telling Mark what that psychiatrist had said,' she explained. 'And ever since then, it's become a family joke. *It is alveys ze fault of ze mozer*,' she added, with a smile.

But Mark hadn't used a German accent when he'd said it. He hadn't smiled sardonically. He hadn't smiled at all. The look he'd given her was cold, and the words hadn't sounded funny.

Across the table, Mark watched as Guy ordered a Sancerre for the table, giving a brief nod of acknowledgement when the waiter presented the bottle. He continued to observe the man as he swirled the wine in his glass and tasted. Guy had a heavy-jowelled face like that of a morose-looking dog, a slightly pop-eyed look about him that suggested a thyroid problem. The way he spoke about his own daughter was infuriating. Sure, the girl was slight and skinny, but so was her mother, for God's sake.

He knew his irritation with Guy was a by-product of his larger fury with his wife.

Their orders arrived and he watched her prise a buttery snail flecked with parsley from its shell and pop it into her mouth, making a little humming sound of delight. Her strained optimism that evening was grating on his nerves. All that steely cheerfulness – couldn't she see how transparent it was? He ate quickly, barely tasting the food, mulling over the rashness of his announcement to her earlier that evening. What had he been thinking? Small ripples of panic continued to reverberate through him from the detonation. It wasn't something he had been thinking about – not seriously anyway. And yet, as soon as he spoke the words, he felt the truth in them – the rightness of his statement. It made sense, what he was suggesting, even if he couldn't quite visualize how it would play out in reality. He tried to block from his mind the look of naked shock that had seized her face when he'd said it, the niggling voice in the back of his mind that the fault was his alone: his inability to be happy for his wife. What was wrong with him? He sat there, joylessly chewing his scallops, washing it all down – the food and the fury – with a long, cool gulp of wine.

'It's hard for teenage girls these days,' Valentina was saying now. 'All the focus on their appearances. It's no wonder they put such pressure on themselves.'

'I know,' Abi agreed. 'And it starts so young. In Beth's year, there's a group chat called Outfit Of The Day. The way they scrutinize each other – it's appalling. We tell our girls to ignore it – to simply decline taking part in any of that nonsense.'

'But it's hard when everyone else in their group is involved,' Valentina countered. 'You don't want them to feel left out.'

The conversation moved on to social media, the pernicious inroads it was making into adolescent development. Mark zoned out. He was thinking instead about his own daughter, Eva. The memory of their afternoon together still glowed inside him. It occurred to him that there would not be many more such opportunities for him to connect with her before she went off to college, if any at all. Already, he felt the bonds that tied her to the family loosening, as if she was even now drifting away.

From the corner of his eye, Mark saw Guy emptying the last drops of the bottle into his own glass, then signalling to the waiter for another. Who was supposed to be driving them home? Mark wondered with a little rise in anger. Pointedly, he emptied what was left of his own wine into Abi's glass.

'I'm happy to drive,' he announced, but she ignored him and the conversation drifted on, some nonsense about installing spyware on the kids' computers to monitor their activities. They had moved on to their main course, various joints of meat and slivers of fish steaming from plates in front of them.

'What about computers?' Abi asked. 'Beth spends so much time on hers.'

'Corinne, not so much,' Valentina answered. 'But her phone—'

Guy grunted, spearing some meat with his fork.

'Instagram,' he said. 'It's all she cares about.'

'We've seen some of her posts,' Abi said. 'They seem charming.'

'Charming!' Guy laughed. 'You are very naive.'

Mark saw Abi's cheeks flush, her back straightening. He knew she was bristling.

'Why? The pictures she posts, they're very playful and girl-ish. And yes, I do think they have a certain charm. They're warm, sunny, optimistic.'

'But they are not real,' Guy declared, enunciating each word carefully for emphasis.

He put down his fork. 'When you see a picture of Corinne grinning by a lake, or swinging "playfully" from a lamppost, waving a bunch of flowers in the air, you think that is a spontaneous moment that just happened to be caught by the camera?' His tone was heavy with disdain. 'No. It is carefully planned. Each image meticulously thought out – calculated. You see a laughing girl jumping in the sunlight and think she just happily skips through her sunny life? But that one picture has involved countless changes of clothes, and perhaps an hour or two of jumping and clicking, jumping and clicking, all in search of this perfect shot.'

'What's wrong with that?' Mark asked. 'Surely there's a sort of artistry to it. A vision, a commitment.' Personally, he liked Corinne's Instagram feed. Some of the images were clumsy and sentimental, immature. But they made him smile.

'Who takes the pictures, though?' Abi asked. 'I've often wondered.'

'Whoever she can persuade. She's very good at it, you know,' he remarked coldly. 'Manipulating others to carry out her demands.'

'That's a bit harsh,' Mark said.

'Is it? You'd like that, would you? Standing around for hours while Corinne prances and poses, all smiles in front of the camera, but out of view always moody and dissatisfied?'

'They're teenagers. What else are they going to do with their time?'

'It's pretty harmless,' Abi offered.

'Harmless!' Guy laughed. 'What do you think this is all about, really?'

'Having fun. Being inventive. Experimenting with the medium.'

'I will tell you what it's about,' Guy said, waving away her list dismissively. 'It's about deception.'

He leaned back while the waiter took his empty plate, and once the table was cleared, he leaned forward again, intent now.

'When I see these images of hers, I do not recognize the girl in them. That is not my daughter. It's a fake.'

'So what if it's aspirational?' Mark interjected. 'Adolescence is about trying on different selves, discovering what you want to be.'

'But why like this? With such dedication. And what about the audience?'

'She has a very big following,' Abi remarked, and Valentina shifted anxiously in her chair, her eyes flickering to Guy who waved his arm with a flourish, and said:

'Another deception! Twelve thousand followers? Please! She bought them!'

'What?' Abi laughed nervously. Guy had grown voluble and people around the restaurant were starting to look over.

'You think I'm joking?' he ploughed on. 'She stole money from us and used it to buy followers. This is real. This is something you can do. You buy an ad that's designed to look like a post that promotes your account. It's called "boosting your profile",' he informed them, making little inverted commas with his fingers, 'so she can become an influencer,' articulating the word with disgust.

'How much did she pay?' Abi asked.

'Two thousand euro,' Valentina admitted, her eyes flashing apologetically.

'Really?' Abi could scarcely believe it.

'You call it art,' Guy said. 'I call it devious.'

'You're very hard on her,' Mark stated. 'She's just a kid.'

Guy looked down, quietly saying: 'You can love your child and still see her faults.'

'It must be hard for Corinne though,' Mark pushed on, 'growing up in the shadow of her older sister.'

'What do you mean?' This from Valentina, an instant

response. The smile was still on her face, but it seemed defensive.

'Well, we've heard all about Anouk, haven't we? Her academic achievements, her sporting success. I mean, a scholarship to McGill? I've seen all the pictures you have of her round the house. I just wonder what it's like for Corinne, trying to live up to her sister. It seems impossible. All these things you've been talking about – Instagram, anorexia, the deception and fakery – I just wonder, might it all be a cry for attention?'

He took a sip of water, his mouth dry after his little speech.

Mark wasn't sure why he'd gone that far. Mostly, to needle Guy. There was something unfeeling in the way the man spoke about his own daughter, as if he'd already written her off. Hadn't Corinne herself confessed to her father's customary detachment?

But now he saw the look that passed between Guy and Valentina.

'You see—' Val started to say but Guy shook his head and she stopped.

It was amazing, Mark briefly observed, how calm and self-possessed Valentina was when her husband wasn't around, and yet in his presence she became watchful and nervy, looking to him for her cue.

She said something now – a low rattle of words fired across the table under her breath – the first and only instance during the meal when they slipped into their native tongue. Mark caught Abi looking at him – an expression of mild alarm there. She'd felt it too: the wariness that had sprung up, the sense that he had succeeded in peeling back a layer to expose a raw nerve.

Valentina leaned her elbows on the table, touched her

fingertips to her closed eyes. When she opened them again, she seemed calm but strained.

'I am sorry,' she began tentatively. 'This is my fault. Guy thought that you should be made aware of the situation from the very start, but . . . It was my decision not to tell you.'

'Tell us what?' Abi asked. She had put down her glass.

'About Anouk.'

Her voice trembled as she spoke her daughter's name. Guy had fallen silent, his chin had dropped to his chest and he regarded her with caution and with what looked almost like pity.

'She's not at McGill,' Mark stated.

'No.' Valentina's voice was dry.

'She is in a hospital near Poitiers,' Guy explained, his voice and expression soft, almost tender. 'She had a breakdown, you see. We do not know when – or if – she will recover.'

No one spoke for a moment. Mark felt a wave of guilty regret pass through him. His needling seemed petty and cruel now; he had sought to embarrass them, but he'd never wished to expose real pain.

Abi reached out a hand and placed it on Valentina's. 'What happened?' she asked, and Val took a breath.

'It was a year ago now. Something changed in her. She had always been such a good child until then. Those things you heard about her were true. She was a good student. She excelled at anything she was interested in – sports, her school-work. And she was happy. Both our girls – they were so close. But then, on her gap year, she went away, did some travelling. We encouraged it, didn't we? We thought it would be good for her.'

'She came back a different person,' Guy said. 'It was like somebody had flicked a switch inside her. She became wild.

Unpredictable. Staying out all night, not telling us where she was, hanging out with all kinds of people, dangerous characters. And when she did interact with us, she became so emotional. She made all sorts of crazy accusations. Wild imaginings.'

'Like what?' Mark asked, but Guy brushed this aside.

'It doesn't matter what. I tell you this just so you understand what we were dealing with. It was very upsetting – for us, for Corinne. For our neighbours and friends. It was like having this ticking time bomb in the room – you would never know when it would go off.'

'We tried to get her to seek help,' Valentina told them, 'making appointments for her with a therapist, but she wouldn't turn up. She disappeared for days at a time, coming home, bruised and filthy. Her clothes ripped. Cuts all over her body. Sometimes she took Corinne with her and that really frightened us. Corinne is so young and impressionable. We worried what might happen to her. These people Anouk had made friends with, they were not good people.'

'It became too much,' Guy said, shaking his head. 'We knew she was a danger to herself, but also to Corinne, who had always looked up to her older sister, but now she was completely obsessed. Corinne lost interest in school, in her friends. All she cared about was Anouk, doing whatever it was Anouk demanded of her, no matter how outrageous these demands became. Anouk was out of control and she was dragging Corinne with her. It could not go on. No parent wants to see their child taken away and put into one of those hospitals. But what was the alternative? Just sit around and wait until one of them got hurt, or killed?'

'I can't imagine it,' Abi said, shaking her head, 'all that you've been going through.'

'Why didn't you tell us?' Mark asked, and he noticed the

crease in Valentina's forehead, the almost sheepish way her expression changed.

'It's been very hard for Corinne,' she explained, her voice dropping almost to a whisper. 'She loves her sister so much. When Anouk went into the hospital, Corinne couldn't accept it.'

'It was her way of coping,' Guy interjected, and Valentina nodded quickly.

'She kept talking about Anouk as if nothing had happened to her. As if everything was just carrying on as normal. She even invented this idea of Anouk being away at college.'

'And you just let her go on making this stuff up?' A little incredulity crept into Mark's voice, and Val heard it. Flint entered her stare.

'Perhaps you think it is my fault, hmm? Always the fault of the mother?'

'No—'

'What could I do? Shout and scream at her? That would only have pushed her away and I had already lost one daughter.'

'You wanted to protect her,' Abi said soothingly, and Val seemed to relent a little.

'I struggled with it, of course. We both did. And when she filled out the form for this exchange, I worried about her going away from us; all the fear we felt over Anouk came flooding back.'

'The phone call you made – on the night before Corinne came,' Abi reminded her. 'That was because of Anouk, wasn't it? Because you were scared.'

Val nodded, wiping quickly at the tears that had sprung in her eyes.

'But we have been so lucky that Corinne found you. That she found your family. It made all the difference to her. She has been happier since her stay with you.'

She reached out and took hold of Abi's hand, smiling bravely as she squeezed it.

'Corinne is a good girl, just a little lost,' Valentina said. 'It makes me wonder what I was worried about. After all,' and her glittering eyes darted around the table at all three of them, 'what could possibly go wrong?'

21

The pain was constant and intense, a sharp burning through the layers of her skin. It reminded Beth of visiting the dentist – the hum of the machinery, the same inner clenching as if holding her breath the whole time. She was crouched over the side of the sofa, hugging the armrest against her chest while Bruno perched beside her, pensive and attentive in his work. She tried to focus on the weave of the rug on the floor, the smell coming off the couch – something vinegary and stale, like old chips – while the top of her spine braced against the vibrations.

'Are you okay?' Corinne asked, bringing something of the freshness of outdoors with her as she knelt on the floor in front of Beth.

'Sure.'

'Not too sore?'

'It's fine.'

The words came out small and remote. She couldn't bring herself to look at Corinne, still stunned by the sudden savagery of the pinching. She felt Corinne's eyes flickering over her bent head, instinctively catching the tiny flame of hurt.

'I had to do it,' she explained, and Beth felt the strain of her optimism. 'I only want to help you. Would you have gone through with it if I had not?'

Beth shrugged, then felt the sharp tap of Bruno's finger on her shoulder, instructing her to keep still.

'You need me to push you, Beth, or else you will never change. You will always be the sad, frightened little girl.'

She waited, but Beth didn't answer. After a moment, Corinne gave a little huff of impatience.

'Fine. Believe what you want,' she said, and moved away.

The pain which had been intense at the start had dulled to a low throb, and when it was done, Beth was surprised by Bruno's tenderness as he dabbed at her neck with a disinfected cotton pad. Beyond the site of pain, she could feel the heat of his breath on her skin as he came close to inspect his work. Satisfied, he sat back, and she heard the rip of surgical gloves peeled from his skin and discarded.

'Come,' he told her, and led her through into the bedroom where there was a mirror on the wall.

He tugged open the shutter to allow in more light, and then held another, smaller mirror up behind her. In the dimness of the room she surveyed the tattoo reflected back at her through the foxed glass. Along the line of her scar, he had made another line – a slender stem, punctuated with tiny thorns. At the top, near the base of her neck was the head of a rose, petals delicately unfurling. The ink appeared wet, as if a brush of the hand would smudge it.

'You like it? You are happy?' he asked her, brisk and curt in his request for approval.

'It's beautiful,' she replied.

This was not altogether a lie. To her untrained eye, there did appear to be a certain artistry. But it seemed alien – the lines so very black and stark against her reddened skin. Something austere and cruel about the spiky little thorns. She had hoped to feel transformed, or even just a bit emboldened, as if the tattoo could protect her, like a carapace, a piece of armour she'd fixed to her person. But instead, she felt a pulse of alarm. The thing was a distortion. It didn't belong to her and yet it had attached itself to her and there was nothing she could do about it now.

Behind her, Bruno waited. She offered a smile, saying:

'Really, it's great. You're so talented.'

But a guarded, watchful look had come down over his face and the compliment bounced off him, an irrelevance. All at once, she was aware of the bed in the room, blankets collapsing to the floor. Her grey bra, the soft childish folds of her belly above her jeans – she stood with her arms crossed, hands tucked into her armpits.

'Well, thanks again,' she said, moving past him back out into the sitting room, where Corinne was reclining on the couch blowing in and out of the latex glove so that it inflated and collapsed like a fingered lung.

Beth picked up her T-shirt, pulled it quickly over her head.

'Wait. Let me see,' Corinne said, sitting up and beckoning her with an impatient gesture, fingers wiggling. Dutifully, Beth went to her, bowing her head while Corinne made her inspection.

'You see? I told you it would be beautiful!' she exclaimed, her approval clamorous and too loud, as if she could lift the mood, compensate for Beth's unspoken misgivings.

She clapped her hands, then lifted Beth's face, swept her fingertips over Beth's hot cheek, saying: 'I told you, remember? Even ugly things can be made beautiful. You just have to be brave.'

She smiled into Beth's face, and for just a moment, it blinded Beth to her doubt.

Then Bruno coughed, reminding the girls of his presence. He slouched against the door frame, said something she didn't understand, and when Beth looked to Corinne for the translation, her friend was smiling at her strangely.

'He needs to be paid,' Corinne said, her face tilted to one side, idly playing with the glove in her lap.

'But, the rum . . . I thought—'

'No, no!' Corinne laughed gently.

The bottle stood on the kitchen counter where they had left it, untouched.

'How much do we need?' she asked, but the jump she felt inside told her it wasn't about money.

Bruno waited and Corinne sat still on the couch. Beth looked from one to the other, her heart hammering.

'It will be quick,' Corinne said. 'And you will be happy you did it afterwards.' She smiled at Beth, but her eyes were steely.

'No. I can't.' Beth's hands slick with sweat, heat prickling like a rash over her body.

'Go on,' Corinne said, nodding her encouragement.

'Corinne, please—'

'You want to grow up, don't you? You don't want to be a baby for ever?'

'No, but—'

'He will show you what to do. Like he showed me. You do trust me, don't you?'

Fear bubbled up inside her, and to her shame tears sprang in her eyes.

'Please. I don't want to . . .'

'Just think,' Corinne said, reaching out and taking hold of Beth's hand. 'How close it will bring us. You said it yourself. How you want to be like me. Look!' she said, turning quickly and pulling up the side of her vest to show the tattoo on her hip. 'Yours is just like mine, no? We are twins, right? Sisters. My first time was with him. Now yours will be too!' Light filling her face, but her eyes remained fixed on Beth, pinning her there for an answer, a submission. When she didn't reply, Corinne's grip tightened.

'Remember the rules,' she said softly but firmly. 'You must do what I tell you.'

Beth felt the lump rise in her throat. 'Please don't make me,' she whispered.

But Corinne was insistent.

'You have to pay him,' she said, her voice low, her gaze intense. 'It isn't fair not to pay him.'

Beth was crying properly now. Childish sobs wracked her chest. She wanted Eva to come back. She wanted Corinne to stop looking at her in that way. Bruno spoke, his impatience and disgust there in the rattling string of words she couldn't understand, and Corinne snapped at him to just wait. But the squalor of the room and the recklessness of Beth's mistake all rose up and overwhelmed her.

'Please,' she said, her voice shaking. 'I can't. I know I should. I know you want me to, but I just can't.'

She pulled her wrist from Corinne's grasp and sat down heavily on the couch, her arms held protectively around her, refusing to meet her friend's gaze. But she felt Corinne's glare, her silent fury. A single moment of silence, and then Corinne stood up, moving swiftly past Beth, almost stepping on her feet. She said something to Bruno, and Beth could tell from her aloof tone and the way Bruno sniggered that it was something disparaging about Beth. And when the bedroom door closed behind them, leaving Beth alone on the couch, a wave of self-disgust washed over her so strongly, it might have obliterated her completely.

In the silence that followed, she rocked herself gently back and forth, trying to calm the storm of emotions inside. Corinne was right, she thought. She was a baby. A child needing a push. And how could she not have understood what would be demanded of her in exchange for the tattoo? Furiously, she raked back over the events in her mind, starting with Corinne's suggestion that first time of turning the scar into something notable – something beautiful – and then to the meeting with Bruno outside the Proxi one evening, the negotiations carried out by Corinne in French, Beth smiling shyly up at him in the sunlight. Pushing aside any thoughts of collusion, she trawled instead through memories of conversations that had followed, seeking out clues she'd missed at the time. Her naivety appalled her. Of course he would expect something in return – hadn't Corinne said as much? So what if she hadn't been explicit? To do so would have been coarse, and Corinne was not like that. Outspoken, yes, with a mischievous streak running through her. But she was not vulgar or crude. And she only wanted what was best for Beth. Hadn't she said as much? Let me help you, she'd offered, and Beth had accepted. So, wasn't this as much Beth's fault as Corinne's?

As she sat there trying to impose logic on to the events that had led her here, from behind the bedroom door came sounds of the bed jacking against the wall. Beth held herself still and listened, ashamed but helpless to it all the same. Her thoughts went to what was going on behind that door, picturing Corinne's lithe body straddling his, all the blankets sliding away to the floor. *That might have been me*, she thought, the fact of this both shocking and strangely compelling. Would it have been so bad if she'd agreed? Shrugging off the mantle of childhood, shedding all her dopey innocence – wouldn't that have been a relief?

She saw now, with a flash of clarity, how Corinne had been right. Beth's failure to recognize this was a sign of her own weakness, her own lack of judgement. She envied Corinne's confidence, the ease with which she moved through the world, but surely, if she wanted to attain the same ease and grace, she would have to surrender her doubts, her crawling fears and inhibitions? She needed to trust her friend.

The noises in the bedroom eased into silence. Calmness came over the room. Beth thought of the stillness that lay within, the lovers entwined, peace falling over the tangle of their limbs.

An act of generosity, that's what it was. Where Beth had failed, her friend had stepped in to make up for her weakness. That was friendship. That was love. Corinne had paid Beth's debt for her in the most intimate, most giving way possible, and Beth also understood that a new debt had been created. An obligation.

The bedroom door opened and Corinne stepped out, fixing the straps of her vest top and ruffling the ends of her hair with her fingertips. She pulled at the waistband of her cutoffs, readjusting them, then yawned, but Beth sensed the jitteriness within her. A brittleness in the air as she pulled the bedroom door closed and crossed the living-room floor. She wouldn't look at Beth, withholding something of herself, enigmatic and haughty, with a loucheness that implied the whole thing was a drag.

'Are you okay?' Beth asked, nerves keeping her voice quiet.

'Sure.'

'I'm sorry.'

Corinne was hunting around for her belongings, gathering up her phone, her wallet, putting them all in the little silver tasselled bag she carried around with her.

'I'm sorry I disappointed you,' Beth went on. 'That you had to do that for me.'

'That's okay. I liked doing it.'

But there was no smile on her face, no hint of any lingering pleasure. For the first time, Beth looked at Corinne and saw the dark void inside her – a frightening emptiness. She had a way of making you feel cold, shutting herself off from you. Beth thought about their morning together in the river, limbs flashing wet under the hot sun. The closeness that had been between them inaccessible now. Beth scrambled for a way to claw it back, went to thank her for what she'd done, but just then, Corinne's gaze landed on the puppies and she swept down and scooped two of them up in her arms.

'Hey, take a picture,' she instructed, nodding to her phone. 'I want to Instagram this.'

Beth did as she was asked, and when she held the phone up and opened the camera function, Corinne fixed her with the full wattage of her sunny gaze and Beth was momentarily startled. How swiftly she'd turned her mood around, snapping on her bright smile like a varnished mask reflecting the light. And Beth thought how later the picture would appear on Instagram – the happy grin, the soft, wrinkled faces of the pups – and there would be nothing of the rancid smell, the squalor, the sex act demanded as payment. All that they'd see and remember of this day was the innocent felicity of new-born pups.

Mark drove them home. Even before they'd left the restaurant, it was clear that Guy was too drunk to get behind the wheel. Silence filled the car as they made their way through the darkened countryside, the road unwinding into the distance, a silvery thread in the moonlight.

Guy was dozing in the passenger seat. In the back, the women observed a thoughtful silence. It seemed to Mark as if the memory of that troubled girl was alive in the air with them. He kept thinking of her photograph on the mantelpiece, the sunlit hair, the clear-eyed gaze into the camera. Something about the account had caused him disquiet, made him think of his own children, their vulnerabilities. Before leaving the restaurant, as Abi settled the bill, he'd taken the opportunity to call Eva. Her phone had gone straight to voicemail, so he'd left a message, and then sent her a text for good measure, just to check everything was okay. Even now, he was glancing at his own phone on the dashboard, watchful for a notification, some response to put his mind at ease.

'Slow down,' Abi murmured, a warning in her voice, and he realized that his foot was to the floor.

'Sorry.'

Unease was making him speed. He was impatient to get home to his own daughters, to make sure they were safe. As he drove, he wondered what had made the poor kid crack up. He couldn't imagine growing up with parents like Val and Guy: she was flaky and uncertain while he seemed untroubled by any sense of affection or warmth.

At that moment, Guy shifted in his seat, letting out a loud belch into the cabin. Mark exhaled with annoyance – he could smell the bilious odour, and lowered his window. Behind him, Abi complained of the draught but he didn't care. Guy was moving in his seat again, clearly discomforted by the big meal he'd just consumed, all that wine. Swearing under his breath, he unclipped his seatbelt, and Mark snapped:

'Put that back on.'

But Guy grumbled incoherently, trying to stretch out his belly to relieve his discomfort.

'Put your seatbelt on, Guy, now,' Mark insisted, the car's sensor bleating out a warning.

He turned his head, glanced across at the man wincing in pain, and Mark half-leaned towards him. He was reaching to grab the seatbelt—

'Watch out!'

The shriek of Abi's voice rang in his ears as he felt the impact of the blow to the bumper and slammed on the brakes. Beside him, Guy jolted forward, his head glancing off the dashboard, before he was flung back against his seat. Movement streaked through the headlights – a fleeting glance of tusks and the reddish hue of animal hides within a rising cloud of dust. The car swerved and skidded to a halt. Wild boars – Mark counted five of them, as they raced across the road in the light of the car's headlamps before disappearing into the darkness. For a moment, Mark just sat there, his heart pummelling his chest. Abi was already out of the car.

'Can you see any damage?' he asked as he joined her by the bumper. She was hunkering down, running her hands over the frame.

'A dent. There's blood. Ugh,' she said, her fingertips glossy with gore. Quickly she stood up and wiped her hand on her dress.

Val had joined them and was looking anxiously from the car to the black field. The air was still sultry with heat from the day, but out here in the middle of nowhere, with only the moon casting its light, it felt lonely and remote.

'We shouldn't stay out here,' Val said, nerves in her voice. 'Boars are dangerous. They could come back.'

'What about the one you hit?' Abi asked him. 'It could be lying there half-dead. Shouldn't we check?'

'And what if it is? What do you propose I do? Finish it off with the tyre-iron?' The adrenaline rush and the strangeness of the incident made him tense and snappish.

'I'd just feel better if we looked.'

'Fine.'

They'd need more light to find the thing if it was even there, which Mark doubted. Leaving Val and Abi peering into the darkness, he went back to the car. Guy remained where he sat in the passenger seat, and this needled Mark even more. It was Guy's damned car and he couldn't even rouse himself to check for damage. And it was Guy's bloody fault that they'd had the accident in the first place. If he hadn't distracted Mark with the seatbelt, then he'd have had his eyes on the road and might have seen the animals sooner.

Mark's phone was on the dash – he would use the torch function. As he climbed into the car to reach for it, Guy slumped forward, a sharp indrawn breath hissing through his clenched teeth.

'Are you all right?' Mark asked.

It was only now that he noticed Guy was clutching at his forehead, and when he sat back suddenly in the seat, Mark could see the large welt just below his hairline, a swollen mass already clearly apparent. Guy's face had turned greyish in colour, and Mark's thoughts moved quickly back to the moment Guy had unclipped his seatbelt. Had the man been struggling for breath then? Was that why he'd sought to release himself?

'Guy?' Mark said, quietly now as fear swept over him.

Guy's eyes were closed and his body was twitching and jerking, his mouth opening and closing as if trying to swallow air.

'Christ!' Mark backed out of the car and shouted to the women. 'Get over here now! He's having a seizure!' his voice roaring through the darkness, the women turning quickly, their faces lit by the headlamps caught in a rictus of fright.

All at once, the car became a site of panic. Valentina grew hysterical, her hands fluttering around Guy like flapping birds seeking a place to land, wildly imploring her husband to wake up, a stream of rapid French. Abi was brusque, instructional. Swiftly, she sat in the car behind Guy and held his head, fearful of any spinal damage caused by the impact.

'Call an ambulance,' she barked, and Mark looked at his phone.

'There's no fucking signal!' he snapped, rushing from the

car, his eyes on his phone, desperate to see a bar or two of signal as he hurried down the road.

The vast emptiness of the French countryside surrounded him, dark and dense, and a great swell of fear rose up inside him. What if he'd noticed Guy was struggling to breathe? What if he'd stopped the car then, avoiding the collision with the boar, Guy's head injury?

'Come on, come on!' he muttered, panicking now. Time was passing – they couldn't afford to hang around.

He ran back to the car. The passenger door was still open, Valentina leaning heavily over her husband, weeping. Abi remained in the back.

'I can't get a signal. Let's just drive to get help,' Mark said as he climbed into the driver's seat. 'Where's the nearest hospital? Châtellerault? Poitiers?'

But Valentina just kept wailing. He reached out and grabbed her arm. 'Valentina? The hospital? Come on! Would you just get in the back so we can—'

'Leave her,' Abi said quietly.

He shot her a look. 'We don't have time for this, Abi! We've got to get him to a hospital.'

'It's too late for that.'

He looked at her again and saw that she was no longer holding Guy's head. Instead, she had slumped back against the upholstery, her face pale and shocked in the dimly lit cabin. She was staring off into the middle distance, but now her eyes focused and she met his gaze. The look she gave him was grave and full of sadness and he found himself inwardly turning away, not wanting to hear her pronouncement, not wanting her gaze on his face as she uttered the words. Sound like water rushing through his ears.

'He's dead,' she said.

22

They left France before the funeral. Even if they had wanted to attend, Abi couldn't swing the extra time with work. They had stayed for as long as they could, the last days of their holiday spent dealing with the police, the coroner, piecing together the minutiae of the night's events leading up to the accident.

Because that's what it was: an accident. It was nobody's fault. Just an awful tragedy on a country road, nature crashing through, a shattering reminder of her power and man's insignificance. If anyone was to blame for what happened, it was Guy himself for unclipping his seatbelt. The police officer leading the investigation had said as much. There would be an inquest, and both Mark and Abi would be required to return and give evidence, but it would be a formality. The outcome was already clear.

Guiltily, Abi acknowledged to herself that she was relieved to get away. Valentina's voluble grief, Corinne's shocked silence, were both difficult to navigate, particularly for Mark, who blamed himself for Guy's death, despite the reassurance of the police, and the clear-cut facts. Abi still remembered how she had put her arms around her husband at the side of the road while the paramedics dealt with the body. He had broken down, noiseless sobs sending tremors through his body, communicated into hers. It had occurred to her at the time that she couldn't remember him crying in her arms like that before. Not even when Melissa died. He had kept his grief inside him then. Perhaps the shock of the night's events had jolted something within him – shaken the grief loose from the tight grip he held it in.

Beth had wanted to stay, and there had been a bitter argument when they'd broken the news of their imminent departure, her small face made ruddy and strange with the force of her angry weeping, but in the end, their course was set. They said their goodbyes, dropped the rental car at the airport and flew home.

That relief lingered in the days that followed. The cool spaces of their house, the breeze rustling through the vegetation in the garden, it was a balm after the arid heat, the airlessness of France.

There was a muteness though. Things that had happened were not spoken of. Occasionally, Mark might ask: 'Any word from Val?' or one of them might wonder aloud about how the Cattos were getting on, but for the most part they didn't discuss it. Avoidance of the issue was their unspoken policy, both of them shying away from the fissure in their holiday – those awful words he had spoken.

Once, during dinner, they had seen a fox run through the garden, pausing in the middle of the lawn, brazen in the daylight, and Mark had said, 'God, remember those boar though?' and all at once they were reliving the night, the car skidding to a halt, blood on the bumper, and then Guy clutching his head. Mark still obsessed over the sound in Guy's throat. He confessed to Abi one evening, the two of them sitting on the patio, enjoying a bottle of Viognier in the last rays of the evening sun, that he woke in the middle of the night sometimes, thinking he could hear the rattle of Guy's breathing in the room with them, the wet gasps jolting him out of sleep, frightening him in the darkness. They were both stretched out on their loungers at the time, a couple of feet apart. Mark had one arm raised, his hand slung across his forehead, and it was this hand that he reached out to Abi, grasping hers in a tight grip, his eyes turned to hold her gaze. 'I'm sorry,' he said, and she felt the solemnity of the words and knew he was referring to his behaviour the evening of the accident. That terrible thing he had said.

He hadn't meant it. This was the conclusion Abi had reached. She would allow him a moment of weakness like that, particularly in light of all that had happened afterwards. But every so often, when she was tired, overwrought from work and the new responsibilities she had taken on, her thoughts would again creep in that direction, and she would find herself wondering: what if he *had* meant it? She didn't want them to be one of those couples who stayed together for the sake of the children, the marriage a sham. She wanted more than a loveless union. Whenever these thoughts came to her, she grew watchful, alert to some clue as to the authenticity of her husband's affection, but it was exhausting and unnatural, like being a spy in her own marriage. So, for the most part, Abi followed her usual approach in dealing with the bigger emotional issues: she ignored it, hoping it would go away.

Occasionally, Abi's guilt prompted her to ring Valentina, and she would listen with concern as the woman held forth on the strangeness of her life with Guy suddenly gone. Val, in those conversations, sounded bewildered but also distant, as if she were observing her own life, her own grief, from a remove. A reversal seemed to have taken place in the time since the death – Valentina's storm of grief had abated, while Corinne's shock had worn off leaving her distressed, pitiable in her new sadness. Abi learned this from Val herself, for in the days and weeks after their return, Corinne's silence had become notable. The calls from France dried up overnight, and whether or not she was still communicating with Beth via Instagram or WhatsApp seemed doubtful. Both Abi and Mark observed an increasing desperation in their younger daughter as she struggled to reach her friend, growing more frantic as the silence stretched on.

'I'm not sure about this, Beth,' Abi gently remarked on one occasion.

She had happened upon her younger daughter slumped over her desk, her whole body wracked with emotion. Beth's hair had grown a little, but it was still a cropped boyish cut and above the collar of her shirt, Abi could just make out the head of the black rose snaking up her spine. Every time she saw the thing, it caused a tremor of revulsion. The row that had followed their discovery of it had been awful. Even now, an echo of that shaking rage came back to her, remarks bubbling up inside: *My God, what were you thinking? Look at that dreadful thing! Your beautiful back, destroyed.* But she said nothing. 'What's the point?' Mark had counselled her. 'It's not like she can rub it out.' They had let it go, and Abi, while not making her peace with the tattoo, at least avoided commenting on it.

Now she stepped cautiously into the room, while Beth sat up, swiping angrily at her eyes, struggling to compose herself.

'I'm fine,' the girl said, not looking at Abi.

'You're not fine. You're crying.'

'I'm okay, Mum.'

'What happened? Is it Corinne?'

'Nothing happened.'

'Did you hear from her?'

'No. I keep calling her, and sending her messages, but she hasn't replied.'

Beth shook her head, biting down on the fresh tears that instantly rose. 'I'm really worried about her.'

'Of course you are. It's natural that you're concerned for

your friend, but – well, perhaps you should give her some space, hmm?'

'I just want to help her, even if it's just to listen. She needs me.'

'Yes, but you have to look after yourself too. How many times this week have you been crying because of Corinne?'

'So?'

'It's not healthy.'

'I'm not made of fucking stone, Mum.'

'Well, exactly. You're sensitive, love, and I worry about you. Corinne will get in touch when she's ready.'

'It's not that simple. I'm her friend. She needs me,' Beth said again, a pleading insistence to her voice that worried Abi. She couldn't help but think that Corinne did not, in fact, need Beth, but rather it was the other way around. In the weeks of Corinne's silence, Beth appeared scattered and lost. Acne had erupted on her face and she often wore the same clothes for days at a time, hair greasy and unwashed. Her whole body screamed with need.

Abi looked at the grim constellation of spots on Beth's cheek and chin.

'She's got her mother to support her,' she said gently, but Beth's face contorted with scorn, and she shook her head with disgust.

'Val's useless.'

'That's not true.'

'Yes, it is! All she thinks about is herself! She doesn't care about Corinne! She doesn't give a shit how much she's damaged her!'

'Damaged her?'

'Oh my God. She's just . . . Look. There are things you don't know. Things about Valentina and Guy.'

'What things?'

For a moment, she saw the indecision playing across Beth's face. But almost as quickly, it shut down. 'I can't tell you,' she answered quietly, half-turning back to the desk, idly spinning her phone over the surface.

'Why not?'

'Because I promised Corinne.'

'I'm not sure I like that, Beth,' Abi remarked, sitting down on the edge of the bed. 'We're a family. We shouldn't keep secrets from each other.'

'We shouldn't. But we do,' Beth said, and her gaze was cool and direct. Abi found herself inwardly backing away.

Beth refused to be drawn on the subject, whatever Valentina's sin was, which was probably nothing anyway, Abi concluded. She was well aware of Corinne's flights of imagination, the creative licence she took with the truth.

'All teenage girls hate their mothers sometimes,' Abi said. 'And that's fine, that's normal. So, whatever Corinne told you about Val, well, I think you'd be wise to take it with a pinch of salt. I mean, look at all the lies she told us about Anouk.'

'That's different!'

'Is it?' Abi tried to keep her voice level. They'd already had the conversation about Anouk, about Corinne's deception. It wasn't worth revisiting, so she changed tack.

'What about your other friends, hmm? Why don't you try and meet up with some of them before school starts?'

'What friends?'

'Maybe give Lisa a call – I'm sure she'd love to hear from you.'

'No, she wouldn't.' Disdain dripped from Beth's voice. 'She can't stand me. She hates my guts, just like everybody else.'

'I don't get it, Beth. You and Lisa used to be such good friends – really close. Is this because of what happened at school? Was she frightened by it?'

'It doesn't matter,' Beth said, her voice dropping away, growing defensive. She was still spinning the phone, a little quicker now.

'I wish you'd talk to me about it.'

'Why? Would that be *healthy*?' The word dripped with sarcasm.

'Something clearly happened between the two of you. I can't help but think it's linked to you hurting yourself in front of the school.' Abi noticed the way Beth flinched when she brought up the incident. It prompted her to continue: 'It's something we never really talked about. Not properly.'

'I spoke to the shrink you fixed me up with,' Beth said tartly. 'Isn't that enough for you?'

'No. No, I don't think it is. I worry there's something unresolved there, something that's still troubling, but you just bottle all this stuff up inside when you should talk about it.'

'I have talked about it.'

'Really? To whom?' But Abi already knew the answer, the knowledge coming instantly along with a small flare of anger. 'Corinne. Am I right?'

Beth shrugged.

'Well, Corinne is in France and you are here,' Abi said, trying to be pragmatic, but impatience with the situation leaked into her tone. 'Wouldn't it be better for you to be friends with girls here, girls you can actually meet up with and have some fun with?'

'Have some fun with? God, do you even hear yourself, Abi? Do you know how shallow you sound?'

Reeling a little from Beth's use of her Christian name, Abi said: 'Shallow? I just—'

'You think friendship is something you just pick up and put down when it suits you. Something disposable and transient, like fashion.'

'Don't be ridiculous.'

'It's true! Look at the way you treated Valentina! When we were in France, you were all buddy-buddy, but then when her fucking husband dies, you can't get out of there quick enough! I mean, have you even called her since we came home?'

'Yes, I have! Several times.'

'Oh yeah. Sure. Just so you can tick that box, pat yourself on the back for being so fucking polite and attentive. But you don't actually listen to anything she's saying, you don't actually care—'

'Oh, and you're full of concern for Val now, are you? Just a minute ago you were berating her for being a bad mother. For damaging Corinne.'

'Hey, I'm not a fan of the woman. She's a liar and a freak and her behaviour repulses me, but that's not what I'm talking about here. I'm talking about you wanting me to hang out with one of those stuck-up cows from school so that you can relax about my fucking mental health and feel better about yourself as a mother and then forget all about me and go back to hob-nobbing with your fucking corporate dildo friends!'

'That's enough!' Abi snapped.

Beth's phone spun off the desk and skittered across the floor where it came to rest by the foot of the bed.

Abi's heart was beating wildly in her chest. She looked at Beth's small face dark with rage, with hatred. An icy finger ran all the way down her back. She had the queerest feeling that she was looking at a stranger. She didn't recognize this girl at all.

'I don't know how to talk to you when you're like this,' Abi admitted, her tone softer now, but her heart was still beating fast. 'I feel like everything I say will upset you.'

Beth didn't respond, but the anger drained a little from her face, the air between them losing its fractiousness.

'Sometimes I think you find it easier to talk to your dad than to talk to me. Since Melissa—'

Beth took in a sharp breath and put both hands to her head, smoothing her hair back in a swift gesture that told Abi she should stay away from that subject.

'We all love you, Beth – me, your dad, Eva. We just want what's best for you. We want you to be happy.' She tried to infuse these words with gentle meaning, but still they came out sounding stiff.

'I am happy,' Beth said with quiet insistence, adding: 'Corinne makes me happy.'

Abi was not convinced of this. Yes, it was true that when they were together, there was a conspiratorial closeness and she thought back to those occasions when she'd heard the pair of them hooting with laughter in this very room. But since Corinne had withdrawn her friendship, Beth had been miserable. And then Abi's mind flitted back to that day by the river when she'd watched the two of them in the water, caught in the dappled shade, twirling slowly, their arms draped around each other's necks, smiling. Peaceful. Content. She knew she had beheld something beautiful.

It seemed risky to say more. Abi didn't see how she could achieve anything further, except to send Beth off on another rant.

At the door, she looked back at Beth, who was already reaching for the mouse of her computer.

'Will you think about giving Lisa a call?' she asked, hopefully.

Beth glanced away from the screen and met her mother's gaze. Clear-eyed, chastened.

'Sure,' she said.

But they both knew she wouldn't.

While Beth was suffering from the withdrawal of Corinne's attention, Eva was troubled by the increasing number of unsolicited texts and WhatsApps from the girl. Mostly, they were inane messages, recounting some small event or raging about a row with her mother. Eva never replied. In fact, since the night they'd hitched a lift back from Bruno's house and Eva had sat in furious silence, she'd hardly spoken to Corinne beyond a few words of condolence after Guy's death. It bothered her, the likeness drawn between Eva herself and Corinne's sister, especially after it emerged that Anouk was locked away in some sort of asylum. Eva shuddered at the comparison Corinne made between her and this deeply troubled girl.

Once or twice, she had looked at Corinne's Instagram account, curiosity and boredom pushing her to it. The images, she noted, had turned melancholy – a leaf floating in water; a wilted geranium, petals scattered on the ground beneath it; Guy's reading glasses, folded and left resting on a book. None of the images were of Corinne herself. Gone was the sunny smile, the goofing around, the carefree poses. On one occasion, she'd posted a picture of Beth's tattoo in close-up – the skin still raw beneath the ink – with the caption: 'Courage' beneath it. Eva had snorted with ridicule, saying: 'Give me a break,' even though there was no one in the room to hear her. Still, it made her uneasy – these messages that Corinne insisted on sending her, all the while she was painfully ignoring Beth.

But whenever Corinne's texts quizzed Eva about her own life, what she was doing, who she was meeting, Eva couldn't help but remember the incident in the field in France, that stupid photograph she'd sent, Corinne's knowledge of it. The picture held sway over her now, and she resented the semi-playful way Corinne inferred the power she had over Eva because of it. *I hope you're being a good girl,* one of the messages had said. Eva had angrily deleted it.

She knew now that it had been a colossal mistake. As soon as she had obtained a replacement iPhone, Eva had texted Ross to explain her silence – a long-winded, wordy message that she agonized over before sending – but after hours waiting for a response from him, then days, she realized the truth of the situation. That they'd gone too far and now he was regretting it, backing off from any contact with her. This suspicion was confirmed as soon as they'd returned to Ireland. On the first day, back in her bedroom, she'd heard voices down below in the garden. Looking out the window, she saw her father chatting to Ross over the fence. Straight away, she'd run downstairs and outside, using the pretext of borrowing her dad's car, but as soon as she approached, Ross had backed away, saying: 'Listen, Mark, good to see you,' then disappeared inside his house without so much as a glance at Eva. The coldness of his gesture, blanking her like that, had cut her to the quick.

She noticed that he didn't linger outside his house any more. She never saw him tinkering with his cars, and when he played with Jo it was inside the house or the back garden. Eva couldn't escape the feeling that he was avoiding her.

The summer was almost over. One evening, after cycling home from tennis, Eva came into the kitchen where her father was getting ready to serve up dinner.

'There you are,' Mark said, two bright red spots high in his cheeks from the steam coming off the pasta. 'How was your match?'

'I lost, but it was close. Where is everyone?'

'Your mum's on the phone to Valentina. I've no idea where Beth is, probably in her room.'

'Valentina? What's that about?'

'No idea. So, your new laptop arrived,' Mark said as he strained the spaghetti at the sink.

To celebrate her offer of a place in UCD studying Engineering, her parents had ordered a new MacBook for her. Mark had also promised to look into buying her a small car of her own.

'Oh cool! Where is it?'

'It's next door. You'll have to go in and ask for it.'

'Next door?'

The sharpness of her response made Mark look over.

'There was no one here when it was delivered so Becca signed for it. Relax, sweetheart, it's not like they're going to run off with it, are they?'

Eva slumped against one of the kitchen stools.

'So? Why don't you go over there now and get it?' Mark asked, adding: 'They're home – I just heard noises through the wall.'

Eva wracked her brain but couldn't think of a good reason not to.

And so, she peeled herself away from the counter, smoothed back her hair in the hall, and a minute later she was at the Campbells' front door, leaning quickly on the bell, her heart pounding, as she waited for a silhouette to appear behind the bevelled glass.

Please let it be Becca, she silently prayed. But the broad shoulders and the bald dome of Ross's head appeared behind the glass, and when he pulled open the door and saw her, the naked shock in his face, the wariness with which he regarded her, seemed to stop up all the words inside her so for a moment, she couldn't speak.

'Eva,' he said, and the sound of her name in his mouth made her feel deeply uncomfortable, waves of embarrassment crashing over her.

'Hi. Sorry to barge in on you,' she said, hearing the high, reedy note of nerves in her voice, knowing her neck was blotchy and red. 'But I believe you guys took receipt of a delivery for me today?'

Awkwardness made her speak formally, but if Ross noticed it, he didn't comment, wordlessly standing back and ushering her into the house. When he closed the door behind her, she caught the scent of his aftershave, suddenly and intensely familiar to her.

'Come on through to the kitchen,' he said, leading the way.

She followed, her eyes casting about the place nervously. From upstairs, she could hear the sound of running water, the high shriek of little Jo's voice.

The laptop was in its box on the kitchen island, and Eva went forward to pick it up, noticing the half-empty bottle of beer alongside it, a second bottle already drained.

Ross waited by the kitchen door, watching as she picked up the box. When she turned back, saying, 'Thanks so much for keeping it for me,' she saw him closing the door behind him, his face grave, and her heart gave out a sudden kick.

'Becca's upstairs with Jo,' he told her. 'We only have a minute.'

'Please,' she began, flustered now. 'I don't—'

'I owe you an explanation. I know you must think I've been avoiding you, and the truth is, I have been. All that stuff, when you were in France – it got a bit too intense, you know?'

'I know. I'm sorry.'

'No! God, I'm the one who's sorry! You've got nothing to apologize for.'

He was looking at her strangely. She saw now how dry and hollow his cheeks looked, a thin layer of stubble over his jaw, his upper lip. But it was the intensity of his gaze that made something catch in her throat – fervent and desperate. She had the strangest impulse to reach out her hand and gently cup his cheek.

The laptop in its box was heavy and awkward in her arms, and she felt weak and a little shaky, so she put it back down on the countertop so she could face him properly.

'I shouldn't have sent you that picture,' she admitted.

'Listen, it was my fault. I should never have encouraged you to do that. Jesus, I feel awful, like some kind of creepy auld fella. But, I dunno, things were not so great between me and Becca, we'd had a row and she'd stormed off taking Jo with her. I was here on my own, having a few beers, feeling a bit lonely – not that that's an excuse. But as soon as you responded, I knew it was wrong. That I shouldn't have done it. It scared me a bit. And I know it was cowardly of me not to reply. I should have at least tried to explain to you.'

He let out a long breath and shook his head, stared at the floor.

Quietly, she said: 'When I didn't hear back from you, I just assumed you didn't like what I'd sent.'

He looked up quickly, an expression of confusion on his face. 'Not like it? My God, that picture was fucking amazing.'

She saw the wonder now in his gaze. 'It was the hottest thing that's happened to me in years,' he told her, and then he put his hands on her waist and kissed her and all her thoughts slowed right down.

His lips felt dry against hers, she tasted beer on his tongue, warmth flooding her bloodstream. It amazed her that this was happening, that he was pressing her back against the counter, the force of his body against her. She lifted her arms and wrapped them around his neck, feeling him press closer to her, his tongue hungrily exploring her mouth, his hands roaming quickly over her back and hips, unable to settle. His wife and child were right upstairs and here Eva was with him, in the kitchen, giving vent to their lustful feelings – the thought of how brazen and wrong it was just made her more excited. When Ross's hand slipped down the front of her jeans, she had to mash her face against the brushed cotton of his T-shirt to muffle the cry that came up her throat. Her hips pushed against him, her pelvis working quickly over the slick of his fingers, shocked and thrilled by the lust that had stirred to life between them.

A sudden clatter overhead made them pull apart.

'Jo's in the bath,' he explained, still breathless. 'It's just one of his toys dropping on the floor.'

'I should go,' she said, hastily fixing her clothes, her hair, then turning to take the laptop in its box.

Before opening the kitchen door for her, he kissed her again, a swift, searching kiss, and when he pulled away, his eyes were deep and serious. 'I'll call you,' he said, and then she was outside in the driveway, holding the box tight against her chest, thoughts exploding in her head as she hurried back home, still thrilling to the realization of what she'd begun.

In the house, there was a stillness and a silence, the smell of fried onion and garlic in the air. She took a moment to compose herself, putting the laptop down and checking her reflection in the hall mirror. Satisfied there were no tell-tale signs of her recent dissipation, she went into the kitchen where the places were set, the food served out, but there was no one there. Instead, they were out in the garden – Abi and

Mark standing opposite each other, Beth sitting on one of the sun-loungers. When Eva stepped outside and they all turned, grave looks on her parents' faces, for an instant she had the frightening thought that they knew what she had just done. That somehow, they had witnessed the act of depravity she had just committed in the Campbells' kitchen. Guiltily, she hung back, but then her father sighed and ran a hand through his hair and said:

'Come here, Eva. You might as well hear about this too.'

'What?' she asked.

'Valentina just rang,' Abi began.

'God, what's happened now?'

'Nothing, nothing,' Abi soothed, but there was tension. 'She's having a hard time, that's all. So is Corinne. Val's asked us to help.'

'Help? In what way?'

She looked from one parent to the other. Her father's magnanimous expression, her mother's optimism and eagerness to please fighting against a rising anxiety. Eva knew at once what this meant.

'She's not coming back here. Is she?'

'Would it be so bad if she did?' her father asked.

'Yes!'

Abi put her arm around Eva, pulled her daughter close. 'She needs our help, love,' she said. 'It will only be for a few weeks.'

Eva heard the reassurance in her mother's voice, normally enough to silence her doubts, but still they crowded her. Her heart was knocking against her ribs and her palms started to sweat. She couldn't account for the violence of her physical reaction, as if her own body was crying out a warning.

And then she saw Beth. Since their return from France her younger sister had worn an almost permanent scowl, a maudlin ferocity making her features sharp and angular beneath her ravaged hair. But now, in the soft evening light, Beth appeared calm, serene. Abi still had her arm around Eva's shoulder, her fingers squeezing reassurance, but Eva drew no solace from it. She looked at her younger sister, the placid smoothness of her expression – something prayerful about it, beatific. Like a believer who'd spent a lifetime waiting, Eva thought, finally to be rewarded by the Second Coming.

Autumn

'Is she alone?' I ask.

Cassins, the detective, raises her amber eyes to me.

'Mark is with her. As a minor, she needs an adult accompanying her during questioning,' she explains, adding: 'She asked for him.'

Watching me to see how that lands.

I nod, remain composed.

'Well, if that's what she wants.' My hands in my lap, kneading my thumb joint hard, waiting for the pop.

She's here in this building. Where? I wonder. In the next room? Further down the corridor? Distantly, I'm aware of noise. The muffled sound of a phone ringing. Perhaps there's a particular room for interviewing the suspect, especially one who's owned up so easily. Who sat cross-legged on the ground, eyes closed, waiting for the police to come, her face tilted towards the sunlight, feeble as it was this morning.

This morning.

It shocks me anew. The space of a few hours and everything is changed. Lives devastated. Destroyed.

She'd sat there on the ground, serene, a yogic pose, the faintest smile on her face – a yogic pose, for God's sake! Nearby the blood trickled and flowed, still warm. And I ran across the grass, screaming.

'To get back to it,' Cassins says, bringing my attention once more to the line of questioning. 'How would you describe their relationship? Would you say it was close?'

'Yes. At least it was for a while. Very close.'

Those two girls in the water, light glimmering around them, arms about each other as they slowly turned. Nothing in the world existing for either of them beyond their own locked gaze. Had I known then what it would be like? Was I wilfully deaf to the whisperings of conscience?

'Was it love, Abi?'

I had thought so, hadn't I? At the time.

'It was too one-sided to be love. Too distant – Corinne always held herself back, made herself aloof. Adoration, that's what it was. Beth adored her.'

Worshipped her like an unworthy devotee.

'But this adoration wasn't returned?'

'No, not really. She liked Beth. At first, we thought Corinne was good for her, showing an interest in her, drawing her out of herself. Beth had been very shy, you see. Not many friends. Well, not any really.'

I think of Siobhan Harte in the corridor, imagine what she'll say about Beth when they get her in a room.

'My daughter had a tendency to form strong attachments to certain people in her life – her friend Lisa. And she was very close to her aunt. To Melissa. She was troubled when she died.'

Disturbed.

My mouth has become dry, and I take a moment to drink from the glass of water they've left out for me. I wonder if she sees my hand shaking.

'But when we went to France,' I continue, 'I began to worry that Corinne was too controlling. That she understood the influence she had over Beth and would sometimes abuse it.'

'In what way?'

The hair, the tattoo, the behaviour. How paltry it sounds when detailed aloud.

'So why did you have her return to you? Why not end the association?'

I snap at her: 'Don't you think I wish we had?'

Instantly, I regret my rage. The emotions whirr inside me, vying to be released. I tell myself that I need to stay calm. It's important that I get through this without losing it. There will be time later to fall apart.

She waits for me to answer.

'Her father had died while we were staying with them. An accident. I suppose we felt we owed it to her . . . And there was never anything to suggest . . . Nothing at all to suggest that she would . . .'

I can't say it. I cannot say the words out loud.

'So, what happened, Abi? When did things go sour?'

'I don't know,' I tell her, but it's only partially true.

'Have you called her mother yet?' I ask. 'Has anyone told Valentina?'

'That's been taken care of.'

'What did she say? How did she react?'

Detective Cassins fixes me with a patient stare. A look that says: how do you think she'd react? An image of a gendarme arriving at La Grange. Valentina opening the door, seeing the uniform. Anouk, she would think, leaping to the conclusion. And then shock, disbelief, the opening out of horror as he tells her, as he explains.

'She didn't want Corinne to come,' I volunteer. 'Did you know that? The first time, I mean. Back in April. Before they'd even met.' I hear the amazement in my tone, and perhaps I am amazed, in hindsight, at the woman's perception. 'She rang us the night before Corinne was to fly. I'd never spoken to her before. She sounded agitated, anxious about the exchange. I thought it was just nerves, but . . .'

I look down at my hands. I've been twisting my rings,

fingering them like worry beads. And now I see the bruising, there on the fingers either side of my rings. Purple smudges. And I remember Ross Campbell squeezing my hand. Holding on to it for dear life. Desperation in his voice as he prayed. He begged.

'Why was Mrs Catto reluctant?' Cassins asks. 'What reason did she give?'

I think about it for a moment, and a sigh escapes me, a hot breath of despair. I bring my eyes up to meet hers, my shoulders rising and falling in a tired shrug.

'Intuition,' I say.

23

Corinne was different now.

At the airport, when the frosted glass gates opened and she emerged, weighed down by her bulging courier bag and dragging a wheelie case behind her, Abi experienced a twinge of sudden alarm. Inwardly, she had prepared herself for the grief the girl would be carrying, but it shocked her to see Corinne looking so small, dwarfed by her luggage. All traces of bubble-gum pink in her hair were gone, replaced by a sober brown, cut short into a straight line that skimmed her jaw. She seemed less defined, as if her outlines had become blurred, her colours faded. The animation which had so enlivened her features had evaporated, leaving her deflated, smaller somehow. She bore herself carefully, with an unnatural calm.

Abi and Eva hung back while Beth laid claim to her friend, gathering her up in an enfolding hug that went on for a long time until eventually Eva murmured: 'Jesus, enough already,' and Abi stepped forward to put a hand on the girl's shoulder.

'Thank you for your kindness,' Corinne told her after they had embraced.

'No need to thank me. We're glad you're here.'

Corinne nodded, her face a blank. 'I am very grateful,' she said in her new flat voice.

This formality felt strained to Abi – unnatural. Behind the veneer, she sensed a gathering storm of grief. She exchanged a glance with Eva, who looked unimpressed. Abi noticed how she made no effort to embrace the girl, and when Corinne expressed surprise that she had come to the airport with the others, Eva replied in a tight voice: 'Yeah, well, I'm only here to practise my driving,' then turned to lead them back to the car.

Abi had reassured her eldest daughter that Corinne would probably not be with them for long. But her ticket was open-ended and as Abi lifted the wheelie-case into the back of the Cherokee, she remembered the paucity of belongings when Corinne had first come to stay, and now began to doubt the reassurance she had given.

They drove in silence, Eva at the wheel with Abi beside her, the two other girls in the backseat. Corinne's gaze was fixed on the passing landscape beyond the window and her body language suggested an unwillingness to be drawn into any conversation. It was as if a shell had hardened around her. A carapace of brittle politeness. It made Abi wary and she was already having second thoughts.

Their decision to take Corinne in had not been easily reached. Mark had pushed for it while Abi had been reticent.

'I'm just thinking about Beth,' she'd argued. 'Is it too much for her to be burdened with? Corinne is obviously grieving. God knows what kind of emotional turbulence is going on inside her.'

'It's a good lesson for Beth. For both of them,' Mark reasoned. 'Teenagers are so inward-looking, self-centred. It won't do her any harm to think about her friend. And besides,' he went on, 'although she doesn't show it, Beth must be grieving for Melissa. A closeness like theirs doesn't just disappear without a trace. Maybe, with Corinne here, Beth might be able to address those feelings of sadness and loss, instead of just burying them.'

Abi listened to this argument with scepticism, but said nothing.

Valentina had told Abi that she could not cope, but she hadn't been explicit about what exactly in Corinne's behaviour she had found impossible to deal with. When Abi had gently raised a concern about this, Mark had waved it away, putting it down to the overwhelming nature of Val's own grief, and the obvious trickiness in the relationship between mother and daughter.

'They don't get on with each other,' he'd remarked. 'It'll be easier for Corinne once she's here. She's different with us.'

Abi hoped rather than believed this would be the case, but she hadn't pushed it. The truth was also that Abi shied away now from any disagreements with her husband, not wanting to upset the delicate equilibrium that existed between them, not until what he had said in France had been safely excised from their marriage.

Still, she couldn't help thinking, as the car hurtled along the M50, how different it had been a few months ago when they had first brought Corinne home. What she recalled of that journey was laughter erupting in the backseat, the sounds of animated chatter between the two girls. There had been a gracelessness to Corinne's eagerness at the time that Abi had found vaguely annoying, but now she found herself straining towards some kind of communication, anything to break the silence.

Turning to Eva, Abi remarked:

'You were out late last night.'

Eva kept her eyes on the road. 'I was just hanging out with some friends.'

'Were you at Alicia's?'

'No. Alicia wasn't there.'

Something careful and measured in the way she said this made Abi pay attention.

'Actually,' Eva said, clearing her throat, 'Alicia has a new boyfriend.'

'What happened to Josh?'

'They split up.'

'So, who's the new man?'

'It's Callum. Callum Ferguson.'

She'd kept her voice light, but Abi picked up the grace note of uneasiness there. She'd thought for some time that perhaps there was something between her daughter and the Fergusons' boy, and wondered now if Eva was feeling hurt, jealous.

'Well, we'll see how long that lasts,' Abi offered.

'What do you mean?'

'I mean, it will be difficult with Alicia heading off to university while Callum has to repeat sixth year.' Her eyes flickered towards Eva. 'You heard about his exams, I presume?'

'Yeah. It sucks.'

'Irene and Craig are so disappointed. After all they'd invested in him. They had such high hopes for him.'

'Jesus, Mum. He failed a few exams, that's all. It's not like he's dead.'

'All right,' Abi said peaceably, aware of the strident note that had entered Eva's tone.

'What about you?' came the voice from the backseat.

Surprised, Abi turned and saw Corinne, her steady gaze fixed on Eva's reflection in the rear-view mirror. 'Do you have a boyfriend?' Corinne asked.

'No. I don't.'

'Really? No one at all?' Her voice sounded arch, disbelieving.

'I just said "No", didn't I?'

Throwing her shoulders back, Eva sat a little straighter in the seat, staring intently over the steering wheel as she capably rounded the corner into Willow Park.

They pulled into the driveway and Abi, seeking to mollify

her daughter and defuse the tension that had sprung up in the car, said: 'The driving test will be a breeze. You've nothing at all to worry about, love.'

'Thanks, Mum,' Eva said, softening. She pulled the handbrake and turned off the engine.

They were about to get out of the car, when Abi looked up and said: 'My God, would you look at them.'

The Campbells' front door had opened, Ross and Becca emerging, the evening light catching the sequins on Becca's dress. It was a flapper dress, and the headband around her sleek black bob shimmered, the purple bow of her lipstick drawn into a broad smile. Behind her, Ross looked rakish and handsome in a white tuxedo, his bow tie loose around the open collar of his shirt. Their babysitter stood with Jo in her arms, both his little hands flapping excitedly as he waved goodbye to his parents.

'I thought you were their babysitter?' Corinne remarked to Eva, a testing tone to her voice.

'I don't have time now, what with university.' She tried to sound breezy, but the words came out defensive.

'Like Hollywood royalty,' Abi said admiringly.

Eva kept her eyes on them but said nothing. And when the others got out of the car and Abi went towards the Campbells, calling out cheerfully: 'Look at you two! God, I wish I had your life sometimes!' Eva didn't follow. She just sat there, as if caught in the reflected glow of the movie screen, watching with eyes fixed, rapt, until the credits rolled.

The first time was in his car.

Eva had waited in the parking lot outside the pool, just as they'd arranged, and with the sky fading to dusky blue, the Mercedes had pulled up alongside her.

'I know a place,' he'd informed her as she pulled the

seatbelt across her chest, thrilling to the fact that they were alone together in the Mercedes in a way that was so different from the driving lessons in the little Toyota. Back then she'd felt the flirtation to be one-sided – a stupid schoolgirl crush. Now they were both complicit.

'I can't believe we're actually doing this,' he'd remarked, shaking his head at his own audacity as the car sped further outside the suburbs, taking the back roads towards the Wicklow hills.

He didn't say where they were going, and she didn't ask. And when he pulled off the darkened road on to an uneven track, she felt the quiver of nerves as the car lurched and rocked over the rough terrain.

'I'll bring the Land Rover next time,' he'd remarked, his brow furrowed in concentration as he brought the car safely to a halt, and a jolt had gone through Eva at the realization that already he was planning on a next time.

With the engine cut off, the car filled with silence. They turned to each other. Nerves made her giggle.

'Is this where you bring all your dates?' she asked, and he looked confused, then stricken.

'No, of course not,' he replied with conviction. 'There hasn't been anyone before you. Not like this.'

'Good. I'm glad. I was just kidding anyway.' She looked about at the darkness of the trees, the whisk of scrub bushes skirting the crumbling walls of an old shed, its corrugated tin roof collapsed. 'This place is so . . . hidden.'

'I haven't been up here in years. I didn't know if it would still be here, still the same, or would the place have been bulldozed and some McMansion built here instead.'

It was only later, when she replayed the whole evening in her head, that she realized he must have come up here with Becca, when they'd first started dating. But right at that moment, Eva wasn't thinking about Becca. Too focused on Ross's mouth against hers, his tongue exploring her mouth, his hands tugging at her blouse, pulling it loose from the waistband of her jeans. When he guided her hand to the buttons of his jeans, she said:

'Can we go in the backseat?'

She lay down across the length of the bench, the leather shockingly cold against her bare skin, although after a moment it became warm, her skin adhering to it as Ross pressed down on her, the weight of his body a revelation. His height made it necessary to keep one of the passenger doors open and now as she felt him move inside her, distantly she was aware of the night rustlings in the forest beyond, an owl screeching as it took to the wing. And it seemed to Eva as if she was observing their coupling from afar, from a great height. Words went through her head: *I'm having an affair with a married man.* And if those words should have provoked feelings of guilt or shame, well, Eva didn't experience them. Instead, she felt a shivery thrill. She had been a good girl for so long. A straight-As student. A star in the pool and on the tennis court. Well groomed, well mannered, the perfect daughter. It felt so tedious sometimes, the burden of perfection. It wore her down. That her act of rebellion should come with Ross, thrilled her. It made her feel reckless and wild in a way she had never imagined. She opened herself up to him, clamping her feet around the backs of his thighs, his jeans around his knees as he thrusted, breath quickening, her body tightening around him so that she pulled him inside her even deeper.

'Fuck!' he cried out as he came, and she held him there jacking and bucking for a moment, until he slid down against her, his head resting, exhausted, against her right breast.

Afterwards, they stayed a while in the backseat, Ross

slouched against her shoulder, Eva tracing delicate lines over his scalp. He kept a sports bag shoved under the passenger seat and took from it now two bottles of beer, uncapping them with the bottle opener he used as a keyring. The beer was warm and hoppy. It felt just right sliding down her throat with the mild night air coming in through the open door, the giant moon hanging in the sky beyond the tall trees. Eva felt like they were both very far from home.

'Were you shocked when that happened? What we did in my kitchen that day?' he asked, and she could tell from his tone that he wanted her to be. That he was pleased with himself for being so daring, so bold. His wife and child upstairs!

'A little. And yet, part of me knew something was going to happen, you know? Like there was always the possibility of it between us, always threatening to explode whenever we were together.'

'You're so fucking sexy,' he told her, amazement in his tone. 'It took every last ounce of self-control to keep my hands off you during those lessons.'

She giggled. 'I bet you feel that way about all your female students.'

'No, I don't. Just you.' He'd become serious again, and it charmed her, how easy it was to shock him into solemnity. Then he roused himself and said: 'The night I picked you up from that party, and you tried to kiss me—'

'God, don't! Please. I was such a mess.'

'No! Don't you see, I wanted to kiss you!'

'Really?'

'Oh my God, yeah!'

When he'd gone home that night, he'd made love to his wife for the first time in months, and for the whole time he'd imagined it was Eva there in the bed beneath him, not Becca. Eva listened, astonished. Could it be true that he fantasized about her, Eva, instead of exotic, perfect Becca? And what did it mean that he hadn't slept with his wife in months?

'Things have been a bit stale in that department,' he admitted to her now, seeing perhaps the look of enquiry on her face. 'It's natural, I suppose, after being with the same person for so long. And things sort of changed anyway – became a bit difficult – when we were trying for a baby and it didn't work out. I always felt that Becca was disappointed in me after that. It's my fault we can't have kids, you see. People always wonder that, don't they? Whose fault it is. One too many kicks in the balls during rugby training!' He tried to make a joke out of it, but Eva could read the hurt that was clearly there behind the false levity. She stroked his head slowly, feelings of tenderness coming to the surface, as well as relief. He hadn't used a condom and she had been too caught up in the moment to ask.

She kissed the top of his head and they stayed like that for a while, Eva thinking about how different it was this time than it had been when she'd slept with Callum. None of the feelings of shame and doubt adhered to her now as they had done then. Callum had been a mistake – a catastrophic error of judgement – whereas being with Ross felt fated, a wonderful conclusion she had been inevitably drawn to. She basked in this pleasurable feeling until Ross's mobile vibrated with an incoming message and he said they'd better get moving. They drove home with all the windows open, the soft wind washing the air clean of any giveaway odours. He dropped her on a corner near Zion Hill, a ten-minute walk from home. They didn't want to risk any neighbours spotting them.

'What about you?' she asked, and he explained he'd go to the gym for a workout and a shower.

'But it's almost midnight!' she laughed.

He looked sheepish. 'I can't go home like this. Smelling of you.'

She thought of that during the walk back to her house, that even though they'd parted – Ross to lift weights in the Y, and Eva to slip in home and up to the quiet stillness of her bedroom – some trace of her remained on him, just as he did in her.

This thought occupied the spaces in her mind, expanding to fill any pockets of doubt, drowning out the niggling whispers of conscience. And when her mother stepped out of the car that day, and went to gush over Ross and Becca in their glamorous Gatsby gear, Eva's eyes moved to the row of cars that lined the Campbells' driveway, her eyes seeking out the Merc, and she thought of what they had done there and it consoled her. Picturing their bodies locked together, the urgent motion of her pelvis working against him, all thoughts of his wife flown from his head.

24

On Sundays, the Hollands often went to the tennis club for the afternoon. Eva frequently had a match and it was an opportunity for Abi and Mark to catch up with friends over Bloody Marys in the clubhouse bar. Beth didn't play tennis, and she hated everything about the club: the bar clotted with middle-aged men in Lacoste shirts and Argyle sweaters; their wives sipping G&Ts, discussing book clubs and Botox; meanwhile their offspring, a bunch of entitled brats, became hyper on the succession of carbonated drinks they consumed, while Sky Sports was projected endlessly on to the widescreen on the wall. The whole thing gave her a migraine and for the most part, she found some excuse not to go. But on that particular Sunday morning, when Abi raised the idea and Eva had chimed in that she'd booked a court for a practice match, Corinne had looked up and said:

'Hey. Can I go too?'

Beth's heart sank.

In her bedroom, after breakfast, she tackled Corinne on the issue, saying:

'I don't think you realize what you've just agreed to. The tennis club is like super-boring. We'll just be sitting around waiting for hours. The whole club is stuffed with losers. Can't we do something else instead?'

But Corinne had just shrugged, saying: 'You don't have to go if you don't want to. I can go with Eva.'

She was sitting on the bed, leaning over her knees to tie her shoelaces, and Beth, watching her from across the room, experienced an unexpected pang of loneliness. Ever since her return, Corinne had been quiet, withdrawn, choosing to spend hours in Mark's studio, silently working on a match-stick miniature cathedral modelled on Notre Dame. In the evening, after dinner, she had sat and watched *13 Reasons Why* with Beth, but Corinne's eyes had been heavy-lidded and dull, and she had sat apart from her in a distant armchair. Beth remembered with a pang the way they used to lounge together on the sofa with their legs entwined, the way Corinne would sometimes play with her hair or run her fingertips along Beth's scar. But now an awkward shyness had crept into their friendship. She missed the old Corinne, her vivacity, her mischief.

'What should I wear?' Beth asked, the wardrobe open beside her, and her own heart open with hope.

'I don't know.'

'But you've to pick for me, remember? It's part of the game.'

Corinne winced, and when she looked up, the expression on her face was one Beth didn't recognize: scornful, cold.

'It was a stupid game for children,' Corinne told her, on her feet now and moving towards the door. 'Make your own decisions, Beth. Grow up.'

The car park outside the tennis club was full, both flanks of the road leading to the club already occupied with SUVs pulled up to the kerb. Mark dropped Abi and the girls close to the entrance then drove off to find parking in one of the peripheral streets. Once inside, Eva disappeared to the changing rooms, while Abi led the girls into the bar.

'Here,' she said, handing Beth a twenty-euro note. 'Get yourselves something.'

Then, seeing Irene Ferguson waving to her across the

room, she began weaving her way through the scattered tables, leaving Beth and Corinne alone.

'Do you want a Coke or something?' Beth asked.

'Sure,' Corinne replied, but her eyes were casting around behind her, as if seeking a way out.

They queued for the bar in silence, Beth wondering what it was she had done wrong. She tried to tell herself that it was Corinne's grief for her father that was making her by turns irritable and subdued. But her thoughts kept returning to that evening in France – Bruno, the squalid house full of dogs. She recalled the brief inflation of fury in Corinne's eyes when Beth had chickened out of going through with the payment, and then the way she had refused to look at Beth when she emerged from the bedroom, the transaction completed. Beth understood that she had broken the rules of their game, and ever since that moment, she had felt the wintery coldness of Corinne's withdrawal, the panicky fear it stoked alive inside her.

They stepped closer to the bar, and she saw that Callum Ferguson was behind the counter, wearing the club's signature red polo-shirt with his jeans, concentrating on the pint he was pulling. It was strange, seeing Lisa's brother working there, the familiar ruddiness of his cheeks. She had overheard her mother on the phone consoling Irene over Callum's disappointing exams, his failure to gain a place on any of his desired choices.

'I guess he must be working here now,' Beth said, having pointed him out, but Corinne acted as if she hadn't heard, or didn't care. She was sullen and distracted, unwilling to be drawn into conversation.

'Do you want to find a table?' Beth asked. 'I can get the drinks—'

At that moment, she heard someone calling her name, and

when she turned to look, her skin prickled with alarm. Sasha, Nicole and Lisa were sitting nearby, still in their tennis whites, their post-match lunches spread out on the table before them.

'Look who's back,' Sasha trilled, her eyes alighting on Corinne, and Nicole laughed. 'Couldn't live without you, huh?'

'Ignore them,' Beth said, but Corinne just continued staring ahead, her face unreadable.

'Hey, Beth!' Nicole called out loudly. 'How's the transitioning going? Had your hormone shot today?'

Sasha spluttered with laughter.

'Fuck you,' Beth snapped, but she felt her cheeks prickling with heat.

They'd had a field day with her hair and tattoo since term started again, taunting her about being gender-neutral, non-binary, a dyke. Unwelcome hands fingering the ends of her hair, jostling with her for a glimpse of the rose on her neck.

'Ah, it's cute,' Sasha went on in her sweetly poisonous tone. 'You two back together again. What an adorable couple you make.'

'Hey, do your parents let you share a bed?' Nicole enquired. 'Pretty open-minded, aren't they?'

'Oh, we're all liberals here, Nicole,' Sasha cooed, taking a bite from her apple and giggling as the juice ran down her chin. 'Hey, didn't she make a pass at you one time?' she asked, turning to address Lisa, who sat up straight, her eyes flashing with alarm.

'What? No, I—'

'Didn't you tell us that she tried to kiss you once?' Sasha continued in her dangerous tone: 'Told you how she adored you?'

Callum Ferguson was looking over now, taking in the

scene, listening to every word. But another voice crept into Beth's thoughts: *My lovely girl. It's our secret, isn't it? Our special time.* The words weaving their own silvery path.

She was willing Lisa to look at her, but Lisa was wrapping her sandwiches back into their tinfoil, her cheeks flushing crimson.

'Hey, is it true your dad killed her father?' Sasha asked Beth. She had put aside her half-eaten apple and was releasing her hair from the tight ponytail that swung from the back of her head. Her gaze slid briefly in Corinne's direction.

'*What?*'

'Didn't he like run him over or something?'

'Of course not!'

'Word on the street is that your parents are on some kind of guilt trip about it. That they're paying for her education as like a form of compensation.'

'That's total bullshit! She's here because I wanted her to come. Because she's been having a really hard time back home and she's my friend.'

But Sasha seemed unconcerned with the detail. Bored of the conversation now, she smoothed her hair and stood up, fixing the strap of her bag on to her shoulder, checking with the others to see if they were ready.

'It's not true, okay?' Beth persisted, unwilling to be shrugged off while the rumour still lingered. 'It was an accident. It was no one's fault.'

'Fine. Like I care.'

Nicole snorted. 'What a dope.'

'I want you to say it,' Beth went on, her voice shaking with emotion. 'Say my dad didn't kill him. Say it!'

People seated at tables around were looking over now, and from behind the bar, Callum said: 'Ladies,' a warning there in his voice.

'Don't say anything, Sash,' Nicole counselled. 'Ignore the stupid cow.'

But Sasha gave Beth a long, forensic stare, like that she'd give a specimen to be dissected in the biology lab. Something particularly disgusting. A bull's eye. A rat.

'I honestly couldn't give a shit about what happened in France. But I do know this.' Sasha took a step closer, so close that Beth could see the flash of a silver chain winking from beneath her open collar. 'You're a freak. You're a fucking lunatic. Who the hell stabs themselves like that? In front of all of us? What, did you think you were Elliott fucking Smith or something? And we all know you would have been expelled if your parents hadn't bribed Bracken to keep you. But you know what I think?' And here she stabbed her index finger into Beth's chest, pressing against her ribs at the point above her heart. 'Next time, aim higher.'

Anger moved quickly inside Beth like the sudden snap of a towel in the air.

'All right, that's enough!' Callum said. His hands were on the bar and he was leaning forward.

But Sasha just laughed and wiggled her fingers, saying: 'Bye bye, freak!'

The long ribbon of their laughter trailed after them as they sashayed out into the foyer. But the rage stayed inside Beth, roiling and churning, her head swimmy like she'd had too much caffeine. Distantly, she heard Callum say:

'Are you okay?'

'I'm fine,' she murmured.

When she looked at him, she saw his brow lowered into a frown, but his eyes were full of concern.

'Don't mind those bitches,' he said.

Something inside her softened.

'That's your sister and her friends you're talking about.'

'Yeah. They're still bitches though.'

'I guess.' The anger inside her was trickling away.

She stepped closer to the bar, and he remarked: 'I haven't seen much of you lately. Did you and Lisa fall out?'

'Sort of.' Her cheeks flushed and she looked down. 'She doesn't talk to me any more.'

'Well, if it makes you feel any better, your sister won't talk to me either.'

The note of injury in his voice made her look up. Any possibility of an explanation passed when he shook his head and shot her a smile. 'Hey, don't mind me. I probably fucking deserve it anyway.' Snapping back into his role as a bartender, he clapped his hands together, saying: 'So? What's your poison?'

'Two vodkas and Coke?'

'No chance. Cokes do you?'

'Sure.'

She paid for the drinks, but when she looked around Corinne was gone. When a quick scan of the room failed to locate her friend, she drifted out into the lobby, her hands cold from holding the bottles of cola. The benches were unoccupied, and it was only when she went down the ramp to the indoor courts that she saw Corinne.

Leaning against the barrier, Corinne's eyes were fixed on the court where Eva swung her racket, bouncing about on her toes as she waited for the return. Something avid in her attention. A hunger that Beth recognized. For a moment, Beth just stood there, silently observing as the Coke bottles sweated in her hands, anxiety moving in her chest, a confused, bristling mass of it.

'Have you told anyone about us?' Ross asked Eva that night as they were driving home.

'No,' she replied.

Still tired from her match that afternoon, now her hips ached a little, her body dry and sore. They'd done it twice that time, the second time a little rough. She didn't mind, but it had chafed and now there was a dull ache. Eva always showered, but she felt a pressing need for a bath, wondered how she might explain that to her parents. It was after midnight.

'You're sure? Not even your friend, what's her name?'

'Alicia?'

'Right.'

'Hardly. We're not even talking at the moment.'

'How come?'

'Remember Callum? Well, Alicia's going out with him now.'

'Right.' He said it in a way that implied a question, like he was waiting for the real reason why they weren't speaking.

'I feel like it's a betrayal.'

'I thought you didn't like the guy.'

'That's not the point. I'd told her everything that had happened, everything that he'd done, and still she's going out with him? I can't understand how she'd do that to me.'

'Ah listen, Eva, I wouldn't take it to heart. That's the way it is at your age. You try people on for size. It's all part of growing up. Don't worry about it.'

She was stung by his casual dismissal but didn't say it. Instead, she sat in sullen silence, thinking of how easy it was for him to shrug her off, to remind her of the age difference between them. She had expected outrage from him at Alicia's callous disregard for her friend's feelings, but Ross seemed more concerned with their relationship being exposed. And while she understood his fear, part of Eva was thinking ahead – people would discover the truth at some point, they couldn't hide it for ever. Privately, she nursed a fantasy about the day Ross would leave Becca so they could set up their own home together, little Jo staying over at weekends. Part of her was convinced it was inevitable so why prolong the wait?

'But I'm glad you didn't tell her about us,' Ross went on, 'because it's really important that no one finds out about this. It's our secret, right? Just you and me – that's what matters. No one else needs to know.'

'I haven't told anyone.'

'Good. Because we'd be in a world of pain if this got out.'

She laughed, but there was an edge of annoyance to her laughter. His warning tone irked her. It gave her an unwelcome Sunday-evening feeling, school the next day, homework not done.

'I'm eighteen,' she reminded him. 'It's not like it's a crime.'

'Maybe it should be,' he remarked grimly, hunched over the steering wheel, staring hard at the road ahead. 'I'm almost forty, Eva.'

'I know how old you are. I don't care.' She reached over and put her hand on his thigh. 'Our ages don't matter. All that counts is us being together.'

'For however long it lasts,' he muttered, and she felt a lick of panic in her stomach.

'What do you mean?' she asked.

'It's autumn now. Soon it'll be winter. We can't keep driving around the Wicklow mountains looking for a place to fuck in the freezing cold.'

He hadn't called it that before. Fucking.

He dropped her off at their usual spot and she stood watching until the tail lights of the Land Rover disappeared around the corner. As she walked home, she thought about the weekend that was over now, and wondered how much these snatched hours together meant to him. Did they register at all, or would his thoughts automatically tilt in the direction of his family: afternoons in the park throwing a ball with Jo, or some fortieth birthday party he and Becca had attended? Eva remembered them in their Gatsby costumes, pictured them sipping from champagne saucers, dancing the Charleston in some bar done up like a speakeasy. It seemed so grown-up and sophisticated, a far cry from the parties she went to: R&B thumping through speakers, rum and Coke in paper cups, always some girl crying or puking, bodies dry-humping on the stairs.

As she reached her driveway, she cast a glance at the Campbells' house and saw the light on upstairs in their bedroom. Briefly, she imagined Becca up there reading or watching Netflix, unaware that for the past few hours her husband and her babysitter were making love in a car up the Dublin Mountains. The thought came to her now that she, Eva, could march right up and lean on the Campbells' bell and when Becca opened the door, naked surprise on her face, Eva could tell her everything. About Ross, about where they'd been and what they'd done. She could stand there and tell that woman that her husband's semen was, at that very moment, trickling from Eva's body, dampening the cotton of her underwear.

The possibility made her feel powerful, but it also frightened her as she pushed through her own front door, closing it softly behind her. The hall was dark and quiet, and she hurried up the stairs, carrying the thought in her head. It filled her so completely that she almost didn't notice the figure lying on her bed, until the shadow moved in the darkness and Eva found herself jumping in fright.

'What are you doing in here?' she snapped, fear making her aggressive.

'Where have you been?' The voice cool and low and very calm.

'None of your fucking business.'

Light from outside reflected in the shine of Corinne's eye. She blinked once.

'You were with him. The neighbour.'

'Get out of my fucking room!'

'Quiet, Eva. We don't want your parents to wake up, do we?'

It was there in the inflection of her voice, the suggestion of a smirk, the latent threat.

'It's late. I'm tired,' Eva said, keeping her tone level but firm. 'Why don't you go back to your room. Go talk to Beth.'

'I don't want to talk to Beth. I want to talk to you.'

'I've got nothing to say to you.'

'Oh, really?' Corinne laughed. 'I think you have a lot to tell me. You've been very naughty, no?'

Fear gathered in her throat. 'You're full of shit, Corinne. Now get out of my fucking room.'

The other girl stood and then came towards her. As she approached, Eva instinctively stepped back. But Corinne reached out her hand and gently pushed the door shut. This close, Eva could feel the warmth of the girl's breath against her face.

'Just imagine,' Corinne said, 'what your parents would think were they to find out what you've been doing. How shocked they would be if I told them about that picture you sent him. The next-door neighbour.'

'They wouldn't believe you. And besides, you've no proof.'

'Or his pretty wife. What do you think she would say if I told her? She could check through his messages – I'm sure he kept it.'

Eva's heart was beating hard now. The room felt small and

oppressive, her mind flitting all over the place, but there was nowhere for her to go. No one to turn to.

'I don't want to fight with you, Eva,' the girl said, her voice softening, but still Eva didn't trust her. 'But I am worried. He is no good for you. I can see that. He doesn't make you happy.'

'You don't know the first thing about it.'

'I see the way you run around after him. Why do you let him control you?'

'I don't. This is bullshit.' But her mind twitched at Corinne's suggestion, thinking of the lectures she had missed just so she could be with Ross. And even when she was in university a part of her felt absent, as if she was just treading water until the time passed and she could be with him again.

'Do you love him?' Corinne asked, and Eva felt the blood rush to her cheeks.

'That's none of your business.'

'Does he love you?'

Did he? There were moments when he looked at her and she felt sure he was on the verge of saying it.

Corinne had eased herself on to the bed again, resuming her reclining pose. Something patient in her manner, her stare, as if suggesting she could wait all night.

'You are not happy,' Corinne observed, words whispered like silk over skin. 'I can help you.'

But Eva didn't trust this. The threat of the photograph lingered in the air between them, like a foul odour that would not dissipate.

'What makes you think I need your help?' she asked.

The girl smiled through the darkness, her eyes shining with a peculiar light, and a feeling came over Eva then of panic, indistinguishable from the suspicion that lapped inside.

'We all need a friend,' Corinne said softly. 'Trust me. Let me be yours.'

25

The first couple of weeks passed, a routine quickly establishing itself in the household. Abi left early for work before the rest of them were stirring. Eva, having started university, was rarely home. Days often passed without Mark setting eyes on her. And with Beth and Corinne busy at school, Mark found himself once more alone.

His studio was tidy now, all of Melissa's effects boxed up and put away or else discarded. A question mark still hung over what to do about her house, but Mark had decided to wait until probate had been taken care of before raising the matter once more. Despite Eva's lofty dismissals, it remained a thorny issue.

On his return from France, Mark had emailed Andrew and informed him of his decision to withdraw from the film. 'There'll be other projects,' Abi had gently suggested, and lately Mark had started putting out feelers, seeking local projects that would not draw him away from home for long.

He tried not to feel bitter about it, and yet it still rankled. That morning, he'd received an email from Andrew, who was on location in the Czech Republic. Photo attachments showed an enormous, sprawling set outside Prague, each image crawling with little ant-like carpenters, electricians and specialist painters. Mark had pored over the pictures with a mixture of awe, criticism and envy. Mostly he felt excluded.

Now, as he read over his CV once more, contemplating ways to jazz it up a little and fill in the gaping holes with something other than 'Fatherhood', Mark realized that the email from Andrew had made him feel shockingly middle-aged. The distance that had opened out between the experiences of the two men seemed vast. While one's career had skyrocketed, the other's had stagnated, Mark's professional life dying a slow, silent death with no mourners, only a vague sense of embarrassment. For the first time it dawned on him that there was little chance of him reviving it. He felt the dearth of his life experience; so much had been wasted. These were the thoughts he was mulling over when Eva's footfall sounded outside the door. Seconds later she appeared in his studio.

'I need to talk to you,' she told him, her voice frosty and tight.

'What's the matter?' he asked wearily.

'That freak was in my bedroom again.' He returned his gaze to the computer screen but still he felt her eyes on him, shining coals of fury.

'You're talking about Corinne, I presume.'

'Who else? It's the third time this week. Why is she always in my fucking space?'

'She's probably lonely.'

'She's got Beth, hasn't she?'

'I suppose.'

'And you,' Eva added.

Mark looked up, thinking he'd caught a note in her voice. 'Me?'

'Come on, Dad. She's always in here, fiddling with that stupid model.'

'That's got nothing to do with me. She's just bored, looking for something to do.'

'Fine. If you say so.'

Last night, after spending a couple of hours with Corinne working on the model, he had gone to bed, satisfied with the progress they had made on the apse of the cathedral – the narrow spindles of the flying buttresses and counter-supports. It was as he was getting undressed that Abi had looked up from her book and asked him: 'Do you think she's attractive?'

'Who?' he'd replied, his back to her as he sat on the bed and pulled off his socks.

'You know who. Corinne.' Her voice was light but the words were loaded.

'She's a child, Abi.'

'So? You can still have an opinion, can't you? You can be objective. The same way you can look at our daughters and say that Eva is without question attractive, whereas Beth . . .'

'I don't see them that way. And for God's sake, don't let Beth hear you say that. She's insecure enough as it is.'

He'd pushed himself away from the bed and finished undressing in the bathroom, hoping that when he returned, she'd have let the matter go.

Still, it came back to him now, as he reached forward and closed his laptop, then swivelled his chair so he could face his daughter.

'You're not happy about Corinne staying with us?'

Eva frowned. 'I just don't get why you invited her back. I mean, she's already had her stint here with us.'

'The girl just lost her dad. Let's try to be compassionate.'

'So that's why you asked her back? Out of compassion? Not because you're feeling guilty?'

Mark said nothing but he wondered, not for the first time, how much of his conversations with Abi were overheard by their daughters. It was Mark who'd said, after the call from Valentina begging for their help, 'How can we not? Every time I think of Guy in the car, clutching his head, I feel to blame. Like if I hadn't hit that boar, if I'd been driving more

265

carefully . . .' Of course, the fact was that it was the man's own actions that were responsible for his demise – the over-eating, the drinking, Guy's own recklessness at removing his seatbelt. But still, it kept him awake some nights, the gurgling sound in Guy's throat coming back to him, amplified in the darkness.

'And I don't know how you managed to swing it with the school,' Eva added. 'Mum probably promised to refurb the computer lab or something.'

This was a low swipe, referring back to that time when Beth had been threatened with expulsion in the wake of her self-harm. In the conversation that had followed with the principal, Abi had lightly dropped the suggestion of some IT education her firm were in a position to offer – free of charge, naturally. A programming course given by trained instructors – Abi would be happy to arrange it.

Mark experienced a brief flush of shame now at the memory, felt the sting in Eva's comment.

'The school are fine with it,' he said coolly. 'And Val is covering the fees for the half-term.'

'It's weird, seeing Corinne in my old uniform. I came home last night and found her lying on my bed.'

'Really?' The surprise sent his tone up a notch.

'Scared the shit out of me.'

'But what was she doing there?'

'Search me. I'm not happy about it, Dad.'

'Point taken,' he said, running a hand over his jaw.

'Will you talk to Beth about it?'

'Okay.'

'She keeps glaring at me as if I'm trying to steal her soul-mate from her. Like it's my fault Corinne's decided to attach herself to me like a leech.'

'It will only be for a few weeks,' he said, trying to soothe her.

She was backing out of the room now. 'I hope so,' she said, and flashed him a warning glance before leaving him once more alone.

The rain had been coming down all day. It streaked the windows of the Home Economics kitchen, shallow puddles forming in the dips of the granite sills where pigeons huddled, ruffling their feathers with indignant complaint. Beth stared at them, at the darkening sky beyond, evening crowding in, and wondered where Corinne was at that moment, whether she was out there getting drenched.

Just before class had started, Corinne had sidled up to her in the corridor, looking groggy, her movements slow and bored. 'I'm going,' she'd said. 'Cover for me?'

'What's going on?' Beth had asked, a low jump of alarm catching in her throat.

Corinne had shrugged. 'Just say I'm sick,' she'd said and turned away.

Beth's solidarity was unwavering, but she felt at times as if Corinne no longer relied on her the way she once had.

'Aprons on and find yourselves a partner,' Ms Quinn barked from the top of the class.

Beth had forgotten her apron, so she took off her school jumper and tucked her tie into her shirt. Looking around, she saw Lisa standing alone. It had been months since they'd spoken to one another, the chasm between them too large to be bridged. But now, while all the other girls paired off, they eyed each other shyly. After a moment, Lisa moved towards her.

'Where's Corinne?' she asked.

'She went home. She wasn't feeling well,' Beth lied, trying to sound casual. 'Where's Nicole?' she asked.

'At the orthodontist. She's getting her braces tightened.'

Beth gave a swift, mirthless laugh, and Lisa frowned.

'Don't,' she softly admonished. 'You used to have braces too, remember?'

Beth looked down at the cluster of ingredients on the table, the nested bowls and measuring spoons, and felt ashamed.

'Sorry. You're right.'

There followed a moment of strained silence, then Lisa said: 'I guess we'd better partner up.'

They listened as Ms Quinn outlined the steps to be taken, all the while Beth concentrated her attention on Lisa's presence. How strange it was to be beside her again. For years she had existed closely within Lisa's orbit, knew instinctively the familiarities of Lisa's corporeal reality – the soft, quiet way she held herself, the sensitivities of her skin, plagued by sudden flare-ups of eczema, the stoic manner in which she trained herself to resist scratching. Glancing down, Beth saw the red rawness of Lisa's fingers and it caused a small lurch of tenderness within her, while at the same time she noticed the plaited leather bracelets that were unfamiliar. Lisa's hair, brown and thin, was worn in a new way. The lank ponytail that used to swing down her back was gone, replaced by a tightly scraped little bun, austere and prim. Beth noticed this with a twinge of sadness and imagined the scene – Sasha saying: 'You have *got* to do something with your hair, Lise. That ponytail is so lame!' Nicole sniggering, 'Yeah. It makes you look like twelve.' Lisa's martyred submission as they refashioned her hair to their liking.

Silence stretched between them as they measured the flour and sugar. Beth, unwrapping a slab of butter, said: 'So Callum is working in the club now?'

'You saw him?'

'He served me. You know, the other day when—'

'Oh, right. I forgot.' Lisa seemed embarrassed, and after a moment, she added:

'Look, I'm sorry about what happened. Those things Sasha and Nicole said . . . It all got out of hand.'

'It's okay—'

'No, it's not. I never meant for anyone to think that you're . . . You know . . .'

'A dyke?'

Lisa winced. 'Not that there's anything wrong with that. They just misconstrued what I said.' The skin at her neck had turned a mottled red. 'I've been wanting to say something to you about it ever since it happened. I feel awful.'

Lisa was looking at her directly now, and Beth remembered with a pang how they used to sit cross-legged on the bed staring intently at each other for hours while they talked. Having Lisa's familiar blue-green gaze fixed on her once more made her feel both happy and sad at the same time, longing and loss mingling together in confusion.

'That's okay,' Beth said, adding: 'Callum was pretty nice to me though.'

'Oh. Well. That's good.'

Then Lisa leaned closer; lowering her voice, she said: 'My dad made him take that job. He's been giving Cal a really hard time since the exam results. They keep having these massive rows, Dad calling Cal an embarrassment and a waster, saying he's ashamed to have a son who's thick and useless.'

'God. Really?'

'He told Cal that the job in the tennis club would be suitably humbling and that if he felt demeaned having to wait upon his friends and their families then so much the better. You know, he's not just serving drinks and that. He also has to clean out the locker rooms, the toilets and everything. Dad said that if he didn't take the job, he'd have to find somewhere else to live.'

'That's awful.'

'You've no idea. Dad hits him sometimes.'

'What?'

'Don't tell anyone I said that—'

'I won't.'

'The atmosphere at home has been toxic.'

Lisa looked down at their hands ploughed into the bowl full of flour, the half-formed dough. She suddenly looked like she might cry.

'I don't know why I couldn't just pick up the phone and talk to you about it,' Lisa admitted. 'We used to spend hours on the phone. So why is it so difficult now?'

Beth shrugged but didn't trust herself to speak.

'Do you hate me?' Lisa asked, and Beth shook her head, no.

She thought back to the phone call after Sasha's party, Lisa ringing to check she was okay, and how Beth had started screaming, accusing Lisa of abandoning her, yelling that she was spineless and two-faced, shallow and weak. She had grown hysterical, but even then, she had known it wasn't the grand betrayal that she had made it out to be.

Her anger had cooled, and then fear set in. Days later, a cold conversation on a bench in Bushy Park, Lisa's spaniel Daisy straining impatiently on the lead, while Beth tried to account for her behaviour on the phone. Lisa sat stony-faced while Beth gabbled on about feeling threatened by Lisa's new closeness to Sasha and Nicole, how she worried about losing her friend, but Lisa had just squinted at her in the slanting light, an eyebrow tilted with scepticism. That was when Beth told Lisa that she loved her. That she missed her. That she was closer to Lisa than anyone else in the world.

Lisa had listened, the dog's tugging on the lead growing stronger and more agitated. Finally, she'd let out a small huff of impatience or frustration and said:

'You're too intense, Beth. You expect me to be everything to you and it's too much. Sometimes I just feel smothered.'

'I know. I'm sorry. I'll try not to be as intense. I'll give you more space.'

But Lisa had sighed. 'You don't get it, Beth. Having just one friend – it's not normal.'

She'd gotten to her feet, pulling on the ends of her scarf, tightening it around her neck.

'I just need a break from you for a while,' she'd said, and Beth had felt a new and sudden desperation gripping her. She stood up and reached out to hug her friend, to embrace her, and that's when she saw it – the expression crossing Lisa's face so swiftly, she might have missed it. Revulsion. An instant recoil.

'For how long?' Beth asked, thinking a week – maybe two.

But Lisa had shaken her head. 'I need to find different friends,' she said, 'on my own. Without you. I don't want to hang out with you any more.'

A few days later, as Ms Philips, their Art teacher, had swept into the room, Beth had opened up her pencil case and found a bloodied sanitary towel among her markers. The class erupted around her into screeches of disgust and howls of laughter and something inside her seemed to crack open, revealing a soft, painful vulnerability. The craft knife was there on the desk. Hardly any thought went into it – an impulse, that's what it was. A way of confusing the pain. A small flesh-wound to distract from the dark chasm opening inside her.

She had almost forgotten what it had felt like. But now, what came back to her was the rumble of emotions, the clamouring of despair, of unacceptable rage at all the burning disappointments, the parade of indignities. And sadness. Immense sadness breaking over her head like a wave.

In the bowl of flour, Lisa's hand moved, her fingers finding Beth's, the gentle squeeze of them as Beth's hand responded, flakes of dough catching in their grip. It only lasted a second or two and then Lisa let go, saying: 'I am sorry, you know?' and Beth nodded, saying 'Me too.'

'I know you think I'm crazy to be friends with them,' Lisa continued after a moment, picking up the thread of their conversation, 'but they're nice, really, once you get to know them.'

'Even Sasha?' Beth asked sceptically.

'She's different when she's on her own, away from the crowd. I know she acts like a princess, but she actually has a pretty hard time at home. Her dad's work sends him abroad like for months at a time, to Saudi, Bahrain, places like that. He's practically a stranger to her. And her mum is really hard on her, constantly putting pressure on her to be perfect. It all got too much for her last year, and she had to go on beta blockers for a while. God, don't tell anyone I said this, okay?'

It was strange how easily they slipped into their old ways of sharing confidences, and Beth felt a twinge of conscience when she remembered what she had been plotting for Sasha, the hours she'd already spent on social media, planting the seed and nurturing it, watching for it to spread.

'What about Corinne?' Lisa asked, interrupting her thoughts.

'What about her?'

'You two seem to be good friends.'

'Yeah. She's cool. We've gotten pretty close. Especially since her dad died.' Even as she spoke the words, she wondered was there still any truth to them. The rupture in her friendship with Corinne was a wound that would not heal.

'Hmm.'

Lisa looked away, busying herself with the textbook, running a floured finger down the page.

'What?' Beth asked, and Lisa chewed the inside of her cheek, considering her answer.

'It's just, some people think it's a bit odd.'

'What do you mean?'

'They think that you've changed since you've started hanging out with her. That she sort of controls you.' Her brow furrowed with the awkwardness of her admission.

'Who thinks this? Sasha and Nicole?'

'Not just them. I do too,' she added.

'She doesn't control me. Is this because of my hair?'

'No—'

'It's just a haircut. Not all of us want freaking hair extensions and fake tan, you know.'

'It's not about how you look, Beth, it's about your behaviour.' Lisa paused, swallowing as if the words were causing her difficulty. Beth remembered with a pang how anxious Lisa became about any sort of confrontation. The mildest put-down could send her into a spin of neurosis. Lisa went on now, cautiously: 'You don't talk to anyone in school except for her, and I mean anyone. I might be the first person you've spoken to all term, not counting that row with Sasha and Nicole. You walk around with Corinne like she's this precious commodity that you have to protect. Even the way you look at her when she's talking, it's like this adoring gaze. And you don't even seem to realize you're doing it!'

Beth's cheeks burned. 'Are you jealous?'

'Not jealous. Concerned.'

She couldn't look at Lisa, but she felt the touch of her hand now at her sleeve, Lisa's voice dropping to a whisper: 'Did something happen to you, Beth? Something you didn't tell me?'

Anger roared within her.

'I tried to tell you,' she snarled but then broke off suddenly as Ms Quinn came towards them.

'My God, girls, is this all you've done? Get moving and roll out that pastry, and Beth, where's your apron?' Beth mumbled an excuse, Ms Quinn snapping her own apron from over her head and tossing it in Beth's direction. 'Put that on or you'll ruin your uniform,' she commanded before moving away.

For a moment, Beth stood there fingering the unfamiliar fabric.

'Here, let me do that.'

She submitted to Lisa, her anger all fallen away, her arms slack at her sides while the apron was tied around her. Lisa's fingers at the back of her neck, tying the apron strings – Beth felt her pause.

'Can I look?' she asked timidly, and Beth said yes, felt the small tug at the back of her collar, Lisa's breath warm against her neck as she examined the ink flower that bloomed there.

'Did it hurt?' she asked, her fingers tentative against Beth's skin.

'Yeah. A bit.'

'Why did you do it?'

'I don't know. I just felt like it.' But even as she spoke the words, she knew it wasn't true. She'd done it because Corinne had told her to do it. Was Lisa right? Had she surrendered all control to Corinne?

'It's very pretty,' Lisa offered.

'Do you think so?'

'Yeah. And your hair is . . . well, it's a bit full on, but I guess I understand why you did it. I think it's kind of brave.'

'You do?'

'Uh-huh. I just miss the old you, a bit.'

She was trying to be kind, but Beth suddenly recoiled from it.

Her submission to Corinne's suggestions – the severity of the haircut, the permanence of the tattoo – had been a statement. A testament of her love, her devotion. But it was also a way of protecting herself – a false front to her vulnerability. That Lisa had seen through this, had glimpsed the desperate longing inside her, made Beth suddenly ashamed.

'Yeah. Well, you're hardly one to talk,' she said, heat suffusing her face. 'The job Sasha and Nicole did on you. That severe little knot they've made of your hair. Just looking at it gives me a migraine.'

Lisa's face moved with a flicker of sudden hurt. The kindness fell away from her eyes and Beth saw the swift recalculation there, the almost instant withdrawal.

'There's something wrong with you, Beth. Something broken inside you.'

The words were searing, causing her to lash out. 'And you can tell that princess Sasha to watch her back. Soon she's going to know what it feels like to be talked about like a fuckup. A freak. A dose of her own fucking medicine.'

'What do you mean?'

But then Ms Quinn snapped at them to stop talking, and for the rest of the class they didn't look at each other, the silence hardening between them.

26

'What is this place?' Ross asked.

He was standing behind her while Eva slotted the key in the lock, a light drizzle falling on them. It was three o'clock in the afternoon. Nerves made Eva glance around at the neighbouring houses, watchful for a face at the window, a figure paused at the end of the drive. But there was no one there, only Ross's Mercedes parked on the deserted street. She pushed the door open with her hip, saying:

'Come in and I'll show you.'

It was strange being back here. The house felt different and yet the same. The same brownish décor, the same dusty airlessness. And yet there was an emptiness to the place that was unfamiliar. No radio playing tinny pop in the background, her aunt humming tunelessly along. The silence was rich and enveloping and she felt the nerve endings along the back of her neck tingling as she led Ross through the rooms.

It felt like they were trespassing – burglars stealing through the house, aware of every creaking floorboard, each groaning step. *This is Beth's house now*, she found herself thinking, but no feelings of jealousy flowed from that thought. She was just grateful that the house was empty and available to them – a place where she and Ross could be alone together.

In the bedroom, Eva looked around at the studded green velvet headboard she remembered, the same curtains with the Laura Ashley print that had been hanging there for as long as Eva could recall; she drew them now against the thin afternoon light. Ross stood in the doorway; his height and bulk made the room feel smaller, the furniture cramped and mean. He seemed to be hanging back, a shyness coming over him that was unfamiliar.

'You sure this is okay?' he asked, eyes darting around the room – the pressed flowers framed above the bureau, the scatter cushions over the worn chenille bedspread.

'Trust me. No one comes here. It's perfectly safe.'

'You don't think it's weird, us being here like this?' He glanced meaningfully at the bed between them. 'I mean, she died there, right? Doesn't that make you feel strange?'

'It makes me glad to be alive,' she said forcefully, and holding his gaze she began unbuttoning her blouse, taking her time, a performance that she was letting him watch, revelling in how his inhibitions loosened and then fell away, how she could tempt him into surrender.

Afterwards, they lay together in the bed, his body spooned around hers, and she felt the weight of his arm over her hip, luxuriating in the sweet slowness of time in this bedroom, so different to being in the car where they could never truly relax.

'You laughed,' he told her, his mouth by her ear. 'When we were in the middle of it, you were laughing.'

She heard the smile in his voice, the question there.

'I was thinking of my aunt,' she told him, 'imagining her here, watching us, what we were doing in her bed.'

'Jesus. You perv,' he teased, and she laughed again.

'She was so uptight, you know. Highly strung. We always had to tiptoe around her, always getting warned about her fucking nerves. Such a drag.'

'I'd say her nerves would be shot, watching what you just did for me,' he chuckled, his hand squeezing her breast.

'Do you really think I'm perverse?'

'You're sexy as hell and you know it.'

She squirmed with pleasure. Maybe there was something perverted about her, some deviant drive within her. Right at that moment, the rest of her classmates would be pouring out of Lecture Theatre L. They had two hours of Thermodynamics on a Thursday and she had skipped it to be here, lying with a married man in the bed where her aunt had died.

Not that she had any regrets. She could always catch up with the work later in the year. And while she was here with Ross, Eva could forget about college, and about the persistent disappointment she had carried around inside her since term began.

Throughout her final year at school, it was driven home to her again and again how her life would change once she went to university. The expectation was raised that it would be challenging, exciting, an adventure into adulthood and independence, a chance to explore the world beyond the limiting confines of school. Why then did she feel so disillusioned? Her other friends all seemed entranced, caught up in their heady new experiences, but Eva seemed immune to the novelty of it all, lost. When she got home in the evenings and saw the hopeful looks on her parents' faces as they asked about her day, Eva felt something plummet within her. It was such an effort to lie and pretend that everything was great, jabbering away about how new and exciting everything was, all the interesting people she was meeting, what a great adventure she had embarked on, instead of the flat loneliness inside her, the cowed feelings of insecurity, of not belonging.

The only time she felt relaxed, completely herself, was when she was with Ross.

'It sucks,' she told him honestly when he asked about college. 'The classes are either boring or confusing, and the other kids are so immature. I think I've made a big mistake.'

'Ah, give it time,' he said. 'It's early days yet.'

'I wish you were there,' she told him, and he laughed.

'Yeah, right. Can you picture it? Me among all those students!'

'Why not? They do take mature students, you know.'

But she couldn't imagine him there. No more than she could picture herself at his friends' fortieth birthdays. The only place it made sense was when it was just the two of them, together. She lived for these stolen hours, when she could let everything go and feel him inside her.

From where she was lying, she could see Ross's shoes on the ground – a pair of Dubarry's, the dark indent of his foot visible inside. She had the strange desire to press her own foot into the shoe, feel how neat and small it felt in the groove his foot had made.

'I wish we could stay here for ever,' she murmured, and felt the hum of his response communicating through her back.

'Maybe we could get Beth to sell it to us, hmm? Can you picture it?' she asked. 'You and me, living together here? Sleeping in the same bed every night. Waking up together. Wouldn't it be amazing?'

He held her close but didn't answer. She pressed on.

'We'd do it up, of course. Put our own stamp on it. And every morning, we could get up early and go to the gym together. Or if the weather was good, we could go jogging, picking up coffees and pastries afterwards which we'd eat stretched out on the grass by the canal. And then we'd come back home,' she said dreamily, 'and shower—'

'Together?'

'Why not? And in the evenings, we could meet for a drink or go for something to eat, and then come back here and make love all night long.'

She turned over, stretching her body against his.

'That's a nice fantasy,' he said, but she could feel him turned on by her account.

'We wouldn't have to sneak around in your car any more,' she continued as he began tracing her breastbone with kisses. 'We could be together all the time, no one between us.'

'Mm-hmm.' His tongue circled her nipple, his hand reaching between her thighs.

'And at the weekends, Jo could come over. We'd have the spare bedroom made up just for him. Little decal stickers on the walls of fire engines and trucks. He loves those, doesn't he?'

Ross had stopped kissing her, his hand moved away. For a moment, he lay propped up on one elbow beneath the covers, a stillness coming over him.

'What?' she asked. 'What is it?'

He said in a quiet voice: 'I don't want you to talk about him.'

'Why not?'

He was looking down, but his eyes weren't seeing her body; rather they were focused on some inward point that she couldn't access.

'What you and I do together,' he said softly, seriously, 'it's separate from my family life. I care about you, Eva, and I value the time we spend together. But I need us to be clear about what this is. It's amazing and exciting and fun. But it's just temporary. You do know that, right?'

Her heart was drumming so loud, she thought he must be able to hear it.

'Yeah, of course. I know that.'

He breathed out with relief. 'Good. Just when you were going on there about us living together and stuff, I was worried that maybe we weren't on the same page—'

'No, no. I get it. Hey, I was just messing with you,' she smiled, trying to make light of it.

'You're sure?'

'Of course! I know what this is. A torrid affair, right?'

'Definitely torrid,' he laughed, but there was a little undercurrent of nerves in his voice, like he wasn't entirely convinced. Then, he added: 'Sometimes I wonder what it is you're doing with me. I mean, right now you should be in college, hanging out with boys your own age, having all your experiences with them.'

'Maybe I wanted a different kind of education,' she said coyly, sidling up to him, watching for his doubt to slip out of sight.

It worried her, though, the risk that was always there: that she might lose him. Sometimes, Eva wished she had someone to confide in about her relationship with Ross. She would have told Alicia once, but not now. Not after her betrayal. The only person who knew was Corinne, who wielded the knowledge like a threat.

She had no choice but to keep her own counsel. And when he kissed her, she convinced herself that everything would be all right. It was just the two of them cut adrift from the real world. They didn't need anyone else.

Mid-October, dark mornings, damp evenings, summer a distant memory now. Their schoolwork became intense, arduous, all the heavy lifting to be done before Christmas, Halloween tests approaching. The time left before Corinne's departure was rapidly shrinking and it pained Beth to think of it.

Friday evening, rain pelting down, Beth borrowed Mark's Visa and booked cinema tickets. *Joker* was showing in Dundrum. They could get the bus there. She had money for

Eddie Rocket's afterwards. Beth had picked her own clothes to wear but still she sought approval. In her bedroom, she waited for Corinne to finish her shower.

Downstairs, the front door slammed, footsteps thundering up the stairs, followed by the sound of Eva's bedroom door closing.

Beth listened, trying to read the silence. The noise from the shower jets had stopped. She could smell spices on the air – her father was making a curry. She thought she heard low murmurs coming from Eva's room and made the assumption that her sister was on the phone. Briefly, Beth considered quietly crossing the hall to put her ear against the door and listen. It was not something she was proud of, resorting to eavesdropping on members of her own family. But Eva was so secretive. How else would Beth find out anything that was going on in her sister's life?

On this occasion, she decided to stay where she was and wait for Corinne. While she waited, Beth scrolled through her social media accounts for updates. Her plan was working, and she took the opportunity now to add a few more crumbs to the trail. It was getting easier at this point – a simple matter of agreeing with speculation, thereby amplifying it. Sasha was involved now, and Beth noted the degree of annoyance and even hysteria that had crept into Sasha's posts – vehement denials, protestations of bullshit – but it was all just part of the game. Briefly, she remembered Lisa's whispered account of Sasha's insecurities: talk of an absentee father and an over-zealous mother, how beneath the nonchalant exterior, medication was required to calm her nerves. For a moment, Beth felt a pinch of conscience, as if Lisa was right there at her elbow, tugging at her sleeve. Still. It was hard to feel sorry for Sasha. 'See how you like it,' Beth murmured to herself while 'liking' another denigrating comment.

Corinne had been gone for a while, and when Beth stepped out into the hall, she heard the rise and fall of voices from Eva's room, the whispered urgency. Opening the door, she found them sitting on the bed, Corinne wrapped in her towel with hair dripping, Eva beside her.

'What's going on?' Beth asked, her gaze falling on Corinne's hand which was wrapped around Eva's wrist.

Instantly Eva snatched her hand out of Corinne's grasp.

'Nothing,' she snapped, rising to her feet.

'What are you doing in here?' Beth asked Corinne, alarm springing up inside as she caught the way Corinne's eyes followed Eva as she paced to the window.

'Leave us, Beth,' was all she said.

The anger came swiftly.

'No, I won't leave you. Not until you tell me what's going on.'

'There's nothing going on,' Eva claimed but Beth shook her head, looking from one of them to the other.

'You're always in here, the two of you. Whispering, telling each other secrets, leaving me out.' A cracked note sounded in her voice, but still she pressed on. 'Why are you doing this to me?'

'God, Beth, no one's doing anything to you. I don't even want her in here with me.'

'You say that and yet you keep letting her back in.'

'No, I—'

'You're trying to steal her from me.'

Eva was shaking her head, staring at her sister's face wet now with tears.

'I'm not, I swear.'

'You are!' She swiped at her eyes with the cuff of her sleeve, focusing once more on Eva. 'It's because of the house, isn't it?'

'What house?'

'Melissa's! You're jealous because she left it to me! And now you're trying to steal Corinne so that you can punish me!'

'Don't be absurd—'

'I'm not being absurd!' She was screaming now. 'Admit it!'

Corinne moved swiftly, catching Beth by the elbow and ushering her out the door, across the landing. There was an urgency to her movements, and Beth felt the painful grip of fingers around her upper arm. Once they were alone in her room, Corinne turned on her.

'What are you doing, speaking to your sister like that? Can't you see she's upset?'

'*She's* upset?' Beth screeched, while Corinne looked around the room with a frown, snatching up her clothes.

'Things are difficult for her in college. It's hard for her, trying to make new friends.'

'Is that why you're in her room so much? So that you can be her new friend?' Beth hated the sarcasm in her own voice but couldn't help herself.

Corinne ignored the question, turning away from her, and discreetly pulled on her underwear underneath her towel. It pained Beth – this new modesty in her friend. She remembered a time when Corinne had felt free to dress and undress in their room without regard to her naked body. This easiness between them – like so much else – had shrivelled and died.

'You should be kinder to her,' Corinne said.

The words grated, as did the sanctimonious tone. Jealousy moved inside her, a malignancy eating away at her devotion. And the rage – always there – simmering beneath the surface.

'I suppose you'll want her to come to the cinema with us,' Beth remarked, and Corinne straightened up and looked at her.

'Beth?'

'We'd better get going,' Beth said quickly, looking around for her jacket. 'There's a bus in fifteen minutes—'

'Beth—'

'But if we miss that, there's another ten minutes later,' she rattled on desperately, trying to ward off what she knew was coming. 'We should still make it on time—'

'I'm not going,' Corinne announced softly but firmly. She was dressed now, standing barefoot, her hair dripping on to her shoulders, darkening patches of damp in the cotton of her T-shirt.

'Why not?' Beth asked, the surge of disappointment making her sound childish and desperate.

'She needs me,' Corinne said softly.

'*I* need you.'

A trembling had started inside her.

'I'm sorry, Beth—'

'But I've booked the tickets!' Biting back her panic, she whined: 'Come on, you can talk to her later. Please. She's just being dramatic to get some attention.'

'You go. Give my ticket to someone else.'

'Like who?'

'I don't know. Call someone. One of your friends.'

'I don't have any friends. Not any more.'

'That is not my problem.'

Corinne turned away as if she was weary, and Beth felt in that moment what a burden she had become to Corinne, a burden her friend no longer wished to carry.

'Is this because of Bruno?' Beth blurted out. 'Because I wouldn't sleep with him like you asked?'

'It doesn't matter why—'

'I'm sorry. I should have done it. I wish I had now. Don't hate me. I was just afraid . . . Stupid . . .' Her tears had started again, and she saw the brief flash of irritation crossing Corinne's face.

'I don't care about that now,' Corinne told her in a voice that sounded heavy with boredom. And the realization came to Beth as she watched Corinne turning away from her for the door, that her friend had grown bored of her. Like a child that had outgrown a toy and now discarded it without a twinge of regret. She couldn't bear for Corinne to turn from her like that.

'Maybe I'll call Lisa,' Beth said quickly. 'She'd probably be delighted to go.' Aiming for defiance but her voice was shaking. 'She worries about me spending too much time with you. She thinks you're too controlling.'

Corinne paused. She had her back to Beth, but Beth thought she saw tension coming into her shoulders, her neck.

'You were talking to her?'

'The other day. We were paired with each other in Home Ec. You'd bunked off, remember?'

Her limbs suddenly ached, like she was coming down with something, and when she thought again of Lisa's fingers reaching for hers through the flour in the bowl, she felt the colour rise to her cheeks.

The words hung there for a moment, a tense silence gathering around them. Then Corinne turned, and scoured the flat plain of Beth's face.

'Do you believe her?'

'No. I don't know.' Beth's voice wobbled, her eyes slid away.

'I have tried with you, Beth. I have tried to make you stand up for yourself. To be brave—'

'I am brave. Lisa thinks I am.' The words emerging in a rush.

Corinne took them in with a look of faint amusement mingling with pity. 'Does she.'

'Cutting my hair, getting my tattoo – she thinks it was brave—'

'Perhaps you didn't tell her who it was that paid for your tattoo.'

The words snapping in the air between them, all of Corinne's animation sharpened to a hard, narrow gaze.

'I miss you,' Beth whispered. 'I miss the way you used to be with me.'

A tear tracked down over her cheek. She put her hand up to wipe it away, felt the hard bump of a spot to one side of her mouth and she remembered the first time they were alone together in this room all those months ago – the tenderness with which Corinne had popped the zit on her chin, the way Beth had thrilled to her touch.

'I have a zit,' she said softly and the look she gave Corinne was full of hope.

The needle was still there on the mantelpiece.

'Look at me,' Corinne commanded.

Nerves crackled beneath her skin as Corinne tested the surface of the pimple with her thumb.

The needle stabbed suddenly, a quick, savage motion. Beth felt the startling heat of it searing her flesh. Tears sprang instantly.

'That hurt,' she cried, but Corinne's hand continued to grip her face, holding her there.

'She liked your tattoo?' she repeated, her voice controlled, steady, but there was wildness in her eyes. 'And did you tell her what I had to do to pay for it?'

Corinne's hand gripped her chin, and Beth felt the controlled fury channelling right through into her body, heat coming off Corinne's gaze. Beth shrank from it now.

'No,' she said quietly. 'I'm sorry.'

Corinne's eyes flickered over her for a moment, then she

drew herself in and released Beth's chin. Beth touched her own face, and when her fingers came away, they were wet with blood.

'You went too deep,' she said quietly.

The door was open now, and just before she left, Corinne looked back at her and Beth could see the pity in her gaze, the profound disappointment, and thought she couldn't bear to be looked at in that way.

'I had to,' Corinne replied, her voice flat and resigned. 'It's for your own good.'

27

Beth didn't go to the cinema. Instead, she walked the route, familiar to her since primary school, to the Fergusons' house on Victoria Road. Rain pelted the pavement, cars sending up sudden waves from water pooling by the kerb, so that by the time she reached the house, her hair was dripping, her denim jacket soaked through. She leaned on the bell, and then waited for someone to come, her Converse trainers squelching as she stood on the brushed mat.

She might have called Lisa first, but what little communication they'd had of late seemed so finely balanced, easily veering off the rails of friendly exchanges into perceived insults, judgement, blame, that it seemed better to talk to her in person. Besides, with all the emotion roiling around inside her brain, a large part of Beth wanted to be outside in the rain, feeling it permeating her clothes. The drama of turning up on Lisa's doorstep wet through and desperate for refuge, for care, appealed to her. The Fergusons' house had always felt safe to her, overheated, like a warm nest. All the lights were on downstairs, sending out their rosy glow into the night.

Beth expected Lisa to answer, or Mrs Ferguson with her silk eyelashes and tight mohair sweaters, her bright look of enquiry. But after a moment's wait, the door pulled back and Callum Ferguson looked down at her, blinking, a sleepy, puzzled look on his face like he'd just been hauled out of bed.

'Is Lisa home?' she asked.

'No.'

He was wearing flannel shorts and there was a red mark on his T-shirt that looked like ketchup. He rubbed his eyes and then regarded her briefly from where he stood inside the threshold.

'You're soaked,' he observed, and Beth felt a creeping embarrassment, hair pasted to her forehead.

'You'd better come in,' he stated, turning away from the door before she could reply, leaving it wide open while he disappeared down the hall, so she had no choice but to follow him.

She closed the door behind her, felt the familiar fug of warmth as she stepped into the house, the soft weave of scatter rugs in the hall, the sweet, heavy scent of coconut from the plug-in fresheners Irene Ferguson had dotted around the house. The door to the playroom was open and Beth followed Callum inside. They still called it a playroom even though it had been years since the room had been home to Callum's Scalectrix track ringing around Lisa's stable full of My Little Pony toys. All of that had been cleared out long ago, replaced with a TV, a stereo, a DVD player and a Wii. There was a slouchy red corduroy couch on to which Callum had thrown himself, his eyes returning to the screen where there was a match playing – American football.

Beth hovered by the door, unsure of whether she should enter. She saw now that the mark on his T-shirt was not ketchup but sauce from the pizza he'd been eating, the remains of which still adhered to the Domino's box on the low table. A six-pack of Hop House 13 sat alongside it, a couple of cans already squashed, lying on the floor.

'Where is everyone?' she asked.

'Mount Juliet,' Callum answered, pointedly articulating the words. 'A round of golf for him, some pampering for her, a spot of horse-riding for the princess, a happy family dinner in the evenings.' Beth thought he sounded bitter.

He leaned forward and took the ashtray from the table. There was a reefer in it, which he proceeded to spark up, reclining against the couch once more, the ashtray balanced on his tummy.

'You didn't go?'

'Ah no. I couldn't, could I? I had to work. And besides,' he went on, in that strained, mocking voice, 'can't have the treats without earning them, can we? And God forbid another guest might ask what the young man is studying at university. Think of the shame.'

His eyes narrowed as he dragged at the joint, then offered it to her. 'Don't just stand there,' he murmured. 'You're making me nervous.'

She came and sat on the other end of the couch, taking a quick drag then passing it back to him. The weed tasted earthy, and the room held the musty odours of old socks and pizza and her own damp clothes. Her feet were sore now, chafed and uncomfortable in her wet shoes. The whole room made her feel light-headed and nauseous. She pressed her head back against the headrest, closed her eyes for a moment.

'I feel so strange,' she admitted quietly, opening her eyes when she felt him get up from the couch.

Wordlessly, he left the room, returning minutes later with a towel.

'Here,' he said, tossing it to her. 'Dry yourself with that.'

Struck by his consideration, she smiled weakly. 'Mind if I take my shoes off?'

'Knock yourself out.'

She felt strange because of the weed, because of the

night's events. But it was also true that the oddness was because of the house, and because of him. He was watching the television on mute, and there wasn't any music playing, no voices drifting in from other rooms, no sound of laughter from Irene on the phone to one of her friends. The house was deathly quiet, lifeless, and she felt like the two of them were creatures washed up on to a rock, refugees from the outside world seeking solace together, some kind of peace.

She eased out of her wet jacket and towel-dried her hair. In all the years she'd been coming to the house, this was the first time she'd been alone in a room with Callum for any length of time. As Lisa's older brother, he had always scorned their company, and they had mocked him and his jock friends, the two girls rolling their eyes at the ignorant jokes the boys told each other, their obsessive and inane conversations about sport, even the fuggy way they smelt. 'The uncleans', Lisa had called them, a sighing acceptance of the fact of their existence, their permanent place in her home.

But his friends weren't here now. It was just Callum with his feet in tube socks up on the table, his unfocused gaze settled on the screen.

'Why aren't you at work?' Beth asked, and the corners of his mouth crept up into a smile.

'Because I quit.'

'You did? When?'

'Rang them this afternoon. Told them I just couldn't do it any more.'

'Do your parents know?'

'Not yet.' He dragged on the reefer, stirred by some inner mirth. 'I can't wait to see the look on the old man's face,' he said, but Beth didn't quite believe his bravado, the way his smile faltered, panic behind his eyes. She remembered what

Lisa had said about the difficult relationship between Callum and his father, something ominous there.

'Well, that's a shame,' Beth told him. 'Cos you were the only thing I liked about that stupid club.'

'You don't like the club?'

'Tennis sucks. It's a stupid sport and the club is stuffed full of white, middle-class, privileged, elitist twats. Just like school.'

'Hmm.' He was looking at her now, considering her points, observing: 'Your sister likes it well enough.'

'What can I say? She found her tribe.'

His mouth twitched with amusement. 'And you? Have you found yours?'

She looked down, a sudden tightening inside as she thought of Corinne, the hard point of the needle stabbing her zit. 'I'm not sure I have a tribe.'

'A misfit,' he mused. 'An outcast.' A taint of sadness coming into his voice, as he added: 'I can relate to that.'

Something had changed about him. Beth saw it now: a heaviness about his face, his complexion usually ruddy with health looked pasty and there was a thickening about his trunk, carrying weight where there had been none before. She recognized his unhappiness; it mirrored her own, and she considered for a moment what it was like for him – all his friends gone off to college while he was left behind. His loneliness was there in the room, and she felt moved to pity him.

'What happened?' she asked. 'With your exams, I mean.'

He looked sheepish, rolling the tiny butt of the reefer between his index finger and thumb.

'I just sort of lost it,' he explained, sounding a little bewildered. 'I thought I would be okay, that I was prepared – I'd put in the time. But then, my first exam, I went in and looked at the paper and it was like all the letters just swarmed over the page. This is going to sound weird, but it felt like the characters on the page were angry, like a nest of wasps disturbed.'

'An anxiety attack.'

'Right.' He gave her a swift look. 'You know what it's like?'

'Your heart races, you sweat like crazy. This wave of emotion swells inside you suddenly and you don't know what to do.'

He was watching her in a new way. 'You've had them too?'

She nodded.

'Well, I'd never had one before. It was all I could do to just stay sitting in my chair, trying to put some kind of answers on the page. It didn't happen with every exam, but enough to make a difference.' He shifted on the couch, jutting out his chin pugnaciously, saying: 'So now everyone thinks I'm either thick or a fruitcake.'

'I don't think you're either of those things.'

'What about your sister?' he asked quietly. 'What does she think?'

'What do you care what she thinks? Aren't you with Alicia now?'

He shook his head. 'We broke up.' Then his eyes flicked to her. 'I only went out with Alicia to make Eva jealous.'

'Why do you like her so much?'

His eyes became glazed with suspicion. 'Why do you ask?'

'Just curious.'

'Did she send you here?'

'No,' she laughed. 'God, you're paranoid.'

He looked embarrassed, and then he considered her question. 'Well, she's fit – that's obvious. And I thought we had lots in common, you know? Tennis, but also ambition, drive. It seemed like we were going along the same path but then I crashed and she zoomed on without me.'

'That's not what I heard.'

A challenge in her voice. He picked up on it, his cheeks colouring, and he sat up a little.

'What did you hear?'

'That it had something to do with a gun?'

Risky saying this out loud, giving away the little snippet of information she had garnered while eavesdropping on one of Eva's conversations with Alicia. But it moved something in him, an alertness entering his gaze, the way he leaned forward suddenly, his feet on the ground now, the ashtray clattering on to the table, one hand rubbing across the back of his neck. The silence stretched between them, until he collapsed it, turning to her, his face serious, saying:

'Want to see it?'

The rain had eased now, leaving only the patter of water from the leaves of the tall trees in the garden. From the tiny windows of the cabin, she could see back up the lawn to the house, all lit up from within. But here, within the clapboard walls and the creaking shelves, it was dim and cold.

The gun sat on a square of green leather, illuminated by the desk lamp.

'Can I hold it?' she asked.

He gestured to it. 'Be my guest.'

It was lighter than it looked, the grip smooth against her palm, but she held it with both hands anyway, nervous in case it slipped.

'It's not loaded,' he told her, feeling the fear in her. 'It's strange, isn't it? The first time you hold it. Like it's going to suddenly go off in your hands, or as if, just by holding it, you're going to suddenly tap into some bloodlust you didn't know you had.'

'Yes!' she laughed. The weed had made her sleepy, but

now she felt suddenly awake, everything impacting on her like she was seeing the world with fresh eyes.

'I like how it feels,' she told him. 'It makes me feel powerful.'

'Steady on,' he laughed, taking it from her hands.

With ease and swiftness, he popped open the barrel, showed her where the bullets went, briefly described how to load it and discharge a round. He clipped it shut, then spun the barrel.

'Have you ever fired it? Like, for real?'

'Nah. Not this one. But I have shot a gun before.'

'You have?'

'Last year, in the States. We were on holiday and Dad took me to a shooting range for the afternoon. Just the two of us.'

He held the gun up to the light, cast his eye closely along the stock.

'What was it like?'

'Pretty fucking cool, actually. I wish I could take this baby out some time. Not to shoot anyone, obviously! But like, to a gun range or something. Somewhere I could try it out safely.'

'Does your dad know you mess around with it?' She nodded to the gun, and he slid her a mischievous look.

'Course not. He'd have my nuts if he knew I was doing this. He thinks I don't know he has a gun, let alone the combination to the gun safe.'

'So why do you do it? Take it out, show it to people. Aren't you worried he'll find out?'

'Part of me wants him to find out, just to see what the fucker would do, you know?' He tried to smile, but it died on his lips.

The air between them grew quiet and serious.

Testing the silence, Beth said softly: 'Lisa told me that your dad hits you.'

'She told you that?'

She nodded, watching him absorb that for a moment, and then he looked at her, his eyes clear and glassy blue. 'Do you know what I was thinking this evening, just before you came over?'

She waited.

'I was thinking what it would be like for him to come home from Mount Juliet and find me out here with a bullet in my brain.'

It shocked her to hear him say it, his voice hoarse with sudden emotion. She thought of him back in the house, on his own watching the telly on mute, the airlessness of the room, the eerie quiet. Something desolate about it, and horribly lonely. Like he'd been abandoned.

'You wouldn't . . .'

'No,' he said, gulping back the tears. 'Too fucking gutless,' laughing mirthlessly at his own cowardice.

He busied himself now putting away the gun. She watched as he closed the safe, running his fingertips lightly over the keypad as if to remove any trace of dust. When he stood up again, she reached out and touched his forearm.

'I'm glad I came here,' she said softly, and he nodded.

'Me too.'

Something had passed between them. Something profound though neither of them could name it.

'I'll watch out for you,' she told him as she stood on the doorstep, her denim jacket a little less damp now although her shoes still squelched.

She wasn't exactly sure what she meant by that, but he nodded as if he understood.

Standing there in the doorway, his hands in his pockets, he watched as she walked away. And all the time, she had the feeling that she had not only saved Callum from himself, but that he, somehow, had restored her. She had toppled momentarily, but he had set her back on her feet again, dusted her down, and pushed her back out safely into the night.

28

Eva was in a tutorial when her phone buzzed with an incoming call. Seeing Ross's name light up the screen, her instinct was to answer. But at that moment, the tutor looked up and said drily:

'Would it be so much to ask for you to drag your attention away from your phone for the half-hour remaining to us?'

She felt the gaze of the row of students in front of her, most of whom she hardly knew. In the weeks since term began, she'd been absent so often that she'd barely exchanged a half-dozen words with most of her classmates.

'Sorry,' she mumbled, stuffing the phone deep into her bag, trying to focus her attention on the tutor.

It was halfway through the semester and she was completely lost, having skipped so many lectures. Ross found it easier to get to the house during the day while Becca was at work. He worried about her missing lectures, so she lied to him about it, making it sound like her timetable was not that full. She told herself that there was plenty of time to catch up on her coursework, whereas what she shared with Ross was too urgent and important to put on hold.

The tutorial ended, the class filing out into the corridor, immediately breaking up into smaller groups. Eva looked around but there was no obvious cluster for her to join. Distantly, she caught sight of Orla, one of the few people she knew in the class, and went to join her at the lockers.

They had met at the start of Freshers' Week, the two of them gravitating to each other on Orientation Day. Orla was small with tight black spiral curls. When she smiled, she revealed a row of straight teeth, a tiny gem winking from one of her incisors. She was feeding books into her locker when Eva stopped to say hi.

They talked for a few minutes about the tutorial and about the test they had coming up next week, a slight coolness perceptible in Orla's responses. And when Eva said: 'So-oo, I was wondering: is there any chance I could borrow your CFD notes again? I promise, this is the last time,' Orla slammed her locker shut, and said quietly:

'What do you think I am, your fucking amanuensis?', her cheeks flushing.

'Of course not!'

'Why don't you just turn up for lectures and take your own notes?'

'I would but . . . It's complicated.'

'Sure it is,' Orla remarked, turning the key in the lock. When she began to move away, Eva caught her arm.

'Please, Orla. Look, I'm not supposed to tell anyone, but the reason I've been missing is that I'm seeing someone. But it's difficult for us to meet. He can only really get away during the day.'

'How come? Is he married?' A question thrown out but not seriously. When Eva didn't answer, Orla's eyes widened.

'No fucking way.'

'I'm really trusting you with this, Orla. Ross would kill me if he knew I'd told you.'

'Is it serious?'

'Yes! We're just so in love and it's incredibly difficult trying to snatch some time together. Any chance we get we just—'

'What about his wife?'

'Well, obviously she doesn't know. I mean, she'll have to

find out sooner or later and we're trying to figure out a way to tell her—'

'Does he have kids?'

'One. A little boy. He's adopted. Not that that makes any difference. Oh, he's so cute though, Orla, just adorable! And Ross is crazy about him. He's such a good dad.'

But then Orla said: 'So, all this time I've been covering for you in lectures, passing you on my notes, you've been having it off with a married man?'

Eva's head jerked back like she'd been slapped.

'What? No, it's not like that. It's—'

'Jesus, you disgust me.'

'Oh, come on! Don't you think you're being a bit puritanical?'

'Fuck you, Eva. Just because I don't want to assist you in your home-wrecking. Well, good luck finding some other sap to help you scrape a pass. Hardly anyone here even fucking knows you.'

The scald of those words remained as she watched Orla walk away. The corridor was empty now, her classmates having disappeared to lunch, to the library, to a snatched half-hour in the thin autumn sunshine. Eva felt very small and alone in the echoey space, the tentacles of Orla's shocked disapproval still painfully prodding her. She needed comfort and reassurance, and then she remembered Ross's phone call during her tutorial and reached into her bag for her phone. Glancing at the screen, she saw seven missed calls from him, and two texts asking her to call him asap, both typed using capitals marking the urgency.

He answered after the first ring, as if he'd been waiting with the phone in his hand.

'Where the hell have you been?' he demanded, sounding breathless and angry. 'I've been calling you for ages.'

'I was in a tutorial,' she explained, taken aback by the alarm in his voice. 'What's the matter?'

'We need to meet.'

'Okay, but—'

'I'm in the Science car park. Come and find me.'

'What, like right now?'

'Yes, now. Jesus, do I have to spell it out?'

His sharpness disturbed her, but she said nothing about it. They made the arrangement and he hung up leaving her baffled at his urgency and unsettled by the anger in his voice – an anger that seemed directed at her.

'What took you so long?' Ross demanded.

Slamming the car door shut, she turned to face him. He sat behind the steering wheel bunched up in his puffa jacket, his jaw livid with a shaving rash.

'I came as soon as I could. What's the matter? Why are you so tense?'

'This is why I'm fucking tense.'

His thumb moved over the screen of his phone, and he held it up to show her. The breath caught in her throat.

The picture had been taken outside Melissa's house. Ross's arm slung around her shoulder, his hand hanging low over her breast, whispering something in her ear, a secret smile on her face. The caption under the photograph read: *Bad boy.*

'Who the fuck is this person?' Ross asked, banging the steering wheel with the heel of his hand.

'I've no idea.'

Her mind raced, jumpy with fright, while Ross cast around for someone to blame, his jaw rigid with frustration.

'Did you tell anyone about us?'

'No!'

'Are you absolutely sure about that? No one at all? One of your friends?'

Guiltily, she thought of Corinne. Hadn't she threatened as much? But how did she get Ross's number? Either way, it wasn't something she wanted to get into right now. Ross would only blame Eva for letting herself get caught in the first place.

'I haven't told anyone! Jesus,' she said, indignation rising inside her.

He was hunched forward in the seat, shaking his head with agitation.

'This is bad. This is really fucking bad,' he intoned. 'Who is this person? What do they want?'

He had tried calling the number, but the phone was switched off.

'I hate this. Not knowing,' he went on. 'Feeling like there's someone watching us.'

Even now, he was glancing in the rear-view mirror, his eyes darting around the car park, scanning the benches that punctuated the pavement outside the Sports Centre. The odd student drifted past, a white Campus Services van cruising slowly by, and each movement stirred up Ross's nerves, fixing his jumpy gaze on every moving vehicle or pedestrian.

She put her hand on his thigh to calm him, but he hardly seemed to notice.

'What are we supposed to do?' he demanded. 'Just hang around and wait for the next message? Are we going to be blackmailed or something? Christ!'

'Calm down,' she urged. 'Let's not panic.' Although her own thoughts prickled with nerves.

She would talk to Corinne when she got home. Find a way to make it stop.

'Yeah, well, that's easy for you to say. It's not you that could lose your family, is it?'

Her hand was still on his thigh and she snatched it away now.

'You think I've got nothing to lose?' The words came out in a low snarl, heat gathering in her chest. 'You think I haven't sacrificed anything for us to be together? I'm supposed to be in the lab right now, instead of sitting out here with you getting grief for something I haven't even done!'

They sat for a moment in their own wounded silences. Eva fingered the frayed edges of the satchel that lay on her lap. She was struck by the thought that this wasn't worth it. The endless piling up of work – an insurmountable obstacle. She had fallen so far behind, catching up seemed impossible. Maybe she should just drop out.

Gathering herself, she calmly suggested that they should wait and see. 'It's probably nothing. Just someone playing a stupid prank.'

He put his hands to his face and exhaled slowly. 'Yeah, maybe. God, I hope you're right,' the tension in him beginning to ease.

'Trust me,' she said, 'it will turn out to be nothing – a hoax – and then you'll wonder why you were so anxious.'

He took his hands away and offered her a look of apology. His face was still drawn and blotchy with nerves, but he was calmer now and she was ready to forgive him.

'I'm sorry,' he offered. 'For speaking to you like that.'

'Hey, it's okay,' she smiled, affection for him stirring inside her again, but when she leaned over to kiss him, he turned his face away.

'Don't,' he told her, a warning there.

'Why not?'

'Someone could be watching.'

'There's no one around. It's just us! Come on, you're being paranoid.' But when she went to kiss him again, he put his hand to her shoulder and gently but firmly pushed her away.

Confused now, she went on: 'Well, let's go somewhere then. Let's go to the house—'

'No way.'

'Let's take a drive. Go back to that place in Wicklow. It's been ages since we've been there.'

He was looking out the front window, concentrating on the water tower that rose up in the distance.

'Eva,' he said, and from the ponderous tone, she knew what was coming. 'I think we need to cool it, don't you?'

She sat back, stunned. 'Okay,' she said, cautiously. 'For how long?'

He winced, still not looking at her. 'It's been fun, but this is all getting out of hand. I'm a married man, for Christ's sake. And you should be concentrating on your education, knuckling down to some study.'

Fun? Is that all she was to him? Just some plaything to distract himself from his stagnant marriage, the boredom that threaded through his days? Anger rumbled up inside her. All she had missed for him, everything she had sacrificed. She looked at him there in the car, still refusing to meet her gaze. He didn't even have the guts to look her in the eye while he dumped her. His cowardice in that moment appalled her.

'You can't even look at me!' she hissed.

And then she got out of the car, slamming the door so hard she feared it might come off its hinges. It cut off the sound of his voice uttering her name, and she knew he was sitting there, watching her the whole time she walked away.

29

The rumour grew.

What had started as a small seed planted on the internet gained traction, gathering pace as the nugget of gossip whizzed along school corridors as well and crackled through the cyber-paths. Whispers by the lockers became full-blown accusations; what was once just speculation acquired the varnish of truth.

It had begun in September, but it was almost the end of October by the time it reached Abi.

'A what?'

'A pregnancy rumour,' Helen Bracken said briskly down the line.

'About Beth?'

'No. Not about Beth, about another student – Sasha Harte.' The coldness in her voice was unmistakable. She went on: 'The rumour that's been circulating is that Sasha had some kind of romantic tryst in France this summer when on the exchange programme and that it has resulted in a pregnancy. Let me be clear, Abi, there is absolutely no foundation to this rumour.'

'Okay,' Abi said, unsure of what this had to do with her. She glanced at her watch. It was almost five o'clock and she still had two more online meetings with clients before she could climb into her car and drive home. Fleetingly, she thought of Mark preparing dinner or maybe idling in his studio, building one of his models, and she felt a brief but intense push of irritation. He was supposed to be the stay-at-home parent yet here she was fielding calls from the school.

'There is no pregnancy, nor was there any French romance,' Helen Bracken continued. 'Sasha is, understandably, very upset by these rumours, and her mother is insisting that the school takes action.'

'Of course. But I don't see how—'

'Comments on Facebook, and on Snapchat. A lot of WhatsApp chatter. Internet forums where this rumour has been dragged out. I'm sure I don't need to tell you, Abi, how quickly these things escalate, especially among teenage girls. This is not the first time I've had to manage a pregnancy rumour and it's my experience that this kind of gossip just rips through the school like fire in a drought. Unfortunately, this rumour has already gone out into the wider world, tarnishing Sasha's reputation beyond the school.'

Abi pinched the skin at the bridge of her nose, a headache coming on.

'Right, fine. I understand, but what has this got to do with Beth?'

She heard the slow intake of breath at the other end of the line, read the disapproval at her obviously tetchy intervention, and then Helen Bracken said: 'It appears that Beth was the one who started the rumour.'

Abi exhaled slowly, a tide of weariness washing over her.

She listened then to a baroque explanation about internet activity and user names, as well as some interviews the principal had conducted with some of Sasha's friends.

'One of them was very helpful,' Bracken informed her. 'It seems Beth let slip to this girl how she was planning on getting back at Sasha over some recent slight. Apparently Beth made some assertion over how soon Sasha would know what it felt like to be ridiculed, or something like that.'

'But that's just idle tittle-tattle. Surely you should know better than to believe every word that comes out of their mouths—'

'Indeed I do. But Lisa Ferguson has always been a decent and honest girl. I have no reason to believe she'd lie about this. If anything, she was upset and concerned about Beth.'

The fact that it was Lisa both stunned and chastened Abi.

'I'll talk to Beth,' she said quietly.

'An apology is required.'

'Of course. I'll get Beth to call Sasha—'

'No, I'm afraid that won't do. This is rather more serious than that. The kind of rumour she's been circulating not only damages reputations, but also causes great distress, not to mention bringing down the good name of this school.'

'So, what do you suggest?'

'I want her to meet with me and the girl she has defamed and offer an explanation of herself. Afterwards, I want her to stand up in assembly and offer a frank and fulsome apology.'

'Don't you think that's going too far? I mean, fine, if you want her to come to your office and talk this through with Sasha. But to demand that she castigate herself in front of the whole school? No. Absolutely not.'

'I don't think you understand, Abi. This was not just a stray word spoken, some idle gossip in the classroom. This was a deliberate campaign of bullying. Time and effort went into this. For months, Beth has been harassing this girl over her appearance – in some chat group they have. But this pregnancy rumour is the last straw. Sasha's mother is so concerned about her daughter's distress that she is considering taking her out of school for the rest of the term. She told me that Sasha intimated that she was thinking about suicide. I am telling you this in confidence, Abi, but I need you to understand why I must insist on a public apology.'

Her voice had risen over the course of the conversation, and now in the pause, Abi felt the blood pulsing in her ears. The word 'suicide' stuck in her head cold as a stone.

When Helen Bracken spoke again, it was in a strict business-like register.

'I think you'll agree that I have been more than patient with Beth in the past. That this school has been very understanding – forgiving, even – of her past misdemeanours. Some might say we were too understanding, too soft. And recently, we have been very accommodating of your family, going beyond the usual boundaries of our admissions policy to allow for Beth's French friend to attend for this half-term, an accommodation, I might add, that seems to be unappreciated by Corinne, who deems it unnecessary to turn up for most of the classes she's been assigned to and frequently absents herself from the premises.'

'I'm sorry, Helen. I had no idea she'd been skipping school.'

'My patience is not unlimited. Corinne's lax attitude is unfortunate, but I am prepared to extend some latitude given her recent bereavement and the fact that she will not be with us for long. Also, I might add, because of Eva's good behaviour over the years. Unlike her younger sister, she was always diligent and attentive – a hard-working student well liked by her teachers and her peers. I know we can't expect sisters to act in similar ways, but I had hoped Beth might do more to live up to Eva's high standard.' She paused here, and Abi felt unspoken questions pulsing in the air between them, questions about her parenting skills, her children, how could one turn out so well and the other become so rotten? 'The more pressing matter is this rumour,' Helen went on. 'It must be quashed, soon and convincingly, indisputably, and the only way that can be achieved is through a public apology. I must speak plainly, Abi – this is non-negotiable.'

The words rang in Abi's ears the whole way home. She was driving too fast, impelled by the burn of humiliation running through her body. The way that woman had spoken to her! But underneath it all ran the deeper, more insistent clamour of anxiety over Beth's behaviour. In the car, she felt the dark form of Beth's troubled mind crowding around her and slipping into the shadows, a sprightly presence, mercurial and unreliable, always pushing Beth on, pushing and pushing until she reached the edge of the cliff. Abi's fingers tightened around the steering wheel, her face set against the road, rigid with determination.

Beth looked into her mother's face – it was drawn and furious.

There was such ice in her voice, such quivering contempt, that it made Beth feel frightened.

'A bully. That's what your school principal called you. That's what kind of daughter I've been raising all these years.'

Even though she wasn't shouting, Beth could see there was something barely controlled about Abi, the way she couldn't stand still, the sinewy pull of muscles in her neck.

'Why on earth would you do something like that? Destroying this girl's reputation. Starting malicious gossip. And the lengths you went to! I'm shocked, Beth. I hadn't thought you could be so cruel.'

'She was cruel to me first—'

'And that justifies it, does it? She was mean to you so that gives you carte blanche to set about wrecking her life? My God, Beth, the girl wanted to kill herself.'

Beth, who had been inwardly raging at her mother, felt her thoughts give a deep, vertiginous dip. 'What?'

'You heard me. She told her mother she couldn't cope, that she'd rather die than face the shame. Her mother was so freaked out she took the child out of school.'

'Christ,' Mark said.

He had hardly spoken a word, just stood in the background with his arms folded, looking grave and disappointed.

'Why on earth did you do this?' Abi beseeched her and Beth felt a wobble in her throat.

'I don't know. It just sort of happened.'

'Oh don't, Beth, just don't,' she said, disgusted.

'It did! I never meant for it to get so serious. I just wanted her to feel what it's like to be picked on for a change.'

'Well, you've certainly done that. My God, I'm ashamed of you. My own daughter. Did Corinne put you up to this?'

'No!'

'But she did play a part in it, right? Or did you do this all by yourself?' Her words dripped with sarcasm, and Beth snapped:

'I am capable of doing some things on my own, you know. I'm not a complete imbecile.'

'Oh, that's not the word I would use to describe you right now,' her mother said, shaking her head madly, and Beth's father spoke up then:

'Abi. That's not helpful.'

But her mother just shot him a withering glance and Beth could see that she was equally mad at him. As if she suspected some sort of collusion between father and daughter.

Mark ignored it, turning to Beth to express his shock and disappointment at her behaviour.

'Whatever possessed you to behave in this way?' he demanded. 'I don't care how much this girl might have annoyed you – provoked you, even – you can't go around scorching someone's reputation like that. It's cruel. Heartless.'

'It was just a joke,' she said weakly.

'A joke?' He almost spat the word at her. 'Do you expect us to believe that? A campaign of online criticism – of bullying – and you say it's just a joke? Don't act like this was some spontaneous one-off occurrence. By the sounds of it, you've been at this for months!'

Again, her feelings lurched, and she looked down at the ground, burning beneath the weight of his furious stare.

'I don't know why you're getting so upset,' she mumbled. 'It's not like you really care about me. All that you really care about is what other people will think of me.'

Mark gave her a long, baffled look. 'Is that really what you believe, Beth? You think we don't worry about our children?'

'You might. But Mum's more concerned with her job than she is with me.'

Abi's temper flared. 'That's unfair—'

'No, it's not! You're hardly ever here and when you are, you're always on your phone, on calls, checking emails. I never have your attention, never!'

'Is that why you did this? To get my attention? Well, you certainly have it now!' Abi shouted, her eyes bulging. 'And I am sick to death of being made to feel guilty about my job! Who do you think pays your school fees? Who pays for this house? Who puts food on the table? Who paid for you to go on this bloody exchange in the first place?'

Her father said nothing, but he was looking at Abi with such coldness that it gave Beth a tiny thrill of pleasure. Abi saw the smile and exploded.

'What the hell are you smirking about?'

The thrill faded instantly, but Beth forced herself to keep staring at her mother with the bemused look that so enraged Abi, even though she was wavering inside.

'Just tell me why, Beth. Why did you do this?'

There was no point in explaining why. It was far too late for that. And something pushed her now to just shrug and say, her voice hard: 'For shits and giggles, Mother.'

Abi's face contorted with rage. It made her look strange, unhinged, and as she stepped forward, Beth was sure her mother was going to hit her. But instead, Abi just stared, her face all twisted in fury, and said: 'When did you become such a little bitch?'

The word ricocheted around the room, and Mark said: 'That's enough!'

He stepped forward and took hold of Abi's arm, pulled her back like he too believed her capable of slapping the girl.

'Let's all just calm down, okay? So, she did something wrong. Something cruel. But she'll apologize to this girl—'

Abi laughed then, a harsh, mirthless bark, and said: 'Oh, she'll do that all right,' and Beth began to feel frightened.

When Abi explained what she had to do, about going before the school, about owning up to what she'd done in front of everyone, a cold, hard fear seized her insides. She shook her head violently from side to side. 'No. I can't. Please don't make me,' she said, stumbling over the words. Then, adding desperately: 'They can't even prove it was me who started it.'

'Oh, yes they can,' Abi snapped. 'You made sure of that once you opened your mouth and boasted to Lisa all about your vicious plan.'

Beth's mouth fell open. 'Lisa?' she whispered, as if she'd been struck.

'You will do what Helen Bracken has asked, young lady. For once, I'm not going to intervene for you and smooth the way.' Adding in a quieter voice: 'God knows, I've done enough of that in the past.'

Her father said: 'Is this really necessary though?'

'I can't, Mum. I don't care if they expel me. I don't want to go back there anyway.'

'We shouldn't have sent her back to that school after the last time,' Mark muttered, and Abi glared at him.

'She can leave that school on Tuesday, I really don't give a shit any more. But on Monday morning, you are going in there,' she went on, addressing Beth again, 'and I don't care if you're sick or dying, do you hear me? You're going to make that apology if it damn well kills you.'

Eva heard the kitchen door close sharply, silence rising ominously from the hall below. Her heart was scudding quickly along, but she remained still, steadying herself against the bathroom sink while her mind raced. She took a few deep breaths, then washed her hands, splashed cold water on her face, before opening the door.

Corinne was waiting for her.

'Are you okay?' she asked softly.

Eva ignored the question, crossing the landing quickly, refusing to meet the girl's eye. And when Corinne followed her into her bedroom, without seeking permission, Eva didn't swing around and bark at her to get out as she would normally have done. Her heart was fluttering in a frightening way, her limbs had gone cold. She wondered if she was in shock.

Corinne closed the door gently behind her while Eva threw herself face-down on the bed, one hand sliding beneath the pillow.

'What's wrong?' Corinne asked softly.

Eva turned her face to the wall.

'Nothing's wrong,' she answered, the pillow muffling her voice. She could feel it in herself – the swell of emotion. Fear rising like dough in her chest, filling out to reach her tingling extremities.

Movement on the bed as Corinne came to sit beside her – something tentative about it, as if bracing herself for Eva's anger.

It amazed her, how Corinne kept coming. In the face of Eva's constant angry rejections, she had shown resilience. Or maybe she was just propelled by desperation – a feeling that was growing familiar to Eva now too.

Eva lay still on her side, thinking furiously. Her head was overfull, it pulsed painfully with the speed of her thoughts. She missed Alicia. The loss of her friend felt like a physical pain, twisting and tangling with her panicked desperation. If only she hadn't pushed her away. If only she hadn't allowed the silence to harden between them. She longed for Alicia's presence, her honesty, her pragmatism, her love.

And then she felt a hand at the back of her head, gently drawing the elastic from her hair, loosening the knot. The ribbon of hair unravelled and fell over the sheet.

From downstairs the silence continued, Beth and her parents in grave dispute. But Eva didn't care about what was happening there. She wanted to stay in this moment for just a little while, the stillness of the bedroom, the calm that was coming over her now as Corinne tenderly combed Eva's hair with her fingers, her scalp prickling pleasurably with the sensation. Any anger inside her was temporarily deflated, and she felt tired – profoundly wrung-out. Corinne lifted Eva's hair and then her hand was on Eva's back, her touch cooling the hot skin between her shoulder blades. Eva closed her eyes and submitted to the touch, the tender press of fingertips, the gentle sweep of palms. A new stillness entered her body that felt like acceptance more than defeat.

When the mobile phone on her desk pinged with a message, she didn't want to get up and risk breaking the spell. But the possibility that it was Ross itched at her brain, and reluctantly she moved away from Corinne's stroking hand and went to retrieve her phone. But on the screen, she saw

Callum's name, his message: *I meant what I said. I really am sorry. Could you meet me? Please.*

A wave of disappointment came over her – that it wasn't Ross, but also at the complex path she had chosen. How had her life become snared up with a married man? Why couldn't she have been normal and fallen for a boy her own age with no baggage, no strings attached?

'It's Callum,' she explained, seeing the question on Corinne's face. She remained sitting on the bed, a still and watchful presence. The feelings perpetually inspired by this girl were ones of irritation and suspicion. But all the fight had gone out of Eva, and besides, she needed a friend.

'He keeps texting me. Saying he's sorry. Asking if we can meet and talk.'

'He wants to go out with you,' Corinne stated, and Eva shrugged, her eyes averted. 'And you? What do you want?'

Outside, from the street, came the sounds of Ross and his son. Jo had a new pedal car and they'd been going up and down the street for almost an hour, even though the light had faded, the boy's excited shrieks cutting through the air, Ross's cheers of encouragement soaring. Eva turned and watched them, a dull ache settling inside her.

'Are you going to meet with him?' Corinne asked.

Eva felt her chin wobbling, tears springing in her eyes.

'There's no point. He won't want me. Not when he knows . . .' Her eyes slid away from Corinne's gaze. Corinne followed them to the pillow.

Part of her knew it was a mistake. But she was so tired. It was a burden too heavy to carry alone.

The atmosphere in the room seemed oppressive as Corinne's hand moved quickly under the pillow and withdrew the wand of a pregnancy test wadded in tissue paper.

There they were, the two pink lines, pulsing with their own importance.

Eva's eyes remained fixed on her, desperate and staring.

'What am I going to do?' she asked. Her voice was very small.

'Will you tell him? Ross?'

Eva shook her head miserably. 'He won't talk to me. He won't even take any of my calls.'

From outside there came a small crash and then a wail rose up. Instantly, Eva turned to look. The small blue car lay on its side on the kerb, one wheel still gently spinning. The boy, swept up in his father's arms, continued to wail but with less urgency now. Alerted by the cries, Becca had come out of the house, and they could hear her making soothing noises as Ross handed the little boy over, saying: 'He's grand, just a little knock.' For a moment, both parents fussed over little Jo, pushing back the fringe of black hair, examining his forehead for a bruise. Becca kissed the boy, and Ross ran his hand down his wife's back, a small gesture of affection. Eva shuddered.

'He'll never leave her,' she said, her voice flat, but beneath the surface resignation, something wilder fought against it. A tightness in her stomach, she couldn't wrench her eyes from them.

'I can help you,' Corinne whispered. She had come to stand next to Eva and reached now to take her hand.

'How? How can you possibly help me?'

'I know something we can do.' When Eva looked at her, she saw a lunatic hope blooming in her eyes. 'Will you trust me?' Corinne asked, tightening her grasp so that Eva winced, startled, and said 'Hey,' withdrawing her hand, her attention suddenly sharpened, some of the old feelings of unease trickling back in.

Corinne started to explain, to apologize, rattling on quickly about how she could save Eva, but then the door opened and there was Beth, moon-faced with bewilderment, her eyes red-rimmed from crying.

'You have to pack,' she told Corinne. 'They're calling your mother. You're going home.'

30

There was a flight from Dublin to Tours the following Monday at lunchtime, and on Saturday morning, Abi went online and bought Corinne's airline ticket. It calmed her a little, the prospect of the girl's imminent departure, a return to some kind of normality. She was printing out the boarding pass when her phone rang, Irene Ferguson's name appearing on the screen.

'Abi, I need to talk to you,' she said and instantly Abi picked up on the hushed urgency in Irene's voice.

'What's the matter? Has something happened?'

'It's Callum. He's missing.'

Abi put down the boarding pass and sat back in her office chair.

'He had a row with Craig – a serious one this time. Ever since the exams, he's been off the rails. I can't tell you how worrying and frustrating it's been for us. Craig has been going nuts.' She drew in her breath, bringing her voice back under control. 'Anyway, when we got back from Mount Juliet last weekend, we found out that Callum had quit his job at the tennis club and that was the last straw. Craig lost the plot and told him to leave.'

She explained how they had only done it to try and force the boy to take some responsibility for himself, to grow up a little. They hadn't meant it as anything definitive or final.

'A few days sleeping on someone's couch,' Irene said, 'and we thought it would bring him to his senses. But he's been gone for a week now, and he's not answering his phone. We've no idea where he is.'

'Have you tried his friends?'

'Yes, of course. He was at Josh's for the first few nights, until Elaine wanted her spare bedroom back. Since then, no one's seen him.'

'It's only been a few days,' Abi said gently. 'I'm sure he'll surface eventually.'

'I'm worried he'll do something stupid.'

'No.'

'That he'll harm himself.'

'Come on now, Irene. Of course he won't.'

'You don't understand. He took some things from the house,' she whispered.

But when Abi asked what it was that he had taken, Irene fell silent.

'If you're really worried, then maybe you should speak to the police—'

'No. We can't. Craig refuses to.'

Abi exhaled softly. 'Well then. I suppose all you can do is wait for him to turn up.'

She heard Irene swallow and thought perhaps she was crying.

Carefully, she said: 'If you want to meet . . . if you need someone to talk to, we could always—'

'No, that's fine,' Irene said with a new briskness, tamping down her show of emotion as if embarrassed by it now.

After the phone call, Abi felt tight-shouldered and stressed, some of Irene's anxiety adhering to her.

'Let's get out of here,' she said to Mark after leaving Corinne's boarding pass on the hall table. 'I could do with some fresh air.'

He suggested the Devil's Glen with its deciduous forest,

the show of colour probably at its zenith now before the inevitable shedding of leaves by Halloween. So they piled into the Cherokee – all except Eva, who opted to stay at home and study – and Mark took the wheel, the car filled with silence as they passed over the Dublin Mountains crossing into the Wicklow hills.

The day was calm and warm for October, light filtered thinly through a sheet of cloud providing a crisp clarity to the autumn colours that drenched the swathe of trees. The forest floor was still wet from the rain of the previous day, a mulch of damp leaves underfoot as they made their way through the quiet terrain, separating into pairs, Abi and Mark walking briskly ahead while the two girls hung back. Every now and then, Mark turned to shout out encouragement, trying to chivvy them along, until Abi said:

'Just leave them. Let them have their time together. They'll catch up with us eventually.'

She herself would have preferred it if the girls had stayed home. Even at a distance of several paces, Beth's presence was a constant reminder, and Abi felt she couldn't shake off her own anxiety. Mark, catching the trace of irritability in her voice, said quietly:

'Are you all right?'

She exhaled. 'Tired, that's all.'

He didn't reply, and after a few minutes trudging along, she began to feel his silence was less contemplative and more interrogative.

'I know you think I went overboard last night,' she said at last. 'But I worry about Beth in ways I never do about Eva. And when she does things like that, I just get so anxious, and it comes out as anger, frustration. Of course, it's myself I'm angry with really, not her.'

'Why you?'

'Because I feel I've failed her, I suppose. Failed to protect her, or – as in this present debacle – I've failed to guide her. I mean, she's supposed to learn these things from us – how to be a good citizen, how to be a decent human being.' She shook her head, pushed her hands deep inside the pockets of her coat, the frustration rising up inside her again. 'When they were little, we always used to say to them: be kind to the other kids. Did that fail to register with her? Or did we just stop saying it and it slipped down her list of priorities?'

'By that argument, we'd be reciting a whole list of commandments to them every morning; they'd never get out the door. We do our best, Abi.'

'I keep thinking about the way Helen Bracken spoke to me yesterday. Like she couldn't fathom how I'd let things slip with my own daughter, like I'd failed to understand what was really going on with her.'

'You think she was judging you?'

'God, yes. We all do it, subconsciously or not. And I imagine it's part of her job, trying to second-guess the parenting skills of people like us whose kids are wild.'

'Beth's not wild!' he laughed, more from annoyance than humour. 'She doesn't give lip to teachers. She does okay academically – not as well as Eva, granted. On the whole, she's a good kid.'

'Yeah, well, I'm not sure everyone would agree. Look at the evidence: her freak-out last year was pretty shocking. And now she's been orchestrating this bullying campaign.'

'She was bullied herself, Abi. You heard her. And that Sasha can be a little bitch – we both know this. Remember, Beth only tells us half of what's going on. I'll bet she's been putting up with all sorts of jibes about her scoliosis, and about . . . oh, I don't know, just the way she looks, the way she acts. She's nerdy. And nerds always get a hard time in school – I should know.'

'So, did you ever do something like this?'

'I did other stuff, I'm sure.'

'Come on, Mark. No, you didn't.'

'All I'm saying is that none of us are angels.'

'It's the premeditation that bothers me. I took a look at the social media posts she put up; one of them had details of abortion clinics in the Netherlands and the UK, marked for Sasha's attention. Where did she even learn about this stuff?'

'Kids these days – they're just more clued in than we were. The internet—'

'Yeah, but a year ago Beth would never have even thought to do something like this. Something happened to her.'

'You've said this before—'

'Well, isn't it a fair assumption?'

She remembered the word Siobhan Harte had used to describe Beth: disturbed. She felt it like a stone lodged deep in her stomach.

'We dropped the ball, Mark. And not for the first time. It makes me wonder what else we haven't noticed.'

'What I haven't noticed, you mean.'

'Oh God, please.'

She was too tired for his sensitivity, too anxious to tiptoe around issues for the sake of maintaining their domestic peace.

'What did you mean when you said you were not going to intervene for her – that you'd done enough of that in the past?' he asked.

'Did I say that?' she answered, cautiously.

He waited for more, and her footfall instinctively slowed as her thoughts speeded up, casting around for something to say.

'It was just the heat of the argument,' she offered weakly. 'I don't know what I meant by it. Nothing, I suppose – just looking to score a point. To wound her. There, I've said it. Now tell me what an awful mother I am.'

'Stop it,' he said, coldness still there in his voice. 'You want me to say: "Of course you're not awful." It's just a way of seeking praise or forgiveness or something, and I'm not feeling particularly forgiving, Abi.'

'I don't even know why we're having this argument,' she declared, before increasing her speed so that she could get ahead of him, get away from him, saying over her shoulder: 'I should have just gone for a walk on my own.'

A river cut through the forest, the path meandering along beside the flow of water. Corinne stared down at the ground as she walked, hardly even looking up once to take in the trees, the turning leaves, the craggy rocks that jutted out into the stream. Both girls were thoughtful and melancholy and Beth, believing the source of their sadness to be the same, said:

'I can't believe you're really going. On Monday.'

When Corinne said nothing, she ventured: 'I fucking hate my mum. She's such an over-reactor. She prides herself on being so communicative, but does she listen? No. As if communication just equals talking. God forbid she'd actually listen to my side of things, actually take into account that there was a reason behind what happened.'

'Is there?'

'What?'

'A reason.'

'You know there is! All those things they said – Sasha and Nicole – about me. And about you. I'd just had enough.'

'You could ignore it.'

'I did ignore it – for years! It got too much.'

It troubled her, Corinne's lethargy, the tired, distracted cast to her voice. Hadn't it been Corinne's idea, to take action against the girls that had made Beth's life so miserable? Wasn't it Corinne who had suggested the plan? Beth distinctly remembered the lilt in her voice when she'd alighted on the perfect idea: a pregnancy. The way Sasha prided herself on her looks, her figure, constantly alluding to her own sexual experiences, listing the guys falling over themselves to get intimate with her, that and her over-confidence. An unplanned pregnancy would be a fitting reward for her hubris, but a rumour would suffice. Corinne, far more proficient on social media channels, had shown Beth how to drop hints in the right places, and then how to warm up the rumour and fan the flames, sitting back to let it ignite. All she had wanted was to inflict a dose of the same pain she had endured, over and over again. She had not stopped to consider the consequences, to imagine how Sasha might feel.

'I can't believe I have to stand in front of the whole school and apologize,' Beth said now. 'You will be there, won't you? I know your flight is at lunchtime, but you will come to school first for assembly?'

'Sure.'

'I don't think I could bear it if you weren't there. I don't think I could do it—'

'It's just words,' Corinne said sharply. She stumbled over a tree root and then righted her footing, casting a glance of irritation at the ground.

Beth, keenly attuned to Corinne's changes of mood, asked: 'What's the matter?'

'All you have talked about is your plan, your apology. It's stupid. Boring.'

Stung, Beth fell silent, her mind swarming over their previous conversation, looking for some clue she had missed.

'Do you think we shouldn't have done it?' she asked, tentative. 'Do you think it was mean?'

Corinne didn't answer, and so Beth continued: 'My mum said Sasha was suicidal. Do you think that's true?' Whenever she turned this thought over in her mind, she felt queasy.

But Corinne seemed untroubled by Sasha's mental state. She was more concerned with getting home to Willow Park.

'How long is this walk?' she asked.

'I don't know. A couple of hours. Why?'

'I should get back to Eva.'

'Eva? Why?' The words, little bullets fired sharply.

'I shouldn't have left her. She shouldn't be alone.'

'She's not a baby. I think she'll manage,' jealousy making her mean.

'She's upset. You don't understand.'

'What's she got to be upset about? So, she was dumped by some guy. So what?' This much she had managed to squeeze from Corinne.

'It's not that simple,' Corinne intoned in a serious way that pricked Beth's attention.

'How come? Has something happened?'

But Corinne didn't answer. The river rushed past, growing louder as they neared the falls.

'Why do you like her so much? I mean, she's not even your age.'

'Does that matter?'

'She's so selfish. Don't you realize that? She doesn't care about you, only herself. She's using you as an audience, because she knows you're just going to fawn all over her.'

Desperation made her say these things, the panic of knowing she was losing Corinne, that she wasn't equipped to compete for her affections.

'You prefer her to me, don't you?'

'So?'

One word uttered so casually. And yet it pierced her heart.

'I don't understand. You never used to be like this about her. But since we came back from France, it's like she's the one you care about, not me.'

'Can't I have more than one friend? Why must you get so jealous?'

'Is it because she reminds you of Anouk?' Beth continued desperately. 'Or is it because I couldn't go through with it with Bruno? I let you down, didn't I?'

'I can't breathe with you around me. You want too much from me. I feel like you want me to be everything for you – your whole world. It's too much. It's not normal!'

The words caught her with a sudden sting, Lisa's accusations echoing up from the past.

'Not normal? What about you? What about your family? You think you're normal? Your sister is a mental patient, and your parents—'

'What about my parents?'

'Come on – you know what I'm talking about. Your sordid secret.' She felt herself unravelling at the edges, the weave coming loose. But Corinne only laughed.

'Oh Beth. You are so stupid.'

'I should tell my mum and dad,' Beth blurted out, a panicked anger pulsing inside her. 'About how you're a freak! About how your parents were brother and sister!'

'It was never true!' Corinne cried. She was having to shout now to be heard above the din of the water. 'It was just a story, something I made up to tease you! But you believed it, because you are a little child! Always asking me what to do. How to act. What to decide. Can't you make up your own mind?'

'No, it's not like that. I . . . I thought we were friends – best friends—'

'So childish—'

'I've learned so much from you, Corinne. It's not that I want you to decide for me—'

'Childish, childish—'

'Listen to me! I respect you, okay? And I need you,' her voice cracked. 'Please, Corinne. She doesn't love you. Not like I do.'

'You love me?' Corinne frowned and the fear opened out inside Beth, hope plummeting as she saw the instant withdrawal in Corinne's face, her features closing down with suspicion. 'You love me but you would tell my secret?'

The waterfall roared. A wind had whipped up – it rushed through the trees and over the surface of the river. High up on the craggy ledge, Beth could see her parents, their brightly coloured rain jackets like flares amidst the dull browns and fading greens.

'Perhaps,' Corinne said now, her eyes narrowing, 'I should tell them yours.'

A sudden plunge in Beth's stomach. 'You wouldn't.'

'Sometimes I think I should. That it would be better for you if I did. A kindness.'

'I wouldn't have told them. I was just saying that because I was upset,' Beth admitted quickly, desperately, blinking away the tears. 'I love you, Corinne. I really do.'

So often, she had thought about saying those words. Even now, as she made the admission, she didn't know how to qualify it. How to explain that it wasn't a sexual thing – she didn't think it was that. It was a need. A huge, hungry want inside her. A loneliness that only receded when they were together. An anxiety that grew calm when Corinne was there.

'I don't know what to do without you.'

A pressure was building inside her. She felt it now as Corinne stepped towards her.

'You need to grow up, Beth,' she said, her voice raised to be heard above the noise of the river. 'Stop playing these silly games. The school, Sasha – rumours on Facebook, fake boys? It's all so stupid and pointless. Don't you see? A waste of time. No one will care. No one will even notice.'

The wind whipped her hair and she turned to free it, her voice getting lost in the wind so that Beth had to ask her to repeat it.

'I said if you want to be noticed you must do something bigger than that,' she shouted.

'But what?'

Corinne's eyes wide, the river rushing behind her. 'You must make it big. Something they won't ever forget.'

31

That night Mark couldn't sleep. They had all gone to bed early, each of them retreating to the separate corners of the house to nurse their bitter feelings, the sour taste of yesterday's argument lingering in the stillness of the air. Outside, a sliver of moon hung in the cloudless sky. The temperature had plummeted, the mildness of autumn ceding to the first promise of winter. Beside him, Abi slept, one hand flung over her head, a trace of a frown lingering in her expression like some remnant of fury. His wife seldom lost her temper, but when she did, she could be ferocious, scathing, like she had been last night. Even when she was in the right, he still found it hard to like her in those moments, let alone love her.

He spent a long time looking at her as she slept and he lay awake, thinking back over their conversation at the Devil's Glen. More and more lately, he was unsettled by the disconcerting thought that they had made a mistake. Their marriage, their life together. No matter how hard he tried to rationalize it, how objectively he tried to look on the matter, it always came back to the feeling that there was something about them that did not click together as it should – a warp in the wood, a snag in the weave.

After a while, he gave up on sleep, quietly rising from the bed and moving to the door. There were no sounds from the other rooms as he stepped silently down the stairs. On the hall table was the printout of Corinne's flight. The sight of it gave him a heavy heart; he felt disappointed by the manner in which her stay with them was ending. Despite everything, he still liked her. But it was settled. On Monday morning, she would go to school with Beth for the last time, say her goodbyes, and then they would drop her at the airport. He doubted they would ever see her again.

In the kitchen, he fixed himself a vodka with ice, then carried it through into his studio where he found Corinne in her T-shirt on the floor, her feet tucked up underneath her, one hand delicately lining up a match to affix to the sculpture that had grown since her arrival, the distinctive towers of Notre Dame's west façade almost finished now. She looked up, startled and shy, then explained:

'I thought I could get it done before I leave. Surprise you. But that was stupid of me. Even if I work on it all day tomorrow, there is too much to do.'

She sounded bewildered, close to tears. He himself felt unbalanced and strange, at a loss for words. For a moment he just stood there, fighting the urge to turn away and take his drink somewhere he could be alone. It felt like he had been avoiding her all day.

'I'm sorry,' she mumbled, putting the matches down.

She rose as if to leave, but he stopped her, not wanting things between them to be left like this.

'Wait,' he said, his voice softening. 'It was a nice thought, Corinne. And I'm sorry you won't be here to finish it with me.'

'Maybe Beth will help you . . .'

But her voice trailed off. They both knew, somehow, the sculpture would be left unfinished until the day arrived for Mark to rouse himself and take it down.

'I'll send you a picture once it's done,' he said halfheartedly.

She nodded, and then sat down cautiously on the edge of the sofa. He noticed she was wearing the Radiohead T-shirt he had given her, and this made him feel strange. His old

T-shirt worn as a nightie. Glancing down at her bare knees, they seemed vulnerable and tentative. The way her eyes widened, seemed to dart about the room, it was as if her coltish beauty had morphed into a startled deer, all bony joints and nervous glances.

The curtains were drawn against the night; the harsh glare from the angle-poise lamp illuminating the matchstick sculpture was the only light in the room. He wanted to sit down but was wary of her physical proximity, in the end, choosing a chair a few feet back from the table.

'I'm sorry things didn't work out,' he said, sipping from his vodka, feeling the burn of it at the back of his throat. 'Will you be all right going home?'

She shrugged but seemed unsure, and he felt a brief stab of worry at what awaited her: Valentina's flakiness and grief, the gaping hole of her absent sister, her dead father. That sound came to him again – the awful gurgling in Guy's throat – and he leaned forward, head bowed, his forearms resting on his knees, the glass of vodka cradled in his hands.

'We thought that having you here with us might act as a welcome distraction,' he said. 'I know what it's like to lose someone. I thought that it would be comforting for you to be within a family environment. But I wonder now if it just made you feel more unsettled.'

She pulled the hem of her T-shirt down over her knees as if aware of them being exposed to his gaze.

'You think I skipped school because Guy died?'

'Is that so implausible?'

Her brow furrowed as if confused, but he sensed that she understood him and was just buying time to think.

'How about you?' she asked, and he sat up straighter.

'Me?'

'You lost your sister. Did that make you *unsettled*?'

He noted the way she articulated the word, unsure if this was because of her unfamiliarity with it, or whether she was needling him in some way. Instantly, he became defensive.

'A little. Then again, we all find our own ways to grieve.' Uncomfortable with the intensity of her gaze, he became brisk, authoritative. 'I hope you will take away some happy memories of your time with us, Corinne. I know that Beth will certainly miss you, as will the rest of us—'

'Abi won't miss me. She hates me.'

'She doesn't hate you. The phone call from the school just threw her. She worries about Beth – we both do.'

'She thinks I am a bad influence.'

'It's not that. Beth is sensitive. Impressionable,' he added carefully.

'And this is how you punish her: by sending me home.'

She spoke plaintively and he acknowledged to himself that there was some truth to her statement.

'Listen,' he began, but then stopped. He hadn't realized she was crying.

'Oh, Corinne,' he said, shaking his head, putting his drink down. 'You mustn't take this to heart. None of this is your fault, you just happened to get a bit caught in the crosshairs.'

'You've always been so kind to me,' she murmured, 'letting me be in this room when you probably wanted to be alone.'

'I was glad of the company.'

She smiled weakly. 'You're just saying that to make me feel better.'

'Well, yes, but also because it's true.'

Something passed between them, a moment of recognition, of shared alliance, and he felt better for it, as though any bitterness between them had been expunged, understanding reached.

'It's getting late,' he told her. 'You should get some sleep.'

'Okay.' When she smiled he saw the gap between her front teeth and it made her seem youthful and fresh, a hint of her old vivacity returning.

'I shall miss you,' he admitted as they both got to their feet.

'Me too,' she told him.

And then she reached out and put her arms about him, and he was gratified by this unexpected hug, this sudden show of emotion. He felt the warmth and thinness of her body, and then she twisted in his arms, turning into him, her face lifted, and he felt her mouth press against his. It was urgent and brief, surprise leaping up inside him as he drew back, aghast.

'Wait,' he said, 'hang on just a second there.'

He had his hand clamped around her upper arm, but he was holding her at a distance away from him, panic surging in his chest.

'You've got the wrong idea,' he began.

'What's this? What's going on?'

He looked up and saw Abi, ashen-faced, at the door.

'Shit,' he whispered. He released Corinne's arm quickly as if it burned, and turning to his wife, he said: 'It's nothing, Abi. Just a stupid misunderstanding.'

'What is she even doing in here?'

'Nothing! Just working on the model—'

'In the middle of the night?'

'I couldn't sleep,' Corinne interjected, her voice quavering with nerves. She was looking from one to the other, twitchy with uncertainty. 'I just wanted some company.'

'Do you think I'm really that stupid, Corinne? That I would fall for that? And as for you,' she said, rounding on

Mark. 'I would have thought you could exercise a bit more judgement.'

'She hugged me. She kissed me,' he told her, emphasizing the order of the pronouns. 'I pushed her away. It was nothing, just a split second. An impulse that I rejected.'

But Abi was unmoved.

'You should have known better. Letting yourself get into this situation. My God, use some common sense! And so should you, Corinne. Think how inappropriate this is! He's old enough to be your father, for Christ's sake!'

The words were out of Abi's mouth before she realized what she had said.

Corinne grew very still, her gaze cold. 'My father is dead,' she told Abi. 'And I won't be lectured by you. You don't even know what is going on in your own house, with your own children, and you talk to me about being inappropriate?'

The words spoken, the tone she used – a challenge there. Abi's gaze narrowed.

'What do you mean?'

'Nothing.'

'Is there something going on that we don't know about?'

The girl was fiddling with the hem of her T-shirt again, putting a finger to her mouth and biting away a hangnail, her eyes darting towards the door. Mark understood that what she'd said was just a ruse. A ruse he could see that she regretted and he felt moved to pity her.

'Go to bed, Corinne,' he said gently but firmly.

'Corinne?' Abi's voice tilted towards sharpness. She was not prepared to let it go.

'It's nothing—'

'No, don't do that. Don't hint at something then back away. If you've got something to say, then say it.'

Abi's tone had grown strident.

'Come on, Abi. Let the girl go to bed. This is all nonsense.'

Ignoring him, Abi ploughed on: 'Is something going on? Is it Eva? Does she—'

'Not Eva. Beth,' she came back quickly.

'Beth?' Abi's voice dropped a little.

Corinne paused, as if briefly considering the effect her words were about to have. Then she raised her eyes to look at Abi and in a cool, clear voice, she told them: 'Beth was abused by her aunt.'

'*What?*'

The word shot out of Mark's mouth like a bullet.

'Your sister, Melissa, abused her,' she said, unfazed by his sharpness.

'That's ridiculous,' Mark scoffed.

'Touching her. Making her do things.'

'Stop it, Corinne—'

'Beth never told anyone. She thought no one would believe her. That you all loved Melissa.'

'That's enough—'

'That you would never believe her. The abuse went on for months—'

'I said that's enough!' he roared.

Anger flared in his brain, unwanted thoughts and images trickling into the corners of his mind. He pushed them away, turning on her.

'I don't want to hear any more of this!' he told her. Aware that he was shouting, he went on: 'This is all just bullshit. You're making this up.'

'I'm not—'

'Why should we believe a word of what you say? All the lies you've told us about your own family, your sister.'

'This is different—'

'My sister loved Beth. And how dare you besmirch that love, make it out to be something sordid and twisted. The woman is dead, for Christ's sake! She can't even defend herself against this crap!'

'It's true,' Corinne protested softly. Her eyes flicked to Abi. '*You* believe me.'

In the heat of their exchange, he hadn't noticed Abi, too focused on his own indignant rage. But now he turned his gaze and saw that she was no longer standing. She was leaning weakly against a chair, all the colour drained from her face.

'My God,' she said quietly, bringing her gaze up to meet his.

Her eyes were large, frightened pools and he saw the creeping realization in them, the horrified belief.

'My God,' she kept saying, over and over.

All this time, his mind had been fighting against the idea, convinced that it was another one of Corinne's stories. But now he glimpsed his wife's thoughts and the gates began to open, unwelcome images creeping in.

The room around him tilted, the furniture looked strange. Could it be true? The words blew up in a storm and there was nothing he could do. He stood in the middle of it all, helpless to ward it off. And then his eyes lit on the sculpture standing on the table – the delicate flying buttresses, the solid twin towers. All the hours he'd put into it – a childhood hobby he'd revived. It flashed across his mind, the long afternoons and evenings he'd spent as a boy with his sister, working side by side. His stomach turned. He lurched forward and with one quick sweep of his arm, the sculpture shattered. For a moment, his eyes widened with wonder at the matches scattered over the floor and the furniture, the broken shards of the foundations remaining on the tray. He couldn't look at Corinne.

'Get out,' he told her.

They talked long into the night. In the kitchen, Mark poured out vodka for both of them and they sipped from their glasses at the table in the window. At one point, Abi said shakily: 'What I wouldn't do for a cigarette right now.'

Neither of them had smoked since the girls were born, but Mark remembered a packet of Marlboros he had found in Eva's schoolbag some years back, and he went into the den now to find them. Pausing for a moment in the doorway, he was arrested by the explosion of matchsticks spread around the room. The aftermath of his fury seemed pathetic and sad – as futile and silly as the whole matchstick building endeavour.

Now, wading through the detritus, the matches snapping underfoot, he felt a great urge to set it alight, the whole damned room, every last stick of furniture in it. So much of what was gathered here had been Melissa's. The musty smell of it filled his nostrils, making him bilious and light-headed. Quickly, he found the battered carton of Marlboros in a drawer of his desk, then exited the room, pulling the door firmly shut behind him.

In the kitchen, Abi lit a cigarette with trembling hands. The smoke escaped her lips in a sigh, and she closed her eyes and rested her head against the heel of her hand.

'Why didn't she tell us?' she asked him now.

'I don't know.'

It was not the first time that night she asked the question. Their conversation kept circling back to the same repeated pleas: When did it start? For how long did it go on? How bad was it? Why didn't Beth tell them? Mark didn't have any answers. And a large part of his mind still fought against it, refusing to accept what Abi seemed so willing to believe.

'It all makes sense now,' she told him.

'What does?'

'Harming herself at school – the violence of that act. She was trying to tell us, Mark. I can't believe we didn't pick up on it.'

He felt the reproach but said nothing. Abi banged her forehead with the heel of her hand – remorse, anxiety, frustration, all coming off her in waves.

'Is that when it started, do you think?'

'I don't know,' he replied.

'How long do you think it went on for?'

'I don't know—'

'What did Melissa actually do to Beth? I mean, what level of abuse are we talking about here?'

'Abi—'

'Corinne said touching, but how intimate was it? Was it rape?'

'Abi, would you listen to me?' He spoke sharply. 'I said I don't know, okay?'

'God, I just feel so frustrated! Part of me wants to run up the stairs right now and wake Beth so I can put these questions to her and get some answers—'

'Hey.' He was gentle now, seeing how worked up she was getting. 'We agreed, right? It's better to wait and talk to her calmly.'

She gave a curt nod but didn't meet his eye, stubbing out the diminished cigarette in the saucer she was using as an ashtray. They had decided to wait before broaching the subject with Beth, until a time when he and Abi would sit down with their daughter, reassure her of their love for her, then gently press her to open up to them. Abi had acquiesced to him that this was the best approach, yet still he could see the resistance within her, impatience and frustration impelling her to follow her instincts and shake the child awake.

'All the allowances we made for Melissa. When I think about it now, the way I'd scold the girls anytime they complained about her coming over . . . Do you think it's because they knew what she was, and we didn't?'

His glass was empty and he wanted to refill it, but his limbs felt liquid, unstable. His head swam with vodka, the strangeness of the night. The two of them sat in silence, nursing the feelings inside them. Mark remembered the suicide note he'd found, the list of instructions that had infuriated him at the time – information about bank accounts and post office savings, phone numbers scrawled down for boiler repairs and roof maintenance. He recalled how he felt when he'd turned the list over and seen the words: 'I'm sorry' scrawled across the back. His disappointment at those words, their flimsiness, their inadequacy. But now he wondered whether she had meant Beth.

Then, a thought occurred to Abi. 'That is, unless it didn't happen.'

'What?'

She looked at him. 'Unless Beth made it up and then told Corinne. She lies sometimes. All kids do.'

'But this? To lie about something so—'

'I know. You're right. It was just a thought.' Then she asked hastily: 'Do you think Eva knows anything about it?'

'I doubt it. She would've said if she did, wouldn't she?'

Abi shrugged. 'A year ago, I would have said yes. But now . . . She's become so distant. I hardly see her these days, and when I do, she doesn't want to talk.'

'She's growing up.'

'Yes. She'll be gone soon and then Beth not long after her.'

Abi gave him a direct look. He had the sense that she was steeling herself.

'Things have gotten pretty bad between us, haven't they?'

Meekly, he nodded.

Her brow furrowed with a new confusion, and she continued: 'So bad that you had to seek comfort in Corinne? A girl no older than our daughter?'

A wave of shame washed over him. 'It wasn't like that, Abi,' he said softly. 'But I have felt lonely for some time now and she seemed to understand that. It was friendship – kinship, maybe. As if we came from the same background – the same place of unhappiness.'

'You said, in France, that you'd leave once the girls had left home. Is that still what you intend to do?'

He was so tired. Too tired to deal with this on top of everything else. And yet, he felt the night had brought them closer together, and that she deserved some honesty from him.

'I don't know,' he told her. 'I thought that was what I wanted, but now I'm not sure. When I said that, in France, I was struggling with the feeling that I couldn't hold things together. It's like I was constantly straining to keep together something that naturally wanted to come apart.'

'And now?'

'Now, I just want to pick up the pieces. To stitch this family back together. To care for it, protect it, nurture it.'

He spoke softly, tenderly, in a way he hadn't spoken in years. They held hands across the table and even though something had been shattered that night, it felt like a tiny chink of light, of hope within the gloom.

32

It was easily done. The pregnancy test slipped into an envelope. In the dead of night, she posted it through the letterbox then crept away.

Eva stared at her reflection in the mirror by her bed. Her face looked puffy and pale like dough pounded into the bottom of a bowl. She hadn't brushed her hair and it fell dishevelled around her shoulders. Her room, normally monastic in its tidiness, was swept with a new chaos: books and lecture notes were spread in disarray on her desk where she was supposed to be studying, bags and shoes and clothes strewn across the floor. The bedclothes were still mussed, her duvet a nest at the centre, even though it was almost midday. Her exams were at the end of the month, but after an hour or so of staring blankly at the pages of the books she'd borrowed from the college library, re-reading the same paragraphs over and over, the words blurring out of focus, Eva had given up, succumbing to the draw of her bed.

All morning, there were doors slamming, phones ringing, the drone of her parents' voices conversing downstairs. Corinne and Beth had gone out, and shortly after their departure, there was the familiar sound of her father's bicycle wheels shushing through the gravel driveway. Looking out her window, Eva had seen him clad in his Lycra, one leg swinging over the saddle as he pushed away for his Sunday morning outing.

She had thrown herself on the bed, her body heavy with

exhaustion. Maybe this was because of the small being that had anchored itself in her uterus, sending out waves of hormones, throwing everything off balance, or maybe it was because she had spent the night lying awake worrying about it. Sometimes she put out a hand and touched the wall that separated her bedroom from the house next door as if Ross's presence could somehow communicate itself through the masonry and into her body, give her some sort of sign as to how he was feeling about her. She told herself that there was the chance that he might be happy about this news – elated. Hadn't she glimpsed his profound disappointment when he'd told her of his infertility – a misapprehension, as it turned out? A child of his own – his flesh and blood – surely this would change things? But whenever she tried to imagine his face when he learned of her pregnancy, all she could envision was him recoiling in shock, horrified at the trap she had snared him in, even though, if anyone had been duped and misled, it was her.

Hunger eventually drove her downstairs. She had skipped breakfast and now it was almost two o'clock, and as she descended the stairs, she wondered how it could be possible that a person could feel nauseous and ravenous at the same time. The house felt empty, a cathedral silence hanging over the hall, but when she came into the kitchen, she found her mother at the table hunched over a mug of coffee. There was no laptop open on the table, no papers spread out, she wasn't scrolling through her phone. Instead, Abi was just sitting with her hands wrapped around the steaming mug, her gaze fixed on the garden outside. Her mother was always busy, always occupied with one task or another, which was why it struck Eva as strange to observe her now simply lost in thought. Her face appeared blotched, a downward drag to her skin.

'Are you okay?' Eva asked as she padded across to the fridge.

'I'm fine,' Abi said. She turned her gaze now to Eva but there was still a distracted air about her.

'Where is everyone?'

'Your dad's gone for a cycle. I don't know where the girls are,' she answered, wearily.

Eva peered into the fridge where her eyes fell on a Tupperware jar of leftovers from last night's dinner. Seized with a sudden hunger, she put the tub on the worktop, peeled back the lid and took a fork from the cutlery drawer and tucked right in. Abi watched her for a moment.

'So, what do you think about this mess at school?' she asked after an interval and Eva glanced up, her mouth full. She couldn't get the food down fast enough, hunger making her light-headed. 'This rumour she's been peddling about that girl,' Abi continued. 'Why on earth did she do such a thing?'

Eva thought the whole matter was a little close to the bone. Her younger sister spreading malicious gossip about a fake pregnancy, while here Eva was with an actual embryo gestating inside her and no clue as to what to do about it. Her head felt dizzy with it all, and she propped herself up on one of the kitchen stools.

'Don't ask me. I've no idea what goes on inside that girl's head.'

'Does she talk to you at all? Confide in you if something's worrying her?'

Eva shrugged. 'Not really. You know Beth. She keeps everything bottled up.'

'But if you suspected something was wrong, would you ask her? Would you try and get her to talk?'

Eva looked up.

Abi went on: 'Sometimes it's easier to tell a sibling than to admit something to a parent. Especially if it's something big, you know? Something you thought might be too painful for a parent to hear.'

There were dark smudges under Abi's eyes. Eva saw how worn out she was. But the line of her questioning caused Eva to hesitate. The desperate look her mother was giving her, like she was willing Eva to admit to something.

'I—'

'Does she ever mention Melissa?' Abi went on, and Eva's heart stilled.

'Melissa?'

'Does she ever talk about her? You remember how Beth was always over in that house. Did she ever discuss with you what went on while she was there?'

'No-o,' Eva said, deeply suspicious now. 'Why?'

Abi bowed her head suddenly, as if overcome. She rubbed her forehead vigorously for a moment and said, as if to herself: 'Leaving that house to Beth. I never could figure out why . . .'

Eva filled a glass with water and came and sat at the table. Her mother said: 'Does it bother you, love? That Beth got that house?'

'Not really.'

'Are you sure? Because it certainly bothers me. God! Everything that woman has put us through . . .'

The bitterness in her mother's voice surprised Eva. Referring to Melissa as *that woman* – it was something Abi hadn't done before.

'It's fine, Mum,' she offered gently. 'I don't want any handouts from Melissa – or from anyone else. I'd rather make my own way.'

Abi smiled wanly, reached out and held Eva's wrist. 'Good

for you, love.' She exhaled, some of the tension draining into tiredness. Then she asked the question Eva had been avoiding for weeks: 'How are things going in college?'

She shrugged. 'Okay.'

'I've hardly seen you these past couple of months. How are you settling in? Are you happy with your course?'

Keeping her eyes on the water in her glass, Eva replied: 'Sort of. I don't know. Some of it is really tough. It's not how I thought it would be.'

'That's natural enough. University is a different level. And you're among peers now who are all very bright, and just as driven as you.'

'Yes.'

'Just be glad that you're there. Look at Callum Ferguson, the mess he's made of things. Poor Irene is distraught.'

'Well,' Eva said tentatively, 'perhaps if they hadn't put so much pressure on him . . .'

Abi considered that for a moment, then said: 'You haven't heard from him, have you?'

'Me?'

'You do know he's missing, right?'

'He probably just wants a bit of space. The way Craig goes on, I don't blame him.'

'His parents are worried sick, Eva. They haven't heard from him in days. If you know anything about where he might be—'

'Okay, Mum. I don't know anything, all right?'

'Fine.' She held up her hands briefly, then let them fall again back down to the table. Eva could see how tired her mother was.

'And don't worry about university,' Abi said, picking up the thread of their conversation. 'It's early days. Things will settle.'

'What if I've made a mistake though?' Eva asked with quiet insistence.

Abi's brow furrowed. 'A mistake?'

'It happens. People realize they've chosen the wrong course.'

'But Engineering was always your first choice.'

'I know. But that was when I was in school.'

'Do you want to transfer to something else?'

'No. I don't know—'

'I suppose you could. If you're absolutely sure you want to. But Eva, think carefully, love. Don't throw away your opportunity.'

'I just feel like I need some time to think. Just a space to get my head clear. I thought maybe I could see about deferring—'

'What? No, love, that's not a good idea. And anyway, it's too late surely.'

'But I'm unhappy, Mum. What's the point in killing myself over this course if I'm not even going to carry on? Wouldn't it be better if I just dropped out now?'

Abi stared at her aghast. 'Are you serious? You want to drop out?'

Eva felt a vertiginous lurch inside her. Her mother was looking at her too directly, and Eva shied away from the heat of her stare, as if it might penetrate through the layers and fibres of her body and discover the real secret Eva was hiding from her.

'What would you propose to do with your time?'

'I could get a job.'

'Waitressing? Working in some clothes shop? While all your friends are at university – is that really what you want?'

At that moment they heard a crash next door. Eva, who had been on the verge of retorting that there was nothing wrong with any of those jobs, fell silent, fear prickling across the back of her neck.

'This coffee is cold,' Abi remarked, getting to her feet. 'I'll make us some more and then let's talk about this properly—'

She was halfway across the kitchen when there was another smash against the wall.

'God, what was that?' Abi asked.

From behind the wall they heard the low rumble of a man's voice, the words indecipherable but the tone was clear – a raised shout of anger. Eva's heart gave out a hard warning beat.

There was another crash and then a woman's scream, and Abi turned to her daughter, her face grave.

'What's going on in there?'

'I don't know.' Eva was holding herself very still, straining to listen, aware that the blood had drained from her face.

'It sounds like they're breaking every dish in the house,' Abi commented, shock in her voice, as they heard another smash above the mangled roar of voices. 'Do you think we should call the police?'

Eva's head jerked back. 'What? Why on earth—'

'It sounds bad. We should at least call to the door to see if everything's all right, make sure they're not killing each other.'

'No,' Eva said firmly.

'I just—'

'Leave them be, Mum. It's none of our business, okay?' Her voice tilting away from firmness towards something far less controlled.

'We really don't need this right now,' Abi breathed, rubbing her forehead, looking harassed.

Distantly, Eva thought she could make out the words: *fucking liar!* Becca's voice bent into a shriek. Abi was standing by the cooker, arms crossed, looking down, clearly listening, and Eva wanted her mother to move away, fearful of what she might overhear. But she herself was rooted to the spot, listening sharply, trying to put herself beyond the wall and into that room, wanting and not wanting to witness the appalling scene, to hear whether her own name might come into it, all that they'd done.

Another smash against the wall, her mother's head pulling back as if the china might come shattering through into their kitchen, and Abi looked at Eva and asked: 'You don't think he'd hit her, do you?'

'No! Of course not!'

'It sounds violent—'

'That's her, not him! Ross would never hurt anyone! He's not like that—'

She broke off, aware how her voice had risen sharply. Abi was staring at Eva; the shock that had been on her face over the sounds from next door fell away now. A new suspicion entered her gaze.

'Eva?' she said, and Eva pushed herself away from the table, moving quickly to the kitchen door.

She broke into a run, taking the stairs two steps at a time, her mother close behind still repeating her name, the question in it growing forceful, pressing down on Eva so that by the time she made it into her bedroom, the tears were flowing, sobs shuddering through her body. She went to the window and wrapped her arms tightly about her waist, attempting to both shield herself from her mother's questions and brace herself for the inevitable relinquishing of the awful truth.

Abi's hands gripped both of Eva's upper arms; her eyes searched Eva's face.

'Tell me,' she demanded, her voice low and very controlled.

'I can't,' Eva wailed, shaking her head.

'You and Ross. You've been having some kind of relation-ship. Is that it? Is that what all that shouting is about next door?'

Eva bit her lip, her face a streaming mess and nodded quickly.

'Sweet Jesus,' Abi breathed. 'For how long?'

'Since the summer.'

'And now Becca's found out. Christ, she's probably killing him in there. Is it serious between you two?'

Eva couldn't answer, couldn't meet her gaze, but she felt her mother's eyes flickering over her, the new understanding filtering into her consciousness. Abi dropped her arms, her hands withdrawing instantly as if scalded by the heat from her daughter's body.

'You're pregnant.'

'Mum—'

'Oh, Eva! Oh, you stupid, stupid girl,' she exclaimed and then her arms were around Eva drawing her into a hug that was almost savage. Love and anger beating away in time inside her.

Eva felt frightened. Even there in her mother's embrace, the fear and shame still thrummed hard inside. But a tiny part of her exhaled with relief. She had told her mother, and she was still alive, still breathing. She wanted her mother to keep holding her like that, to feel the protective strength of that love, to feel the real truth in the words Abi had told her from the time she was a little girl: *I will always love you, no matter what.* But then there were voices outside, and she felt her mother's attention moving towards the window.

Hurried footsteps across the driveway, Becca screaming: 'Don't you walk away from me! Don't you dare!'

Both Abi and Eva moved instinctively to the window.

Looking down, she saw Ross walking quickly, his face set, determinedly ignoring his wife who continued to screech at him: 'Who is she? I have a right to know!' Becca, normally so groomed and composed, looked wild and unhinged.

Eva put a hand to her mouth, an acrid taste of vomit at the back of her throat.

'Don't you dare tell me it's not true! You're a fucking liar!'

Ross was at the car now, flinging open the door of the Range Rover and climbing in, but Becca prevented him from closing it, her agitation charged now with a new emotion, a searing rage. 'You got her pregnant, you bastard! Don't try to deny it!'

Eva's heart seized with sudden shock.

Ross slammed the door shut, insulating himself from his wife's frenzied accusations.

Her thoughts tangled in confusion, and that's when her mother started banging on the window.

'What are you doing?' Eva asked, appalled, but Abi didn't hear, hammering the pane with the heel of her hand.

Down below in the driveway, Mark was wheeling his bike towards the house. Eva saw him and thought that her mother was hammering to get his attention, as if trying to warn him in some way. Mark looked up at them, his expression perplexed. But Abi didn't see him. She was staring intently at the Campbells' driveway, her eyes wide with alarm, the hammering becoming furious as she shouted 'No! No! No!'

Ross was in the car now, the car door shut, the engine starting, Becca with her face to the glass, roaring at her husband to stop.

The child's blue car was moving now, little legs pedalling. None of the rest of them had seen him. Not Mark staring up at his own house in dazed confusion, not Becca caught in a swarm of furious weeping, not the child's own father, lost, his vision blurred, too panicked to glance in the rear-view mirror as he put the car in reverse. Only Abi, screaming and banging at the window as if this could stave off catastrophe, as if by her furious actions she could save him, believing until the last second when she stopped, stilled by her own horror.

The car reversed. There was a sickening crunch and then a long silence.

33

The boy was dead. In the moments while they had waited for the ambulance to arrive – agonizingly long, although when he checked his watch it was only five minutes – Mark had seen the boy's life slip away. A small lapse in the panic, a moment of quiet, and then the little body took on a new quality of stillness, just as the ambulance heaved into view, and Mark knew – he just knew. He didn't think he would ever forget the way Becca Campbell pleaded for her son's life – as if the paramedics had it in their gift to bring the boy back from the dead. Maybe they did on some occasions, but not this one. By the time they lifted him inside the ambulance, Becca was hysterical. When Ross reached out to touch her, she turned on him, ferocious, batting him away, and Mark, who had never really thought much of his neighbour, felt a rush of pity for him. Becca had gone alone in the ambulance, and Abi had immediately offered to bring Ross, who had wordlessly accepted. A numbness to the man, like the lifeblood had been drained from him, staring ahead zombie-like as Abi had started the car and pulled off.

Mark realized, after he stepped back inside his own house, how cold he was. Shivering. The sweat on his body after the bike ride had cooled, and now he was freezing. He needed to shower, but he needed a drink first, to calm his ragged nerves. In the kitchen, the whiskey was already on the counter, and he stared at it, confused, until Beth said: 'For Eva. She was in shock.' Adding: 'It was Corinne's idea.'

He hadn't seen her there, sitting in the snug – he hadn't

even realized she'd returned home. She looked small and pale, her hair tousled as if from sleep, and for just a moment, she was his little girl again, sitting quietly in her nightie at the breakfast table, diligently scraping out her cereal bowl in the early-morning light before school.

'Beth,' he said, his heart filling a little just at the sight of her.

'Is Jo dead?'

He exhaled. 'Yes, love. He is.'

She said nothing and he came towards her, putting his hand to the back of her neck, squeezing it gently.

'It was nobody's fault. Just a horribly tragic accident.'

He wondered how the Campbells would live with it. How could any parent carry on after such a thing? He remembered again Becca's pleading – the desperation in it – and was suddenly overcome.

'Beth?' he said, his voice wobbling a little. 'Give your old dad a hug, will you?'

Dutifully, she got to her feet, and he felt her arms go around him as he clasped her against his chest. He just needed to feel her close to him, to know that she was his child and she was alive and protected.

'I love you, Beth,' he said, his voice breaking a little as he tried to control his emotions. He didn't want to frighten her, but something was impelling him now. 'You do know that, don't you?'

Within his arms, she mumbled her yes.

'I'd do anything for you, anything to protect you, to keep you safe. And I'm sorry . . .' He almost couldn't say it. 'I'm sorry if I didn't protect you in the past. If things happened that you couldn't tell me about . . .'

He felt her stiffen, but still he went on: 'You should have told me, love. You should have come to me. I know you think that because she was my sister . . . but if I had known she was hurting you—'

She drew away from him, shocked. The look she gave him — her dark brows drawing together into a frown, her eyes fierce beneath them. He put his hand to her shoulder and said:

'It's all right, love. I know.'

She shook her head quickly.

'Corinne told us,' he said gently. 'She was worried.'

Her eyes flared, and she took a step back from him, away from his reach.

'Beth—'

'No. No!' she cried as he came towards her, putting her hands up as if to ward him off.

'Please, love—'

But she backed away, stumbling against a kitchen stool, sending it clattering to the floor, but she didn't stop to right it, hurrying out into the hall, the door slamming in her wake, the quick crunch of gravel as she ran.

'Christ,' he said to the empty room, and as he reached down to pick up the fallen stool, he felt a rush of blood to the head and with it came the realization that he had failed her again.

On the drive to the hospital, Ross Campbell had prayed. Abi had been taken aback by that, never having considered him to be a religious man, and perhaps he wasn't. But under the circumstances . . . He'd said the *Hail Mary* over and over again, and she had found herself joining in. Her eyes fixed on the road ahead, uttering a prayer she hadn't said in years, and with that man, of all people! A man whom, barely an hour before, she had hated – *hated!* A man who had taken advantage of her daughter, abusing his position, betraying their trust in the worst possible way. This man was the father of her grandchild, she realized now. If Eva decided to keep the baby. She heard the fervor with which he prayed, his head bowed, the knuckles of his hands white as he clenched them beneath his chin, and when she'd drawn the car up outside the emergency department, he had reached for her hand and squeezed it hard. She felt the painful press of her rings against the bones of her fingers.

'My mum knows about the baby,' Eva said.

This was some hours later. They were lying side by side on her bed staring at the ceiling. The jagged peaks of her hysteria had dulled and faded. Outside the window the day had darkened, evening drawing in.

'You told her?' Corinne asked.

'She guessed.'

'Was she shocked?'

'Shocked. Angry. And disappointed.' She sighed and ran her hand absently over her belly. The hunger that had seized her earlier in the day had left, and now she just felt hollow and empty. She thought of the lonely occupant of the dark cavern of her womb.

'She'll want me to get rid of it, I just know it. I probably should too.'

'And your father? Will she tell him?'

Eva frowned, her hand resting heavily on her tummy.

'I don't know.'

Her mother still hadn't returned from the hospital. She'd heard her father on the phone a while ago, his voice still grave with shock.

'Do you think he told Becca?' Eva asked now.

'Maybe.'

'He must have. How else would she have found out?'

Then she remembered the day he'd picked her up in UCD, how upset he'd been over that text. She had almost forgotten about the anonymous sender, the photograph taken outside Melissa's house.

'You didn't tell Beth, did you? About me and Ross. About the baby. Did you?'

'Of course not. I promised I would not.'

Eva glanced across at Corinne, saw the seriousness on her face. She was lying so still, the two of them wrapped in a companionable hush. There was something soothing about Corinne's presence, so different to the jumpy animation of before that Eva had disliked about her. It made Eva wonder if the quirkiness and clownish act had been just that – an act. And Eva felt bad then, because the whole time she'd just been talking about herself. She hadn't once spoken to Corinne about how she was being shunted back home, her stay with them abruptly cut short.

'How do you feel about going home?'

Corinne bit her lip but didn't answer, and Eva believed she saw a trace of agitated fear cross her face.

'Beth will really miss you,' she offered, and Corinne made a small sound of derision.

'Don't tell her I said this, but I am a little glad to be leaving her. She is very . . . I don't know the word—'

'Clingy?'

'Yes. She wants more from me than I can give her. Some-times I catch her staring at me so hard, it scares me a little. It's like she's not really a full person, you know. Like there is something missing that she wants me to fill. It is too much. When I'm with her, I feel she wants even the air I breathe.'

'You feel suffocated?'

'Yes. But I don't feel that with you,' Corinne said, softening.

Eva exhaled. Darkness had crept over the room. She

wanted to get up and turn on the lights, but part of her didn't want to break the relaxed mood they had fallen into.

'At least you will get to visit Anouk again. Maybe she'll be better now,' she said, wanting to offer the girl some sort of hope. Whenever Corinne spoke of her sister, a helpless optimism came into her voice, a tenderness to her recollections.

'I don't know if she will ever get better.'

'Don't say that, Corinne. You can't give up hope.'

'The day before I came here – the first time, at Easter – I went to see Anouk. She was so bad that day, I couldn't stand it. I told Guy and Valentina that I believed her. The things she was saying – even the really crazy shit – I believed it. That it was true, and they had locked her up just for telling the truth.' She shook her head. 'I must have seemed crazy to them too.'

'That's why your mum rang that night,' Eva said, and Corinne nodded.

Eva felt for Corinne's hand and squeezed it, and Corinne kept on holding Eva's hand, turning to look at her. 'You remind me of her,' Corinne said, her voice softening. 'Anouk, how she was before. As soon as I met you, I felt I knew you already.' She smiled shyly. 'When I'm with you, it's like I have Anouk back again, the way she used to be. The sister that I loved – that I adored.'

There was an intensity about the way she was looking that made Eva uncomfortable. She was suddenly aware of the clamminess of their hands, but she didn't want to offend the girl or push her away. Not after what Corinne had just admitted to, all she had shared. Instead, Eva tried to lighten things, saying:

'We both have crazy sisters, huh? You heard what Beth did to herself at school? Stabbing herself? Fucking nuts.'

She turned her gaze back to the ceiling, and then she remembered something, frowning to recall it correctly. Corinne, seeing the frown, said: 'What is it?'

'Something my mum said. Before everything kicked off today.' She tried to bring her mind back, to access the exact words spoken. 'We were talking about Beth, and then she started asking me all this stuff about Melissa. About what I thought of her, and what did I think Beth used to do anytime she was over there. She was talking like Beth had been abused by Melissa or something . . .' Her thoughts ran on, even though her words had stopped.

Corinne's eyes flickered over her. The grasp of her hand tightened.

'And?'

'And it was weird because years ago Melissa did something that creeped me out. I was twelve or thirteen, I can't remember exactly, and I was in her house and I'd spilt something over my clothes. She started fussing, wiping the dress and then she told me to take it off, that she would put it in the wash. I was embarrassed and I said no, but she insisted. She kept on insisting and I kept refusing, and eventually I just shoved her backwards – I was so furious! I called her a pervert or something, said if she ever came near me again, I'd tell my parents.' Eva stopped, a sort of unease coming over her. She had almost completely forgotten.

'Did you tell anyone about it?'

'No. I didn't. But I made sure I was never in a room alone with her. And after a while I just forgot.' She shook her head, amazed at how it had almost become lost to her, this memory. Now, something new crossed her mind. She looked at Corinne: 'Why? Do you think I should have told someone? My parents? Beth?'

Anxiety stirred to life inside her, but Corinne just smiled and stroked her hair, and said: 'Let's not think about the past any more.'

And Eva closed her eyes and allowed her hair to be stroked, feeling the day falling away. Neither of them heard the footsteps moving back across the hall. The sound of a door closing, a sob suppressed.

After a while, they slept.

34

The morning was dark when Mark arose, his breath clouding out on the air as he dragged the bins down to the kerb for collection.

One by one they drifted down for breakfast. Abi, hunched over a coffee at the table, heavy-lidded with exhaustion, watched Eva, who was waiting by the toaster. Mark, still ignorant of their eldest's condition, finished his cereal, then put his bowl in the sink. He didn't speak to any of them, apart from offering to refill Abi's cup. When Beth came into the kitchen, they looked at each other for a moment, and he felt there was something shuttered about her gaze, but then it passed. She turned from him to pull open the fridge. Corinne stayed upstairs, packing.

It was a lunchtime flight, and Mark had agreed to pick her up from the school mid-morning and go from there to the airport. The girls would say their goodbyes on the school grounds – better that way, he thought, than a tearful scene in the departures lounge, all the drama of wheelie bags and closing gates, the long, lonely drive home. But then he remembered what Beth had to face that morning. In all the mess of their weekend, he had forgotten about the crisis at the school – the public statement of *mea culpa* that Bracken had demanded. And he realized that Beth's pallor, the tightness of her face, was attributable not to imminent loss, but to fear.

'Listen, love,' he said in the hall, as she was putting on her coat. 'You don't have to do this. I know your mum put her foot down the other day about taking responsibility for your actions, but after what's happened this weekend, no one expects you to go through that.'

She didn't say anything, didn't look at him. Just went on silently buttoning her coat.

'I can ring the school,' he continued, 'I'll tell the principal what happened. She'll understand, Beth.'

'It's fine,' she told him quietly, then reached down for her schoolbag and went to wait by the car.

But Mark was worried.

Throughout the drive to school, he kept glancing in the rear-view mirror, catching glimpses of Beth's face in profile as she stared out the window, that blank, closed expression persisting. Corinne was also silent, and he noticed the way they didn't look at each other, didn't sit close together or hold hands as they once might have done.

When he drew up alongside the school gate, he turned and said:

'I'll be back for you, Corinne, at ten thirty, okay? I'll pick you up here.'

She nodded and got out. He looked at Beth.

'It's not too late, you know, sweetheart. If you don't want to do this, just say the word. I can go in right now and talk to Mrs Bracken.'

She stared at him, and it was a long look full of wavering, he thought. And then she leaned forward and kissed him on the cheek close to his mouth, and he felt the enervating charge of that kiss.

Later, this would come back to him, the solemnity of her look, the finality of that kiss.

'Bye, Dad,' she said, and then she was gone.

*

Abi rang the office and told them she'd be working from home that day. She cancelled her meetings except for one critical lunchtime face-to-face which she rearranged to conduct via video call instead. After checking her emails and setting these arrangements in place, she closed her laptop and went upstairs, gently knocking on Eva's door before letting herself in.

Eva was lying on her side, fully clothed, facing the wall.

'I suppose you want to have The Talk now,' Eva said, but she did not sound angry. There was a muted tiredness about her – resignation, Abi thought.

She came and sat beside her daughter, resting her hand on Eva's hip.

'How are you feeling, love?' she asked tenderly.

'Kind of shitty.'

'Did you sleep?'

'Yes.' And then she turned and lay on her back, meeting Abi's gaze, and sheepishly admitted: 'All I seem to want to do is sleep. It's like I can't stay awake.'

'I was like that too, during my pregnancies. Swamped with exhaustion. I remember wondering if anyone in work would notice if I just crawled under my desk for fifteen minutes to take a nap.'

Eva gave a watery smile.

'What am I going to do?' she asked and Abi felt her heart contract with a fierce, protective love.

'I don't know, sweetheart.'

'I keep thinking about Becca, how she's just lost her child. And here I am with this baby growing inside me, and she's right next door, watching. It's stupid, but part of me thinks that maybe I should have this baby and just give it to them, and then I can go back to my life and they'll have some kind of consolation to make up for Jo . . .'

363

Abi rubbed Eva's tummy, the way she used to do when she was a little girl. Whenever she was upset or in a rage about some perceived injustice, Abi could always calm her child with the slow, circular movement of her palm. And now somewhere buried in the tight flesh of this girl was a grain of cells, circling and growing, embedding itself deeper and deeper into her. Abi looked down at her hand and Eva's flat tummy beneath it with silent amazement.

'But I just don't know if I'd be able to go through with it,' Eva continued. 'And what about college? And when I think about what Dad's going to say ... Have you told him yet?'

'No.'

'Are you going to?'

'We can tell him together.'

Eva nodded, and Abi saw the spark of fear in her eyes.

'He loves you.'

'But it won't be the same,' she said quickly. And Abi thought that perhaps this was true.

In her bedroom, the phone was ringing.

'I'd better get it,' she told Eva, explaining it might be the office.

But it wasn't the office. It was Mark.

'I've just had a phone call from Ursula Ford,' he told her, and for a moment Abi was completely confused.

'Who?'

'Melissa's neighbour. You know – the lady with the cats.'

'Oh, right.'

'She said there's something up with the house. Some banging going on. She thinks someone's in there.'

'Someone's broken in?'

'I don't know,' Mark said. He sounded irritated more than anything. 'I'm going around there now to check it out.

Listen,' he went on. 'I don't know how long this might take. If I'm late for Corinne—'

'It's fine,' she said. 'If needs be, I can take her to the airport.'

'You're sure?'

Abi assured him she was. And when she hung up, Eva was standing there at the bedroom door, her hair mussed, zipping up her tracksuit top.

'I can take Corinne,' she said.

Strange the things she noticed. A fleck of lint on the lapel of Mrs Bracken's black suit jacket. A dint in the wood panelling at the front of her desk like someone had kicked it, hard, splintering the varnish. A nick in the smooth skin of Sasha's shin just above her sock – a shaving cut, perhaps.

Sasha's legs were crossed, one leg swinging with impatience, her mouth tight with self-righteous fury. Beth sat demure, hands in her lap, reciting her apology, looking at Bracken but not really seeing her. In the same way she said the words but didn't really listen to what was coming out of her mouth. Instead she was noticing the light falling through the window of the office, so bright and clear that morning, a greenish hue to it.

She said the words and Bracken listened with her arms crossed, a look of distaste on her face, like she'd ordered something at a restaurant and what had arrived at the table was exactly what she'd requested but it wasn't quite right, somehow – it just didn't taste the way it should.

Sasha huffed when Beth had finished, and Bracken's mouth twitched.

'I'll say it better when I'm in front of the school,' Beth said.

*

Ursula was waiting for him when he pulled the car up outside the little house on Beaufield Court.

'I was going to call the police,' she explained, hurrying up the path in Mark's wake. 'But then I thought it might be a builder, some tradesman you had in doing work. And you know, there's been a lot of coming and going in there recently. Those schoolgirls coming by. And that man—'

'What man?' Mark asked, fishing for the keys in his pocket.

'The bald man. Stocky. I've seen him here with your older girl.'

He stared at her.

'I don't know what they're up to. But last night,' Ursula went on, 'there was some noise around ten o'clock. I went to bed, and it was silent. But then, this morning, all that banging started. There!' she said, her eyes brightening with conviction, holding her hand up for him to listen. 'Do you hear it?'

They were standing by the front door, and he could hear a rumble from upstairs, a kind of dragging sound. And when he turned the key and pushed the door, the sound got louder, an urgency to it now. His heart was beating a little faster as he called out: 'Hello? Who's there?'

He followed the sound upstairs, aware of Ursula close behind him. It was coming from Melissa's bedroom, and as he reached the door, the noise inside grew frantic, a muffled shouting, a tremulous shake against the wall. He felt his hesitation, and then pushed the door open quickly.

His mouth fell open.

Behind him, Ursula Ford said: 'Sweet God in Heaven.'

They came now, like a procession. Bracken led the way, brisk and important in her black professorial robes, eyes darting about at the girls – her charges – alert for errant behaviour. Sasha next, head up, shoulders back, a regal wounded air as she absorbed the attention. Finally, Beth, head bowed – the penitent. She felt the brief hush come over the assembly hall as they moved through the crowd to the place at the centre of it – a microphone, three chairs.

'Come Holy Spirit, open our hearts . . .' they recited in unison, and Beth felt her mouth forming the words, but there was no pulse of meaning in it. The school prayer echoed around the hall and up to the ceiling, and Beth felt herself to be at the centre of a blizzard of words. They rose up around her, swarming into a mass. One of the doors on to the courtyard had been left open and the curtain billowed in the breeze.

Mrs Bracken was speaking now, sermonizing on the values of loyalty and kindness, the importance of friendships, and Beth thought that there were different types of loyalty, different sorts of friendship.

'I'll watch out for you,' she'd told Callum.

And when she'd texted him to check he was okay, and he'd responded: *Nowhere to go. I need help.* – hadn't she shown generosity? Compassion?

'Are you sure this is cool?' he'd said, looking around the little house, the brown furniture, the chenille bedspread. 'Won't your parents mind?'

'It's nothing to do with them,' she'd told him, watching as he set his rucksack down on the floor. 'This is my house. Mine.'

The last time she would sit in this hall, the last time she would feel the hum of other bodies around her, breathing the same air as all these girls, inhaling the mingled smells of sweat and deodorant and dust and, distantly, the mown grass of the pitches outside.

Courage is a choice, Corinne had said. One of the things Beth had learned from her. She had decided, right from the start, that Corinne had something to teach her, that the French girl was someone to be studied. And so, she had watched and learned and allowed herself to be led, to be moulded. Instinctively, her hand went up now to the back of her neck, fingertips feeling for the soft ridge of her scar. A source of ugliness, Corinne had drawn it out, made it something to be celebrated. The inked flower bloomed but Beth could not feel it.

That day in France, the flower newly inscribed on her neck, in that house with the dogs, she remembered the challenge in Corinne's stare, the brittleness of her smile. A payment had to be made, and Beth had watched Corinne steeling herself for it, like an actor entering the character they were to play – she could become another person in that moment, sealing off her feelings. It was a transaction, nothing more.

Someone was saying her name. Once, twice – the second time sharply. Bracken was staring contemptuously at her, standing back to clear the way.

Beth summoned that same spirit now. She got to her feet, feeling it settling against her – the cold weight of it – and wondering if any of the girls staring at her could sense it. Her nerves steady, she moved towards the microphone.

Eva drove the car through the gates and into the car park, pulling to a halt in a space next to the edge of the grass. She looked across at the familiar building of the school, the horseshoe shape with the courtyard at its centre. The tall glass doors of the assembly hall where she had gathered with her peers every week for years. How distant and strange it all seemed now.

'We're a few minutes early,' Eva remarked. 'Dad told her ten thirty.'

But Abi was impatient. Her video call was at lunchtime and she was cutting it fine already.

'Text her that we're here,' she told Eva. 'We'll give her five minutes, and then you go in.'

The boy couldn't stop crying. Even after Mark had untied his wrists and ankles, taken the gag from his mouth, he kept gulping for air.

'Get him a glass of water, will you?' Mark asked Ursula, and while she was downstairs in the kitchen, Mark sat on the edge of the bed, and asked:

'What happened? Who did this to you?'

Callum inhaled sharply, trying to control his breathing.

'Your parents are worried sick about you,' Mark told him. 'Not knowing where you've been.'

'She said I could stay here,' the boy said. 'She told me it would be all right for a few days.'

'And this?' Mark asked gently, nodding to the ties he'd removed from Callum's wrists and ankles.

'She came over last night. We were just talking. She was upset – we both were. I had some weed, and she made us cocktails. I felt she understood something about me. That we were alike—'

'Slow down,' Mark urged, seeing how worked up Callum was getting.

'We were just talking. She said there was something she needed to do. Something big that people would never forget. I remember her saying that. But I think I blacked out. She must have spiked my drinks.'

He'd fallen asleep. And when he woke, groggy, he'd found himself bound and gagged.

He began to cry again. 'I thought no one would come. I thought I'd die here.'

'You're all right. You're safe,' Mark said, but his heart was pounding.

'How could she do this to me?' he asked, and Mark shook his head.

'I don't know, Callum. I really don't. I thought you and Eva were friends. I'm shocked that she would do—'

'It wasn't Eva.'

'It wasn't?'

'No. It was Beth.'

Mark stared. He could hear Ursula coming back up the stairs, and he ran his hand over his face, recalibrating his thoughts, trying to understand. At that moment, Callum got up from the bed, moving quickly across the room. His rucksack was on the floor, and he began rummaging through it, his search becoming frantic.

'Oh no, oh no,' he said, his voice rising on a jagged ridge of panic. He spilled the contents on to the floor, sifted through it.

'What is it? What are you looking for?' Mark asked.

Callum looked up at him, his eyes round with fear. 'Oh shit,' he said.

It was love. Standing up there, saying those words, steadying herself for what was to come: it was all done for love. *Make it big*, Corinne had said, and Beth would do just that.

All those faces staring up at her, watching while she professed her regret, while she invoked sorrow at what Sasha had suffered as a result of her actions. They were just words, after all, they meant nothing compared to the desperate love that moved inside her. She scoured the crowd as she spoke, knowing that Corinne was there, waiting, watching.

The curtain moved once more, but it wasn't the breeze. A figure entering through the open door, head bowed, making herself small as she moved swiftly around the back of the hall.

'And I . . . I want to say . . .' Beth went on, stumbling now, her eyes narrowing as they followed Eva through the room.

'Carry on,' Bracken said sharply behind her.

'I . . . I . . .'

Eva stopped, crouched low, and then Corinne was on her feet, the two of them shuffling through the hall.

Wait, Beth thought. *Wait! Look at me!*

And then she was actually saying the words out loud, into the microphone.

'No! Stop! Don't go!'

But they had already gone through the doors.

'Don't take her away from me!' Beth screamed.

Laughter rose up from the hall. Behind her, Sasha said: 'Oh, for fuck's sake!' And Mrs Bracken was at the edge of the crowd barking at them all to be quiet. But the air was threaded with a giddy streak that would not be silenced.

Beth's heart was strobing the way it sometimes did when she woke in the night to the sound of her aunt's raspy breath, feeling the dry tingle of those rough fingertips passing over her skin. In those moments, she could scarcely breathe, like a damp hand clamped over her mouth, the darkness bearing down on her: the weight of a body pressing hers into the mattress. And all along Eva knew. She *knew*. And she had done nothing. Nothing! She hadn't even told Beth, hadn't warned her. Despair had taken hold of Beth when she held her ear close to the door of Eva's bedroom and discovered her betrayal. And now, the laughter of those girls roared in her ears, their faces distorted into parodies of themselves, clownish, gaping mouths stretched open. She couldn't stand it.

'What the fuck?' someone said, and the ripple went through the crowd, laughter mutating to breathless awe.

Her hand was shaking. She looked through the crowd for Corinne, but she was gone, the curtain swinging in her wake. No goodbye. No chance to witness. She was gone and now it was too late.

Someone said: 'Is that thing real?'

Panic soared inside her, mingling with rage, confusion, a swirl of emotions rising like a tornado. She turned to Sasha who was out of her chair now, stumbling backwards, propelled by fear, shoving aside the other girls in her bid to get away. Still Beth's hand shook. It would not stop shaking. The panic inside her was in the room now, passing swiftly like an infection. Chairs overturned, girls screaming, the thunder of feet all moving towards the doors. And there in the crowd was Lisa. Lisa who wasn't running or shouting or jostling to escape. She was just standing there, her plain, simple face staring back at Beth, cold with wonder.

Abi drummed her fingers on the handbag that lay on her lap. Where were they? Overhead, she could see a fading grid of contrails marking the cold blue sky.

Her phone rang and it was Mark, breathless, upset.

'What is it? What's wrong?'

'Where's Beth?' he said.

Corinne walked slowly, her courier bag slung over one shoulder, Eva a pace ahead. They didn't have much time. A couple of minutes before they reached the car where Abi was waiting.

'Can I ask you something?' Eva said, as they crossed the courtyard, past the sundial where the class photos were always taken. The windows of the lower year form rooms shone brightly against the autumn sunlight.

'Okay,' Corinne said, glancing behind her, as though regretful at having left early.

'Was it you?'

'What?'

'Was it you who took the photo of me and Ross, leaving the house?'

Corinne looked down, avoiding Eva's gaze.

'It was you, wasn't it?'

'He's not right for you. He doesn't deserve you,' she declared.

Eva stopped, overtaken by a wave of rage.

'And Becca? Did you tell her about us? Did you tell her about my pregnancy?'

Corinne's pace slowed and then stopped. Panic flashed across her face.

'You did, didn't you?'

Corinne whispered: 'I thought it would help, if she knew.'

The doors behind them burst open, girls streaming out.

'Help? Help who?'

'You. Us.' Desperation in her voice as she grasped for meaning. 'I thought if she knew then there would be no chance of you staying with him. He is not good for you, Eva. You don't need him.'

Around them: rushing and screaming, the wave of panic sweeping out on to the forecourt. Distantly, Eva thought: *fire*.

'That little boy,' Corinne said. 'I didn't know . . . Eva, I'm scared.'

The ground tilted. Eva was aware of screaming. She tried to make sense of the moment, to realize the full implications, but the question resounded inside her: 'Why?'

'Because I care for you! It is like we are sisters. Family!'

Words shakily spoken. An uncertain offering. An untrustworthy account.

'Don't you feel it too?'

A voice behind them, a strange shout. Beth. Eva hadn't noticed, hadn't seen until the last minute. The round O of surprise made by Corinne's mouth. Her sister's face ruddy and peculiar.

'You didn't even wait,' Beth said, her breath wild. 'You didn't wait for me!'

Eva was reminded, then, of when they were little girls and she, the faster of the two, would run on ahead, mindless to anything but her own joy at the speed in her legs, the air whistling in her ears as she ran. And then Beth's tears and recriminations when she caught up, the wail at her abandonment.

But there was a strange cast to Beth's face now that Eva did not recognize, the gasping tears, the streaked pallor, rage making her savage.

'Who are you talking to?' Eva asked.

A gun in Beth's shaking hand.

Corinne. Dearest friend. Trusted confidante. Deep well of mysteries.

'Tell me a secret,' she had whispered. 'The one thing you could never tell anyone.'

And Beth had dug deep inside and opened up about Melissa, about what had happened the morning after Sasha's party.

'She ran me a bath,' Beth had said, her voice reedy and unsteady.

While it was running, her aunt took Beth's blood-stained clothes away to soak.

'I had just gotten into the water when she came back.'

The words were difficult to say – like dislodging stones embedded deep within her.

'She sat down in a chair next to the bath. It felt a bit strange because it had been years since anyone – Eva, my parents – had been there with me when I was bathing. But she started talking about how she used to give me and Eva baths when we were little. Then she picked up a facecloth and dipped it in the water and began washing me.'

All the while, Melissa talked, using calm, soothing tones. She talked of how much Beth had changed but how she would always be Melissa's 'special little girl'. The flannel running over her scar: 'a sign of beauty, Beth. Your special mark.'

'She was the person I trusted more than anyone in the world. A sacred bond between us. And it felt so weird, but it would have been worse to say no, to make her feel like I was uncomfortable about what she was suggesting, that I was scared.'

Easier just to lie back, to steel her body to her aunt's touch which was still gentle, still caressing. Beth had fixed her eyes on the light fitting hanging from the ceiling so that she wouldn't have to confront the softness of Melissa's gaze travelling down her body. The faltering smile. Those fingers touching, probing, the flannel floating to the surface of the water, drifting away.

Words spoken. Painful, like peeling back layers of skin. Turning herself inside out – vulnerable, exposed.

Her father's voice: 'It's all right, Beth. I know.'

His arms tight about her, squeezing the life from her.

'Corinne told me,' he'd said, and she'd stumbled away from him, reeling.

She was still stumbling, still reeling, falling out of the hall and into the daylight, pulled along by the current, the tide of girls streaming away from her. It felt like being underwater, everything indistinct, reality refracted and distorted so even the daylight seemed bent, crooked, the grass and sky, the pavement beneath her feet watery, her movements slow. Wading through it, she looked up and saw them there – two girls standing together – and the blood rushed thickly through her veins, everything clarified. The hurt. The betrayal. She had been tossed aside, discarded.

It was like a synapse snapping suddenly to life – so real she almost heard it inside her own head. For such a long time she had been unable to form judgements, to make decisions, as if that part of her brain had atrophied, grown slack and useless. It was Corinne's guidance she had craved and without it she was helpless and adrift.

But now, she saw them together, trapped in a doomed light, and everything became clear. She heard herself speaking the words: 'You didn't wait for me.'

Her sister's face. So known to her, so familiar, and yet it was like Beth was peeling away from herself, stepping back from the scene: an observer, impartial, bloodless, unmoved. Watching from afar as the gun went off, once, twice, the snapping cracks through the air, the dull thud of flesh meeting the pavement. And then slowly, lowering herself, mindful now of the smell of the earth, the warm sweetness of decaying leaves, and the heavy press of her bones on the paving stones as she sat serenely between the two girls, waiting. Her mother screaming across the grass.

35

It's late when they let me see her.

The corridor has emptied. There's still noise around the desk, the occasional slam of a door, the squeak of footsteps, a throat cleared, sudden laughter. But the place feels quieter now; the heightened atmosphere of earlier has deflated.

She has confessed, I've been told. A full statement. There will be a court appearance tomorrow morning for the arraignment, followed by a psychiatric evaluation in the days to come. She will be taken to the juvenile detention facility at Cloverhill, they informed me, to await the shrink's report, and from there . . .

I think I faded at that point. To not have my daughters at home with me tonight. It was too much, peering too far into a frightening future that I'm not yet ready to face.

I follow the officer down the corridor and she stops at a door, raps on it briskly, before entering the code on a keypad. I steel myself, take a deep breath as if I'm about to plunge into icy waters, needing to summon courage for what lies ahead. Entering the room, I see Trevor Byrne, our solicitor, getting to his feet now, my eyes sliding away from him to Beth. There she is with her father. The two of them at the table, and I catch my breath because she looks so young. So frighteningly small and vulnerable. She's still in her school uniform and it's a shock to me – incongruous after what she has done.

The look she gives me is wary and sullen – and then she lowers her gaze, eyes sweeping the blank surface of the table.

I feel there is a degree of shame in that look. Nerves too – her knuckles whiten, squeezing her father's hand. Beside her, Mark sits with his head bowed, and I notice how thin his hair has become, shadows under his eyes, a greyish cast to his skin. He looks older, and I think how much we have both aged on this day – decades stolen from us, as if the last vestiges of our youth resided in our children and now there is nothing left but deadened time.

'Oh, Beth,' I whisper, and the string of names we have called her from the time of her infancy, most of them long dormant, runs through my head: my Elizabeth, my baby-Beth, Betty-Bettina, little doll, angel-child. I try to impose these names on the girl sitting before me with her tousled hair, her berry-black eyes, the grim little stud at the corner of her nose, as if those baby names from the past might soften her, as if they might restore the girl I knew to me. But there is a new name now – an epithet – and it whispers around us, demanding recognition. *Murderess.*

My body reacts, even though my mind is frozen, and swiftly I cross the room and put my arms around her, pulling her into my embrace. As soon as I touch her, I fall apart. Flesh of my flesh. Fruit of my womb. I hold her against me. She is still in her chair, and I am standing, leaning over her, as if with my body I can protect her, fold her into me, keep her safe, undo what she has done. But it's too late for that now. I feel the heat of her head against my chest – a hot living thing – and it stokes to life a boiling fury inside me. *A hot living thing.* I had held Eva in my arms while the life poured out of her and now she lies beneath a sheet on a stainless-steel table or slotted away in a refrigerated drawer. Fury boils up through me. 'How could you do this?' I ask of her, the words spoken into her hair, squeezing her to me. 'Your own sister! How could you do this to her?' I am screeching the words, my hands like claws digging into her flesh, loving her, hating her, a furious love careening through me, as Mark peels my hands from her, his voice breaking, saying: 'Don't, Abi! Please! For God's sake . . .'

We look at each other then, breathless, bewildered, and I see behind his watery gaze that something has broken in him. Later, I will find out that he has already been to the morgue to see Eva. His grim duty to identify her body. To come from that and then be forced to sit alongside this daughter – this murderess – and offer his support. To be a father to the one who killed his child. Whatever resources he called upon, whatever inner depths he has plumbed, it has taken something from him. There's an absence now. A bewilderment. Neither of us can fathom it.

Trevor Byrne stands up and offers me his seat. I pull it around so that I can be next to her. I try to take her hand, but she won't let me. Instead she holds herself stiffly, arms folded over her chest, staring furiously at the table, her mouth a hard little bud. How miserable she looks. But underneath the bravado, there is deep fear. I can see it.

'Beth,' I say softly. 'I know you're frightened. I know what happened today was awful, and that there must be a reason why you did such a thing. If you would only tell us—'

'Why? Were you shocked?'

I stare at her, like I've been slapped. The cut of meanness in her voice. She's looking at me now, small-eyed, watchful. Taking in my reaction. And I realize that I am frightened of her. That I have been frightened of her for a long time.

'Of course I was shocked. My God, Beth, you—'

'I didn't think *you'd* be surprised at all.'

My eyes flicker over her, then cut to Mark. We both caught the emphasis. He's looking at me strangely, I can't make out the meaning of his stare. I feel the weight of Cassins' gaze and that of the other detective in the room. Trevor Byrne's, and all the unseen eyes peering at me from behind the mirrored glass. What a sight we are. What a family tableau.

'I love you, sweetheart,' is what I tell her. 'No matter what you've done, you're still my little girl.'

'All grown up now, though, aren't I?' She tries to smile but it dies on her face, the mask slipping.

'I thought you loved her,' I say. 'I thought you were close. Why?'

She holds my gaze for a moment and shrugs; her eyes fill with tears.

'They left me behind,' she says simply. 'I couldn't stand it.'

'But—'

'She was *my* friend!' she blurts out, her voice breaking. 'Mine! Not Eva's!'

With that, she withdraws into herself. Her anger shrivels before my eyes. She shrinks around what's left of it, stares sideways at the wall, says to no one in particular:

'Are we done here? Can I go now?'

I look at her, amazed.

'Go? Where do you think you're going to?' I bend down, on my knees in front of her, imploring her to look at me, to penetrate the part of her brain that remains shuttered, wilfully apart. 'Beth, you can't come home, do you understand that? You can't come home.'

I start to cry then. Because I know it will be years. *Years.* She will be grown. She will be a different person. Both our girls, gone.

But when they take her from the room, she looks back at us, and the expression on her face is so clouded, so unrecognizable, that I think to myself: *She's a stranger already. My own child. No one I know.*

*

Eventually, Trevor drives us home. I don't know where my car is – at the school, perhaps. God knows if I'll be able to go back there to retrieve it. How I'll ever be able to show my face again. What I want now is to curl up in a hole so deep no one will ever find me.

I look out at the blackness of night, all the houses, the neat gardens, windows lit up against the dark. Box hedging, plantation shutters, SUVs in the driveway. Basketball hoops bolted to garage walls, trampolines on the lawn. Everything neat and safe and tucked up, secure. This slice of suburban life. Tennis clubs and swim teams. We thought we were insulated. All these things we have, everything we've accumulated, thinking it could protect us. But the enemy was here all along, living among us, making itself comfortable in our house.

And I think now of all those other parents out there. I think of Craig and Irene Ferguson – shocked, appalled, furious at their son for involving them in this way. They will have charges to answer too, about the gun, how it came into Beth's hands. But tonight, I know their anger will give way to relief. A prayer offered up in thanks. Their boy is alive. Safe within their home. He survived. He was spared.

And Siobhan Harte. In her mock-Tudor mansion with its tennis court, its home cinema, her ear burning against the phone as she relays the dramatic sequence of events to yet another friend, the gratifying shock resounding in their response. 'It could so easily have been Sasha. When I think about it – the two of them up there in front of the whole school, Sash and that little psychopath. She pointed the gun right at Sash, you know . . .'

There but for the grace of God, they will say. Holding their own children a little closer tonight.

People will look at our house and shudder. *That's the house,* they'll say – *those three girls: two of them dead and one in prison.* Walking on quickly as if chased by a cold wind.

'Will you come in for a drink?' Mark asks, as Trevor pulls into our driveway.

But the engine is still running, and Trevor has the look of a man who wants to escape, to try and expunge what he's learned today, contaminated by the knowledge.

'I'll leave you two alone,' he says, adding: 'Be good to each other, won't you? What you've gone through today is just about the worst thing any parent could go through. You've got to be kind to each other now.'

How like a priest he is in that moment, counselling us, fearfulness present in the shine of his eye. I lean in and kiss him on the cheek. Does he have any idea how fervently I wish he could drive me away from here? Can he guess from my face at the great seam of emptiness that opened within me when that gun went off – as if my own body absorbed the bullet?

The house is dark now, and cold. Inside, the air feels very still. Mark goes into the kitchen, but I hesitate in the hall. I look at the coats hanging on the row of hooks, and the shoes lined up neatly in the racks. Everything in order. Nothing out of place. And I think of the limbs that won't fill those clothes now, the feet that will no longer step into those shoes. The house phone sits on the hall table, and I remember a night, hurrying down this staircase to answer the call, Valentina Catto's hesitancy on the line, her vague reluctance. A feeling, she said. An intuition. Some blurred outline of threat like dark forms gathering just beyond the field of her vision. A premonition? But I had casually waved it aside, knocked it over with the force of my optimism, talked her into ignoring her own sense of dread.

After a minute I follow my husband into the kitchen, watch while he pours himself two fingers of whiskey, flinging his head back as he swallows it down. It is almost midnight. 'You want one?' he asks me, and I nod my agreement. *I don't know how to do this*, I think. *I don't know how to be.* Mark pours us both a glass, but he doesn't knock this second one back. Nor does he come and join me where I sit at the table in the snug. Instead he stands there swirling the liquor in his glass, looking as if he is about to say something, and a hard push inside me wants to shout: *Don't! Just, don't!*

'I keep thinking,' he says, 'of that dinner we had. In France, with Val and Guy.'

He is speaking softly, his voice dry and hoarse.

'I keep thinking of that story you told them – that anecdote about the child psychiatrist you met. Back when Beth was a baby.'

'It is always the fault of the mother.' I say the words calmly, but there's a fire in my head.

'I don't know why it came back to me.'

It's been there in the background ever since we exchanged that glance above Beth's head. I had seen it in his eye: the flash of disquiet, the hardening of a soft doubt that was already there. I know he's going to ask me now.

'Why did Beth say that to you? How she didn't think you'd be surprised by what she'd done. What did she mean by that?'

'Mark—'

'Did something happen? Something I don't know about?'

He is looking at me so intensely that it almost frightens me. Can he read it in my face? Can he see it in my eyes, this thing I have buried so deep inside me, I thought it might never be found?

'Abi?'

Seven months I've kept it hidden. Seven months I've kept

it safe. But I feel the press of his stare, his hunger for this knowledge even though by sharing it I will only compound his pain.

Falteringly, I tell him: 'I remember the last time I spoke to her.'

'Beth?'

'Melissa.' I meet his eye, see something waver behind it. 'I was in work. It was a Friday afternoon.'

She had sounded upbeat – that was what surprised me. My sister-in-law with her anxieties and neuroses; so often in our phone conversations I was aggravated by how morose she could be.

'She told me she felt like a change – a complete change. She said that she felt she'd been locked up in a dusty room for too long and now she wanted to fling wide the windows and doors, let the light in.'

'She said that?' There's disbelief in his eyes, but I can see he's listening, intent on what I'm telling him.

'It was like she suddenly realized that there was still life left in her and she was anxious to make the most of the time. She started talking about travel – Melissa, who never went anywhere! She'd harboured a dream of seeing Rome, she said, and I found myself offering to go with her. Mark, she was so happy at the prospect, it made me feel guilty I'd never thought to offer before.'

I had promised to look into flights and accommodation, but I was still at work and eager to get her off the phone.

'I arranged to call over to her house the next morning, so we could discuss various options and make a plan. Just as we were making the arrangement, she became distracted. There was someone at the door, she told me. So, we said our good-byes, and I was hanging up the phone when I heard her greet her visitor.'

It's you, she had said, sounding surprised. *I didn't know you were calling over, love.*

'Instinctively, I knew it was Beth. From the tone of Melissa's voice – I just knew. And I didn't think anything of it at the time.'

There was no flash of intuition, no slow chill of doubt. I turned my concentration to my work and forgot about it.

'Later that evening, when I asked Beth about her afternoon, and she told me she'd gone to the park with Lisa and some of the others from school, I didn't think to pick her up on it. To ask her had she not been to Melissa's? Teenagers can be secretive. Reluctant to share details of their lives, especially with parents. I suppose I was still happy to think that Beth had someone she could talk to. Someone to support her. So, I let it go.'

The next day – Saturday – Mark had taken both girls to the Tennis Club, and I had spent some time online, looking at flights, browsing through various websites for accommodation in Rome.

'I compiled a few different pages, but when I went to print them, I found the printer was jammed. A page was stuck, and once I'd freed it and reset things, the printer resumed, working its way through the print queue.'

It was when I took the sheaf of printed pages off the printer and started leafing through them that I found the letter.

'What letter?' Mark asks, his forehead creased with concentration.

'It read like a suicide note,' I say carefully, watchful now while he takes this in.

To whoever finds this . . . I have struggled for some time . . . This disease is killing me . . . please understand . . . I'm sorry.

'It wasn't signed. And it didn't make any sense. *This disease?*'

But it was enough to worry me. And of course, I thought of Beth. How could I not, given her history? Was she having suicidal thoughts?

'I went into Beth's room and turned on her computer. It wasn't hard to find the document – there were several drafts of it. A notepad to the side of the keyboard was open, and I saw on the page various scribbles and I recognized at once the sharp peaks of the M. It was Melissa's signature, or an approximation of it. The same scrawl I'd read year after year on birthday cards, Christmas cards, various notes.'

The feeling of unease was growing inside me, a panic starting in my brain as I clicked into the internet and opened the browser history.

'It was all there,' I tell Mark now. 'Searches about fatal overdoses, about what quantities of various drugs would be required – sleeping pills, paracetamol, along with more specific searches about the various MS medications Melissa was taking. I couldn't believe it. How *forensic* she had been. And her research seemed to have been going on for quite some time – there were scores of related searches.'

'What did you do?'

'I picked up the phone and called Melissa.'

I remember the coldness that came over me – like being doused in icy water. I felt it penetrating right through to my very heart. Because I knew she would not answer. Already, I knew she was dead.

The first thing I did was wipe that suicide note from Beth's computer. Then I cleared her browser history. Later I would destroy the computer, replace it with another, but I didn't have time for that then. I got in my car and drove over to Beaufield Court. And it was as I reached the house that I realized I would have to make a performance of it. I would have to go through the motions of discovery and shock and alerting the authorities, all the while concealing the fact that *I knew*.

'I knocked on the door for several minutes, before taking the key from under the flowerpot and letting myself in, calling out her name lest some neighbour happened to walk past, making it all look . . . normal. She was upstairs, in her bed, lying there, perfectly peaceful. But the air in that room — my God. A thick, heavy pall, like it hadn't been aired in weeks. I could hardly breathe.'

There was a bottle of whiskey by the bed — Bushmills, Melissa's favourite — and an empty glass, along with some pill bottles — sleeping tablets, mainly. They were almost empty. And propped up by the bottle was that letter.

'I knew I couldn't leave it there. I couldn't risk it. Something about the wording was so clumsy, and I was in a panic, thinking of Beth's fingerprints on the letter, how would we explain it?'

I took the note and stuffed it in my bag, and then I looked around the house quickly, searching for any evidence of Beth, anything that might incriminate her.

'But that note still bothered me. Or rather the absence of a note. And then I remembered Melissa's list of instructions — she had shown it to me once. When she was first diagnosed and she became maudlin and depressed, she got it into her head that she needed a document detailing all the practicalities concerning household bills, her finances, that kind of thing. Don't you remember her telling us about it? How it would be there in the drawer of her little desk if we ever needed it?'

But Mark is staring at me, baffled, like he's gone beyond memory to a darker place, a frightening reality. He's looking at me like he barely knows me any more. My heart clenches and I force myself to continue, my voice weaker now.

'It was right there in the desk, just like she said it would be. And I thought: That's the solution. Something simple and straightforward. That letter Beth had written – it had jarred because it was too much; Melissa would never have been so forthcoming, never explained her feelings. It made more sense to have something terse, enigmatic.'

I'm sorry about everything. Mx

So easily done. I hardly had to think about it. The work of a moment.

And then I put it back in the desk and went through the motions – calling an ambulance, ringing Mark, bracing myself for everything that was to follow.

'Did you ever talk to her about it?' he asks, his voice hoarse, and I can see how close he is to the edge. 'Did you ever ask her why?'

'I tried,' I say gently. 'Not straight away. You must understand that I couldn't do anything that would draw suspicion towards her. I was completely focused on shielding her from that. It felt like a risk even being in a room with her – I was so worried that I would say something to her, or even look at her in a way that would reveal to someone else what I knew she had done.'

'Even me?'

'Especially you!' His eyes flare a little when I say this, but I press on: 'Melissa was your sister. And Beth – she was always your favourite child. How could I tell you when I knew it would break your heart?'

He bows his head, and his shoulders slump. I see the exhaustion in him, how he is hanging on by a thread. After a moment, he comes and sits opposite me, his eyes scanning the table as if the scuffed surface of it – the site of so many family meals – will reveal some meaning to him in all this.

I did speak to her. Eventually. After the will had been read, and we had discovered that Melissa's house had been bequeathed to Beth and Beth alone. We had come home, and Eva was in her room, sulking. Mark had gone for a walk, needing to clear his head. It felt like the first time we had been alone – just me and Beth – since the morning of Melissa's death.

'She hadn't spoken much,' I tell Mark now, 'after the will was read, and so I asked her how she felt about it, and she just sort of shrugged, like it was no big deal. Her reaction infuriated me. I felt for Eva, the injustice of it, and it annoyed me, Beth's casual response. So, I told her that she ought to make some recompense to Eva – that they should share the property, it was only fair. And that's when she looked at me, such coldness in her eye, and she said: *Why? Why should I share with Eva?*

I think I spluttered some explanation about righting a wrong, keeping the domestic peace, but my heart was hammering.

'I said to her then: "Why do you think Melissa left the house to you?" She said: *Because I earned it.* Such hardness in her voice. She refused to elaborate when I pressed her on it, just clamming up. And when she went to leave the room, I called her back. I had to ask her. I needed to know.'

My heart hammering.

'Why?' I asked. 'Why did you do it?'

And we looked at each other, regarding each other for a long moment. And then she said: 'I don't know what you mean.' But it was a lie. She knew. And then she smiled. Dear God, that smile. A needle of ice went into my heart.

Did I know then that today would happen?

That needle of ice lodged in my heart.

Outside in the hall, the phone begins to ring.

'Leave it,' Mark says, his voice leaden.

But something compels me to go. A need to get away from this table. To escape the crushing atmosphere in this room.

In the dim light of the hall, I tread quickly, feeling an ache in every part of my body. I reach out, put the receiver to my ear.

'Hello?' I say, my voice hollow.

Silence on the other end of the line.

Heat rushes through me. It floods my throat, my face on fire. Because I know it is Valentina. Even though she says nothing, the silence unspools like an accusation.

I knew what my daughter was, and I let that girl come. Aware of the poison that lurked in my house, I opened the door and ushered her in.

I hold the receiver to my ear and try to speak, try to summon words – an apology, some scrap of meaning from this mess – but nothing comes. There is nothing there. I am scraped dry.

I can feel her listening at the other end. Both of us listening, into the silence, waiting, waiting, for the line to go dead.

Acknowledgements

I am deeply grateful to Jonathan Lloyd, my amazing agent, for continually steering me in the right direction and for being such fun with it; thanks also to Hannah Beer, Lucy Morris and everyone at Curtis Brown. Huge thanks to the dream team at Michael Joseph, especially Joel Richardson for his patience, clear-sightedness and thoughtful guidance; Maxine Hitchcock for her support and all-round brilliance; Grace Long who came up with the title and so much more; thanks to Emma Henderson and Sophie Shaw; and at Penguin Ireland, thanks to Carrie Anderson and Louise Farrell.

I was blessed to be able to spend the latter half of 2019 in western France, which is where I began writing *Stranger*. I am grateful to the communities of Saint-Pierre-de-Maillé and Angles-sur-l'Anglin for welcoming me and my family to their beautiful corner of the world; thanks also to Joyce and John for lending us their lovely home – it was simply magical.

For all the walks, talks and Zooms that have sustained me this past year, I thank Aileen O'Dwyer Papp, Ciara McGowan, Merche Marsá, Ruth Cronin, Emma Murphy, Tara Ryan, Alison Weatherby, Rowena Walsh, Tana French and all the members of the B-Step Squad. Special thanks to the incomparable ladies of the Exclusive EU Book Club, and a shout out to Wine Club too.

I am so grateful to my mother, my extended family and my in-laws. This last year, with all its difficulties and sadness, has made me appreciate you all the more.

Finally, deepest thanks to my husband, Conor, and to our daughters, Rowan & Freya. Writing *Stranger* took me to some dark places in my mind – how lucky I am to have you guys to let in the light.

He just wanted a decent book to read ...

Not too much to ask, is it? It was in 1935 when Allen Lane, Managing Director of Bodley Head Publishers, stood on a platform at Exeter railway station looking for something good to read on his journey back to London. His choice was limited to popular magazines and poor-quality paperbacks – the same choice faced every day by the vast majority of readers, few of whom could afford hardbacks. Lane's disappointment and subsequent anger at the range of books generally available led him to found a company – and change the world.

'We believed in the existence in this country of a vast reading public for intelligent books at a low price, and staked everything on it'
Sir Allen Lane, 1902–1970, founder of Penguin Books

The quality paperback had arrived – and not just in bookshops. Lane was adamant that his Penguins should appear in chain stores and tobacconists, and should cost no more than a packet of cigarettes.

Reading habits (and cigarette prices) have changed since 1935, but Penguin still believes in publishing the best books for everybody to enjoy. We still believe that good design costs no more than bad design, and we still believe that quality books published passionately and responsibly make the world a better place.

So wherever you see the little bird – whether it's on a piece of prize-winning literary fiction or a celebrity autobiography, political tour de force or historical masterpiece, a serial-killer thriller, reference book, world classic or a piece of pure escapism – you can bet that it represents the very best that the genre has to offer.

Whatever you like to read – trust Penguin.